Praise for Jo Beverley's magnificent Malloren novels

"Beverley beautifully captures the flavor of Georgian England. . . . Her fast-paced, violent, and exquisitely sensual story is one that readers won't soon forget."

—*Library Journal*

"Jo Beverley has truly brought to life a fascinating, glittering, and sometimes dangerous world."

—*New York Times* bestselling author Mary Jo Putney

"Delightfully spicy . . . skillfully plotted and fast-paced . . . captivating."

—*Booklist*

"Delicious. . . . [A] sensual delight."

—*New York Times* bestselling author Teresa Medeiros

"A fast-paced adventure with strong, vividly portrayed characters. . . . Wickedly, wonderfully sensual and gloriously romantic."

—*New York Times* bestselling author Mary Balogh

"Romance at its best."

—*Publishers Weekly*

"A fantastic novel. Jo Beverley shows again why she is considered one of the genre's brightest stars."

—*Affaire de Coeur*

"Storytelling at its best!"

—*Rendezvous*

Don't miss these Malloren romances!

Winter Fire

Devilish

My Lady Notorious

Secrets of the Night

ALSO BY JO BEVERLEY

Skylark

Winter Fire

St. Raven

Dark Champion

Lord of My Heart

My Lady Notorious

Hazard

The Devil's Heiress

The Dragon's Bride

"The Demon's Mistress" in
In Praise of Younger Men

Devilish

Secrets of the Night

Forbidden Magic

Lord of Midnight

Something Wicked

Jo Beverley

A SIGNET BOOK

SIGNET
Published by New American Library, a division of
Penguin Group (USA) Inc., 375 Hudson Street,
New York, New York 10014, USA
Penguin Group (Canada), 10 Alcorn Avenue, Toronto,
Ontario M4V 3B2, Canada (a division of Pearson Penguin Canada Inc.)
Penguin Books Ltd., 80 Strand, London WC2R 0RL, England
Penguin Ireland, 25 St. Stephen's Green, Dublin 2,
Ireland (a division of Penguin Books Ltd.)
Penguin Group (Australia), 250 Camberwell Road, Camberwell, Victoria 3124,
Australia (a division of Pearson Australia Group Pty. Ltd.)
Penguin Books India Pvt. Ltd., 11 Community Centre, Panchsheel Park,
New Delhi - 110 017, India
Penguin Group (NZ), cnr Airborne and Rosedale Roads, Albany,
Auckland 1310, New Zealand (a division of Pearson New Zealand Ltd.)
Penguin Books (South Africa) (Pty.) Ltd., 24 Sturdee Avenue,
Rosebank, Johannesburg 2196, South Africa

Penguin Books Ltd., Registered Offices:
80 Strand, London WC2R 0RL, England

Published by Signet, an imprint of New American Library,
a division of Penguin Group (USA) Inc. Previously published in a Topaz edition.

First Signet Printing, December 2001
10 9 8 7 6 5 4 3 2 1

PUBLISHER'S NOTE
This is a work of fiction. Names, characters, places, and incidents either are the product of the author's imagination or are used fictitiously, and any resemblance to actual persons, living or dead, business establishments, events, or locales is entirely coincidental.

To my agent, Alice Harron Orr,
who is supportive in every way.

Chapter 1

London, June 1762

"I'm going to miss you." Lady Elfled Malloren went into her twin brother's arms, determined not to cry.

"Now there's a change," he said gruffly. "It's going to be strange all over again after this year together."

Captain Lord Cynric Malloren was dressed for official travel in full red-coated military glory, including powdered hair tied back neatly with a black bow.

Beneath a frivolous lace cap, Elf's hair glinted its natural sandy gold, and she wore a white gown scattered with embroidered forget-me-nots.

Even so, the resemblance was unmistakable.

"I wish you weren't going so *far,*" she complained. "Nova Scotia. It will be years—"

He put his fingers over her unsteady lips. "Hush. I've been away for years before, and you'll soon be absorbed in your own life again."

She pulled a face and moved out of his arms. "Don't *you* start preaching of the benefits of the wedded state!"

He glanced smiling at his wife, waiting tactfully by the hall door, chatting to his brother, the Marquess of Rothgar. "Marriage suits me, and you and I are very much alike."

Are we? Elf wanted to ask, but now was hardly the time to raise troubling questions. "Then I'll consider the applicants again," she said lightly, adding with a teasing grimace, "—of course it might help if my devoted brothers didn't chase off all the more interesting ones!"

He winked. "Takes a scoundrel to know one. We'd

best be off." But he made no move to leave, even though a coach and six restless horses waited outside.

"Go. I hate long farewells." She kissed him quickly, then dragged him toward his wife and the door to adventure.

She kissed her sister-in-law, Chastity, on the cheek. "Write before you sail." They hugged, clinging for a moment, for they'd become close friends. "Take care of him," Elf whispered, having to fight tears all over again.

"Of course." Chastity pulled free to blow her nose. "If I thought there was any point, I'd ask you to take care of Fort in turn." She referred to her brother, now Earl of Walgrave.

"I can well imagine *his* reaction to such a suggestion."

They shared a look, for Chastity's brother hated all Mallorens.

Behind them, two footmen swung open the big double doors, letting in summer sun and birdsong. The marquess and Cyn moved onto the steps outside, waiting.

"Keep an eye on him, at least," Chastity said.

"My dear. The places he haunts? I'd lose my reputation in a moment!"

"Not these days." Chastity pulled a face. "I never thought to complain about a brother's reform, but Fort as a careless rake was a great deal more pleasant than Lord Walgrave, the cynical moralist." She pulled on her gloves. "I do worry about leaving him like this. He's not the same since Father's death."

Elf linked arms and led her to the door. "Then I will play guardian angel. If I hear he's in the suds—about to be beheaded for bloody-minded arrogance, for example—I'll charge to his rescue like Joan of Arc!" With a grin, Elf added, "Mainly to annoy him."

Chastity chuckled, but added, "He's not so bad, Elf. It's just—"

"It's just that he thinks all Mallorens lower than worms, and treats me accordingly."

Chastity sighed and abandoned the argument, turning

to join her husband and the marquess, who was traveling with them to Portsmouth.

Too soon all was ready. Elf watched from the steps as the three settled into the gilded coach. At a word, the coachman cracked his whip and the six horses took the weight of the splendid vehicle. Soon it turned out of Marlborough Square, both Cyn and Chastity leaning out for a final wave.

Passersby had stopped to watch the departure. Now they clicked into motion like clockwork toys—idlers strolled on, servants resumed their tasks, and children returned to games.

As the world filled the space where Cyn had been, Elf bit her lip, regretting the fact that she'd chosen to say good-bye here instead of at the ship. But she did hate lingering farewells, and in the end it would have hurt just as much.

She thought she'd gone through the worst of this seven years ago when Cyn had virtually run away to join the army. For a while she'd even hated him for leaving her, though she'd known he could never settle to the life Rothgar had planned for him. The law, for heaven's sake. One of her oldest brother's less perceptive ideas.

Cyn needed action and challenge.

He'd been home four times in seven years, and she really had thought she'd grown up and detached enough not to miss him. But when he'd come home last year, he'd been deathly ill, and for the first time she'd faced the prospect of really losing him. His recovery had taken months. Then his marriage, and the arrangements for his new post as aide to the governor of Nova Scotia had taken more.

The tendrils had grown deep into her again.

Now it was like losing a part of herself, and losing him more absolutely because of his marriage. She loved Chastity dearly, and didn't begrudge either of them their happiness, but it did sadden her that her twin had someone else in his life, someone, perhaps, as close as they had been.

She realized that she was standing staring at nothing, the two footmen waiting like statues to close the doors. With a sigh, she turned and reentered her home.

As she did so, she finally admitted to thoughts that had lurked in her mind for some time.

She envied her twin.

His life made hers painful.

In some ways, she was glad that Cyn was going far away.

As the footmen closed the door behind her, shutting out sunshine and birdsong, she acknowledged that her beloved twin had been a very uncomfortable presence over this past year.

Listening to his stories, enjoying his adventures, it had gradually dawned on her that she had done *nothing* with the past seven years. Oh certainly she had attended any number of balls, routs, and musical evenings—and arranged a good many of them too. She had traveled between London and Rothgar Abbey in Berkshire, and even—mad adventure this!—to Bath and Versailles.

Some would think she lived a full life, for she managed her brother's homes and was blessed by many good friends. But listening to stories of travel to foreign lands, of battles won and lost, of shipwreck and snake bite, she had come to see that she had done nothing even slightly challenging.

With a start, she realized that yet again she was standing staring into space, this time in the middle of the paneled hall. Picking up her delicate skirts, she climbed the sweeping stairs, heading for the privacy of her suite of rooms.

Movement, however, didn't stop the thoughts from tumbling out of the dark corners of her mind, taking on clarity and a frightening form.

Cyn was newly wed and setting off on another adventure. At twenty-five, he was considered to be on the brink of a promising and fruitful life. She, however—at the same age—was seen as an aging spinster destined to spend her life in a boring round. She would care for her brother's homes, love her siblings' children, but have neither home nor children of her own.

And she was a virgin.

Her steps quickened, and she rushed into her pretty boudoir to close the door behind her, to lean against it as if pursued.

Why had her virginity become the crystalline heart of her unhappiness? How nonsensical.

After all, Cyn had never kept much from her, and she'd known they'd differed in this for years. He'd enjoyed his first woman at seventeen—Cassie Wickworth of the Abbey dairy. Later, he'd visited some select brothels, and even enjoyed a brief, hilarious affair with an older married lady, though he hadn't told Elf her name. In the army, she was sure he'd not been celibate.

Such matters had never made her feel deprived before. These things were different for men and she'd been prepared to wait for marriage to be enlightened.

Accepting that the door did not need guarding, that the enemy was in fact within, she went to sit on her cream brocade chaise. It was Cyn's marriage, she decided, that had given her own celibacy such splinter-sharp edges.

She'd never before had to witness him going nightly to a woman while she retired to her solitary state. It hadn't helped, of course, that she'd learned about some of the adventures he'd shared with Chastity before their marriage. That, added to their open love and delight, to their way of touching or just looking at each other, had driven home the fact that Elf was missing a very important part of life.

And that she probably always would.

After all, a lady's virginity was a hard thing to lose outside marriage, especially when the lady had four brothers who would kill any man who obliged her.

She rose to study herself in her long mirror. With her decorous hairstyle crowned by a white lacy cap, she was the very image of a spinster lady. Of course, her white dress decorated with tiny forget-me-nots made her into the very image of virgin, too.

A *youthful* virgin.

It seemed absurd, though she couldn't imagine how a virginal spinster of twenty-five was *supposed* to dress. Since everyone agreed she had no taste in these matters, she left it all to her maid.

She turned away to pace the room, thinking of the simple solution to all her woes.

Marriage.

That was Cyn's prescription, but he'd found his soul mate and she hadn't. She enjoyed the company of men, and didn't lack for suitors. She had never met any man, however, who created magic in her; never one who could push her beyond the cool control of her mind into doing something foolish.

Something wicked . . .

Was it ridiculous to expect it?

Cyn had found it. His willingness to risk anything for Chastity, their abandonment to each other outside marriage, stood as proof of the power of love.

Another of her brothers, Bryght, had fallen into the magic stew with Portia St. Claire so that his brilliant, logical mind had been unable to do anything but work to win her.

Her friend Amanda was besotted with her husband, and miserable whenever he had to leave for a few days on government business.

Elf had never experienced anything close to that kind of madness. Surely, if it lay in her destiny, it would have happened by now.

Unless she lived too tamely to open herself to Cupid's magic arrow . . . ?

Turning back to the mirror, she pulled off her demure cap and tossed it aside, scattering pins so that her sandy curls bounced around her shoulders.

But then she sighed. She was no man's secret fantasy.

How unfair that Cyn was prettier than she was! He had inherited their mother's remarkable green-gold eyes and thick lashes as well as her russet-gold hair. Elf's eyes were a duller version of that color, and her lashes the same sandy brown as her hair. They both had their father's firm chin. It looked well on a military officer, but less so on a lady.

Impatiently, she shrugged off these pointless thoughts. Chins and eyes could not be changed, and she wasn't about to try dyeing her hair. Perhaps face paint . . . ?

"Ah, milady! Vous être prêt?"

Elf started, and turned to her maid. Of course, she was to spend a few days with Amanda. Her sedan chair was doubtless waiting.

"Bien sûr, Chantal."

As always when they were alone together, maid and mistress spoke French. Chantal was French born, and Elf's mother had been French, raising her children to be perfectly bilingual.

Elf continued in that language. "Have my things been sent around?"

"Of course, milady. And your chair awaits. But what has happened to your cap, milady?"

Elf knew she was blushing. "Oh, it looked a little crooked."

Chantal tutted, steering Elf to her dressing table so that hair and lacy confection could be restored to perfect order.

Elf pushed away her troubling thoughts. They were merely a passing cloud brought on by saying good-bye. A few days with Amanda would drive away the blue devils.

The next morning, Elf entered Amanda's boudoir to find her childhood friend sitting at a small breakfast table, but gazing morosely out of the window.

"Is something the matter?"

Amanda started. "Oh, Elf! Well, it's a blessing you are here or I would be deserted indeed!"

Amanda Lessington was a handsome brunette, of similar height to Elf but much more rounded. She was blessed with dramatic dark eyes and full lips that Elf had always envied.

Elf sat down opposite her friend. "What's happened?"

"Stephen's gone. Something *dreadfully* important has come up in Bristol. Bristol, I ask you!" With a wave of her hand, Amanda dismissed one of England's major seaports.

Elf knew Amanda's problem with Bristol was simply that she hated her husband's frequent journeys. "It will doubtless only be for a few days."

"A week. A whole week. And you don't realize the implications! The wretched man has left us without dependable escort. Unless," she added with a sharp look, "your brothers can be dragged in to do duty. It would serve Stephen right if I spent the evening on Rothgar's arm!"

Elf suppressed a grin. "Is that your secret fantasy? I wish I could make it true, dearest, but he's traveling to Portsmouth with Cyn."

"Bryght?" asked Amanda hopefully.

Elf shook her head. "Down at Candleford, and pretty well fixed there now Portia's close to her time."

"Brand?"

"Gone north on family business. That's part of the reason I'm here. They weren't happy at leaving me alone."

"Alack," said Amanda with a moody sigh. "So we are both cruelly deserted."

Elf helped herself to a slice of ham and a brioche. "Not exactly . . ."

Her discontented thoughts had not gone away. They'd kept her from sleep half the night and this new scenario seemed to feed them like dry logs on a fire. As she poured herself some chocolate from the china pot, she contemplated exciting, terrifying notions.

"Not deserted, Amanda," she said at last. "Without protectors."

"Isn't that the same thing?"

"Not to my mind." Elf cut a piece of ham, then savored the spicy taste along with the spicy ideas dancing around in her brain. "I've always been afraid of involving one of my fire-eating protectors in a duel, so I've had to behave with complete propriety. But now, none of them are around. Perhaps I can finally have an adventure."

"Adventure?" asked Amanda warily. "What kind of adventure?"

"Oh, something wicked, of course." Then Elf grinned at her friend's expression. "Not really. But let's go to Vauxhall."

"Vauxhall? That's hardly a wicked adventure. We've both been there a score of times."

"Without an escort. Tonight. To the Midsummer Night's masquerade."

Amanda gaped. "You're not serious!"

"Many members of society attend such masked events."

"Many *men,* you mean."

Perfectly aware of surrendering to a wild mood, Elf asked, "And why should they have all the fun?"

"I'm not sure it sounds like fun."

From whim, the notion had become insistent. Elf felt she would go mad if she didn't do *something,* something different. She leaned forward. "Let's, Amanda. I promise not to be madly rash. We'll wear dominoes. No one will know us." She took Amanda's hand. "I just want to see what it's like to be someone else for a night."

"Who?" Amanda wailed.

"I don't know. But not Lady Elfled Malloren, sister of the mighty Marquess of Rothgar—*Beware who trespass here!* Just an ordinary woman . . ."

After a moment, Amanda squeezed her hand. "Elf, I haven't seen you like this since we were children. I always thought Cyn was the ringleader in all our pranks."

"Perhaps Cyn and I are very alike."

"Perhaps you are, indeed."

"Amanda, I need to do this."

"So I see . . ." But Amanda frowned in concern. "I am responsible for you in a way."

"I'm six months older than you!"

"But I'm the married woman." She eyed her friend, brown eyes serious. "You promise we'll stay together?"

"Of course. Where's your adventurous spirit? You were never so timid when we were children."

"Because we *were* children. I *don't* think it will be fun. I think it will be crowded, sweaty, and noisy." She studied Elf for a moment, then smiled. "But if you want to have an adventure, my dear, an adventure you will have."

Ten hours later, Elf raised her silken skirts high to step out of the boat and onto the stone of Vauxhall Stairs. Excitement bubbled in her in a way she'd not experienced since she and Cyn had been wild youngsters together.

Both she and Amanda were dressed *en grand domino*—hooped gowns hidden by loose silken cloaks, white-powered hair concealed by deep hoods. Molded white leather masks covered their faces from hairline to lips. Even if they were unfortunate enough to encounter a close relative, they would not be recognized.

Amanda's domino was silvery blue, Elf's a vivid scarlet. In fact, they had switched for the night.

Elf suspected this might be her only chance for wild adventure and she was determined to make the most of it. Chantal—a tyrant supported by everyone Elf knew—insisted strong reds were impossible with pale skin and gingerish hair. Even if Elf purchased red clothing, it always disappeared.

Tonight, however, with her powdered hair and anonymity, Elf had persuaded Amanda to switch dominoes. Then she had insisted Chantal find a certain scarlet-striped dress with coquelicot-red petticoat. Of course Chantal—the wretch—had protested it was stained beyond hope.

"And how," Elf had demanded, "could it be soiled when it has never been worn?"

Chantal, despite her unadventurous taste, was impeccably honest. She had eventually found the gown and petticoat in a box in the attics of Malloren House. When commanded, she had even found some red-and-white striped stockings and a certain stomacher of black-and-red satin trimmed with gold lace. But there had been tears in her eyes as she unwrapped the latter. "Not with the coquelicot, milady! Please!"

Elf had been resolute, though even easygoing Amanda had blinked at her ensemble and suggested that perhaps the stomacher might be *de trop*.

Elf, however, had worn it all. She might never have another opportunity to dress just as she wished. She might never have another opportunity for adventure. She intended to enjoy tonight to the very last drop.

Tonight she was not Elfled Malloren, well-behaved lady, but a new creature entirely.

Lisette, she had christened the scarlet lady in the mirror. Lisette Belhardi, which translated roughly to bold-and-beautiful. Mademoiselle Lisette, visiting from Paris, and bolder by far than Elfled Malloren could ever be.

So now Elf felt wonderfully like a newborn person in a mysterious land. Even Vauxhall Stairs was different, being specially ornamented for Midsummer Night. Hanging lanterns glinted rainbow reflections off the dark, rippling waters of the Thames. Over nearby chatter and the impatient calls of the boatmen lined up on the river behind, she could hear the orchestra in the Grove.

"Welcome to Vauxhall, ladies!" cried the grinning young man who assisted Elf and Amanda up the steps and received a penny from each for the favor. With a wink he added, "I'm sure two such lovely darlings'll soon find gallant escorts on a night such as this."

Amanda pulled her blue hood farther forward. "Elf," she whispered, "are you sure this is wise?"

"Ne craignez rien, Aimée," Elf said, reassuring her

friend but also reminding her that they were to speak in French to further avoid recognition.

She tugged Amanda forward, continuing in French, "And anyway, we cannot leave. There are so many boats waiting to land passengers there's scant chance of one leaving for a while. Come along."

Elf guided Amanda into the stream of visitors heading toward dark Vauxhall Lane. She'd visited the gardens many times and knew the lane was a mock danger, too short and crowded to present any hazard. Its real purpose was to make the glittering splendor of the illuminated gardens burst dramatically upon the eye.

Even so, her heart beat a little faster as she entered the shadows, for this *was* an adventure because they were unprotected. Amanda had insisted on carrying a very serviceable knife in her pocket, and made Elf wear a bodice dagger, but they had no man with them to scare off other men.

This novel situation didn't make Elf at all nervous. In fact, she was relishing it like a fine wine. Secretly, she hoped to meet an exciting rascal tonight now that her brothers weren't around to scare such men away.

After all, there had to be exciting men somewhere in the world.

In moments, she and Amanda spilled out of the dark lane into the light of a thousand lanterns. Colored lamps festooned tall tress, garlanded high arches, and snaked around Grecian temples and ancient grottoes. Nearby a fairy glade had been created, with costumed actors posing as characters from *A Midsummer Night's Dream,* including a donkey-headed Bottom.

" *'I know a bank whereon the wild thyme blows . . .'* " Amanda quoted, at last caught by the excitement. She did not resist being swept up by the chattering, laughing throng of masked and costumed merry-makers. "Oh, you were right, Elf. This is great fun!"

"Lisette," Elf reminded her.

"Lisette, then."

"And you are Aimée."

"I know, I know. Though I think using made-up names is taking this to extremes." Amanda made the complaint in an offhand manner, however, being far more interested in everything around them. "I declare, I wish I had worn a costume rather than a domino. Look at that Titania!"

The lady in question was having trouble managing large, floppy wings, but her costume was remarkably pretty. Elf admired the imagination but did not regret her choice. She had not abandoned all caution, and even the most inventive costume gave less disguise than the Venetian domino.

After all, they said the domino was designed so a man could dance with his wife and never know it. And vice-versa. There were many men here in dominoes tonight.

Letting the noisy crowd carry them along, Elf wondered how many members of Polite Society were here, how many gentlemen were in danger of seducing their own wives. Or vice-versa.

Intrigued, she wondered at what point such lovers recognized each other, and if they were pleased or disappointed. Could an enchanting partner become distasteful when the mask came off?

What then created the enchantment?

Perhaps just the adventure, the wickedness.

Something wicked, she had said to Amanda. Of course, she didn't intend to do anything truly wicked. She merely wanted *change.*

She became aware of Amanda tugging at her cloak.

"Elf . . . Lisette. The Grove is that way."

In the Grove, the heart of Vauxhall, an orchestra played and refreshments could be purchased. It contained booths and pavilions in which guests could sit to eat and observe others. Rothgar had a private pavilion in the Grove and on previous visits Elf had spent most of her time there. She could use it tonight if she wanted to.

Safe.

Bored.

Oh, no. Tonight would be different. Elf put an arm

around her friend's waist to steer her firmly down the wide South Walk and away from security. "How can we have an adventure in such a place?" Just to tease, she added, "Perhaps we should seek out the Druid's Walk?"

Winding away from the well-lit main walks were ill-lit paths known to be the resort of all sorts of wickedness.

At Amanda's shriek, Elf laughed. "Be easy, dearest. I don't *think* I intend to be so rash."

"Elf—"

"Lisette," Elf reminded her. "Stop being such a mouse, Aimée! You have to admit that preparing for this escapade and escaping your servants has been quite the most diverting sport we have enjoyed in years."

"Indeed, it has been fun," Amanda admitted, but she again pulled her hood forward. "But the Druid's Walk—?"

"I was teasing, love." Elf pushed her friend's hood back. "You'll walk into a tree like that. Amanda, your *mother* wouldn't recognize you at the moment! You're the married lady here. You should be bolder."

"You're the Malloren. I always thought you were unlike your brothers, but now I wonder."

Elf drew her friend to the side, into a quiet spot beneath a spreading beech tree. "Do you truly want to go home? We will if you must."

After a moment, Amanda shook her head. "Of course not. I sometimes yearn for adventure, too." Her full lips set into a pout. "And I want to pay Stephen back for neglecting me."

"You shouldn't have married a political man, love. But at least he is completely devoted to you."

"I know, but . . . I just *miss* him. Even when he's home, he's so busy . . ." Then she shook her head and pushed her hood completely off her powdered hair. "On to adventure, then! But do let us be a little cautious, Lisette—see, I remembered! I've seen a number of men eyeing us."

"Indeed, I hope so." Elf led the way back into the crowd. "I don't consider myself past ogling yet. Why, look over there! Is that not Lord Bucklethorpe? He must be sixty if he's a day and he seems to think himself a very dashing fellow still."

The elderly earl was costumed as Charles II.

"Do you think he hired the Nell Gwyns with the costume?" Elf asked, staring at the expanse of naked bosom showed by the two orange-sellers hanging on the earl's arms.

"I think he'll be paying them a fee for the night one way or the other," muttered Amanda. "Do let's be careful."

Elf flashed her friend a soothing smile. "I promise not to hang on any man's arm for money, dear. In fact," she declared, "I vow not to attach myself to any man here unless I find the hero of my dreams."

Amanda glanced wryly at the boisterous crowd. "Then we are surely safe. Pray tell, my dear Lisette, what kind of hero haunts your dreams?"

As they strolled along, Elf pondered the question. "A knight in shining armor? Or perhaps a dashing cavalier in a long-plumed hat." She studied an illuminated Chinese dragon. "Perhaps a dragon slayer . . ."

"Lud!" Amanda raised her entirely ornamental quizzing glass and surveyed the crowd. "You will certainly never find such a man here tonight."

"I never expected to," Elf lied, knowing Amanda was right. Anyone with the fee could attend Vauxhall, and this public masquerade clearly attracted a particularly wild set. She looked around at bosky young bucks, city adventurers, and furloughed soldiers.

Not a dragon slayer in sight.

"I don't suppose any lady meets a dragon slayer," Elf said, "unless she first meets a dragon."

"And who would want to do that?" Amanda demanded.

A lady who wanted to meet a man like her brothers, thought Elf, but she kept it to herself.

Chastity, desperate to get her sister Verity to safety, had played the highwayman and held up Cyn's coach.

Then the three of them had dashed cross-country, avoiding enemies and even the army.

Portia, Bryght's bride, had been auctioned off in a brothel to pay her brother's gaming debts, and only been rescued by quick-witted Bryght. Then she'd been imprisoned by her relatives and had to escape by the window.

Elf knew both ladies had been in real danger, and very frightened at times. She certainly wouldn't want to be hunted by the army, or sold in a brothel . . .

But she wanted *something,* and she wanted a dragon slayer.

There were no dragons at Vauxhall, however, except gaudy Chinese ones, and the heroes—the would-be heroes in costume—were just as ornamental.

Despite her disappointment, Elf had no intention of backing out of her adventure now. Just being anonymous in such a crowd provided amusement, and there was no real danger. Even those four wet-behind-the-ears, would-be rakes over there, calling out suggestive invitations to herself and Amanda, could be ignored.

She noticed the group of drunk and glint-eyed gallants steering a course toward them, and instinctively gave them a frigid Malloren stare, the look she'd direct on any encroaching mushroom. Even through the mask it had its effect, for they halted, sniggered nervously, and went in search of more willing game.

Elf laughed at herself. How was a lady to have an adventure if she frightened off any man who showed interest?

A very tall, broad-chested military man stepped forward to block her way. "Hello, my pretty poppy. May I buy you some wine?"

Because of her thoughts, Elf stopped herself from glaring, consciously lowered her standards, and smiled. "I am not thirsty, sir, but—"

Amanda pushed between them, snapping in French, "Come, Cousin, we will be late for our appointment!" She seized Elf's arm and dragged her onward.

Elf permitted it but complained, "How am I to have fun if you won't even let me *speak* to a gentleman?"

"That gentleman wanted to do more than speak, believe me!"

"Aimée, I might be unmarried, but I'm not stupid. I know what he wants. I know, too, that he cannot force it as long as I remain in the principal walks. In fact, staying in the principal walks promises to be rather dull . . ."

Amanda confronted her. "Elf . . . Lisette . . . oh, whatever! I am no hand at these deceptions! But there I draw the line. We are *not* going into the side walks. Have you not heard the stories of those places? The crudest improprieties. Robbery, rapine—"

"Exaggerations, I'm sure," retorted Elf, being deliberately perverse. "After all, no place here is far from a public spot. Screams would be heard."

"But would they be attended to?"

Elf cast an acknowledging look at her friend. Amanda was no fool. It hadn't occurred to Elf that people might deliberately ignore cries for help, but in this shallow, tinsel-glitter crowd, she could believe it.

"So," said Amanda, pushing her point, "we stay on the main paths, or we return home."

Elf huffed out a breath. "You're no better than my brothers."

"And despite outward appearances, you're the same wild tomboy who used to create mayhem when we were children."

"But of course," said Elf. "I'm just in disguise as a lady." She sidestepped a drunken, weaving couple. "But I'm not a child anymore. It would be pleasant to find out who I really am."

"Ma'am . . ."

Elf assessed the young man trying to introduce himself. Weak-chinned and probably a merchant's sale clerk. She gave him the Malloren look and he slunk away.

"I've said it before, Elf. You need to marry. It can't be for want of offers."

"You've said it too often. I'll only marry the perfect man."

Elf realized they'd lapsed into English, but she didn't protest. Amanda was clearly uncomfortable in the foreign tongue, and this whole enterprise began to seem foolish.

"Lud!" declared Amanda. "If you're waiting for a man like your brothers, you'll rot on the shelf. And trust me, an ordinary man will be a great deal more comfortable."

Elf stopped to confront her. "Are you saying there's something wrong with my brothers?"

Amanda raised her hands. "Pax! Of course not. I've made up some pretty daydreams about them myself. But they're strong meat, Elf. When it comes to reality, there's a lot to be said for a comfortable man by the fireside. Of course," she added, as they strolled on, "I have wondered what it would be like to have a Malloren in my bed . . ." Then she covered her mouth in alarm.

Elf chuckled. "Don't worry. I'll never tell Stephen." She saw a booth selling lemonade, and steered toward it. When they had a glass each, she asked, "Which would you choose, Amanda? An exciting bed partner who was a bother the rest of the time? Or a steady, comfortable man who was merely steady and comfortable in bed?"

"If you're implying that Stephen—"

"I'm implying nothing. So," she asked wickedly, "which is he?"

Amanda glared at her, but her lips were twitching. "He's entirely wonderful. The trouble with the man is he's too rarely at home, and too often tired after long hours at Whitehall. That's when my mind starts wandering to forbidden fruit. Like Rothgar."

At that wistful mention of her oldest brother, Elf's brows rose.

"He's not exactly handsome," Amanda mused, "but there is something about him . . ."

"Probably the fact that he doesn't intend to marry,"

said Elf practically. "The sense of being unattainable is a powerful attractant."

Amanda chuckled. "True enough! But now, since I've told my darkest secret, you should tell me one, too."

"Darkest secret?" Elf drained the lemonade, which had been thin and much too sweet. Did she even know her own darkest secrets? Aware that trouble lurked in the deeper corners of her mind, she consciously kept them closed off.

"I've told you of my restlessness," she said. "Of my dreams about a dragon slayer."

"And what exactly is that?"

"A dragon slayer? Oh, he's Saint George, I suppose . . . No. No, he's not saintly at all. He's a dark, dangerous man. A man who would kill to defend me, but who is, of course, no danger to me. Except to my heart . . ."

Amanda made a purring sound of approval.

"Really, Amanda! For a sensible matron, you can be extremely foolish."

"As a sensible matron, I am allowed to be a little foolish. It's unmarried ladies who must be impeccable. I still don't think I've heard your darkest secret. Is there not some particular man about whom you think wicked thoughts?"

"Dozens, starting with the miller's boy when we were young."

"Oh, yes! Such muscles! We used to hide down by the weir and drool over him . . ."

Elf hoped she'd distracted her friend, but Amanda asked, "And now?"

"Walgrave," said Elf to get it over with. "I have strange, erotic thoughts about the Earl of Walgrave."

Chapter 2

"Lord Walgrave?" Amanda looked at Elf in mild surprise. "He's our age, handsome, eligible, and unmarried. I don't see anything wicked in that."

"He's also insufferable and a sworn enemy to my family!" Elf put down her glass. "Come along. Standing leaning against a tree is a complete waste of time and opportunity." She dragged Amanda back into the stream of revelers. "If we go this way we might at least find a good place from which to view the fireworks."

Amanda hurried alongside. "But isn't the earl Chastity's brother? That makes him your brother-in-law in a way."

Elf might have known mere movement wouldn't throw Amanda off the scent. "That hasn't engendered brotherly love, I assure you. We're all civil, more or less, for the sake of Cyn and Chastity."

"Goodness! It's just like Romeo and Juliet!"

Elf stopped dead, causing a group behind to collide with them. When everything was disentangled, she said, "Romeo and Juliet! You are deranged. He despises me. He likes women pliant and pleasing. And I despise him. He's a rake who has the nerve to preach propriety to me."

Amanda tugged Elf over to a bench which a couple was just vacating—vacating to head off down one of the wicked walks, Elf noted. She let her friend pull her down onto the seat, knowing she was about to be interrogated.

She wished she'd held her tongue. She'd thought Walgrave a safe topic. After all, it was true. She did despise him, even if he had cool blue eyes and an aura of energy that she feared was entirely sexual. He made her nerves tingle, so she sometimes tormented him from the safety of her brothers' protection.

She thought about him entirely too much, however, and even dreamed of him sometimes. Why, she had no idea. These days, the man never smiled, except cynically, and was bedeviled by a violent temperament.

She was mad.

"Preach propriety?" said Amanda like a prime hunting hound stuck to the scent. "Perhaps he's just having trouble settling into his role. He used to be a carefree young man—something of a rake, I'll grant you, but not a vicious one—then suddenly he was the earl. It can't be easy to step into the shoes of the man called the Incorruptible."

"He's trying, though. Trying to be as insufferably pompous as his father."

Amanda gave her a look. "And failing, I assume. I don't see you having fantasies about pomposity." She thought for a moment. "Didn't the old earl die at Rothgar Abbey?"

"Yes. A seizure."

That wasn't true, but it was the tale told the world. The earl had in fact fallen into a fit of madness and tried to kill the king's mother. Someone had shot him in time. Probably Rothgar. The current Lord Walgrave certainly seemed to blame Rothgar for his father's death, and seek out any and all means to harm the Mallorens.

It had been hushed up, of course. After all, attempting to kill a member of the royal family was treason, and that would have meant utter ruin for Walgrave's whole family. The old earl's title and possessions would have been confiscated and his two sons and two daughters cast out of decent society.

Amanda tapped her lorgnette against her lips. "You must have had a number of occasions to meet the new earl. The wedding. Doubtless other affairs."

"Few, but too many, I assure you. Amanda, if you are

even thinking of matchmaking, desist. Two less likely partners would be hard to find."

Amanda did not look discouraged. "Walgrave seems to be handling his responsibilities adequately. Stephen says he's surprised at the amount of attention the earl is paying to affairs of state and the sensible positions he's taking in Parliament."

Elf feigned a yawn. "I'm pleased if it's so, but do let us talk of something more interesting."

"Elf! You admitted to having fantasies about him. He is deliciously handsome. Almost as handsome as Bryght." She stared into the distance and gave a theatrical sigh.

Elf seized the chance to change the subject. "First Rothgar. Now Bryght. Next you'll be telling me you have heated dreams about Cyn!"

"No," said Amanda with a laugh. "For some reason, having spent summers in the mud with him catching sticklebacks puts him more in the status of a brother." She put her arm around Elf. "Perhaps because you are more like a sister, and he is your twin."

Elf returned the hug, hoping her unwise confidence would be forgotten.

But Amanda did not forget such things. "So," she said, "why not turn your fantasy into reality? If your brother can marry Walgrave's sister without the sky falling in, you could marry him."

Elf pulled free. "You have maggots in your head. I told you. We dislike one another thoroughly, and he seems determined on finding a way to destroy Rothgar. There'd be no comfort by the fireside in such a marriage."

Amanda grinned. "But think of the bed!"

Elf leaped to her feet. "You are a wicked woman. But no, I can imagine no comfort in the bed either in the midst of such hate."

Amanda sighed as she rose to join her. "You are doubtless right. It is a shame, though. He's the right *type* for you."

"Mad?" Elf flicked her skirts back into line. "Oh, let's head back to the boats. If we're going to share girlish secrets all night, we might as well do it at home in comfort."

Amanda didn't protest. "Have I spoiled this for you, Elf?"

"No." Elf linked arms with her friend. "It was just foolishness. I'll have to think of a more sensible way to change my life."

Retracing their steps meant fighting the flow, for most of the crowd were pushing toward the place where fire works would soon be set off. At first, Elf thought the obstacle came from the pressure of the crowd, but then an arm slid around her waist, pressing her into a musty woolen uniform. She looked up and recognized the much-braided captain.

"Monsieur!"

"Still alone, pretty poppy?"

"Je ne comprends pas."

He switched into clumsy but adequate French. "If your party has lost you, I'd be happy to be escort in their place."

"I suspect you plan to be a boarding party, sir, rather than an escort." She pulled against his hold, but made no impression on his mass and strength.

He laughed and squeezed her, squeezed a bit too hard so that she worried he might absentmindedly crush her ribs. But then the hint of danger sparked in her spirit like the first flashing lights from the fireworks.

She smiled at him.

"El . . . Lisette!" hissed Amanda, pulling at Elf's cloak.

"Hush, Cousin. Can you not see that the gentleman and I are talking?"

The captain grinned, showing large teeth that seemed healthy and whole, even if his lips were rather thick and red. "What a shame I came without a friend, Mademoiselle Lisette. Then your companion would not be so distressed, I'll go odds."

Elf decided to play her part and assumed a simper. "You are doubtless correct, Captain. But as you see, she is attached to me in all ways."

The captain turned and pulled Amanda within the compass of his other strong arm. "I'm a big man," he declared with a deep, resonant laugh. "I can handle both of you, have no fear!"

"I am sure you can, sir," Elf purred, rather enjoying the play-acting. She stroked his hairy hand. "I do so like a big man."

Amanda's dark eyes were flashing urgent messages from behind her mask, but Elf just smiled. They were both armed. They could handle even such a big man as this if they needed to, and this was an adventure of sorts.

She didn't want to go home without the tiniest adventure.

The captain steered them through the crowd, ably making a path and protecting them from the crush. He kept an arm about each, but most of his attention was on Elf. She didn't find the situation unbearable, for he had some conversation and talked pleasantly enough of the gardens, the weather, and his recent posting in Holland.

Then, without warning, he squeezed Elf close and kissed her.

Though she swayed back and twisted her head, his lips found their target. Hot onion breath swamped her and she struggled angrily against his hold.

Alarmingly, to no effect.

She had never before been in a strong man's power, and found she didn't like it at all.

Her struggles had forced him to release Amanda. To Elf's horror, she saw her friend pulling out her dagger. Struggling harder, she tried to warn the captain of the disastrous attack, but his wet lips sealed hers. In fact, he was working hard at forcing her mouth open to get his tongue inside.

Gemini, but Amanda would end up in the Roundhouse for murder, and the scandal would be appalling!

With a bellow, the captain jerked back, freeing Elf's mouth. Clearly, Amanda had struck.

"*Aimée, non!*" Elf cried, seeing her friend's hand raised again.

People nearby had paused to stare at the angry captain and the two women. Before someone decided to interfere, Elf flung herself back into his arms, snapping, "*Aimée, arrêet!*"

Amanda slid the knife away looking exasperated, but also shaken by her own action.

"It is only that she is jealous, monsieur," said Elf soothingly, switching into heavily accented English and touching the slash in his jacket sleeve. "Are you hurt most terribly?"

The captain stood taller. "A mere fleabite. But I could have the law on the woman for cutting my coat!"

He pulled out a handkerchief, and she helped him tie it tight around his arm to stop the bleeding. Elf couldn't help but admire his disregard of a wound that must have gone in at least an inch.

"Be merciful, *Capitaine*. She is so easily excited, you see."

He grinned and pulled Amanda back to his side. "Now that sounds promising, and may earn you a pardon, my pretty vixen." He turned back to Elf. "What about you, little poppy? Are you easily excited too?"

Elf realized that now she had to humor him until the nearby crowd lost interest and they could escape. Suppressing a sigh, she snuggled close. "I do not know, monsieur. I am not very experienced at these things."

A mighty chuckle shook him. "I'm just the man to expand your experience, my pretty. Oh, yes, I'll expand you well, I promise."

Amanda pinched Elf and whispered, "Have a care!"

Elf ignored her and smiled up at the man. "It seems you will have to expand the experience of us both, *Capitaine*."

His big dark eyes were hot, and he licked his moist

lips. "I could handle a dozen and still need more, my lovely."

"El . . . Lisette!" Amanda hissed. "He's leading us into the Druid's Walk!"

Elf wished Amanda would show faith in her common sense. Of course she knew the captain was taking them into one of the poorly lit paths. How could they break free in the middle of the crowd? When they were in a quiet shady location, she'd befuddle the lustful idiot until they could escape.

Bantering risqué words, she let him lead them farther and farther from the bright lights, into the realm of shadows and secrets. Finally, when a bend concealed them from the South Walk entirely, she eased away from the officer, pretending to study him in admiration. "*Mon dieu, Capitaine,* but you are a fine figure of a man," she crooned. "You must be the most tall man in your regiment."

He let her go entirely and flexed his muscles. "One of them, aye, and the strongest. And," he added, patting his bulging crotch, "built everywhere in proportion." He moved to pull Elf back into his arms, but she evaded him and went to inspect him from the back.

"Such wide shoulders. A Hercules among men! *Bien sûr,* you can carry a cannon, single-handed."

"Pretty close, pretty close." He turned to face her, but she moved to stay always behind, leading him to turn in circles. "Hey, my beauty, stay still so I can admire you, too!"

"There will be time for that. Plenty of time. *Maintenant,* I want to admire your so wonderful physique . . ." She kept him turning for a few more moments, then, judging her moment, said, "You should kiss my cousin, *Capitaine,* or she will turn jealous again."

She'd succeeded in dizzying him, so when he turned back to Amanda, he misstepped. Elf pushed him as hard as she could, then grabbed Amanda's hand to run back to the lights.

But he was more massive than she'd thought, and only

staggered under her thrust. Amanda faltered for a second before reacting and was snatched out of Elf's grasp.

Elf stopped, poised to return to the rescue, but Amanda ripped free, ending up on the other side of the captain, closest to the crowded South Walk. "Run!" she screamed and set off herself for the well-lit area.

With a laugh of pure excitement, Elf picked up her skirts and fled down the deserted Druid's Walk, hearing the captain bellow behind her.

Lanterns were deliberately scanty here and the paths twisted and divided. Elf passed an entwined couple on a bench, and some thrashing bushes that she didn't care to contemplate.

After a few moments she paused, breathing heavily. Devil take it. Her years of being a perfect lady had sapped her strength!

Then she heard pounding feet. She'd not lost him yet.

She plunged between dark bushes into the shrubbery that lined the paths, struggling her way through as quietly as she could. She heard silk rip and feared for Amanda's lovely domino. At least she didn't need to fear for Amanda unless her friend ventured back into the walks to help.

Dense growth and deep shadows formed a frightening otherworld, but she came across occasional open spaces. Whether natural or contrived, they had a purpose. She almost tripped over a couple *in flagrante delicto.*

Her instinctive apology was answered by an abstracted curse from the heaving gentleman. With difficulty, she suppressed a fit of the giggles and hurried on.

Once out of earshot of that encounter she paused to listen.

In the distance, fireworks crackled and banged. Closer, her rejected lover was still bellowing her name. But now other voices chimed in, telling him to shut up and go away. Faith, but the bushes must be alive with lovers!

The captain, however, had clearly lost track of her. Her plan had worked.

Then he became silent and she started to worry again.

She'd made a fool of him, and she didn't think him the sort to overlook that. Nor did she think him a fool. She suspected that he, too, was standing still listening, waiting like a good hunter for some sound of disturbance to mark her place.

She began to ease away from where she had heard him last, trying to make as little sound as possible, and alert for more clandestine lovers. In some places she could pass between shrubs or slip between tree trunks, but in others dense growth forced detours. Soon she was hopelessly disoriented.

She paused in the total darkness of a dense clump of yew to consider her situation. The fireworks had stopped, and no sound guided her.

Amanda would be safe, she thought, as long as she didn't plunge back into these paths in search of Elf. And practically speaking, Elf could do nothing for her friend other than return to the South Walk as soon as possible.

To do that safely, she feared she'd have to avoid the paths. That meant pushing through the bushes in the hope of hearing the orchestra and getting her bearings. It worried her that she could not hear it now, for that meant she must be far from the heart of the Gardens.

Try as she might, she could not even hear any writhing lovers. She felt as if she were alone in the midst of the country.

The dark, silent, ominous country . . .

She realized then that she no longer had any reason to stay away from the paths. As long as she was alert, she could return to them, merely being prepared to plunge back into the bushes if she spotted the captain.

Oh, her poor cloak. What a sight she would be when she finally emerged into the light!

Then she had an idea. Trying not to make much noise, she unfastened the voluminous garment and eased it off. Then she reversed it, putting it on again with the dark, cloth lining outside. Not only would it resist damage, it would be less visible than shining red. And when she finally emerged, she could flip it around again and appear relatively untattered.

That done, she had to make herself move onward. But as she began to work her way out of the yew, footsteps scrunched on the nearby path.

"This should do." A man's voice, speaking low and soft.

Lud, was she going to have to listen to a sordid seduction scene?

"It's quiet enough." Another muted male voice. "Now, what did you want?"

Despite her ladylike life, Elf knew the ways of the world and for a moment she feared she was to be audience to a sodomistic encounter. But the next words dispelled that.

"Your commitment to the cause has been called into question, my lord. There is considerable uneasiness."

"By whom?"

Elf felt the faintest twinge of recognition of that well-bred voice, with its slight drawl. But it could be anyone. She knew nearly every lord in England.

"By those with more to lose than you."

"I doubt any of you have more to lose than I."

"Aye, and that is maybe the cause for concern." The speaker's voice began to show a Scottish lilt, and turned markedly less respectful. "What will be your gain when we succeed, my lord?"

"That right should prevail," said the "lord," audibly dismissive of all concern. "The restoration of the Stuarts to their rightful throne."

At those words, Elf felt as if someone had poured icy water down her back.

Treason.

They were talking *treason*!

But surely the Jacobite cause had been crushed seventeen years ago by the Forty-five. The heads of the last lords to support that cause still rotted on Temple Bar.

Elf had stood statue-still from the first, but now she tried to even cut her breathing to the minimum. Amorous captains were a minor hazard compared to plotting traitors. If these men found her here, they'd slit her throat.

Inch by inch, and wincing at every faint rustle from her garments, she eased her bodice dagger out of her stomacher. Though only a tiny thing, with a blade no longer than her hand, it was still a weapon and better than none.

"I doubt you are driven by ideals, my lord," said the Scot. "Perhaps you think to gain a position of power under the new regime. But you must know there are many others with a claim to it, a claim going back generations."

"My family has a claim, too."

Could he be a Scottish lord? There were a few English who had ever supported the Stuarts, and some Scots lords lacked an accent.

The lord spoke again, with audible disdain. "If you don't want my help, say so. I'll not force it on you. But how you're to get close to the king without me I cannot imagine."

"You know too much to be allowed to walk away, my lord."

A new menace wove into the air and Elf's heart pounded. Murder? Could she really stand here and do nothing about a murder, even of a traitor?

The lord arrogantly dismissed danger, however. "Don't threaten me, Murray. I've left detailed descriptions of the plan in case of my untimely death. And I'm well able to take care of myself." Elf heard the lethal hiss of a sword being drawn.

The long silence might have convinced Elf she was alone except that they couldn't have left without making some noise.

"Put up, my lord," said the Scotsman at last, an edge of nervousness in his voice. "There is no need of swords. It is just that as the time comes nigh we're all on edge. After all, you could be a government man. An agent provocateur."

The lord laughed. "Absurd. You're a more likely one. Surely a man would only take such a role for money, and the one thing I do not lack is money. Are we finished here?"

The lord had obviously regained control of the situation, for the Scottish voice positively groveled as it said, "Aye, my lord."

"Then do not request any more such meetings. We only have a short time to wait, and incidents such as this are both dangerous and inconvenient."

"Aye, you are doubtless in the right of it, my lord."

Then, at last, footsteps on gravel told Elf they were leaving.

She sucked in a deep breath, beginning to tremble in reaction. Dear heaven, what should she do? Someone was planning to do something terrible to the king, doubtless intending to follow it by armed invasion!

She had to prevent it.

As her heart steadied, Elf realized a true adventurer would have found a way to peep out and identify that English lord. She, like a terrified rabbit, had stayed frozen in place. Now, while the impression danced fresh in her mind, she tried to fix a name or face to the voice. Though she was haunted by familiarity, nothing settled.

He had been speaking very low, but something in the tone had been familiar. A young man. She could almost see a proud stance, a haughty look . . .

No, it would not come.

Perhaps it would spring to mind when she stopped chasing it, or when next she met him. For the moment, she must escape from this situation, find Amanda, and get safely home.

She would go direct to Malloren House to tell Rothgar—

Then she realized he wasn't there. None of her brothers was close by. Her freedom from protectors had now become a significant problem.

Calculating how long it might take to get a message to any of them, she cautiously pushed out of the hedge onto the nearby path. As she stepped free of the shrubs, however, she saw a man in the nearby shadows, deep in thought. He was stocky, plainly dressed, with palish hair beneath a tricorn.

She froze, then started to ease back into concealment. But it was too late. He looked up and saw her.

She'd never seen this man before, but since he wore only a small mask, she'd recognize him again.

And he knew it.

Livid alarm replaced surprise. He leaped at her, seizing her arm. Remembering the dagger, Elf stabbed his wrist to the bone. Even as he howled, she fled for her life, praying she ran in the right direction.

The man had choked most of his cry of pain and now the only sound came from his feet pounding behind like a menacing drum.

Or perhaps her struggling blood was the drum in her ears . . .

Breathlessly lost in the twisting paths, Elf thought of taking to the bushes again. But her pursuer gasped close behind. What she needed was people.

Any people.

She'd throw herself on top of a copulating couple to get their protection!

She'd be ecstatic to see her captain.

Pausing at the junction of three paths, stealing a moment to suck in a deep breath, she searched for sound. She heard the orchestra dimly over her pounding heart, but there was no evidence of people nearby.

A frantic glance showed the man almost on her so she desperately took to her heels again, heading toward the music.

Turning a bend, she saw light!

Ahead, the crowded South Walk glimmered like paradise, but her pursuer grunted inches from her back.

A hand snagged her cloak.

She ripped it free and raced on, heart pounding fit to burst, dagger clutched tight in her hand.

If she stopped she was dead.

Nearer than the light, a person turned to face them, a dark silhouette against distant lanterns.

A tall man in dark clothes.

She didn't care who it was. "Help me!" she cried and flung herself against his chest.

Instinctively, his arms came around her as he rocked with the impact.

At the last moment, with heart-stopping relief, she recognized him, despite a narrow black mask. "Thank God!" she gasped.

She'd thrown herself into the arms of her brother-in-law, the Earl of Walgrave.

She was safe.

She was safe . . .

Collapsed against his strong chest, she wheezed for breath.

"She heard everything," panted the Scottish voice behind her. "She must die."

Chapter 3

Elf froze with horror, at last recognizing the hauntingly familiar voice.

She'd thrown herself into the arms of her brother-in-law, Lord Walgrave, but he had turned traitor.

It made no sense.

No sense at all.

What need did one of the most powerful and wealthy men in the kingdom have of Stuarts and rebels? But then she remembered his father had leaned toward the Jacobites during the invasion of 1745. That folly had given Rothgar a hold over the old earl, which in the end had driven the man mad.

Her breath-starved brain struggled for a new strategy. She doubted Walgrave would recognize her. Would he stand by and see an unknown woman murdered?

Would identifying herself help?

He hated Mallorens.

She gripped her dagger, even though she had no faith in its effect against two strong men.

At last Walgrave spoke. "Die?" he said lightly, his arms settling more firmly about her. "Zounds, man, this pretty bird doesn't have the wit to understand anything more serious than the trimming of her caps. Unless," he added with meaning, "you insist on forcing her mind toward the subject."

"You know her, my lord?"

Elf ventured a peep and saw that the Scot had not put away the long, menacing dagger in his hand.

Walgrave sighed as if bearing burdens. "She's my current mistress, and tiresomely jealous." Elf found her chin forced up by a none-too-gentle hand. "I shall have to punish you for this, puss. I really can't have you following me around and interfering in my affairs."

A tremor passed through her, for genuine fury glinted in his eyes. Apparently it wasn't murderous fury, however, and so she must follow his lead.

"Je suis désolée, monseigneur," she sniffed, not having to force the nervousness into her voice. She continued in French, "I was so sure you'd come here with *her.*"

With easy fluency, he replied in the same language. "Even if I choose to consort with other women, you have no right to spy or object, do you?" He enforced the words with a truly painful squeeze so she squeaked.

"No, my lord!"

"You see," he said to the other man in English, "she presents no problem."

The Scotsman's knife glinted. "With all due respect, my lord, she could do harm even by mindless chatter."

"Her English is not good enough, but I intend to keep her close. Don't concern yourself. She won't speak to anyone about anything until it's too late to matter."

With that, ignoring the threatening blade, the earl steered Elf firmly toward the lighted South Walk.

Though Elf's heartbeat was steadying, her legs still trembled. It was no hardship to cling to Walgrave and whisper, *"Merci, monseigneur!"*

"Don't thank me too soon." Once more, he spoke in French. His command of the language lacked her perfect accent, but it was excellent. "My Scottish friend is doubtless following, and I meant what I said. You are my prisoner."

"Prisoner? You can't do that!"

"What is to stop me? Whoever you are, you little minx, you have escaped your attendants and engaged in a feather-witted adventure. Which means I can easily make you disappear. Put away that toy," he added, glancing at her dagger. "It will do you no good."

Elf slipped it back into her stomacher but muttered, "It saved me from that man."

Her nerves were beginning to steady. Relatively speaking.

They still quivered like twanged harp strings, but strength had returned to her limbs and she could think.

Walgrave hadn't recognized her.

That was hardly surprising when she was masked. The main danger lay in her voice, for they'd met often enough. If they only spoke French, however, perhaps that would be enough disguise.

As they blended once more with the festive crowd, she prayed for it. His feelings toward the Mallorens were so fierce that if he discovered her identity, he might toss her back to the murderous Scot. Moreover, when she escaped him, he must never know whom he had saved, especially if he was involved in treason.

Treason!

Lud, but it made no sense. She'd thought him a rake, an unfeeling brother, and a malicious enemy. She'd never thought him deranged.

She'd puzzle that through later. First, she must continue to fool him until she could escape. She hoped he was still enough of a rake to be intrigued by a flighty Frenchwoman.

"Please let me go home, my lord. Don't be cruel!"

"Cruel? Faith, child, I'm being a very gentle, perfect knight. It goes against my nature, so don't question the blessing."

"Oh, I don't, my lord! Thank you, my lord! I think you're being wonderful!" The sillier she sounded, the less wary he'd be. She reminded herself of Amanda, and looked around the crowd. This enterprise had been Elf's idea, and she had to be sure her friend returned home safely. Try as she might, however, Elf could catch no glimpse of a silver-blue domino.

Walgrave was making a way toward the exit like Moses parting the Red Sea. Though incognito and dressed in plain dark clothes, something in his manner seemed to make the lesser mortals slink out of his way.

Where was Amanda?

She had to be sure her friend was safe. She also needed to ensure that Amanda didn't raise the hue and cry. By dawn, Elf hoped to be safely home with no one aware of her folly, but if Amanda raced home to cry the alarm, they'd be deep in the suds.

Elf began to despair, but as they came close to the river, even Walgrave had to slow his imperious progress. Elf could search more carefully, and she finally spotted a lady in a blue domino standing on a bench beneath a tree, desperately scanning the crowd. Amanda had even taken off her mask and looked frantic.

Elf focused on her, as if she could snag Amanda's attention out of the air. Twice her friend's eyes traveled by. Then Elf realized Amanda would be looking for bright red, and she was still wearing her inside-out cloak. Quickly, she pushed back the hood, exposing red silk.

Amanda's eyes traveled over her, twitched back, and fixed.

With a bright smile of relief, Amanda waved and jumped down off the bench. Elf hissed in annoyance. Amanda could be dashing into danger, particularly as Walgrave might well recognize her.

For a moment she wondered if she could use that to free herself. Surely he wouldn't try to imprison both of them. But then she remembered the murderous Scot. She couldn't let Amanda, clearly identified, fall into the circle of danger!

With his gaze on the crowds before them, Walgrave steered Elf onward, but she kept her eyes fixed in the direction Amanda would have to come from. As soon as her friend pushed through the crowd, she raised a hand in a command to stop. Amanda paused, a questioning look on her face. Elf made a shooing gesture, hoping Amanda would understand it as "go home."

Again, at the very mouth of Vauxhall Lane, Walgrave

was halted. He muttered a curse, his attention focused on the people blocking the tunnel ahead of them.

Elf turned her head and mouthed, *Go home. I'm safe.*

Amanda frowned, squinting at Elf's escort. Then her lips parted in surprise. After a moment her eyes widened in horrified amusement.

That expression stayed with Elf as Walgrave found a way through the crowd and swept her into Vauxhall Lane. For heaven's sake! Amanda thought she was heading off willingly for a night of passion with the earl of her dreams.

As they emerged and headed for Vauxhall Stairs, Elf saw one good side to the ridiculous situation. Amanda wouldn't approve, but she wouldn't sound the alarm and risk ruining Elf's reputation forever.

And Amanda should be safe. It was merely a matter of hiring a boat to take her to the steps close to Warwick Street. A footman had been instructed to wait there all evening, ready to escort the ladies back home. Of course, there would only be one lady, but surely Amanda could come up with some explanation for that.

For now, Elf had to concentrate on her own safety, and this bizarre matter of treason.

She needed her brothers, but it could take days for one of them to arrive. She had no idea when the plot was supposed to take place. Walgrave had implied that she'd only be a prisoner for a matter of days. The Scot had said the time was nigh.

She clearly couldn't just wait for her brothers. She would have to do something herself. Underneath worry and fear, she admitted to a tingle of pure excitement.

She was about to be challenged at last, and her Malloren soul delighted. She finally understood why her twin had felt compelled to seek a difficult and dangerous way of life.

Probably for this tingle in the blood.

So, what should she do?

Allowing Walgrave to guide her down toward the

boats, she skimmed over options. She would send for her brothers, but in the meantime, she must act.

Elf drew up a mental list of things to be done, just as if she were preparing for a grand entertainment.

First, escape from Walgrave without letting him know whom he had in his power.

Second, find out as much as possible about the plot.

She wondered if she should reverse those. If she stayed with Walgrave, perhaps she could find out more about the plot. But no. She suspected the earl had plans for their time together that didn't include discussion of his political leanings.

Third? Balk the traitors and see them brought to justice, she supposed. Without Walgrave ending up on the block.

She remembered only yesterday promising Chastity that she'd prevent such a disaster, and hysterical laughter threatened.

The penalty for treason was to be hanged, drawn, and quartered, though the Jacobite peers had been beheaded. She glanced up at the man beside her—clear-cut, arrogant features, brown wavy hair disciplined by a black bow. Was that handsome young head to be severed by an ax and left to rot on a spike in a public thoroughfare?

She could not bear the thought.

Nor would he be the only one to suffer. A traitor automatically fell under attainder, which meant that his title was annulled and his heirs deprived of all his property.

Chastity would fall under the cloud of shame, as would Cyn. A traitorous brother-in-law would play hell with his military career!

The dangers and widespread implications of the situation leached Elf's belief in her ability to cope. She hadn't any idea what to do. She truly wished Rothgar were close by. She would weakly toss all this into his capable hands and go back to planning grand entertainments.

But she was the only one here to do what must be

done, and so she must do it. The first thing was to escape.

She felt the earl's arm relax. Taking the chance, she ripped out of his hold. He reacted instantly, however, crushing her to him so ruthlessly she feared for her ribs.

"Give me trouble," he said flatly, "and I'll hurt you worse than this."

Shivering, Elf knew he told the truth. Though willing to rescue a foolish young girl, he'd control her with pain if he had to.

She wished she knew him better and could anticipate his moves. Before Cyn's involvement with Chastity, however, the Wares and Mallorens had rarely met. Lord Thornhill—as Walgrave had been then—had certainly not haunted the same spots as a lady. In fact, report held him to be little more than a rakish idler.

He had not—as the saying goes—improved upon acquaintance. Elf thought him quick-tempered, arrogant, and uncaring about people in his path. Coming from a close-knit family, she had been shocked that he'd given so little thought to his sisters' welfare. Rothgar had forced him to admit that they were victims of their father's ruthless ambitions, but Walgrave had not been particularly grateful.

After his father's death, he did appear to have reformed his morals, but he'd grown colder and revealed a dark, simmering malice toward all things Malloren.

Heaven knows why.

He couldn't, surely, claim to have loved his power-lusting father, and even if he did, why blame Rothgar for the fourth earl's death? Even if Rothgar had pulled the trigger, he'd been forced to it.

Whatever the truth, Walgrave seemed to be trying to fill his father's shoes in all ways, including enmity to the Mallorens.

It was, as she had said to Amanda, quite lunatic to feel a physical response to the man. Yet even now, literally a prisoner in his unkind arms, she could feel that erotic energy, feel it along her nerve endings and deep inside, where a wanton part of her stirred hopefully.

Oh, foolish creature, she told herself. *Stop it!*

As Elf was pushed toward the Stairs, she glanced back, wondering if Amanda would be following. What she saw, however, was three ominous figures close behind. All wore dark cloaks, tricorns, and masks. Despite the masks, they looked not one bit like merrymakers.

They looked like assassins.

"Yes," Walgrave said, still speaking French. "You really are safer with me. They will slit your pretty throat without a care."

And these were his conspirators? How could he be so foolish?

"Don't be afraid, though," he added without warmth. "If you do as you're told, no harm will come to you."

Boats were still depositing merrymakers, but by now there were plenty waiting to take revelers home. Elf began to ponder ways to use the boatmen in order to escape. At Walgrave's approach, however, a powdered footman separated from a group of waiting servants and blew on a silver whistle. Immediately, a personal barge glided toward them under the power of six sturdy oarsmen.

Elf watched with dismay. These were the earl's own men in his livery. She should have expected it. Rothgar generally traveled the river in this style.

The center of the boat contained an enclosed area curtained in green velvet adorned with Walgrave's crest and lit by hanging lamps. He pushed her into it, then took his place beside her, drawing the curtains as the boat shot off into the center of the wide river.

The area could seat about eight, so two didn't crowd it, especially since Elf sat on one side while the earl lounged on the other. She still felt trapped now she was alone with him. She had no illusions about being able to fight him off. He was twice her size and she knew he enjoyed all the usual manly sports, including the new one of pugilism.

"What are you going to do with me, my lord?" she asked, easily able to sound nervous.

"An interesting question." He took off his mask and dropped it on a cushion. It had been merely a strip of black silk, but without it he looked a little less menacing. That did not mean, however, that Elf underestimated her danger.

"Take off your mask," he said, studying her in a most disconcerting manner. Could he recognize her?

Elf put her hand up as if to hold her mask on, but in reality to cover her mouth and chin. "Oh no, my lord!"

"Why not?"

"I'm embarrassed, my lord. Truly, I'm a good girl. It was just a silly adventure . . ."

"Do you think you can stay masked for a week?" A trace of amusement crinkled his eyes, making him look quite the stranger . . .

Then his words penetrated.

"A week!"

"I can't allow you out of sight until certain matters are finished."

Treason, she remembered. How could he be so deranged?

"And," he added, "if you're thinking of trying to escape, be aware that those other men will catch you and kill you. It may be a strange notion, but you are far safer with me."

Elf looked away, worried now far more than afraid. Amanda might not raise the alarm tonight, but if Elf didn't return home tomorrow, she'd call out the military!

Therefore, she had to escape Walgrave tonight.

She parted the curtains, peering out at the dark water, at the bobbing lanterns of other boats, and the distant lights of wharves and buildings on the riverbanks. No escape there, and the assassins could be following.

"I'm sure they're there," he said lazily. "So. The mask?"

Elf turned back. "Let me keep it a little longer, my lord. Please. I'm so scared."

He shook his head. "You're a foolish creature. How old are you?"

"Twenty," she lied.

"Old enough to know better, then. Give me a name. I'm sure it will be false, but I need to call you something."

"Lisette. And it is real."

Unconvinced, he said, "It will, at least, suffice." He held out a hand to her.

Elf instinctively responded as she would with any gentleman. She placed her hand in his. Instead of kissing it, however, he gripped it and jerked her over onto his lap.

With a cry of alarm, she braced her arms against his chest to keep her distance, but with a sharp blow, he knocked them up and trapped her against his body. "We have a journey ahead, Lisette, and I require entertainment."

The wretch! As Lady Elfled Malloren she wanted to slap him, but she had to play her part as silly Lisette. What's more, now they were so close, the danger of recognition was much greater.

She twisted her face away. "Where are you taking me, my lord?"

"To my house."

Which lay close to the river and could well have private steps. Elf began to worry that it might, after all, be possible for him to keep her prisoner. She couldn't escape from the boat without drowning in the Thames. At his private steps, with his servants waiting and six sturdy boatmen nearby, she couldn't imagine breaking free. Once in his house, she might be caged.

She thought of one way to improve the odds. If he believed she was flattered by the attention of a noble seducer, and if he became sotted with lust, then his vigilance might slacken.

Could she do it?

After a moment's cool thought, Elf decided she could. The safety of the nation apparently lay in her hands.

She turned back and relaxed against him. "I've never been in a lord's house."

To keep her head down, she acted coy, fiddling with the carved jet buttons on his coat. It was black too, for these days he wore deep mourning at all times—a simple black frock coat and breeches. Her fingers brushed against the finest quality wool, though. Even for treason, Lord Walgrave did not dress poorly.

"Never been in a lord's house?" He already sounded less alert. One arm stayed tight around her, but the other slid up to stroke her neck. "Then it will be an adventure, my dear." His teasing touch sent shivers down her spine. "You can order the servants about, bathe in milk, and take breakfast off golden plates. If you please me, that is."

That was bringing matters to a head with a vengeance. But she supposed women fell at the crook of a finger from such a handsome young aristocrat. Or at the touch of a finger. The brush of his hand traveled to a spot just beneath her ear, causing a sensation so truly remarkable that she shivered.

"Oh, my lord, I'm a good girl," she protested again, without much hope of convincing him. Wouldn't a "good girl" find his touch repulsive?

Perhaps not.

"Virgin?" he asked bluntly.

She nodded, and in truth she *was* embarrassed now.

"I'll take care with you, then. You won't find it too unpleasant, and after the first time, it will get better. Now," he said, ceasing his teasing touch and raising her chin, "tell me truthfully, do you have family who'll kick up a fuss?"

If you only knew! Elf hoped that didn't show in her eyes.

"At my being missing, my lord? I am visiting from France, living at the house of my English cousin. A married lady." She took the opportunity to lower her head again. "I don't think she'll raise the alarm just yet—"

"How very obliging of her." His voice had a cynical,

knowing edge. "And what will happen when you don't return in a day or two?"

She traced the braid down the front of his coat. "If I were with a fine lord . . ."

"They'd not be unduly upset. Good." His fingers slid into her hair again, but this time to twist her face up to his. "I dislike scenes, Lisette. Let us be clear. I have no intention of marrying you. If you get with child, I'll pay for its care, but I will not marry you. I am not even interested in a permanent mistress. When I tire of you, there will be a generous parting gift, but I'll expect you to take your dismissal without a scene."

Elf shut her eyes. She hoped he took this for shock, but she needed to hide pure fury. The arrogance of the man! And how wretched that many women accepted such terms every day.

"Well?" he demanded.

He really didn't care, which was another cause for fury. "Lisette" could be one of a hundred young women. She just happened to be the one to hand.

Elf told herself that the fact that Lisette was Lady Elfled Malloren had nothing to do with it. But Lady Elf was definitely not accustomed to being treated just as someone conveniently to hand.

Concentrating on appearing overwhelmed and flustered, she opened her eyes. "Of course you would never marry me, my lord. I would never expect it! But it's a terrible step to take, to give my purity—"

"Sell," he corrected. "Five hundred guineas when we part. Enough to make a future husband ignore any little details."

Elf had lived her life among wealth and position and feared she could be just as arrogant in her own way. Her brothers were surely capable of this cold bartering of the flesh.

Viewed from the other side, however, it appalled her.

"Well?" he asked again. "I won't rape you, but if I must keep close guard on you for a week, some sensual experiments will help pass the time."

She reminded herself that she would use this to escape and snuggled closer. "If you promise to be kind, my lord," she whispered.

"Good girl." His hand rubbed against her neck, a comforting stroke now, as a person might stroke a cat. "You won't believe how kind I can be, Lisette. Now, let's see a little more of you."

He unfastened the ribbons that held her domino closed and pushed it back. Then he blinked at her gown. "My dear Lisette! You need lessons in taste."

Elf pushed away. "How *dare* you!"

"Offended you at last, have I?" he said with a laugh. "My dear, that is the most appalling ensemble I have ever seen."

Now Elf did want to hit him, but she feared she'd let her ingenue manner slip. "These are my very favorite garments," she informed him with a sulky pout.

"Then thank heavens I don't intend to present you at Court." He touched her angry lips. "Dress in the colors of the rainbow for all I care, poppet. I'll even buy them for you if you want. But mostly I'll want you naked . . ." Then he tilted her head back and brushed his lips over hers.

Despite her outrage, Elf couldn't really object at this point, and so she let him tease her out of her annoyance.

He knew the tricks, did Lord Walgrave, and as he said, he could be kind. He did not force a kiss on her, but played with her lips while stroking her body, until she relaxed and responded without conscious thought.

Elf had been kissed a time or two, though never—being Lady Elfled Malloren—with such confident finesse. Even her boldest suitors had kept their senses alert for Rothgar.

Walgrave did not know he needed to be alert for danger. In fact, at the moment, none threatened and he was supremely at ease.

Having overwhelmed her first reluctance, he tightened his hold and brought his tongue into play. Elf struggled for a moment, but then relaxed. She was being thoroughly kissed by a master of the art and might as well enjoy it.

Taking a hint from his own practices, she slid her hands up to his shoulders and caressed his neck as he teased her mouth. She didn't know how it felt to him, but touching his skin was almost as pleasurable as being touched.

The texture beneath her fingertips blended with the taste of him in her mouth, and with the feel of his body close to hers. The pleasure built faster than she'd imagined possible . . .

Then she realized he'd slid his hand between them to rub against her breast. Even through layers of stomacher and shift, the pressure tormented her. He unhooked the front of her open gown so it parted, leaving only her lace-frilled stomacher and scarlet satin petticoat to protect her.

She pulled her mouth free, intending to protest, but he laid his fingers over her lips and said, "Shhhhhh."

To her bewilderment, she did.

Those eyes were the culprit, those bright blue—almost kingfisher blue—eyes smiling down into hers. She'd always known they were dangerous and she'd never seen them smiling before.

He should smile more often.

And now the aura surrounded them both, that aura of erotic energy she had always been aware of. It had been strong even in casual contact. Now it overwhelmed her, dizzying her as if with a fever.

Was it a smell?

No. A slight aroma surrounded him—a musky perfume and a subtle personal smell. But the aura could not be detected by anything except the especial part of a woman designed to respond to a man.

His hands had slid behind her, the touch on her ribs and spine sending shivers through her. With a few expert tugs at her stay-laces, he loosened her stomacher so he could ease it down from her breasts and fully touch one nipple.

Elf had definitely traveled into unexplored territory.

She knew she should protest, should fight, but it felt so utterly wonderful!

And would this ever happen again? She had escaped Elfled Malloren, who must be treated with respect at all times. Here she was just a woman being pleasured by a man. And such a man . . .

She relaxed against his arm and smiled.

He smiled back, looking so unlike her brooding, critical brother-in-law that she could almost be persuaded he'd traded places.

Traded places with the man of her dreams.

"Like that, do you, puss? And there are more wonders to come." He eased her nipple up over the stiff stomacher and lowered his head.

At the first flick of his tongue, Elf gasped. When his teeth touched her, she squeaked and seized his hair, thinking to stop him.

Then he sucked at her and she whispered, *"Juste ciel!"* and held him closer.

"Ah," he murmured softly against her flesh. "You recognize heaven, do you, little one." He moved to torment her other breast.

Elf realized she was clutching his silky hair so tightly she was pulling it out of its ribbon. She relaxed her tense fingers, but then became aware of a throbbing itch between her legs that she understood all too well.

Never before, though, had she experienced hot desire quite like this. She wanted, needed, a man in a way she had never imagined possible.

Oh, she had certainly missed a great deal!

A purring noise startled her, especially when she realized it came from her own throat. That shocked her back to reality. She was in danger of falling into the trap she'd intended for him. She'd soon be so muddled she'd forget entirely that she planned to escape!

Escape, she reminded her dazed brain.

That meant she must fuddle him.

How, she had not the slightest idea. A wanton part of

her body whispered that she could let him fuddle her entirely and see what happened next.

Still suckling at one, he touched the other exposed breast with delicate fingers. Oh yes, thought Elf, purring again, she could just let him enlighten her. After all, she'd wanted to experience this, and Walgrave clearly possessed useful skills.

Then her wits cleared. She could never make love and keep her mask on, yet to reveal her identity would be disastrous. Quite apart from scandal and his feelings about Mallorens, she didn't want a traitor to know Elfled Malloren knew his secrets.

Traitor.

Treason.

Think, Elf!

So Elf did her best to ignore his sensitive attentions, drag her wits together, and find a way to turn the tables.

As a well-raised lady protected by four brothers she lacked experience, but having grown up with four brothers—one a frank-talking twin—she was not entirely ignorant. She had some theoretical notions of how to go on. Did she have the courage?

Of course she did.

She was a Malloren.

Shifting slightly, she pressed her hand to his chest. Then, while he continued to drive her mad with his skillful lips and fingers, she slid her hand down his front till she found the solid shape she sought.

A solid shape, she knew, meant he was at least half fuddled.

Lud! He must be almost entirely fuddled.

He raised his head and looked at her, amusement warm in his eyes. "I thought you were an innocent little bird."

"Oh I am, my lord! But not entirely ignorant . . ." She had no idea what to do next, so she tickled with one fingernail.

He laughed. "Your imprisonment and education promise to be delightful, Lisette." But he removed her hand and sat her up. "We must delay it, however. We're here."

With the calm efficiency of a well-trained maid, he tucked her breasts back behind the stomacher and tightened her laces. Then he hooked her gown, rearranged her cloak, and pulled her to her feet.

Elf let him handle her like a puppet, stunned to realize that the boat had reached the stairs and been tied up without her noticing a thing.

Fuddled indeed!

She shivered, nerve endings raw with arousal and fear. She'd have to be a great deal more careful if she wanted to even *recognize* a chance to escape.

He climbed out and turned to hand her onto the well-lit private stairs leading to Walgrave House. Glancing back, looking for the enemy, Elf saw only the dark river dotted with the bobbing lights of other boats. There was no way to know if the assassins were still close by.

She looked around, hoping against hope for some escape path. The head-high walls of the gardens of Walgrave House surrounded her, however, and ahead loomed the solid mass of the house itself. Some windows glowed with welcoming light, but it looked like an effective prison to her.

Don't be a fool, she berated herself, as she walked along the path beside Walgrave, torchbearers before and behind. Chastity had escaped from a most efficient prison, and Bryght's Portia had climbed out of an upper-floor window! There were always ways.

If she were left alone.

She flicked a glance at her captor. He smiled at her in a way that suggested he was not intending to leave her alone.

Oh, Gemini. Perhaps her best plan would be just to cry the alarm.

But they were in the house by then, and she doubted his servants would rush to her aid.

* * *

Out on the river, Michael Murray nursed his bandaged hand and watched Walgrave and the doxy walk toward the great mansion. When they were out of sight, he told the boatmen to take his party on to the Whitehall Stairs. His three companions relaxed, knowing no violent action would be needed in the near future.

Murray couldn't remember being relaxed, and now tension clamped like a vise around his shoulders and neck. The earl had kept his word thus far; he had the wench safe. It didn't feel right, though. It didn't feel right at all.

A French titty. Murray himself spoke excellent French, and there were always French people in London, but it struck him as suspicious.

And she hadn't acted like a hardened whore. Not even like a regular mistress. A woman moved in a special way with a lover.

He rubbed his wound, remembering how she'd not hesitated to strike at him. Hardly the behavior of the flighty wench the earl had claimed her to be.

His sixth sense told him something was awry, and this close to the time, he couldn't endure it. He'd be easier with the woman dead beneath the bushes in Vauxhall. A lot easier. He'd like the earl dead beside her, but he needed his help.

And a dead or even missing earl might stir up trouble.

Murray began to weigh the earl's usefulness against the danger he presented. By the time his boat nudged the steps at Whitehall, he had reluctantly decided that the benefits outweighed the risks.

For now.

Once the toy was in his hands, though . . .

He paid the boatmen and led the way up to Whitehall, analyzing ways to reduce that risk.

"Kenny," he said, "you and Mack go watch the earl's house. I want to know if he lets that scarlet piece go in the morning."

"Then why canna we go back in the morning?" Mack grumbled with a yawn. "I'm fair forfochten."

"Because this whole business tonight might have been a ruse, in which case he'll send her on her way as soon as he thinks we're gone."

"That one?" Mack chuckled. "She had promising ankles, that one did, and we all ken the Earl of Walgrave can follow ankles upward. She'll go nowhere the night."

"We cannot risk the chance that you are wrong." Murray tried to keep distaste out of his voice. His men used whores. Even his beloved leader, Prince Charles Edward Stuart, was unchaste. Michael Murray would not so sully himself, but he knew the others would laugh at him for prudery, undermining his authority.

Mack scowled, but accepted the orders. "So, what do we do if he does send her on her way? Follow her?"

"Of course not. Kill her."

Chapter 4

Elf had never been in Walgrave House before. Until Cyn and Chastity's inconvenient attachment, the Mallorens and the Wares had definitely not been on visiting terms.

Elfled Malloren would never gawk at anything, but as silly Lisette Belhardi she felt free to stare as much as she wished.

Gloomy, she decided, looking around the large square hall. Ponderous, even. Dark paneling covered the walls and ceiling in a fashion at least forty years old, and the only ornaments were four large marble statues. No fashionable classical nudes here. Instead four eminent men of Rome loomed stern-faced and rigid, fully dressed in togas and laurel wreaths.

She detected the hand of the old earl, the Incorruptible. This was doubtless his vision of himself.

So, how did the new earl see himself?

She wasn't given much chance to stare or ponder. Walgrave steered her toward the curve of the massive oak staircase, clearly not in the mood for delay.

Discarding most of her vague plans for escape, Elf seized on Portia's trick. "Oh, my lord. I hesitate to bother you, but I do need to relieve myself."

"Doubtless. Come along."

He continued up the stairs and led her to a room.

A bedroom.

She'd never been in a bedroom with a strange man before! Then she made herself relax. This was just part of her plan. He'd leave her alone, and she would escape.

He helped her off with her domino, then indicated the closestool behind a screen. "There you are. I'll be back in a moment."

The room had two doors—the one through which they had entered, and one into an adjoining room. He locked the latter and pocketed the key, then left by the former. She heard the key turn in that lock too.

The window. Portia had escaped by a window.

He'd undoubtedly meant what he said about only giving her a moment, so Elf ran to the window and flung it up. One glance killed hope. A sheer brick wall ran down to the ground.

Portia had used cording from the bed to form a rope, but this room offered no such conveniences, and besides, Elf knew she had no time. Hearing footsteps, she closed the window and ran behind the screen, only reaching it as the lock turned.

"Still at it?" he asked, with a great lack of delicacy. "I hope you're not of a gut-tied disposition."

Elf found she did need to use the convenience. Partly to cover the embarrassing noise of her action, she called out, "Not at all, my lord. I was just tightening my laces."

"A singular waste of time." His comment reminded her that she faced a fate worse than death with no sign of escape. Nervous tremors began in her belly.

She'd never believed it would actually come to this.

It was all very well to *think* about experimenting with sex, but now it was close and real, she had no taste for it at all. She didn't want such intimate relations with a man she hardly knew, especially when what she knew of him, she didn't like.

Moreover, he was showing no particular warmth or fervor. She shuddered at the thought of such indifferent invasion of her body.

And what of the possibility of getting with child? The mere notion of having to tell Rothgar she was pregnant with the Earl of Walgrave's bastard was enough to give her a case of the vapors!

Still, she had to pretend to be coyly willing and pray for a chance to escape.

She hastily tightened her laces. Then, making sure her mask was firmly in place, she emerged. "I'm so sorry for keeping you waiting, my lord."

"No matter. We have plenty of time." He was relaxed and smiling, but she judged it more a case of good manners than warmth. She supposed it would be churlish to scowl at the night's bed partner.

He unlocked the adjoining door and gestured that she should go through it. Obeying, she found herself in another bedroom, rich with the light of two branches of candles. This was doubtless his own bedroom, since a number of personal possessions scattered it his razor case on the washstand, a powdered wig on a dummy head, a line of books between gilded bookends.

She turned to watch him stroll to a walnut side table which held a crystal decanter and glasses. He poured deep amber wine into beautiful goblets. "Come, Lisette," he said, offering her one. "You'll enjoy this as much as my suckling."

Feeling her cheeks flare red beneath the mask, Elf took the wine, admiring it as she played for time. "Oh, my lord What a pretty glass!"

Could she get him drunk? She doubted it. His capacity must equal her brothers', and they could drink remarkable quantities of claret and port without progressing beyond bosky.

She sipped. As expected, she tasted excellent port, but she pretended surprise. "Oh, my lord! What a fine wine! What is it?"

"Port. One of the few good wines that do not come from your homeland. Perhaps I can educate your palate as well as other parts of your body."

"Oh, my lord . . ." Elf simpered, sipping slowly and seeking desperately for a way out of her predicament. Something in Walgrave's manner suggested that he had only one goal and would not lose sight of it. Could she use her dagger on him?

She took another tiny sip and smiled at him.

He drained his glass, put it down, and came over to her.

"Getting to like it?" He plucked the glass from her hand and tossed it carelessly to roll and spill on the carpet. "That's a fine augury."

Elf stared shocked at the glass, relieved it hadn't shattered, but concerned about wine stains in the carpet . . .

Then he seized her.

"My lord!"

She was tight in his arms, and his lips sealed hers.

Elf struggled free. "Stop! My lord, have pity!"

"Why?" His expression showed absolutely no uncertainty.

"I . . . I'm afraid."

"It won't hurt too much."

"Not that, my lord! But it's a mighty step, to lose my virginity. I want to think on it!"

"Don't be silly," he said, and kissed her again.

Elf lost her temper. She kicked his shin with all her might. Since, unlike the captain, he wasn't wearing boots, he cursed and dodged back.

But he held on to her arm.

She made a fist and swung at his bulging breeches.

He twisted and took it on his hip, bruising her hand. The next thing she knew, she lay facedown on the bed, her wrists gripped behind her, with a heavy knee in the small of her back.

"What the devil's the matter with you?" he snarled.

"I don't want to do it!" she wailed, hastily returning to her character. "I'm frightened." And now she spoke the truth. She was helpless.

"You're a cursed vixen. Very well, Lisette, have it your own way. But you'd have found swiving a great deal more comfortable than what's going to happen now."

He released her hands, but with his weight pinning her to the bed, she could scarcely breathe, never mind struggle. He raised her skirts.

She began to struggle then, kicking and twisting, but he pulled loose first one garter, then the other. Then he captured her hands again and tied them together.

When Elf realized he wasn't going to beat her or do something even worse, she stopped fighting. He pulled down her stockings and used them to tie her ankles together. Then he picked her up and carried her into the next room. There he placed her, quite carefully, on her side in the middle of the big bed. He even pulled the covers from under her so she lay on the sheet.

She stiffened when his hands went up under her skirts again, but he just untied her hoop laces so he could pull off the cane contraption.

"There," he said, tossing it aside, then pushing back his disordered hair. "That's the best I can do, you silly creature." He flipped the covers over her. "I'll be sleeping in the next room with the door open. If you change your mind, just say so."

She watched him go, thinking she surely should have been able to handle this whole affair better.

Elf didn't know how comfortable swiving would have been, but it could hardly have been less so than her predicament. Her bound arms began to burn and a mad need to stretch her legs plagued her. Twitching around, she managed to roll onto her front, making matters worse. Now she was sunk in the feather bed having to strain her neck in order to breathe.

A hundred times she was tempted to call him, but she managed to resist.

Instead, she tried to consider her options.

If she became the earl's lover, she might have a chance to escape. But she couldn't imagine becoming his lover without being recognized.

If she revealed her identity, he probably wouldn't try to seduce her. He'd always seemed to dislike her saucy tongue and irreverence toward his sex. He certainly wouldn't let Elfled Malloren escape, however, to tell Rothgar about the plot.

Elf wriggled a bit and managed to get her head into a slightly more comfortable position. Really, this was such a ridiculous situation! Was there any hope she could tell her brothers about the treasonous plot without revealing her string of follies? Gloomily, she concluded there wasn't.

Thank heavens Cyn was well away. He'd be disgusted with her.

After much thought, she concluded she'd have to continue to be Lisette, the reluctant French mistress. That way she might manage to avoid recognition and escape in the morning. If only she could persuade him to untie her.

Then she realized she still had her bodice dagger.

How to use it, though?

She very much doubted she could stab Walgrave with it, but it would serve to cut her bonds. If she had use of her hands.

Or had her hands at the front.

It was a risk, but she took it.

"*Monseigneur?*" she called, remembering to use French. After a moment, she called again, louder. "*Monseigneur!*"

He'd left the door open, and she heard movement in the next room. Then light flared. In a few moments, he appeared, a branch of lighted candles in one hand.

Elf's plans were momentarily fractured by the sight of him.

He must sleep naked.

He'd clearly just pulled on a long, black silk robe, loosely tying the sash at the waist. She realized she was staring at his magnificent chest and hastily looked up. The sight was no less distracting. His brown hair curled loose to his shoulders, endearingly disheveled from sleep.

Something about his appearance made her think of angels, warrior angels such as Michael. As he stepped forward, the thin robe clung to his body, and even parted to show a warrior's legs.

Elf stared, stunned by an alarming desire to kiss various bits of his magnificent anatomy.

"Come to your senses, Lisette?"

She forced her mind back to her purpose. "Oh, my lord. I'm in such discomfort. Will you please untie me?"

"Of course not. Is that why you woke me?"

"I can't get any rest," she sniveled. "Could you not at least tie my hands in front? I rolled like this and can't roll back."

His expression relaxed into a wry smile. After placing his candles on a table, he settled on the edge of the bed to rub her back in a disconcertingly gentle manner. "Poor Lisette. I suppose you're thoroughly scared. And, as you say, uncomfortable. You see what comes of going on wild adventures to Vauxhall."

"I do, my lord. I'll never be so foolish again." And that was true. After this night, Elf wanted no more adventures.

"But I can't risk your running off, you know. I'm not sure you won't tattle of things that can't be spoken of. And there's a chance those men are watching the house. I've no mind to have an innocent life on my conscience."

Surprisingly, he sounded sincere. This was a Walgrave she did not know.

"I understand, my lord. But if you could just tie my hands in front . . ."

He rubbed her back for a few more moments, and when he stopped, Elf almost protested. "Very well," he said, and untied her wrists. He rolled her onto her back, and even gave her a moment to stretch and rub away some of the pins and needles before seizing her wrists to retie them at the front.

Despite her discomfort, despite the danger, Elf couldn't help appreciating the beauty of him so close in the candlelight. Framed in jet-black silk, the muscles of his chest and neck were clearly defined. She'd never thought men's necks of any particular interest.

She would dearly like to see the whole of him, to see if it matched the promise of the visible parts . . .

"Changing your mind, sweetheart?" The lazy voice pulled Elf out of her wanton thoughts and she looked up at him, embarrassed. "By the expression on your face, you want to eat me."

He'd retied her almost unnoticed! And even with the mask, he'd read her wicked thoughts. Perhaps she'd been licking her lips!

"Well?" he said, stroking her jawline. "It's not yet one o'clock. We've plenty of night left." Light as a feather, he brushed his thumb across her lips. "You're ripe for it and you know it. You know I can please you . . ."

Could someone take over another's mind, using a soft, persuasive voice to shape thoughts to his will?

Or was he merely speaking the truth of her desires?

Though she couldn't quite form a denial, Elf managed to shake her head. Reluctantly. Very reluctantly. She couldn't believe how much she wanted to accept his offer when but a short while since she'd fought him.

She'd never anticipated the power of unexpected kindness when applied to an awakened body.

Bodies could be very wicked.

He shrugged and stood. Then, with a disarming glint of mischief, he untied the belt of his robe and let it fall open.

Elf looked.

She looked up at his face, then down again, her mouth turning dry and her heart thundering.

He let the black silk slither down his arms, then caught it in one hand.

He reminded her of a statue, but not a stern Roman senator—a nude Greek athlete. Sleek, solid muscles were perfectly arranged around long strong bones.

"Are you *quite* sure, Lisette?" She looked up to see a gentle teasing that threatened to melt her reason. "As my lover, you'd be allowed to do all the wicked things you're imagining, and some you haven't even thought of yet."

Oh yes. Oh please . . .

But then the many powerful reasons why it would be insanity managed to make themselves heard. Though she could have wept, she shook her head again.

He shrugged, picked up his candles, and strolled back to his room, his beautiful naked back constant temptation to change her mind. She could imagine the feel of his firm, round buttocks beneath her hands . . .

"By the way," he said, presumably from his bed, "if you call me again, I'll take it as a demand that I satisfy your all-too-obvious appetite no matter whether you shake your head or not."

The candles were extinguished and silence fell.

Elf lay on her back, shaken by lust and consumed with embarrassment.

Vague hungers based on kisses and men's clothed bodies had now taken concrete form. Her desires were no longer dreamy. They were firm, urgent, and centered on Fortitude Harleigh Ware, Earl of Walgrave, the least likely man to satisfy them if he discovered who she was.

Well, she tried to tell herself, she'd known she was feeling this restlessness, this dissatisfaction. Mere accident had thrown her in with her brother-in-law tonight. Her feelings would surely have been the same for any other handsome man who'd rescued her from death.

She wasn't sure she believed it, and the temptation to take him at his word and call out again astonished her. He would strip off her clothes until she was as naked as he. Then he'd lie beside her and touch her as he'd touched her on the boat, but more so. He'd suckle her again, and stroke her.

And she would be able to touch him, to enjoy the rough and smooth of him, the hard and soft.

The taste.

The smell . . .

No!

Elf blew out a long breath and concentrated on lying still, on listening to the clocks in the house sound one, and then the quarter, then the half.

Then she began her escape before she did something impossibly wicked.

First, she reached up to work her dagger free. That was when she realized that the cunning man had tied her hands back to back so her fingers couldn't work together.

She worked away with just her right hand, thankful that the dagger fit on the outside of the wooden stay down the front of her stomacher. At least she couldn't stab herself in the heart. When she had it free of its sheath, she lost her grip so it tumbled onto the bed. In fumbling for it, she jabbed her hand and hissed at the pain. She hadn't realized just how sharp it was!

But she had it at last.

Then she discovered that with it in the grasp of her right hand, she could not reach the garters binding her wrists. Blast the cunning man's eyes! She could reach her ankles, however, and soon had her legs free.

She sat on the edge of the bed in almost pitch darkness, trying to find a way to cut through the garters binding her wrists. All she managed was to pierce her skin again and again so blood ran down her arms. She needed to get the blade between her hands to cut there.

It was impossible.

Then she had an inspiration. Gripping the hilt of the small dagger in her teeth, she brought her bound wrists up to work against the blade.

It was surprisingly difficult, and she could have screamed with frustration. Her teeth couldn't hold the dagger steady, so she couldn't apply much pressure. Saliva gathered, and she kept having to take the knife out to swallow. It was hard to find the right angle, and she nicked herself again and again.

Despite the mass of burning cuts, she would not, could not give up.

The silk parted so suddenly that she gasped and the knife tumbled to the floor. She froze, listening intently to the next room.

Only the ticking of clocks broke the silence.

With a deep shuddering breath she flexed her hands, pressing at the sore cuts with the sheet. In the dark, she couldn't see the damage, but she didn't think it was serious. Just painful.

Re-sheathing her dagger, she slipped off the bed. She considered leaving her hoops behind, but without their support her skirts hung perilously long, so she took the time to tie them on again. Then she put on her cloak, dark side out, pulling the hood up over her white-powdered hair.

Her stockings and garters were beyond hope, but she considered whether they might identify her. She couldn't imagine how. She was dithering, so she picked up her shoes and faced her challenge. She had to leave this room and escape the house, then cross London in the middle of the night, with murderers quite likely lurking in the shadows.

She was tempted to go into the next room, Walgrave's room, where she might find a pistol. She couldn't take such a risk, however, even though she would have loved to have a weapon.

Shrugging, she reminded herself she was a Malloren.

As her brother often said, with a Malloren, all things are possible.

She crept across the room and tried the door to the corridor. The knob turned in well-maintained silence, and the door opened without a sound into almost total darkness.

Feeling her way toward the stairs, she tried to convince herself that no one would leave an obstacle in the middle of the corridor. She couldn't see well enough to be sure, however, and so crept along with tiny steps, hands extended. The last thing she wanted was to crash into anything.

By the time she reached the top of the stairs, her heart was pounding and her nerves were in shreds. A fine adventurer she was turning out to be. If she had a way of calling for her brothers to come and protect her, she'd take it in a moment!

Sucking in a few deep, steadying breaths, she peeped over the stair rail. Some grand houses kept a night footman in the hall, for security and in case of unexpected callers. Such a footman, however, would have a lamp. The hall of Walgrave House lay dark beneath her, apart from a pale shaft of moonlight from the fanlight above the door.

Elf crept downstairs, testing each step for squeaks before putting her full weight upon it.

Each was solid as rock. Hardly surprising. Until six months ago, this house had belonged to the old earl—the Incorruptible. He'd been a stiff-rumped old tyrant who would no more let a stair squeak than he'd let his daughter marry against his wishes.

Even so, she sighed with relief to step onto the cool tiles of the hall floor. Now she could think clearly.

Outside, there might be waiting assassins. Before leaving the house, she must find a weapon.

Aided by the weak moonlight, she methodically checked rooms until she found the one she wanted—Walgrave's study, where she had the best chance of finding pistols.

The curtains were drawn, so she had to take the risk of opening them, wincing at the rattle. That gave her light enough to search the room. In some drawers beneath a bookcase she found a pistol case containing two beautiful dueling pieces.

From his spot in the shadows in the lane between Walgrave House and its neighbor, Kenny watched the curtains in one window draw back. Unfortunately, his head was a few feet below the windowsill, so he couldn't see into the room. A rum do, though. The servants were surely long since in bed, so it must be the earl.

Rum. Very rum.

If Kenny had that round-heeled wench in his power for the night, the earl wouldn't be wandering around the house fiddling with curtains.

Kenny shared his leader's suspicion of the haughty

earl, and this business didn't seem right. He wished he had something to climb on so he could look into the room.

He hadn't, though, so he shrugged and went back to picking his teeth, keeping even closer watch.

In the study, Elf thanked heaven for a twin who'd liked to teach her everything he knew. Taking up one pistol, she poured in the right amount of powder, dropped the prepared ball into the muzzle, and rammed it home. Then she filled the pan with fine priming powder. When it was ready, she settled it carefully in her right-hand pocket and prepared to face the outside world.

Peering through the window, she saw it looked out onto the narrow lane between the houses, a promisingly pitch-dark area. The sill was a good eight feet off the ground but she should be able to drop that far without injury.

She hesitated only because of the night doorman who surely sat outside the main doors. She didn't give much for her chances of scrambling out and landing so silently that he didn't hear. She also had the pistol to think about. In theory, it couldn't go off until cocked, but gunpowder was chancy stuff.

No, she'd have to ignore the tempting lane and take her chances with the servants' quarters.

Mack slouched against a wall in the lane leading to the mews. Lanterns glimmered outside the nearby stables whose lofts were full of sleeping grooms and coachmen, but the mews lane itself lay dark and silent.

Mack leaned back, watching the gardens of Walgrave House, but he was having a hard time staying awake. He'd been up all last night, dicing, then tumbling a wench or two, and he'd rather be in his bed asleep.

Waste of time anyway, this was. If the earl hadn't wanted the titty, he'd have taken her somewhere else.

He wasn't going to change his mind an hour later and throw her out.

In Mack's opinion, Michael Murray worried too much.

Truth to tell, Mack didn't have much feeling over this business. He was heart and soul for the Stuarts, who by God-given right should be kings of Scotland and England. He'd inherited that from his father and grandfather, who'd both fought for the cause.

But he wished he'd been born in a time when a man could prove it with sword and blood. Instead, here he was, sneaking around London spying and pilfering, and yawning against a rough wall in the dead hours of the night.

Elf eased open a paneled oak door at the back of the hall and found herself, as she expected, in the much plainer servants' quarters. She made herself wait and listen, but when she heard no trace of movement, she went through and closed the door gently behind her.

With the door open, she had seen a corridor. With it shut, she stood in pitch darkness. Again, she moved forward cautiously, trying to use other senses to guide her. The darkness pressed, and she began to imagine the walls closing in to smother her.

She stopped and sucked in a deep breath, forcing control.

There. A ticking clock! That had to be the kitchen. She groped toward the sound, feeling along the wall until she found a door. She should have paused. She should have been careful, but her need to escape the suffocating darkness drove her. She turned the knob and went in.

Light.

It was only the glow of the banked fire, but it seemed like bright sunlight after such blackness. She gasped for breath, trying to do it silently, for she'd already seen the humped shapes of at least three servants on mattresses on the floor.

A shape stirred.

Her calming heart scurried again.

A cat meowed.

It came over to weave around her ankles, threatening to trip her. She scooped it up and stroked it, making subdued soothing noises.

None of the servants seemed to have woken. Working morn till night, they'd not rouse easily from their rest. She just had to be careful not to bang anything, and here that wasn't so easy. Certainly she had the firelight to help her, but the room was full of furniture and utensils.

She didn't dare put down the cat, which lay heavily contented in her arms, so she couldn't manage her wide skirts and cloak.

Oh well, she could see a small window and a door beside it. More than likely that door led to the outside. If she woke anyone, she'd make a run for it.

She began to thread her way between bodies and furniture, forcing herself to go very slowly. Three-quarters of the way to the doorway, a servant heaved over with a mumble.

She froze.

The man settled to sleep again, still muttering.

Elf risked putting the cat down, and ignored its brushing warmth against her ankles as she went the last few steps and turned the knob.

The door didn't move!

It took a few moments for common sense to overrule panic. Of course they'd keep the house locked.

Grasping the heavy iron key, she tried to turn it gently, but the lock was too stiff. In the end, she had to use all her strength and the *click-clunk* of the lock echoed through the room.

She froze again, pointlessly holding her breath.

One servant half sat up, muttering, "Wha—?"

Elf stayed statue-still, though she felt her thundering heart must be audible.

After a moment, the man settled down again, but she couldn't be sure he'd returned to deep sleep. She made herself count slowly to two hundred before she risked turning the knob again and easing open the door.

For a blessing, the door didn't squeak but opened silently into a small yard. She went through, eased the door shut again, then leaned against the high stone wall, shaking.

Oh, how she wished for a magic wand to waft her out of this situation.

Adventure was actually no fun at all!

She wanted to be safe in her luxurious bedchamber, with servants to attend to every wish. She wanted her brothers, and their protection solidly around her. Instead, she had escaped an imprisoning house only to be out alone in the middle of the night with murderers quite likely hovering nearby.

Her teeth were chattering, surely loud enough to be heard if anyone was nearby.

But then she managed to control the panic. She didn't have a choice, and as the old saying went, "What can't be changed, must be endured."

And she was a Malloren.

With a Malloren, all things are possible.

She'd come to think that the bane of her life, being a Malloren. It meant every act was of interest to society. It meant having four brothers determined to protect her from every hurt, and well able to do so. It meant she stepped with care through life because she didn't want men out at dawn trying to kill one another.

She'd learned that lesson at eighteen when she'd foolishly encouraged a dashing young rake, underestimating his intentions. When she'd resisted his seduction, he'd tried to force her. He'd been lucky. Rothgar's sword had merely disabled his right arm.

Permanently.

Though Scottsdale had deserved his punishment, Elf had learned her lesson. She'd put no more men in danger, especially her brothers. After all, there must be swordsmen in the world even more skilled than the Mallorens.

She'd seen Walgrave fence and knew he was good, though not as good as her brothers. He'd apparently been training hard since Cyn beat him, though. He'd almost managed to force her brother Bryght into a duel last year. Presumably he'd love to confront Brand or Rothgar over rapiers, over her.

Elf had no intention of being the cause of more death or maiming, so she'd have to get out of this entanglement by herself.

Taking a deep breath, she forced her heart to calm a little more. Thus far, she was living up to her Malloren name. She'd succeeded in the first stage of her escape.

Clearly no one lurked in this small yard, which by the smell contained only the privy and some slop buckets. She couldn't hear any nearby sounds of movement, which meant no one was coming to investigate the noises she had made.

So where could she expect to find watchers? One at the front and one at the back? Which direction should she choose?

"Oh, the pox on it!" she muttered, borrowing her twin brother's language, hoping to get his confidence, too.

She pulled the pistol out of her pocket and cocked it. Then she slipped out into the small garden, trying in weak moonlight to distinguish path from shrubbery. A touch on her ankle almost made her scream, but then she saw the cat's bright eyes and heard its friendly purr.

"Shoo!" she hissed, but it stared up at her as if devoted, weaving around her ankles.

With a muttered complaint to fate, Elf put the cat out of her mind and headed toward the mews. With her dark cloak, she felt confident of not being seen unless she bumped into someone.

At the cast-iron garden gate, she paused to check the dark lane beyond.

There, she saw her enemy.

The heavily built man in a slouch hat leaned against a wall. He could be asleep, so slumped he seemed, but she doubted he'd miss the opening of the gate.

Elf shrank back into deeper shadow, raising her left hand to her agitated chest.

That man wanted to *kill* her!

After a moment, anger drowned fear. The wretch was willing to murder an innocent young woman just because she might be an inconvenience. If not for the noise it would make, she'd put a ball in him as he stood!

What she had to do, however, was find a way past him. When the persistent cat brushed her ankles again, she picked it up and placed it on top of the six-foot-high wall. It sat there, blinking at her, purring. Hoping against hope, she made shooing gestures at it. It stirred, but only to ready itself to leap down to her again.

"Sorry," she muttered, and pushed it off the wall.

It squawked a protest as it landed, and the man twitched up straight. Possibly he *had* been asleep, but he wasn't anymore. Scanning the area, he pulled a pistol from his pocket.

Elf heard the click as he cocked it.

Now what?

The cat brushed up against the gate. Surely the man must realize someone was here! But then, thank heavens, it showed itself to be promiscuous with its friendship and went over to court this new human, purring loudly.

"Be off!" the man snarled, fending the cat off with his foot.

Elf could have told him the kitty was not so easily dissuaded. His attention was focused on the cat, however, and some clouds scudded across the moon. She seized her chance. Pulling her dark hood down over her face, she eased the latch down. In a moment, she was through the gate, and had closed it behind herself.

Then she slid into a deep shadow nearby and stood still.

As if the gods smiled on her, the clouds thickened, plunging the area into almost pitch darkness. Holding her breath, and praying that the cat wouldn't remember her and chase after, she sidled down the wall.

When she was passing the gate of the next house, she

heard a squawk and feared the man had kicked the cat. Then she heard a curse and hoped the cat had scratched the man. Whatever was happening, she was past the worst.

Being careful where she put her feet, expecting pursuit at any moment, Elf worked her way down the lane until she could turn into a street and finally be out of sight.

With a prayer of thanks, she leaned against some railings in front of a tall house, drawing together her tattered courage for the next trial.

She didn't even know where she was. How stupid that she'd always been taken around in a carriage or sedan chair and didn't know her geography. But Walgrave House was on Abingdon Street, which meant this might be Morpeth Street. Perhaps she had some idea how to get to Amanda's house from here.

The elegant street was deserted, but flambeaux burned in front of many of the houses to provide light for passersby. Elf hurried down it, her heeled shoes too loud on the flagstones, all senses alert for lurking footpads and other villains.

All the same, she couldn't help but grin with success. She'd done it. She'd achieved the first part of her escape! Now she just had to make her way through London in the middle of the night without being robbed, raped, or murdered.

That sobered her. She'd never been out alone by day, never mind in the dangerous night.

She paused and looked back toward Walgrave House, her experiences there already dreamlike.

What should she do about all this? By rights, she should tell someone in authority about Walgrave's involvement in treason and let the government deal with it. If the man was foolish enough to meddle in such matters, he must take the consequences.

And yet, and yet . . . it would be a terrible thing to see him hang, to perhaps be drawn and quartered. In France not long ago, a man who had tried to murder the king had been torn apart by four horses.

Elf shuddered, trying to imagine Walgrave's magnificent body mangled in any of these ways. Surely she could find some way to save him and do her patriotic duty, too.

As she headed for Amanda's house, she pondered the problem. No brilliant solution occurred to her, but at least she didn't experience much trouble along the way.

There were people about, but only one bothered her. A one-legged man crept out from some steps where he doubtless slept, whining for coins.

He might have been an innocent beggar, but Elf took no chances. She showed him the pistol and told him to "Cut it," in a rough accent, hoping he'd think her a tough specimen.

It worked. He scuttled back into his hidey-hole, and she hurried on her way thinking that the night streets were not quite as dangerous as she'd been taught.

Of course, probably few women went abroad well-armed.

Which raised the interesting question of why not? Men always thought women needed protection. Would it not be rational, therefore, to ensure that women could protect themselves?

Against men, she thought with a wry smile. Doubtless, therein lay the catch.

Perhaps women should take their defense into their own hands.

This thought so intrigued her that she arrived in Warwick Street before she knew it. Amanda's neat, modern terraced house was the only one with lit windows, which meant she was still up. Elf supposed it would be surprising if she'd gone to bed, but at least the house didn't look to be in a state of alarm.

She hurried up the steps and used the knocker gently, praying Amanda stood ready to open it.

She did.

She opened it cautiously, however, since she wore her night robe, then grabbed Elf and pulled her in. "Thank heavens! I've been pacing the floor for hours. How could you . . . ?"

On a stream of whispered complaints, she swept Elf up to her bedchamber. As Amanda shut the door and leaned against it, she seemed to run out of breath.

Elf hugged her. "I'm sorry! I promise not to go adventuring again."

Amanda regained breath. "You certainly won't persuade *me* to it again! I have never been so terrified . . . And when you ran off into the Druid's Walk with that man behind you . . . So, did the captain catch you?"

"Of course not!" Elf realized she could finally take off her mask, and did so. "Thank heavens for that," she said, rubbing her face. "I've been so hot and uncomfortable."

But Amanda came forward and seized one of her wrists. "You're bleeding! What on earth happened?"

Bother. Elf would rather have kept most of the details secret, at least until she'd had time to consider her options. As she snatched up a towel and pressed it to the small open cut she said, "I was tied up and had to escape."

"Tied!" Amanda stared at her. "But I thought . . . Wasn't that Walgrave you were with when you left?"

Bother again. "Was it?" Elf asked innocently.

"I was sure of it! In fact," she said with a stern look, "I *am* sure of it. He was hardly disguised at all! I thought—"

Elf raised her brows. "That I'd decided to live through my fantasy? Nonsense. He just rescued me. He is part of the family, after all."

"Oh, really!" Amanda took the towel to dampen it in the bowl of washing water. "Having found a safe champion, was it not a little thoughtless to leave me to fend for myself?" She came to dab at Elf's wrist. "And it still doesn't explain your captivity or your wounds."

Elf quickly assembled a story. "Walgrave didn't know who I was, you see. He was rescuing a stranger, and fancied a seduction."

"Well, of course he did! Really, Elf—"

"When I objected, he tied me up."

"The wretch!" Amanda cleaned the dried blood off the other wrist, then looked up, somber. "And?"

"And what?"

"When he'd tied you up, what did he do?"

Elf studied her wrists. The cuts were superficial, but they'd still scab for a few days. How fortunate her sharp-eyed brothers were away. "He went to bed."

Amanda gripped Elf's hands. "Dearest, you don't have to lie to me. If you've been unwise, I'll help you."

"Unwise? It was certainly unwise to go to Vauxhall."

"Elf!" Amanda almost shrieked. "What did the man do?"

Elf tugged free. "I don't think it's quite proper to demand these details, Amanda. I don't ask what you and Stephen do."

"Ah! So he did something."

"Well, of course he did. He was trying to seduce me. And," Elf added thoughtfully, "it was surprisingly pleasant. He kisses rather well."

"*Kisses* well." Amanda collapsed into a chair. "Are you saying Lord Walgrave tied you up and then did nothing but kiss you?"

"He didn't kiss me *after* he'd tied me up. That would be rather dastardly, wouldn't it?"

Amanda sank her head in her hands. "I hesitate to destroy your innocence, but even gentlemen are capable of being dastardly, you know."

Elf supposed they were. With distance and leisure, she could see that the earl had behaved rather well. Once he had her in his power, he could have assaulted her with all kinds of touches. All he had done, in fact, was to save the life of an anonymous innocent and not press his attentions when she said no.

Elf found it hard to be thinking so kindly of her brother-in-law.

"And he doesn't even know who you are," said

Amanda, shaking her head in wonder. "You seem to have escaped scot-free."

Which reminded Elf of the inconvenient Scots and a small matter of treason. Lord, what a tangle. She needed time to think it through before she said anything to anyone.

"Goodness, I'm worn out," she said, unhooking her gaudy overdress and shrugging out of it. She turned her back. "Spare me having to ring for Chantal, Amanda, and help me with my laces. I'll be grateful for my bed."

Amanda came over, but then said, "Are you going to tell me you usually wear your stays so loose?"

Bother, bother, and more bother! "He loosened them."

"I thought so." Amanda tugged at the bow. "Men never retie them tight enough."

"I don't like them tight anyway."

"You have the good fortune of a naturally trim figure."

Amanda loosened the laces so Elf could step out of the boned, cotton stays. "That's better. But you have a full figure that men admire."

"You have a delicacy that men admire, inconstant creatures that they are. So?" Amanda asked, clearly in trigued. "What think you of Lord Walgrave now?"

Elf was happy to be able to laugh about it. "That he can be pleasant, I admit it. But only because he thought me a silly ingenue called Lisette. If he'd any idea of my true identity, he'd have throttled me." She gently turned her friend toward the door. "Off you go to bed, Amanda. I'm safe now, and you must be exhausted. I'll tell you the whole story in the morning."

Once alone, Elf untied the laces that held her two pockets around her waist. She'd been aware of the pistol in the right one, and prayed that Amanda not notice the bulge. She didn't need any more peculiarities to explain.

Now she knocked the powder out of the priming pan, wishing for a safe way to return the weapon. Walgrave could afford to replace it, of course, but she knew men treasured such guns. She traced the mother-of-pearl and gold design on the grip. The weapon had doubtless been custom-made to fit his hand exactly with precise balance, and she had, in effect, stolen it.

A fig for such silly scruples. She placed the pistol in the back of a drawer. She'd return it if she could, but the man was a black traitor, and deserved no consideration at all.

But still, she thought, as she unfastened her silk petticoat and let it fall to the floor, he had been kind after a fashion.

And he was very beautiful.

Her brothers were each beautiful in their own way. She'd never been aware of seeking beauty in a husband, but now she thought perhaps it was important to her. It seemed a trivial thing, but she responded to it, indeed she did. The picture of her brother-in-law's body, so wantonly displayed to her, teased at her mind.

Washing her face and hands, it still teased her, and lingered as she unpinned her curls to brush some of the powder out. Her hair would have to be washed tomorrow to get rid of it all.

Of all the men in the world to be stirred by, why the Earl of Walgrave?

Fort. That's what his intimates called him. What Chastity called him.

She paused, staring sightlessly at her reflection in the mirror, imagining murmuring that name to him in the dark as she licked his skin. She'd never before thought such a thing about a man.

Perhaps it would be different now. Perhaps she just needed awakening to these desires, and now she'd feel drawn to other men. More suitable men. After all, Fort in dishabille had been quite a revelation to her. Presumably, if she married, her husband would come to her lightly clothed, hair loose, and she would feel the same wanton desires . . .

Elf rose to pull off her shift and slip into her cotton nightgown, stroking her hands over her awakened body.

Honesty commanded her to remember that she'd been stirred by Fort in the full armor of gentleman's dress. Stirred more than by any other man of her acquaintance.

But it was completely impossible. Not only was he enemy to her family, he was a traitor. Stupid, stupid man.

She climbed into bed intending a logical analysis of the threat to the realm. Immediately, however, she remembered lying in Walgrave's house, listening.

She remembered being tempted to call out to him again . . .

Had he discovered yet that she had gone?

No, she thought he wouldn't check her again until the morning.

Would he just shrug, assuming silly Lisette had returned to her home? Or would he be concerned for her safety?

Would he care that she had left him?

No, probably he'd mostly be concerned about what she knew. That meant he'd have to try to find her again, to recapture her so she couldn't chatter about his affairs. Her heart raced with nervousness. Surely he couldn't find her. He'd shown no sign of recognition, and she'd left behind no clue.

She hoped that was true, for if Walgrave could find her, perhaps those Scots with knives could, too.

She pulled the covers up around her head, lusty desires chilled by fear. If only none of it had happened. If only she'd never gone to Vauxhall in the first place.

Something wicked, indeed.

Something completely foolish. And now she must face the consequences. She knew about things that could not be ignored, and she could pay for it with her life.

Chapter 5

Fort awoke when someone rattled back the curtains at his bedroom window. Blinking his eyes against sunlight, he saw the offender was not an impudent servant he could dismiss on the spot.

"Gad, Jack. What the devil do you think you're doing?"

"Waking you," said the rangy young man cheerfully. "Late night, Fort?"

He had a lean, humorous face, and mousy brown hair, tied back casually. His dress, too, was casual—plain breeches and coat, suitable for riding.

"Not particularly." Fort stretched lazily, then tensed when he remembered the night.

A quick glance showed him the door to the adjoining room still stood ajar. Was the chit awake? Though Jack Travers wouldn't make trouble, he'd rather his friend not know there was a bound damsel in the bed next door. He'd be hard-pressed to come up with a believable explanation.

He rolled out of bed naked and rang for his valet. "Why don't you go down and command breakfast, Jack? I'll join you when I'm ready." He turned to frown at his friend. "Why the devil *are* you here at this ungodly hour?"

"Pettigrew. Ham. Tickle-me-quick."

This cryptic string of words enlightened Fort, and he glanced out of the window to check the weather. Another fine day. No chance of getting out of his commitment to ride out to Ham this morning with Travers and

Pettigrew to observe the paces of Tickle-me-quick, a promising Ascot runner.

What on earth was he going to do with troublesome Lisette? He didn't want to leave the poor girl tied up all day.

He turned back to repeat his suggestion that Jack go down to breakfast, just as his friend pushed wider the half-open door into the next room. It was a meaningless fidget, really, but Jack paused, then walked in.

Fort waited, expecting voices or perhaps a scream.

Silence.

Then Jack strolled back, dangling red-and-white-striped stockings, and lacy garters speckled with dark stains. "What have you been up to, my friend?"

Fort snatched the garters and confirmed that the stains were blood. He pushed by his grinning friend, but saw what he expected. The little bird had flown.

He looked at the sheet. More blood. For a moment he wondered if Murray and his men had somehow invaded his house and murdered the wench. It took only a moment to dismiss that. The blood was mere spots, and Murray would have left the corpse.

What the devil had the silly chit done to herself?

"The bodice dagger," he muttered, then remembered that he had an audience.

He cursed himself silently, though, for forgetting Lisette's weapon.

Thinking back, he could see he'd been far too interested in the silly widgeon, far too stirred by her, far too frustrated by her sudden panic. He'd hidden it. He didn't show anyone that kind of need. But it had dulled his wits.

These days, he couldn't afford dulled wits.

He glanced at the clearly intrigued Jack, but before his friend could voice his curiosity, Fort's valet scratched and slid into the room as if attempting to be invisible.

Dingwall was a thin, prudish, humorless man who had been appointed by Fort's father years ago. Gliding over the carpet, the valet placed hot water silently on the washstand, then stood beside it, as patient as a statue and almost as inanimate.

Jack was observing Dingwall in fascination. He'd seen the valet many times before, but everyone tended to stare. As well, everyone asked why Fort didn't get rid of the strange man now that his father was dead.

There were reasons, but not good ones. Even he knew that. It was petty to jab at Dingwall when his father was beyond reach. It was foolish to keep the Incorruptible's tool around just because Fort felt haunted by memories and guilt. After all, the valet could no longer send reports back to his father, unless he had a means to talk to hell.

Fort strolled over to the washstand, ready to jab at Dingwall, petty or not. If only the valet's feelings were more obvious. If they were, he'd show his disgust at the sight of naked bodies. No flicker of emotion moved the still, pale features.

Plague take it, Fort had let the man find him in bed with a whore once or twice. Dingwall had not so much as twitched. Two whores once, now he came to think of it.

He'd think the man indifferent if he'd not found the years of reports of his every action. Dingwall had related every sin, had described every debauchery in detail. Always he had implored Fort's father to correct his wickedness.

Fort knew what sort of correction Dingwall had in mind, for the man had been hired before he'd grown too old to be beaten.

Now, Fort dangled the stained scraps of cloth in his valet's line of sight. "Dispose of these."

Ah, for once Fort saw a betraying trace of hesitation before the valet took the garters and stockings. "Immediately, my lord?"

"Immediately."

Dingwall glided out of the room.

"You really should—"

"—dismiss him," Fort completed. "Perhaps he amuses me."

"Only if you've a devilishly strange sense of humor. He makes me feel as if someone's walked over my grave." Jack dropped lazily into a chair. "Now, tell. Whom did you have tied up? And, more importantly, why was she so eager to escape? Must be losing your touch, my friend!"

Fort soaped a cloth and began to wash. "A virgin who got cold feet, that's all. I'd no mind to go out again to take her home, but feared she'd run given the chance. The silly creature would never have survived the night streets." He rinsed the cloth and re-soaped it, frowning. "I didn't think her desperate enough to cut free. I hope she's safe."

Jack surged out of his chair to face him. "No, you are *not* spending the morning checking on her. You have a commitment."

Fort eyed him for a moment, then shrugged. "I wouldn't know where to start, anyway." Dingwall oozed back into the room, so Fort added, "Do go down, Jack. *I'm* not going to run off."

An hour later he rode along Whitehall, strangely tempted to abandon Jack and search for Lisette even though he knew it was hopeless. He was annoyed but comforted by the knowledge that she'd run off with one his pistols. He truly didn't want her to have fallen into the clutches of Murray and his associates.

He saw another angle to it all, however.

Innocent young ladies—French or English—didn't go out for the evening with a blade tucked down their stays, nor did they sneak around the dark walks of Vauxhall.

Innocent young ladies weren't likely to cut themselves free at cost of some skin, either. They were even less likely to arm themselves with a dueling pistol and head off into the night streets of London.

Therefore, despite appearances, Lisette was not an innocent young lady.

Which raised two important questions.

Who was she working for?

And why had she not become his mistress when given the chance?

Daylight had forced Kenny and Mack to move farther away from Walgrave House, but it didn't prevent Kenny from seeing the earl ride off with a friend.

He went to find his companion. "Nothin'?"

Mack rubbed his gritty eyes. "Nae a scabby thing. I need some sleep."

"Aye, me too." Kenny yawned. "Rum do, though, isna it? He's gone off. So what's he done wi' her?"

"If she really is his fancy piece, perhaps she's lyin' on silken sheets, sippin' chocolate out of fine china."

Slowly, Kenny grinned. "Then perhaps she'll come out later—go shoppin' or some such—and we can scrag her then. I'm away back for a word wi' Murray. I'll send Jamie along to relieve ye. It's definitely worth keepin' an eye on this place."

Elf wasn't lying on silken sheets but she was sipping chocolate out of fine china. She was in Amanda's boudoir, wondering how to evade her friend's persistent curiosity. Her hair was still damp from washing, so all outward trace of her adventure had disappeared. Except for some scabs on her wrists, of course.

Those scabs were outward signs of inner turmoil and a restless night.

"Well?" asked Amanda, buttering a bun. "Have you decided to tell all?"

Elf focused her attention on the serious matter of stirring chocolate. "Why do you think I didn't tell all?"

"To begin with, you said nothing of how you escaped that captain."

Elf looked up, relieved to have a question she could answer. "Oh that! I merely took to the bushes. Amanda," she added, leaning closer, "the shrubbery was *alive* with lovers!"

She succeeded in distracting her friend for a while

with a discussion of the scandalous nature of Vauxhall, and the possible identity of some of the people there. But eventually, of course, Amanda steered back to her questions.

"So, how did you end up with Lord Walgrave? It looked to me almost as if he had taken you prisoner! If you hadn't indicated otherwise, I would have sought help *instanter*."

"What a scandal that would have caused!" Elf decided that the best way to diffuse Amanda's curiosity was by appearing to be honest. A mischievous childhood had taught her that a story should stay as close to the truth as possible.

"Lord Walgrave saved me from the captain," she said, "and then wanted to return me to my party. When I had to admit I had none, he came to the reasonable conclusion that I was a doxy and offered to buy the night."

"Elf!" Then Amanda put down her bun and whispered, "You *didn't*!"

"Of course I didn't!" Elf knew her cheeks had turned bright red. She only hoped Amanda took it accurately as embarrassment and not as guilt over a lie. "But the captain was hovering, so I took up Walgrave's offer so as to get away. I'm sorry for abandoning you, Amanda, but I thought you'd manage."

"Of course I managed. It was nothing to return home. But then how did you end up bound?"

Elf rolled her eyes. "The man is no fool. When we arrived at his house, I said I'd changed my mind, expecting him to throw me out. He, however, said he'd not throw a silly little innocent onto the streets at night, but he'd not leave a chit like me to roam his house and steal the silver. So he tied me up. I managed to keep my mask, but I wasn't sure I could keep it in the morning, and I'd no intention of being taken home in his coach. So I escaped."

Amanda had been listening to this mouth agape, and now she pressed a hand dramatically to her chest. "Elfled Malloren, you must have an angel watching over you!" But then she stopped her histrionics and a glint entered her eyes. "All in all, it sounds as if Lord Walgrave acted very well toward a silly young creature."

"Yes, I suppose he did." That was one of the thoughts that had disturbed Elf through the night. It was disconcerting to have her opinion of a person so completely overturned.

"But that doesn't incline you to consider him as a potential husband?"

The flashing image of a fine body, eyes full of tempting passions, had Elf's cheeks fiery again. "Amanda, he hates all Mallorens!"

"He hates your brothers. I doubt he hates you." Amanda licked chocolate off her lips, staring into the distance with a silly smile. "I was right. It's just like Romeo and Juliet."

"I do hope not," Elf said tartly. "They ended up dead. Now, I need to visit Malloren House."

It took Elf some effort to visit her London home without Amanda, for her friend was bored and ready for any diversion. But by pleading she had family matters to discuss, she managed it. She knew Amanda was suspicious when she ensured that one of her footmen escorted Elf's sedan chair to Marlborough Square.

Amanda couldn't suspect serious problems such as treason, so she probably thought Elf had planned a tryst with her dangerous earl. Her astute sense for such matters was quivering, but this time in a wrong direction.

Despite his physical appeal and kindness to chance-met women, Walgrave was still arrogant, selfish, and an enemy. She would have nothing more to do with him, even in silly fantasies.

All the same, she'd do her best to save him from his folly. After all, she'd promised Chastity not to let her brother end up on the block.

The servant who sat in the niche outside the big double doors of Malloren House leaped up to open the door for his mistress. Elf walked into the large marble-floored hall with a pleasant sense of homecoming.

Then it hit her. This wasn't really her home. Her destiny was to marry and make some other house her home. Despite his declared intention not to marry, Rothgar might one day bring another woman to rule here.

As she gave her hat, gloves, and pelerine into the care of a servant, she wondered why this thought had come to trouble her now. Perhaps because she'd never stayed anywhere else while in London. Visiting here from Amanda's house made her feel as if she didn't completely belong.

She brushed her thoughts away as foolish. She was probably uneasy because none of her brothers was here just now to make this house a home, a place in which she could find the help she needed.

Instead, she had to handle her problems alone, and she couldn't deny a touch of excitement. After all, none of her brothers would blink at the idea of Cyn coping with such matters. Why should it be thought beyond her competence?

Elf waved away a footman and headed down a corridor toward the back of the house. There, she opened a door and entered the main office of the marquessate's business operations.

Most people would have been astonished to realize just how businesslike the Mallorens were. Society assumed the family's increasing wealth and power came about through some kind of luck or government patronage. In fact, it was the result of hard work by all the members.

Well, nearly all the members. That was another thing that had started to rankle with Elf. She had the job of organizing the domestic affairs of her oldest brother's estates, but any spinster sister would be expected to do that. She had never been offered any part in the real business here. Was she not capable of managing property, studying investments, or keeping an eye on impending legislation?

She pushed such resentments aside for the moment and smiled at the four men working at paper-laden desks. Three of the clerks nodded and returned to their work. The fourth stood, prepared to help her.

Elf waved him back to his seat and progressed to the next room, where two accountants and two computing clerks slaved away over ledgers. One of the accountants asked a silent question and again she indicated that it was not him she wanted. She opened the door to the next room, the office inhabited by Joseph Grainger, the family's young but extremely competent man-of-law.

Another room lay beyond this, but that was the preserve of her brothers and thus empty at the moment. Grainger was the highest level of help available to her, but he was a servant, and she must be cautious.

"Lady Elfled," said the wiry, dark-haired man, standing, "how may I help you?" He was dressed as always in a neat suit of plain dark cloth with the most moderate of lace at neck and cuffs.

Elf sat in a chair. "In many ways, Mr. Grainger. I need to send messages to my brothers."

"All of them?" The man's brows rose, but he said, "Of course, I will make the arrangements."

"Thank you. Not Cyn, of course, since he should be embarking about now. But I am hoping to catch the marquess before he crosses the Channel."

"That may not be possible, my lady. There is some problem?"

"A minor one," said Elf, knowing he wouldn't believe her for a moment. "Bryght is at Candleford, I assume."

"I'm afraid not, my lady. I just received word that he has traveled into Worcestershire. Something to do with a Titian becoming available."

"Bother." Elf had relied on the fact that one of her brothers was only a day away. "Do we know where he's gone?"

"To Sir Harry Parker's, but he does say he might travel around the area."

"And Brand is wandering the north country. How very disobliging of them both, to be sure."

"Perhaps I can help you, my lady."

The suggestion tempted her, for he was a very clever man, but Elf knew it would not do. "Not at the moment, thank you." With a coy smile, she added, "It is a personal matter." There, that should diffuse his interest. "Please just send messages asking them to return with all speed, Mr. Grainger."

"Of course, my lady."

His smile, however, was patronizing, and he clearly thought she was acting foolishly. She felt a strong urge to give him a thoroughly Malloren set-down, but restrained herself.

"Is there anything else I can do, my lady?"

"Yes." Elf had reached the delicate point. The marquessate retained an excessive number of servants. People put it down to Rothgar's insistence on excellent service at all times. He certainly did demand that, but the abundance of staff was also because some of them possessed special talents.

"I want some people set to watch Lord Walgrave."

"Indeed, my lady?" His brows rose. "And what would they be watching *for*?"

"Anything out of the ordinary."

His face twitched with suppressed derision. "I will see to it, of course. Do you wish to see the reports when they come in?"

Teeth clenched, Elf did give him a Malloren look, though a mild one. "They will report only to me, Mr. Grainger. There is no need for you to be involved at all."

"My lady—"

"Would you question one of my brothers' orders?"

Color touched his cheeks, and it was probably anger. "Your brothers will expect me to take care of you—"

Elf stood, back very straight. "I do not need taking care of. I take full responsibility for this, Mr. Grainger, and will discuss it with my brothers when they return.

Are you going to follow my orders, or do I have to discuss *that* with them as well?"

He rose, too, tight-lipped and intensely disapproving. "I request that you put these orders in writing, my lady."

Elf sucked in a deep breath. "What do you expect? That I'll lie and say you suggested all this?"

Clearly, he thought just that.

"Paper," she snapped.

He handed it over rather warily. Perhaps at last he saw the Malloren in her. About time too. She sat and hastily scrawled the outline of her instructions, signed, and dated it. "There, Mr. Grainger. Have the appropriate people sent to me in the inner office to receive their instructions."

"Yes, my lady." Elf had reached the door when he said, "My lady . . ."

She turned, braced for another battle. "Yes?"

"We have two people in Walgrave House."

Elf's anger simmered down a little. "How careless of the earl."

"They were there in the old earl's time. Do you wish me to contact them?"

For a panicked moment, Elf feared they'd know about her time there, but then she reminded herself that they'd only know about Lisette. "Ask them to report to me at Lady Lessington's. I would like to talk to them." Since he had made a concession, she made one too. "Thank you for your assistance, Mr. Grainger."

In the inner office—almost entirely the territory of Rothgar and Bryght—she paced around the ornate desk and circled big, comfortable chairs, walking out her irritation at Joseph Grainger and at herself.

She had no real right to be angry. She'd never given him any reason to think she had interests beyond furnishings, food, and servants.

As she calmed, she saw it in another light. Poor Grainger was doubtless terrified. If Rothgar came back and found his sister had come to harm, a lost position would be the least of Joseph Grainger's problems.

Elf couldn't even feel outrage at that. Rothgar would feel just as deadly if disaster entangled one of her brothers. He was ferociously protective of all his siblings.

She looked at the picture over the mantelpiece and smiled. It was the charcoal sketch done by the artist for the grand portrait of her brother that hung in the hall. He always said it had captured his worst features, and that the artist had flattered him in the final product.

Elf wouldn't say that, but the sketch captured Rothgar at his coolest. Dark and lean featured, he seemed to be looking out at the world as if he were an all-seeing and all-knowing creature. The spare charcoal lines failed to capture his soul and thus made him seem cold, almost devilish.

But a damned handsome devil, as Cyn had remarked on first seeing it.

Rothgar did sometimes seem all-seeing and all-knowing, even to his family, but they all knew a passionate devotion lay behind his powers. If he had become vigilant and powerful, it had been to protect them.

In most noble families, the younger children had to make their own way in the world. Rothgar, however, on inheriting the marquessate at nineteen, had set about building power and wealth so as to provide magnificently for them all.

Doubtless because of the tragedy of his mother.

Elf turned to a side wall to study the portrait of a woman there, the only portrait of their father's first wife.

Dark-haired and dark-eyed, she looked very like her son except for an expression of confused intensity. It could be the first hint of the madness that had seized her after the birth of her second child. New or old, that madness had caused her to murder the baby despite the attempts of her young son to prevent it.

Elf turned away. It had formed Rothgar, that moment. Perhaps it had caused the wildness that had marked his early years. It had certainly created his excessive protectiveness toward his half-siblings, especially Elf and Hilda. None of them would come to harm if he could help it. He had been driven almost beyond reason by Cyn's determination to join the army.

So, what would happen if Elf came to harm through this business?

It would not be good, so she must be careful. But she couldn't just let things lie until Rothgar returned. The king was in danger, and Walgrave's involvement could not be ignored.

Someone knocked on the door, and she turned as seven people filed in—a powdered footman, two maids, and four men who were either gardeners or grooms. They all had the proper demeanor, and yet they were not at all nervous at being summoned to this room. They also looked like people who could act on their own. She'd never doubted it. Her brother chose all his servants with great care.

"Good morning," she said. "I have some work for you. I wish a close watch kept on the Earl of Walgrave. I want to know where he goes, whom he meets, what he does. I don't want him to know he's being watched, however. Can you do this?"

They all nodded as if it were the most common request.

"I must warn you that some other people might be watching the earl as well, and I am particularly interested in them. One of them is a Scot called Murray. He's in his mid-thirties, with mousy-blond hair and a stocky, average build. The others may be Scots, too. If you detect anyone watching the earl, I want their names and places of residence, all without raising their suspicions."

She had no idea whether this was possible or not, but their lack of alarm was promising.

"My lady?" one of the men asked.

"Yes?"

"Should we be prepared for danger?"

Elf hadn't thought of that. "From the earl, probably not. From the others, yes." After a moment she added, "Kill them if you have to, but try not to bring it back to us. I'd rather no one be aware of Malloren involvement until the marquess or one of my other brothers returns. Any other questions?"

One of the maids said, "Who are we most interested in, my lady? The earl or the others?"

Again Elf had to think about it. Her concerns were focused on Walgrave, but in truth, the Scots posed the true danger. "The others," she said. "I need to know how to find them. Other questions?"

After a silence, she added, "You are to report to me, and to no one else, at Lady Lessington's house in Warwick Street. Keep away from this house. If you are detected, I'd rather you were traced to Lady Lessington than to here. Lord Lessington is away at the moment, and no one takes women seriously." She accompanied the latter with a smile and saw the maids' lips twitch.

With a wink, one of them said, "Comes in useful at times, my lady."

One of the grooms scowled and said, "Watch your tongue, Sally."

But Elf shared a smile. "Indeed it does come in useful. Off you go, then. If you need funds, Mr. Grainger will provide them, but you are not to talk of the details of this matter, even to him."

Alone again, Elf took a moment to worry about set ting this machine in motion. She couldn't be sure what it would do, what trouble it might cause. It had to be, though. Murray had said the time of treason was close. Walgrave had spoken of a week.

A mere week!

When Rothgar returned, time would be short. This way, she might have some useful information to pass on. And if the plot began to heat up, she might become aware of it and know she had to act on her own.

She rubbed her hands nervously, hoping it never came to that.

And still she fretted about Walgrave. She had to keep him clear of this!

Simply for Cyn and Chastity's sake, of course.

* * *

Elf returned to Warwick Street to find Amanda sifting through invitations. "I'm trying to decide what to do tonight."

"And no possibility appeals?"

Amanda grimaced. "I planned to attend Lady Tollmouth's salon, but after Vauxhall, it seems rather tame."

"I think after Vauxhall we want tame, don't we?"

"But in this case, T stands for Tamest of the Tame. Middle-aged writers reading from works about morals and reform. To add spice to the evening, there will doubtless be some analysis of ancient documents."

"Lord! Why had you ever planned to attend?"

"She's Stephen's aunt."

"Oh."

Amanda considered the invitation for a moment, then tore it in two. "So much for Lady T." She pushed the pile of cards over to Elf. "You look."

Elf riffled through, practiced at spotting the dull, the pretentious, and the outlandish. Then she paused and stared at Amanda in amazement. "Sappho?"

The woman who called herself Sappho was a poet and freethinker who moved on the fringes of society in the manner of one who does not care to be involved any further. And there were other things . . .

Amanda looked as if she would snatch the card back. She even blushed. "I met her recently. I don't know why she sent me the card. I would hardly attend . . ."

Elf picked it up. "Why not? It's a respectable address."

"She's beyond the pale!"

"Is she? I feel she's more in a pale of her own. Where did you meet her?"

"At Mrs. Quentin's. I thought we were to raise money for destitute women, but it turned out to be more about the *rights* of women."

"Perhaps women have a right not to be destitute . . . How fascinating, though." Elf read the card. "Poetry readings here, too. But I'll go odds they'll be more interesting than those at Lady Tollmouth's. Let's go."

"Elf!" Amanda leaned closer, though there was no one else in the room to hear. "They say that she . . . that she prefers women to men."

"So do I much of the time."

"In bed!"

Elf looked at the card and then at her friend. "I don't think so. My understanding is that she's Rothgar's mistress."

Amanda collapsed back, staring. *"What?"*

"Not for gossip, Amanda."

"As if I would!"

"I just wanted to make it clear. Let's say that Rothgar spends rather more time with Sappho than he does with other women, and sometimes spends the night. I've always wanted to meet her."

"It's hardly proper."

"Why not? I've hesitated before because I've had no invitation. And because I would hate to create embarrassment by turning up there to find my brother *en déshabille.*"

Amanda fanned herself with her hand. "The mere notion of Rothgar *en déshabille* is enough to make me swoon!"

"Restrain yourself," said Elf with a chuckle. "But see how ideal this is. I have an invitation—or rather, she can hardly refuse to admit me while I'm with you—and Rothgar is safely out of town. It's perfect."

"It's trouble," said Amanda gloomily. "I can sense it."

Late in the afternoon, at the Peahen Inn he used for such meetings, Murray—there known as the Reverend Archibald Campbell of the Church of Scotland—summoned Kenny and Mack. He kept rooms here, and always dressed in the black clothes and powdered bob wig typical of the Kirk.

Kenny, Mack, and Jamie knew his true identity, of course, but the other minor pawns in the game did not. If the plot fell awry, the authorities would still not connect it to Michael Murray, poor connection of the mighty Earl of Bute, with rooms in the earl's mansion.

"The wench escaped sometime in the night," he snapped.

Kenny stood straighter. Mack scowled. They both said the same thing, "She canna have!"

"She did. I have just been sipping a lambswool with my good friend Mr. Dingwall. For all his sanctimonious airs, he likes a gossip with someone he thinks as righteous as he. This morning, the earl had him dispose of a pair of stockings and two garters. Red-striped stockings just like the ones that vixen wore. He brought them to show me."

Kenny and Mack exchanged a glance. "So?" Kenny ventured. "She took off her stockings and garters."

"There were bloodstains on the garters and sheets."

"That's nae surprisin', is it?" asked Mack.

"Fool! The earl claimed she was his mistress. If that were true, she would hardly be a virgin, would she? More to the point, she is not in the house, and Dingwall assumes the earl was holding her against her will and she escaped." He glared at the two men. "How did she escape?"

"Nae by the front," Kenny stated with a scowl. "I kept close watch all night."

"Mack?"

"Are ye saying I didna keep watch? I did. And nothin' stirred except a damn cat." He stuck out a hand, showing swollen scratches. "Unless she turned into a cat, she didna get out the back."

Murray clenched his fists. "I do not like this. I do not like it at all. It feels wrong. Nothing can be allowed to go wrong now. Go find Jamie and arrange a tight watch on the earl's house. Round the clock. I want to know everyone who goes in and comes out. *Everyone.* And every little thing Walgrave does."

"It isna' possible wi' just the three of us," Kenny protested. "Not wi' all the other things in hand. The stone and the toy—"

"You can take turn and turn about. And I have recruited a bunch of street monkeys. They live like rats in the garden of an empty house in Abingdon Street, but they are sharp enough. They do not know anything of what is toward, of course, but they will take over the watch for a sixpence now and then, and report to me if anything particularly unusual happens. Perhaps things you will miss?"

Then, realizing his worry was making him harsh, Murray made himself relax. "Just a few more days, my friends, and our great enterprise will be under way. We cannot let a little detail spoil it now, can we?"

Chapter 6

Trouble, Amanda had predicted.

Even in the coach that evening, she continued to forecast disaster, but when they arrived at Sappho's, nothing could be more normal. Her house proved to be a terraced one on a fashionable street, and tonight for her entertainment, every window was lit.

As was usual, scattered groups of the lower orders hovered to gawk at the people arriving by carriage, chair, and on foot. The guests were being admitted by well-behaved servants.

Amanda and Elf shared a look and descended to enter.

In the elegant white-plastered hall, a maid and footman stood ready to take their cloaks and guide them to the stairs. Elf noted that though the hall was conventional, the paintings and ornaments were not. She studied a grimacing mask that appeared to be made out of beaten gold, wondering where it came from.

She could see, however, that her brother might find this place intriguing and congenial.

At the top of the stairs, another servant directed them to the drawing room, which already spilled the chatter of a well-behaved but happy crowd. At the door, Sappho stood greeting her guests. Elf needed all her self-discipline not to stare.

She was tall. Perhaps six foot. And though not dark skinned, her complexion was not English. Wide cheekbones and slightly slanted dark eyes made Elf think of a Russian count she had met who claimed Tartar blood.

Her heavy, thick, brown hair fell to her knees, merely held back by jeweled combs, and her outfit seemed almost medieval. Or perhaps Byzantine. She wore a loose bronze gown under a tunic encrusted with gold and jewels, and a great many unusual rings.

The peculiar thing was that Elf—correctly attired in corset, hoops, petticoat, and overdress—suddenly felt ridiculous.

Sappho turned and smiled at Amanda. "Lady Lessington, I am so pleased you could come." If she was surprised, she hid it. "I think you will find people here you know." She turned to Elf, and Amanda made the introductions.

Sappho's dark eyes stilled for a moment. "Lady Elfled. An unexpected pleasure. I hope you will enjoy the evening. Please let me know, either of you, if there is anything I can do to increase your comfort."

Then she turned to the next guest, and Amanda and Elf moved on into the room.

It was not a large house, so the drawing room and anterooms were pleasantly full with just thirty or so people. They would soon be a little crushed, but that was the sign of a popular entertainment.

The decor here was more ordinary, with furniture similar to that in most fashionable houses. The company, too, seemed quite normal except that some of the women shared their hostess's taste for loose garments.

"If we were looking for the outrageous," Elf murmured to Amanda, "I doubt we'd find it here. You might have warned me about her looks, however."

"Why? She's tall and foreign. At Mrs. Quentin's she was dressed normally. Her dress tonight suits her better. I'm not surprised that Rothgar—"

"Hush." Elf turned and greeted an acquaintance.

As she strolled through the rooms, she realized that the people she knew here were some of the most interesting of her acquaintance. Also, the strangers here seemed to be people she would like to know.

Very intriguing.

She did wonder, however, why Rothgar had never invited Sappho to Malloren House.

Of course, she had never met Sappho in any of the more normal places. Either she didn't receive invitations or chose not to attend. None of the people here were the most straitlaced members of society. Perhaps Sappho would be snubbed. After all, she could well have the taste for female lovers. Why else take the name of Sappho, the Greek poet killed for that amorous tendency?

A trio of female musicians played in one corner. Soon Sappho clapped her hands and commanded attention for the music. The three played very well indeed, and were soon joined by two vocalists who sang beautifully.

The music gave Elf opportunity to look over the company, spotting new people.

The Earl of Walgrave rather leaped to her eye.

Among the peacock colors of fashion, his black clothing set him apart. It was eccentric, really, to still be in deep mourning seven months after his father's death.

Of course, it was mourning of the most magnificent type.

Tonight, his black coat and breeches were of brocade, heavily embroidered in silver, as was his dark gray waistcoat. His silver buttons and buckles glittered with what were doubtless small diamonds.

The dark magnificence suited him, and made those blue eyes even more startling. Elf's memory of him in that black robe, his hair loose and wild, gave this elegance a strange new power to arouse.

She pushed that folly aside. *What on earth was he doing here?*

A hundred suspicions flew into her mind, but she had to dismiss them. He couldn't have known she planned to be here. She'd scarcely known it herself. And anyway, he'd be more likely to avoid Elfled Malloren than seek her out.

He surely couldn't suspect the identity of Lisette.

So, could he be planning to strike at Rothgar through Sappho?

Trying to be subtle about it, Elf kept Walgrave under observation. He seemed his usual chilly self, listening to even a frivolous piece of music as if it were a funeral dirge. But when the piece ended, a young woman by his side turned and said something to the group nearby. Everyone laughed, and Walgrave . . . Well, perhaps he grinned before suppressing it. The lightness certainly lingered.

She observed him chatting to those around, and though his manner could not be called warm, it was far from the sneering disdain she was used to. The reactions of the others—at one point he made them laugh—showed he was not being unpleasant.

In fact, he reminded her too much of the man who had held her prisoner last night. A strange tightness in her chest almost made her dizzy. Perhaps Chantal had laced her too tight.

"Goodness," said Amanda from behind her fan, "isn't that Walgrave?"

Elf hastily looked away. Amanda had enough silly ideas in her head. "I can't imagine why he's here."

"Perhaps for the excellent music. I confess, if I'd known, I'd have begged an invitation sooner. He is a fine figure of a man," she added, still studying Walgrave around the edge of her fan.

"I never denied it."

"A very shapely leg. Though it's possible, I suppose, that he wears calf-enhancers."

Elf looked at that leg, clear in black silk stockings and well-fitting breeches, and could remember it naked. "Don't be foolish."

"Ah! You know for a fact that his shape is all his own."

"In those stockings, all the world must know it. I think men should wear skirts."

Amanda chuckled, but before she could pursue the conversation, the poetry began.

After a while, Elf realized that all the readers were to be women. She glanced around to see if the men found this strange, but none appeared to. As best she could tell, the work was very good.

Throughout it all, however, Elf's attention largely stayed on Walgrave. Discovering her brother-in-law here was rather like discovering the parson in a brothel, and said equally much about character, but in this case creditably.

It was another indication that there might be more to the earl than she thought.

She remembered Chastity protesting that her brother had been quite a pleasant person before the events surrounding their father's death. And Portia, who had known him in her youth, claimed him as a friend, a friend she'd trust. Portia, however, feared Walgrave's hatred of Mallorens had become a sickness that could destroy all the good in him.

Was he only hateful with Mallorens, then? That hardly seemed fair. His father had been responsible for all the troubles, and Rothgar had sorted them out so Walgrave's sister could marry Cyn. Admittedly, the old earl had ended up dead . . .

Her thoughts had caused her to stare. Perhaps he sensed it, for he glanced over. Immediately, any trace of lightness drained from him.

He raised his brows and gave her the look with which she was all too familiar. The one that saw her as an enemy, and an unattractive one as well. He certainly hadn't recognized Lisette!

Elf was a tiny bit disappointed. What a fool she was. Had she actually expected him to be pining for his lost doxy, and instantly able to sense her presence?

Yes, she had.

What things she was learning about herself.

She wanted a hero, a dragon slayer. She wanted him decadently beautiful. She wanted him mad with lust.

For her.

For Lady Elfled Malloren, who was not without charms, but who had never driven any man mad with lust.

He looked away and smiled again for those around him, but Elf could sense an effort now. Portia was correct. The earl's feelings toward the Mallorens were like a sickness, one infecting his whole world.

She began to wonder if he could be cured, for it was not in her nature to ignore a suffering creature . . .

When refreshments were served, Elf sought out her hostess and said, casually, she hoped, "How surprising to see Lord Walgrave here. Does he come regularly?"

"Moderately so, my lady. It offends you?"

"No, no!" Elf declared. "But I have always thought him more inclined to gaming and sportsmanship than to poetry and music."

"Perhaps he is a more balanced person than you suspected. Or perhaps it just amused him, when his father was alive, to consort with people the Incorruptible particularly disliked."

"He didn't consort with my brother."

Sappho smiled, perhaps in acknowledgment of the many layers to the statement. "Fort always inquires, before coming here, whether your brother is likely to be present."

Elf had to suppress a spurt of outrage that this woman used his first name so easily. "Lord Walgrave does seem to have taken on his father's dislikes along with the title," she remarked.

"Not at all. He doesn't dislike *me*." Sappho halted a passing maid and took two glasses from a tray, handing one to Elf. "Men can be very foolish, my lady. A wise woman keeps out of their affairs."

Elf sipped the excellent milk punch. "Really? What if a woman cares for the man?"

Sappho's lips turned up slightly. "A wise woman does not care for men."

"Are you saying you do not care for men?"

"Did I ever say I was wise? But men have codes quite adequately designed to manage their disagreements. It can be dangerous to interfere."

"Men sometimes kill one another in those disagreements, codes or not."

"True." The notion did not seem to disturb her. "Whom do you wish to protect? Your brothers or Lord Walgrave?"

"My brothers of course."

"I wonder."

What on earth did the woman see? One-handed, Elf flicked her fan open and wafted it protectively. "I have no desire to see harm come to Walgrave either. His sister is married to my brother, after all. But if it came to a choice, I would choose my brothers."

"Perhaps." With that, Sappho moved on and Elf, impelled by some insane force, sought out her dangerous earl, Amanda by her side.

Elf had to admit that for her to be in the same room as Walgrave and not speak to him was close to impossible. It had been that way since their first meeting. The compulsion had resulted in nothing more than a string of barbed exchanges—unless one included the time as Lisette.

What would happen this time?

He stood in a loose group of people and she found it easy to move beside him. "How surprising to find you here, Walgrave."

He started as if she had in truth jabbed him with a barbed weapon, then turned to face her as if she were an enemy. "How even more surprising to see you here, Lady Elfled."

"This is my first visit." Despite his tone, Elf determined to be calm and polite. Surely it was possible. "A pleasant event, is it not?"

"Indeed. But I wonder if Rothgar will permit other visits to this house."

"Rothgar does not control my movements." Already they were sparring.

"Rothgar controls any damn thing he can."

"Then perhaps I cannot be controlled."

His lips twitched into a sneer. "Doubtless true. Perhaps you do serve a function—as a cross for him to bear."

With difficulty, Elf resisted the urge to fall into a full-fledged quarrel. She took a calming sip of her brandy-laced punch and tried again. "Why so heated, my lord? In truth, I don't think I've ever done you harm."

He, too, collected himself. "How true. And in this company, to visit the sins of the brothers on the sister would be foolhardy."

He bowed, and would have moved away had Elf not stayed him with a hand on his arm. It surprised her as much as him and she had to scramble for a reason.

"I wondered if you had word yet from Chastity and Cyn."

He raised his brows. "I would have thought your brother more likely to write to you than my sister is to me."

"Women are generally better correspondents. And anyway, Rothgar is out of town, so I am staying with Lady Lessington. If there are letters at Malloren House, I might not know of it. It was an impulse only, to ask you." And a foolish one. She must sound like a babbling idiot.

He delicately removed her hand from his sleeve, rather as if it were a louse or some similarly unwelcome intruder. "You are overmuch given to impulse, I fear."

"And you are overmuch given to criticism!"

As usual when they had these spats, he looked as if he'd like to throttle her.

"No," he said tightly, "I have not received any letters. It is, after all, only three days since they left for Portsmouth, but I believe they planned to go onboard about now. They will doubtless send letters just before sailing. As you know, sailing can often be delayed. I will inform you as soon as I have any news."

With that, he turned and walked away. In fact, he went to speak to Sappho, then left. Sappho glanced across at Elf with mildly amused interest.

Mild did not describe Elf's feelings. Her hand tingled

where he had touched it, even if only to remove it from his person.

"I was wrong," Amanda murmured. "It's not Romeo and Juliet, it's Benedick and Beatrice. If he ever discovers he's kissed you, he'll wash his mouth!"

"Oh, do stop being so foolish," snapped Elf. "I want to leave."

In the coach on the way home, however, Elf couldn't help thinking of Lord Walgrave relaxed and in good company. Another side of him she'd never expected.

"If I hadn't been there, Amanda, could you have found Lord Walgrave's company pleasant?"

"It's possible," Amanda admitted. "He's handsome enough, and has remarkable style. He moves well . . ."

"I wasn't asking if you wanted to bed him!"

Amanda grinned. "Such thoughts tend to arise when discussing a handsome man. But yes, when not speaking to you he seemed pleasant enough. Quite a different person, in fact. Most of the time, however, it was hard to tell because of the noise and smoke of open warfare. At least he didn't recognize Lisette."

"That's true."

And, thought Elf, that could be at the root of her discontent. Deep in her heart, she felt he *should.* He should at least have felt the vibration, the excitement that plagued her whenever she was in his presence.

Surely it couldn't be entirely one-sided.

Amanda relaxed back in her seat, fanning herself lazily. "I must say, I was wrong in my misgivings. Your foray into wickedness is proving to be most entertaining. I'll let you choose all our activities from now on."

Elf wished she could tell her friend this wasn't a game, and that any silly reactions she might have toward Lord Walgrave were completely irrelevant. Of course, it would help if she could persuade herself of it!

The Scots, she reminded herself sternly.

Treason.

A possible threat to the king.

Those were the important things, not the way Lord

Walgrave made her skin tingle or the beautiful shape of his legs!

She feigned a yawn. "I must decline. It is too exhausting to be always seeking the unusual. Let us be strictly conventional in the future, my dear."

Fort berated himself for leaving Sappho's so abruptly. Irritating though Elf Malloren was, she hadn't put him on the run before. His nerves must be on edge because of this business with Murray, damn the man.

Or perhaps because of Lisette. The fate of the silly chit still bothered him, though it was none of his fault. He'd done his best.

Lisette bothered him in other ways, too. He wasn't satisfied she was an innocent, and she seemed to have stirred his dormant interest in women. He'd even found himself sexually intrigued by Milady Elf, burn it! Elf was just the sort of bold chatterer he detested. He liked his women lush, silent, and very experienced.

Or had, before he'd gone off sex entirely.

Pox on it, he hadn't thought about any female this much in months, and now he had two wretched specimens living in his head. If he could only put his mind at ease about Lisette, the other disturbing notions would surely disappear.

So, the next night, when he attended a dinner at the home of Sir John Fielding in Bow Street, he set out to deal with it. As the ten gentlemen waited for dinner to be served, he asked an opportunity for a quiet word with Sir John, London's chief magistrate.

"Trouble?" asked the grizzled man, who wore a silk scarf around his sightless eyes.

"Of a minor nature."

Sir John chuckled. "That's what everyone says. Or they say they're asking for a friend. What can I do for you?"

Fort smiled, knowing Sir John could pick up every nuance of tone and the smile would carry into his voice. "My *friend,*" he said, "was in company with a young woman two nights ago. She ran off alone and he's concerned for her safety. I wondered if any female bodies have turned up."

"None that I know of, Walgrave, though it's always possible for unfortunates to be washed up from the Thames some time after their death. Name?"

"I have not the slightest idea. Gently bred, though."

Sir John cocked his head, turning toward Fort as if he could study him. "Then her family will have raised the alarm."

"Has any such alarm been raised?"

"No."

"She's foreign—French—and visiting relatives here. She claimed they might be slow to announce her missing."

"Silly titty," growled Sir John, understanding the implication that the woman had been looking to become a rich man's mistress. "And shame on you, my lord, for preying on her."

"My *friend,*" said Fort, "behaved with considerable propriety under the circumstances. She would be completely safe had she not run away."

"Humph! As I said, I've not heard of any suspicious deaths of young women. Give me a description, though, and I'll have it checked."

"Thank you. Middling height and build. Fine boned but rounded in the right places. She was masked, but her chin was a little square, though her lips were delicately shaped. She could be pretty . . ." Fort realized his voice had become almost dreamy because he was recalling Lisette lying on the bed, eating him with her eyes. "Last seen," he added briskly, "she was wearing a lurid gown of scarlet stripes over a scarlet petticoat, all covered by a poppy-red domino worn inside out."

Sir John shook his head. "There's no use in that, Walgrave. If she came to grief, she'll have been stripped to the skin. Clothes like that are worth money." After a moment the magistrate added, "To the poor, all clothes are worth money. If her killer didn't strip her, the slum-carrion would. Hair color?"

Walgrave found himself deeply disturbed by the thought of Lisette limp and naked in a gutter. After all, it would be his fault for letting her slip. "I don't know. She wore powder."

"Well, a powdered corpse would cause some stir, I assure you! I'll let you know if I hear anything, but if she's not caught in a brothel, she's safe with her relatives. And we can pray she's learned something from her fright."

A brothel. Why hadn't that possibility occurred to Fort? London abounded with women eager to sell their bodies for coin, but virgins were the fashion. This meant many brothels sought the helpless or hopeless as long as they were unbroached.

As he moved on to speak to other men, he berated himself for overlooking this.

When dinner was announced, Sir John called Fort back to his side. "I could hire you a Runner, Walgrave. Remarkably clever, my men are, at finding people."

It tempted him, but was far too dangerous. Part of Fort worried for silly Lisette, but part of him suspected her of being much more than she seemed. If she were working for Murray, he couldn't let Fielding get within sniffing distance of her.

Fort offered the older man his arm into the dining room. "Thank you, Sir John. I'll consider it."

After the meal, as the contented men sat around enjoying brandy and tobacco, Fort found opportunity for a moment or two with George Grenville, the powerful Secretary of State. It wasn't hard, because Grenville was just as eager to speak to him.

"So, Walgrave?" asked Grenville in a quiet corner. "Any notion of when these Scots villains plan to do it?" A neat man in sober clothing and a tidy gray wig, he took his brandy with abstemious sips as if it were a bitter medicine.

"It's to be soon, but I can tell you no more than that.

Murray keeps me in the dark." Fort offered his silver-and-obsidian snuffbox but the older man waved it away. Fort took a pinch himself. "From what I can gather, he keeps everyone in the dark as to the whole plan."

"But he'll use this toy, this pagoda?"

"So he says, and I've managed to remove it from Rothgar Abbey for him. It's at my house under guard. A shame really. It's an exquisite piece, perfectly made. When wound, all the little figures around it and on balconies spring into motion, performing their tasks. It was the centerpiece of a masquerade ball Rothgar held last year."

A ball that Fort would never forget.

The ball at which his father died.

"So?" said Grenville. "It's a toy."

"It doesn't make it any the less dangerous."

"It offends me to have it at the center of serious matters. Indeed it does."

Fort hadn't told Grenville that the pagoda had been his idea. The main reason Murray had risked contacting strangers at all was because he didn't know how to get a lethal object close to the king. Fort, playing his part of willing conspirator, had pointed out that it should be a gift the king wanted, and that he knew just the thing.

The king had not been present at the calamitous ball at Rothgar Abbey, but he'd visited a few days later to grace Chastity's marriage to Cyn. He'd seen the automaton and expressed a veiled desire for it. It had clearly just been a matter of time before Rothgar presented it as a gift.

So, when Murray asked about an object that could be sent to the king, the pagoda had sprung into Fort's mind. It was perfect, mainly because Rothgar would end up entangled in a Jacobite plot. There was such seductive neatness to it. The toy that had tinkled as his father died would bring the revenge Fort thirsted for.

When Murray had given Fort the word, he had used his knowledge of Rothgar Abbey to have the toy stolen. Now it was hidden in his cellars until the time came for the Scot to make it lethal. He should have been relishing the next steps, but instead he found himself increasingly uneasy.

"I don't trust Murray," he told Grenville. "I certainly don't trust him to tell me the truth about his plans. He's clearly suspicious." He gave an edited version of events at Vauxhall.

The older man shook his head. "Can't have been pleasant for you, Walgrave. My thanks for playing this part."

"I am happy to do my duty." Fort pondered the situation a moment longer, reluctant to give up his weapon against Rothgar. But it wouldn't do. The risks were too great. "It is my opinion," he said, "that the king must be warned about the pagoda."

"No, no." Grenville leaned forward, color touching his cheeks.

"Why the devil not?"

"Because the king's too fond of Bute."

Fort knew Grenville hated Lord Bute, confidant of the king and now Prime Minister of England, but he didn't follow this. "Surely His Majesty could be warned not to tell anyone."

Grenville snorted. "His Majesty tells Bute every time he empties his bowels. He'd tell him about this, believe me. Bute's loose-mouthed, too. He'd go home and chat to everyone, including his cousin, Michael Murray."

Both Fort and Grenville had been considerably surprised to find that Michael Murray, traitor, lived openly in London in the house of Britain's Scots Prime Minister.

Fort had expected Grenville to order Murray's arrest. The Secretary of State had other ideas, however. He wanted Murray caught in the act. He pretended he wanted to catch him red-handed so the plot would be quashed forever, but Fort knew he also wanted to ruin Bute.

Grenville and Bute were rivals for power in the kingdom.

It was all a devilish mess.

"You know what would happen if we warn the king," Grenville continued persuasively. "Bute would talk. Murray would take to his heels. But he'd be back again another time without us being in on the plot." Grenville leaned forward. "It was sheer good fortune that the man approached you, Walgrave, and that you had the wit not to reject him outright."

Fort often wished he had thrown Murray out and not ended up in this tangle.

"Don't worry about the king," Grenville continued. "He's safe. We've told his people to be particularly careful about unexpected gifts. And with you involved, we're alert and ready. They can't act until they take possession of that toy."

Fort wished he shared Grenville's confidence. "Why not just take Murray in and force the details out of him?"

"It's hard to get anything out of these fanatics, and the days of rack and pincers are over. Without proof, there are too many to cry 'injustice' and 'habeas corpus.' Have you heard about Wilkes's new venture?"

"That blusterer? What now?"

Grenville's face creased into lines of distaste. "He's starting a news sheet called the *North Briton* merely to stir trouble against the administration and the king. He'd love to open with a story of an honest Scot being tortured merely on vague suspicion of treason. No, my lord. We need to catch the villains in the act."

"It's devilish risky."

"We have people watching Murray."

"If only we could find out what's really behind it all," said Fort. "What point in killing the king, when he's got two brothers and a child on the way? It seems like an act of spite."

"Perhaps that's what it is."

"Murray doesn't strike me as a mindlessly spiteful man. He's more like a zealot with a cause. Once or twice he's mentioned a stone. The Stone of Destiny. Do you have any idea what that might be?"

"An amulet, perhaps?" But Grenville waved the words away. "If it's supposed to protect him, he'll find it of little use when we catch him in the act. Damme, sir, we'll tear him apart with four horses as the French did for attempted regicide."

"Just so long as it's not for *successful* regicide," Fort said dryly. "His Majesty does not deserve an early death. But I'm afraid my part is mostly done. I have the pagoda. When they come for it, I'll alert you. The rest is up to you."

Fort moved on then to chat with other men. At the moderate hour of ten, he left Sir John's house, intending to head home and check yet again on that damned pagoda. Even though he'd put two armed men to guard the door turn and turn about, he still worried about it being moved without his knowledge.

He felt as if he was living on top of a powder magazine surrounded by fire.

Fort suspected Rothgar intended to give the automaton to George upon the birth of his first child, sometime in August. But he could imagine the enthusiasm with which the king would receive such a gift at any time. He'd probably be in an unregal hurry to have it wound and set in motion.

At which point, the explosives with which Murray intended to pack it would send shot and fragments into the bodies of all nearby.

Fort wanted to be completely certain that His Majesty's aides and attendants would never let any item near the king without careful inspection. He wasn't. George liked his own way.

If only Murray would unlock his damned mouth and simply explain the whole plot!

Fort had tried to draw him into his social set, hoping to create a time of drunken ease in which the Scot would tell all. Murray, however, drank like a nun, and did not game at all. He had no interest in women. God knows what he did do with his time. Read the Bible?

How could Bible reading go hand-in-hand with callous slaughter?

And what did Murray's apathy toward women mean for Lisette?

Fort would have laid his fortune on her being a genuine innocent panicked by the prospect of sex. If so, she was unlikely to be Murray's puppet. But then, who had she been, this bold innocent who stole a gentleman's pistols?

With a sigh, he realized he'd sunk back into fretting over the damned woman. He rapped on the roof of the coach with his cane and commanded a change of direction.

He would do something to lay one of his fears to rest.

Soon he entered the handsome establishment of Mirabelle, London's premier madam. Heavy chandeliers illuminated her grand salon, where men gamed and drank, often with a woman in their lap. On the many raised daises around the room, thinly draped beauties assumed suggestive poses to titillate any still-jaded appetites.

Fort indicated that he wanted to speak to the proprietress privately, and was ushered into her elegant boudoir. Soon the handsome if hard-faced Mirabelle joined him. Her dark hair was elegantly arranged, and her ruby-red silk gown would not have disgraced a duchess. Nor would her jewels, though she always wore too many at a time.

The madam was clearly disappointed to discover that one of her richest patrons hadn't come in search of pleasure, but she was willing to sell information, too. She knew the usefulness of friends in high places.

"You know I don't deal in slaves, my lord."

"But you know who does. Would you have heard if a new girl was being coerced?"

"I have no interest in such things." She fingered the diamond necklace spread over her white-powdered chest. "I could find out."

He gave her a smile that carried promise of payment. "Do so. I'll be grateful."

She smiled back. "I count on it." As he turned to leave, she said, "Are you sure we can't entice you, my lord? As you know, we have anything a person might desire."

From the way she stressed *anything,* he suspected she was delicately offering a pretty boy. His recent lack of attendance must be puzzling her.

"Thank you, Mirabelle, but no."

He made no further explanation, but as he strolled through the crowded salon toward the doors, he gave a moment's thought to his strange celibacy.

Before his father's death, his attitude toward women had been enthusiastic, but cheerfully uncomplicated. As long as a wench was willing and likely to be free of disease, he'd enjoyed her, doing his best to give her pleasure in turn. He'd always appreciated a restless body more than a passive one. In fact his ideal was to enter a woman already wild with orgasm, to ride her writhing hips . . .

With some surprise, he realized the image was having no effect on him at all.

It was taking time to escape Mirabelle's, for friends and acquaintances constantly hailed him. He had paused with a group of men to watch one of the women on a dais give an excellent representation of orgasm with an invisible lover. His companions were staring hot-eyed, slack-lipped, some even rubbing at their crotch.

Nothing.

He felt nothing.

He'd shackled his interest in women months ago, but he hadn't realized how thorough he had been. Perhaps he would never desire a woman again.

But he'd desired Lisette.

That thought jolted him. Had he reached the state where he needed a frightened innocent to stir his jaded palate? If so, his palate could stay jaded. Trembling virgins were too much trouble.

He quietly slipped out of the group around the demonstration, and left Mirabelle's wondering just when his interest in sex had died. He could remember a time not long ago when his interest had been strong, even excessive.

After his father's death, he'd discovered that his sexual appeal had suddenly increased. A surprising number of society matrons found the youngest, handsomest earl an enticing curiosity. For a while, he'd obliged them.

If he preferred a whore, his purse was bottomless, and in London anything, absolutely anything, could be bought. For a while he'd thought he might find oblivion in exhausting and inventive sex, or perhaps he'd foolishly thought to find something more.

Whatever he'd sought, he'd found only hell.

When the writhings of pleasure ceased to explode his mind, he'd progressed to the writhings of pain. Lady or whore, they never complained—some even seemed to enjoy his roughness. But one day, seeing the bruises he'd left on a countess's lush body, he'd hated the person he had become.

As his coach rolled up and he climbed in, he hoped none of his thoughts showed on his face. The coach moved off, heading back to Walgrave House, and he suddenly remembered Portia. Here in this coach he'd threatened to rape his childhood friend simply because it would be a blow against Bryght Malloren, her husband.

At the memory, he raised his fingers to massage his temples. It had been the ancient instinct of man to attack his enemy through his women.

But Portia.

God, *Portia.*

Of course he wouldn't have done it, couldn't have done it.

He'd forced a kiss on her, though. The sort of kiss that had nothing to do with tenderness or even lust. An assault of anger and power.

He'd stopped there, thank God. But sometimes, lying sleepless in the dark, he wasn't sure rape had been impossible. Could he, in fact, have blocked out who she was, blocked out the fact that Portia was a person at all. Could he have hurt her, defiled her . . .

Frightened by himself, he'd taken very few women after that, and soon stopped entirely. He knew his friends worried that he was turning into a simulacrum of his prudish, pride-ridden father.

Perhaps he was, at that. His healthy interest in women seemed to have drained away, leaving only warped tastes he would not nurture.

But then, there had been Lisette . . .

Irritated, he pushed thoughts of the tiresome chit away.

Sometimes he felt that every healthy part of him had rotted away, leaving only a warped formless thing that should not survive. A thing guilty of the most heinous sin . . .

Plague take it!

He had *everything*. He should be able to do something with it. Something worthwhile.

But what?

He didn't want to be a copy of his father. The Incorruptible, though admired by many, had cared not a jot for wife, sons, or daughters. He'd been driven by pride and his own grandiose plans. In the end, he had even proved to be corruptible in pursuit of pride and plans.

Fort had pride and plans of his own, noble notions of using his wealth and power for good purposes, of making reparation for the evil his father had done.

Beneath, however, lurked another plan—no, a need—to destroy the haughty Marquess of Rothgar just as the marquess had destroyed him.

He knew one plan conflicted with the other, but was fiercely determined on both.

He was aware that these obsessions could drive him as mad as his father had been at the end. They could push him over the edge as his father had been pushed—by Rothgar, who played people like the helpless figures on his damned Chinese pagoda.

Rothgar's sister Elf popped into Fort's mind and he remembered her lively face as she bandied words with him at Sappho's. How typical that Rothgar let his sister run wild, verbally crossing swords with anyone she didn't like. He'd thought once or twice of using her in some scheme of destruction.

It would mean his death, he knew that. But death in the cause might be welcome. This was hardly a life he lived. And he had a brother.

Immediately after their father's death, Fort had sent seventeen-year-old Victor to Italy. Whatever happened, he would come through it in some shape to take on the responsibilities of the earldom. This left Fort free to pursue revenge.

Through Elf Malloren?

Fort's eyes focused, and he saw his reflection in the glass window of the coach, saw his own wry smile. He hadn't been able to use Portia in his war, and he doubted he could use Elf.

She was a troublesome creature, but something about her made her hard to hurt—perhaps the fact that she had a genuinely kind heart. Sometimes, when she was teasing rather than taunting, it was damnably hard not to mellow and forget she was a Malloren at all.

He muttered a curse.

Kind thoughts of Elfled Malloren.

An excessive interest in that silly Lisette.

Perhaps Mirabelle was right to be concerned about him. Probably a night of exhausting, unusual sex with a few of her most skilled whores would be the cure to all that ailed him. After all, would he be thinking so much about Lisette if she hadn't been the first woman to truly stir his sexual appetite in months?

And that made her doubly, triply dangerous.

He made an instant resolution to put her out of his mind. Rather than returning home, where he'd be likely to think about the wench, he needed company.

Back to Mirabelle's? No, that kind of sex still did not appeal.

One of his clubs? The main activity there would be gaming, and he was not in the mood.

A coffeehouse? Late-night denizens of such places were always sunk deep in philosophy or politics. The last thing he wanted was to think.

He needed distraction and regretted that the theaters would be closed by now. A romping, foolish farce would fit the bill.

Then, ahead on Piccadilly, he saw the glittering lights of Devonshire House and remembered receiving a card for the duchess's ball.

Dancing would provide mindless distraction for an hour or two. With luck, by then the strange mood would have passed.

Chapter 7

Elf spotted Walgrave the moment he appeared at the entrance to the duchess's crowded ballroom.

Of course, in this glittering company, anyone dressed in funereal black would stand out. There was no question of some sixth sense alerting her to his presence. Of course there wasn't.

She couldn't deny, however, the disturbing flutter in her stomach, and that her hands were suddenly slick with sweat on her fan.

Oh dear. This was becoming ridiculous.

She forced her attention toward young Lord Northrop and smilingly accepted his invitation to join the next set. As he led her forward she refused to allow herself to watch the earl.

Some of the flutters in her stomach were nervous ones, however. She wasn't accustomed to bumping into Walgrave all over town. What if he recognized Lisette?

As the music struck up and she curtsied, she assured herself that his identifying her was next to impossible.

Tonight, turned out to perfection by Chantal, she was completely Lady Elf. Her sandy curls were unpowdered and scattered with tiny blue flowers to match her pale blue watered-silk gown. No gaudy black-and-gold trimming here, but instead a cobweb-fine confection of white and silver, trimmed with seed pearls. For jewels, she had chosen a pearl-and-sapphire parure which Lisette could never afford if she saved for a thousand years.

Though this outfit was exactly the sort she found boring, she knew society thought it elegant and perfect. She knew, too, that she was a pleasing companion well liked by nearly everyone. Yet Fort, who had been kind and sometimes charming to silly, gaudy Lisette, would sneer at Lady Elfled Malloren as if she'd slithered out of a marsh.

Despite her good intentions, her eyes flickered around in search of him.

He was talking to Minnette de Courtances. No, not talking. *Flirting!* Minnette was a charming young woman, but how unfair that he flirted with *her* when he never did anything but glare at Elf!

"Is something the matter, Lady Elf?"

Northrop's words made her realize she was frowning. She hastily smoothed it into a smile. "Nothing of moment, my lord. Just one of those fleeting concerns."

He raised their arms so she could pass beneath them, then turn. "Is there any way I may assist you?"

Elf smiled. "Thank you, my lord, but no. Now tell me, what do you know of Nova Scotia? My brother is posted there, you see."

That settled him comfortably off on another track.

Northrop was one of the men who would make her an offer of marriage if she gave him the slightest encouragement. As they chatted and went through the movements of the dance, she wondered why she did not. He was young, well set-up, intelligent, courteous . . .

He did not, however, make her flesh tingle when he touched her, and he never made her think of sex. In fact, she thought, rather shocked at herself, try as she might she couldn't imagine lying naked in a bed with him, something she found all too easy—and too stimulating!—to envision with Fort.

When had she started thinking of him as Fort?

The set ended and she asked Northrop to take her to sit by her Aunt Kate. Otherwise, he would be obliged to keep her company until a new partner appeared. Having thus liberated them both, she chatted to her aunt while keeping a hunter's eye on Fort.

She wanted to be with him—she didn't try to lie to

herself about that. But she had an altruistic purpose, too. This unreasonable enmity between the Mallorens and the Wares was dangerous and she intended to put an end to it.

Tonight.

Minnette was stolen by another gentleman and Fort stood alone, his dense black making him seem apart from the company. It could not be pleasant to be so alone, Elf thought in sudden awareness. Not pleasant at all.

On the other hand, his decision to continue in black so long after the funeral was his own choice. For the first time she wondered why he chose to dress so. Yet another problem to be solved.

With an excuse to her aunt, she rose, gathered her nerve, and set off toward him. Partway, however, she was intercepted by Lord Bute, extremely grand in white powder, red satin, and the blue ribbon of a showy Order. She wondered if he were consciously sporting such patriotic colors. The handsome Scottish lord was Prime Minister of England, but everyone knew he'd obtained the post simply because the young king was fond of him. Or perhaps because the king's mother was even fonder.

"Lady Elfled, how charming you look tonight."

Even as Elf smiled and curtsied, she knew his smile was false. He did not care for Mallorens, for Rothgar was one of his rivals for the affection of the young king.

He took her hand, making it impossible not to walk with him for a while. She cast a cross look in Fort's direction and saw him chatting to some male friends.

"Now," said Bute, "tell me how your family goes along, my dear lady. I haven't had the pleasure of seeing the marquess for some time."

"Surely only for a week or so, my lord?" said Elf, resigning herself and putting on a smile. "He attended Court quite recently. But since then, he's traveled to the coast with Lord Cynric, who is off to Nova Scotia. Rothgar planned to go on to Versailles."

"And other places, I suppose."

"Oh, doubtless. We have estates in France, you know." As she chattered on about their vineyard near Bordeaux, Elf puzzled over his tone. It was almost suspicious. No, not suspicious. Insinuating. And he looked almost smug.

When she fell silent, he said, "The Mallorens are astonishingly prosperous, Lady Elf. When the marquess returns, the king must ask his advice on financial matters, I think."

With that, he kissed her hand and departed, leaving Elf distinctly uneasy. Though always courteous, Rothgar and Bute were rivals, so why would Bute suggest that Rothgar become even closer to the king?

Fanning herself thoughtfully, Elf remembered Rothgar remarking that Bute would do him harm if he could. But, try as she might, she could see nothing in her recent conversation that warned of harm. Except that aura of smug insinuation.

Oh, hang it. She didn't need yet more puzzles on her mind!

As she threaded her way back toward Walgrave, however, Elf couldn't shake off the uneasiness. Other places in France? What other places? Astonishingly prosperous?

Good heavens! Did Bute suspect the source of the Malloren wealth?

What an arrant case of the pot calling the kettle black! Bute's money came almost entirely from the public purse. Rothgar did not refuse the occasional gift from the Crown, but most of the family's money came from well-tended land, trade, and shrewd investments.

The fact that Rothgar didn't try to dip into the young king's purse was doubtless one reason George found his company so pleasant.

Fort's male companions moved away, and Elf slipped into place beside him before someone else could do so.

"Lord Walgrave, will you walk with me?" It was a bold request, but not unreasonable since many couples strolled about the room waiting for the next dance to start.

He turned slowly to face her, clearly considering refusal. That, however, would take matters between them into outright rudeness, which they generally tried to avoid. After sufficient pause to almost be an insult, he extended his hand.

She stared at it, unsure why she felt shocked. Then she realized that from his austere style she had expected his hand to be like her older brother's, like Rothgar's. Fine-boned and pale. Instead, it was square-nailed, solid, and brown. He clearly neglected gloves when out riding.

How strange that she'd not noticed his hands before. But then, during their most recent encounter she had been distracted by the whole of him.

Not an elegant hand, no, but astonishingly pleasing, especially when thought of in contact with her skin . . .

He raised a brow and she read his suspicions as clearly as if he'd voiced them. He thought she played some petty trick and was about to snub him!

Hastily, she placed her hand in his and they began a stately progress around the ballroom. Though suddenly nervous, Elf had achieved the first step of her plan. Promenading in this way, no one would try to join them.

So, if she could ignore the distraction of his flesh against hers, she had her chance to thaw the ice.

"Is it your plan now to surprise us all, my lord?" she asked in a playful manner.

"Surprise, Lady Elf?" Thaw was the right term. His voice could frost one of the nearby hothouse plants!

"We so rarely see you at these *normal* society affairs." She plied her fan gently and stole a look at his cool face. Perhaps she could tease him into warmth. "If I were a vain woman, I might think you were pursuing me, Walgrave."

"Because I arrived here tonight after you?" He turned to look at her, brows raised. "But then, my dear sister-by-marriage, you must have pursued me to Sappho's, mustn't you, since you arrived second." He stared at her as if struck by a revelation. "You did! There's no need to be coy, dear lady. If you lust after me, just say so and we'll attend to it directly."

Thrown off balance, Elf snapped, "I doubt you have the nerve for that, my lord."

He laughed, but it was not pleasant. "Try me. Oh, try me, Vespa. Here on the ballroom floor, if you want."

Elf fled for the cover of a simple question. "Vespa?"

"It means wasp."

"Then I wish you would not be so rude, Walgrave."

"It suits you. You like to sting."

He stopped their progress by a large plinth crowned with flowers and turned to face her. Disconcertingly, he raised her hand for a flirtatious kiss. "Well?" he asked, smiling, blue eyes completely without warmth. "Many ladies like to pursue and torment the object of their adoration. Do you adore me, dearest Elf?"

He could almost have posed himself for effect, with a spray of cream blossoms brushing his black shoulder, and the heavy perfume of roses all around.

Elf did not let herself be swayed and assumed an equally false smile. "I adore you to the exact extent that you adore me, dearest Fort, for you torment me just as I torment you."

"Torment? I? When have I ever even sought you out? Whereas you seem drawn to me like a wasp to sweetness."

"Sweetness? Lud, my lord, but you are as sweet as my doctor's favorite nostrums."

Frantically fanning her hot cheeks, however, Elf had to accept some truth in his observation. She had a history of seeking him out. Plague take the man. She would have walked away if not for the suspicion that he wanted her to, that it would mean victory for him.

It was time for her plea for peace. Not only was it right, it would save her face. Before he could think of a new dart to throw, she placed her hand on his arm and compelled him to resume their promenade.

"You mistake matters, my lord." Deliberately, she

fanned herself in a slow calming rhythm, smiling at friends nearby as if this discussion were of no importance. "I am a peacemaker, that is all. Your sister is married to my brother and thus you are, in a sense, part of my family. I cannot abide enmity in the family."

Carefully, she did not look at him.

"Peacemaker. Then why are we always at war?"

"It is not of my making."

"No? On the few occasions when we've been forced together, you have not hesitated to sting me."

"I?" Elf inclined her head to the duchess. "I cannot recollect a one."

"Think back to when we first met. You immediately accused me of being a heartless brother."

Elf was so startled that he remembered that she looked at him. "Since you had utterly failed to support poor Chastity in her time of need—"

"The whole world thought her an unruly wanton. She'd been found with a man in her bed! In fact, I *saw* her with a man in her bed."

"My brothers would not abandon me in such a case!"

"We can only pray that your faith is never put to the test. And in the end," he added, "I *did* duel with her scoundrely seducer, as is my fraternal duty."

"You dueled with *Cyn,* you wretch, rather than with that horrid Vernham!"

Why, oh why, did they *always* squabble?

He sobered. "I knocked Vernham out. Your damned brother prevented me from killing him. It did not mesh with his intricate scheme."

"Rothgar's scheme worked," she pointed out. "It brought about Cyn and Chastity's marriage."

"Yet ended with my father's death."

So, suddenly, they were spun from bickering into somber reality. "It could not be helped," she said quietly. "He went mad and tried to kill the king's mother."

"Driven mad by your brother."

"No. Driven over the brink, perhaps, but he was already mad. Chastity told me about her imprisonment in

Maidenhead, about the way your father tried to beat her, and that you stopped it."

He looked away. "It is not mad for a father to beat a wayward daughter."

"Was he sane at that time, then?"

She could sense tension in him, as if he fought invisible bonds. Fought to leave, or fought to stay? Or just fought memories? "No. No, he was not sane. He enjoyed hurting her. He would have enjoyed killing her, I think. But—"

"But you did not want him dead, for he was your father. I understand."

He looked back then and even wore a smile, but a wry one. "You understand nothing, Elf, being blessed instead of cursed." Again he paused, but this time by a window, far from blossoms and perfumes. "Cease this peacemaking. You are destined for disappointment. My father was a troubled man and your brother used him and me as if we were puppets. In the process, he destroyed us both. I will not forget."

"Your *father* was at fault, not my brother."

"But my father was my father, while your brother is your brother. You believe in family. You expect your brothers to support you, even if you are in the wrong. That is not a virtue reserved for the Mallorens, you know."

For the first time they were speaking seriously, and she was failing in her task. "But he's *dead,*" she protested. "It's past. Can't time heal all wounds?"

"It would appear not. Blood can be a soothing salve, however."

"I will *not* let you duel any of my brothers!"

It was a ridiculous statement, but she was surprised when it summoned a faint smile from him. "You'll sting me to death to prevent it?"

This was not the Walgrave Lisette knew, but the hint of him made Elf's lips unsteady. "I'll do anything to prevent it. You are part of our family, deny it as you will. I will not let you kill in such a cause."

Suddenly his expression turned blank. "Are you saying your concern is for *me*?"

"Well of course it is! You never asked to be entangled in any of this, and it isn't fair that you suffer so. I can't imagine that you will feel better if you manage to kill Rothgar, and it certainly won't be easy to do."

"I might feel better if he killed me."

The flat tone caught at her heart. What could be so dire that he wished to be *dead*? Had his plan to force Bryght into a duel last year simply been an attempt at suicide?

"Poor Elf," he said, almost gently, touching her cheek, "you've turned pale and I am a wretch for invading your blithe existence with my dark soul."

After her time as Lisette, such a fleeting touch should not have startled her. It was the first time Fort had done such a thing to Elf Malloren, however, and her whole body quivered like a brushed harp string. His expression was different, too. Still somber, but not cold.

"Take comfort, then," he said. "I will cease trying to harm the Mallorens. I have been considering the matter for some time and you have just opened my mind. There are more kindly ways to carry my new responsibilities. Unless your brothers offend again, they are safe from me."

Trapped in incoherence, Elf could only say, "Thank you."

" 'Tis nothing," he said lightly. "And it frees you to devote your energies to stinging yourself a husband before you crumble entirely into dust."

With a brief kiss on her knuckles, he bowed and left her tumbling in a torrent of emotions.

When she realized she was just standing there, Elf forced a light smile and strolled back toward her aunt as if supremely at ease. For comfort, she seized on the easiest emotion. Anger. Plague take the man for getting in the last word!

That was such a minor part of it, however, that it hardly mattered.

Suicide. He had considered killing himself or putting himself into a position where someone else could be depended upon to do it for him. Was that time past? His talk of more kindly ways offered hope, but it didn't really address self-destruction.

And what of his promise to end the feud? That should be unalloyed delight, and yet her heart ached.

Absorbed by her thoughts, she changed course, for the ladies' retiring room, hoping it would be empty and a suitable spot for contemplation.

Apart from two maids who stood ready to offer assistance, it was deserted. Elf settled on a sofa, fanned herself, and looked into a bleak future.

How strange that the most meaningful conversation she had ever had with Fortitude Harleigh Ware could quite likely be their last.

Where in the future would they meet? Despite his appearance here, Fort had little taste for balls and soirees. Elf rarely attended masculine events to do with sports or politics, and she certainly didn't visit gaming houses and brothels.

She should be delighted by the end of the feud. Considering the dangers caused by Fort's enmity, she should be relieved that he had abandoned it and would cease meddling in her family's affairs. Instead, she was painfully upset because they would rarely meet. Clearly her feelings for him were more serious than she had ever imagined.

And he thought of her as a stinging pest.

She considered two recent occasions when the whirling social eddies had thrown them together. Guiltily aware that her family was in some way at the root of his gloom, she had tried to lighten it. Perhaps she had become a little barbed as he clung to bitterness, but had she really been *waspish*?

Perhaps she had. But if it took a sting to shock him out of his dark isolation, she didn't regret it. In fact, she would apply it again!

Truth was, she thought wistfully, she'd enjoyed their

few encounters even when she'd thought him surly. From first meeting she'd been intrigued by him, and aware of her physical response.

And now, because of Vauxhall, his insubstantial attractions had very real form. His body, his mouth, his taste could be summoned at will. In fact, they crept into her mind, will or not, at unlikely moments.

More powerful perhaps than her knowledge of his body was that she had come to know *him*. She had seen him, really seen him, at ease with others. A phantasm of the man he could be, should be, haunted her mind. Not a saintly man, but one capable of consideration, kindness, and humor.

One capable of joy.

With a wry smile, Elf remembered both Chastity and Portia claiming Fort had those virtues. They had been proved correct.

But what should she do in the future to help that promising young man triumph over the dark, embittered cynic?

With a start, she remembered the Scots and treason. It was all tangled up together, though, for in the end she wanted Fort to be a carefree young man. She doubted he'd be that when facing noose or ax.

She rose and checked her appearance in the mirror. Duty called. She must apply her mind to catching the traitors.

Then, perhaps, just perhaps, she would sting Fort again and see what happened.

Fort's visit to the Devonshire ball had not cured his restlessness, for now Elfled Malloren was even more of a distracting presence in his mind. Perhaps his father's insanity had been the type to run in families.

Elf Malloren!

No less suitable lady could be imagined, but for a moment there he had wanted her. Not physically, though she was well enough he supposed, but possessively. He'd wanted her for his own.

The madness had struck when she'd said she was worried for *him.* He'd thought her devotion, her cheerful affection, reserved for her family. He'd envied them that. His sisters cared for him, but their family past left scars on all of them. Theirs wasn't the unquestioning love Elf wrapped around her brothers.

The thought of having that warmth for himself, of having someone who would believe in him, trust him, who would care, and smother every shadow in smiles and chatter . . .

Gads. He'd used to think her chatter irritating, hadn't he?

Now, however, he realized it was her weapon of choice.

Fort muttered a curse and rapped the roof of the carriage. When his coachman opened the trap, Fort directed him to drive to the establishment of Signor Angelo, the most noted instructor in duello in England. Even at this late hour, Angelo would not turn away his wealthiest student.

Fort had become a regular at Angelo's, practicing to kill Mallorens.

"Why at this hour, my lord?" asked the Florentine, leading the way into his practice room, a large, plain chamber. The only decoration here came from the masks and weapons hanging on the walls. The empty space echoed their movements like a cavern.

"Whim," said Fort, stripping off his coat and waistcoat. "Ten times your normal fee, Angelo."

Dark eyes bright with interest, the swordsmaster bowed and went to light the wall sconces all around the room.

Fort took off his shoes, chose a mask and a foil, and stood ready.

"Whom do you want to kill now, my lord?" asked Angelo, moving *en garde* opposite.

"Perhaps you."

Angelo laughed, saluting with the foil. "*Buone fortuna!* But I will not kill you for your impudence. I agree to your excessive demands, my friend, only because I do not want to see you dead at the end of a sword before you have found your way." He lunged, Fort parried, riposted, and the bout was on.

"Tonight," said Fort, pressing his attack, "I do not want to kill. I am just restless."

"Aha!" cried the Italian, dancing backward, blade clicking and hissing in counterpoint to Fort's. "It is a woman. At last, my friend, it is a woman!"

"Damn your eyes, it is not!" Fort shouted, but then saved his breath as the swordsmaster executed a lightning move and he found himself hard-pressed.

Chapter 8

To evade Amanda's perceptive eyes, Elf breakfasted in bed the next morning.

She tried to keep her attention on treason, but found thoughts of Fort exploding in her mind like fireworks, making everything else invisible. It was his pain, she decided, picking at a currant bun, that had brought her to this state. At the Devonshire ball Fort's cynical mask had slipped to show her he suffered. She couldn't bear anyone to be in such pain.

Pondering it through a sleepless night, she'd decided that the roots of the problem must lie in the matter of his father's death.

Before inheriting his title, Fort had been brash and fun-loving, if inclined to easy anger. With his family in crisis, anger had taken over, but there still had been none of this dark bitterness. That had only emerged after the tragic masquerade ball.

Grief for his father?

She didn't think so. He lived under something darker and more twisted than grief.

With a grimace, Elf wiped crumbs from her fingers with the linen serviette. She hadn't eaten a morsel, and had no appetite to try.

Thinking back to the masquerade in November of last year, she realized that she'd paid shockingly little attention to the fourth earl's death. She'd not been in the hall when the shot had been fired. Immediately afterward she'd been busy tending to Princess Augusta and some other women who had fainted. As soon as the ball ended, she'd thrown herself into arranging Cyn and Chastity's wedding.

Now she wondered exactly what had happened to affect Fort in such a malignant way. She would have to find out. She suspected there would be no peace for anyone until she did.

With frustration she realized this too would have to wait until one of her brothers turned up to tell her exactly what had happened.

Where on earth were they? Three days had passed since she'd sent messages. At least one of them should be here by now. Everything was becoming too complex and intertwined, too hazardous for one person to handle, even a Malloren.

What were those servants up to? She'd heard nothing. Suddenly she wondered if Grainger had ignored her instructions and kept reports from her. If so, she'd have his head! She rang for Chantal, then slid out of bed and dashed a note to Grainger demanding a report.

The maid's first command was to take the note to a footman to be delivered posthaste.

Once dressed, Elf went downstairs to find that Amanda had gone to visit her old nurse, leaving a pile of invitations for scrutiny. Elf flicked through them without interest. The social whirl seemed increasingly pointless, though she was restless enough to want entertainment.

She was restless enough to pace the room for hours, waiting for word from Grainger, but instead she forced discipline upon herself. She sat in the sunlight with a piece of delicate stitchery, just as a lady should.

Thus innocently occupied, she set to a tight analysis of the treasonous plot and her choice of actions. Instead, her mind kept twisting away to Fort as if seeking something in particular. Suddenly she tossed down her needlework and hurried back to hunt through the pile of invitations.

Aha! She pulled out the one teasing her mind. Lady Yardley was holding a masquerade. Lady Yardley was a very proper matron and her entertainment would be nothing like Vauxhall. Why, then, had it caught Elf's interest?

Then she realized where her wanton mind was traveling.

Lady Yardley was Fort's aunt. That might mean he would put in an appearance. More to the point, at a masquerade she could be Lisette again. If he attended, he might recognize her scarlet and gold and seek her out. Perhaps in that setting Elf could meet the smiling, kindly Fort again.

Of course, she would risk exposure, which would be embarrassing and could even be dangerous.

Excitement warred with nervousness, holding her there staring at the engraved card until she was jerked out of her thoughts by a knock at the door.

Amanda's footman entered. "A person by the name of Roberts wishes to speak with you, milady."

Roberts?

Who was Roberts?

Then Elf remembered he was one of the Malloren servants set to watching Fort. She puffed out a breath, relieved to have something practical to drag her out of insanity.

You have a possible threat to the king in your hands, she silently berated herself as she hurried after the footman. Yet all you can think about is dressing in scarlet and seeking out a wicked night with Fort Ware!

With luck, Roberts knew where the Scots were living. That would give her some control over the situation.

The footman took her to the housekeeper's parlor, where Roberts waited, dressed in the breeches and frieze coat of a respectable tradesman. He must surely blend into the crowded streets without trouble. It was comforting to see such expertise.

His words were no comfort, though.

"Nothing much to report, milady, I'm afraid."

"Nothing?" Elf subsided into a chair in disappointment.

Roberts shrugged. "The earl's doin' what an earl does,

milady. And the people in 'is house agree with that. Nothin' fishy at all, really, 'cept that a few nights ago he brought home a doxy who gave him the slip. Or at least," he added, rubbing the side of his nose, "she wasn't there in the mornin' and he seemed put out about it."

Elf prayed her cheeks weren't turning pink. "I can't see how that is of interest."

He took it as a rebuke. "Sorry, milady."

"What of watchers?"

"Nothin', milady, though it's a busy street so it'd be hard to tell if they're clever about it. They might even have a spot in a house nearby. A couple of the girls say they *sense* somethink. But you know women—" He broke off, diplomatically studying the wall.

"Indeed I do," said Elf dryly. "So, they think there might be watchers but none of you has detected them. Is no one watching the house at night? I'd think that would be easy to spot."

"Beggin' your pardon, milady, but why would they watch his house at night when he's in his bed? If anyone's interested in his doings, I'd think they'd follow him as he goes about by day, and that's not easy to spot with so many others around."

"So there's nothing." Elf felt almost sick with disappointment and worry. Perhaps the time had come to go to someone in authority and tell what she knew.

Tell what, though? That a man named Murray had discussed what sounded like a Jacobite plot to kill the king. And that the Earl of Walgrave was involved. And that she'd learned all this while in the Druid's Walk at Vauxhall, pretending—for no adequate reason—to be a Frenchwoman called Lisette Belhardi.

They'd toss her in the madhouse!

" 'Cept a room in the cellars the earl keeps guarded."

Elf started out of her thoughts. "What?"

"Seems the earl 'ad somethink put in a room in 'is cellars a few days ago, milady, and 'e's set two men to guard it. They don't know what's there, though. No one does."

"Could it be a person?"

Roberts shook his head. "No food nor water goes in. And it wasn't no bigger than a baby anyway, wrapped up in heavy cloth. Want us to try to get a look at it?"

Elf tried to imagine what it might be, and failed. "Could you, without creating a stir?"

He rubbed the side of his nose again. "It'd be tricky, milady. There's only one key, you see, and the earl keeps it on 'im. And the men he 'as guardin' it are honest. But I can ask one of our people in there to try."

"Do that, then, but they're to take no risks. I don't want the earl to even suspect he's being watched. Now, what about the Scots? Did you make inquiries at all the inns?"

"Aye, milady. There's any number of Scots around—they not being so scarce these days, more's the pity—but none of 'em match your description of this Murray."

Elf puffed out a breath. If a plot truly existed it could be rolling ahead at speed and she was no further forward. She'd been beginning to think it all a phantasm, but that mysterious package at Walgrave House revived her concerns. She tried to imagine what a mighty earl might keep in a locked and guarded room to which only he had a key. It would have to be something important and potentially very dangerous.

Fort, after all, had servants to handle nearly every aspect of his life, even the most personal. He would only be so directly involved in something intensely secret.

Something treasonous.

She had to know what Fort was keeping in that locked room.

She realized she'd risen to pace the small, cluttered room, and that Roberts was watching her curiously. Be damned to that. Her mind had found an intriguing and dangerous path.

One person might be able to find out what was in that

room—a certain scarlet lady named Lisette. But only if Lisette became Fort's mistress.

She stopped, staring sightlessly at the empty fireplace. Her mouth had dried and her heart raced, but a tingle of delicious delight danced along her skin. Almost complete, a plan was forming in her mind that meshed her earlier longings and her duty to the king.

It promised all kinds of benefits.

It also threatened danger.

It required that she do something very wicked indeed, but something she'd been wanting far longer than she'd ever dreamed . . .

"I think we should try to draw them out," she said, amazed at herself.

"Beg pardon, milady. What did you say?"

Elf considered the plan again, and sucked in a deep breath. "Tomorrow, Lady Yardley is holding a masquerade ball at her house in Clarion Street. The earl will almost certainly put in an appearance since Lady Yardley is his aunt."

How calm she sounded, yet her heart was racing like a mad thing.

She continued: "A woman will attend dressed in a scarlet-striped gown over a scarlet petticoat and a black, red, and gold stomacher. At some point before the unmasking at midnight, she will leave with the earl. If any of these Scottish gentlemen are watching, they will quite likely try to take some action then, if only to follow the couple closely. This will give you a chance to spot them."

Roberts scratched his nose, understandably dubious. "Who is this woman, milady? And why would these Scotsmen come out of hidin' as soon as she appears?"

Elf put on a frosty Malloren look. "She is another servant of the Mallorens, that is all you need to know. Just be sure that if the Scots show themselves, you do not lose them. If they should attack the woman, you must protect her. But try to take prisoners rather than to kill."

It felt extremely strange to be speaking so calmly of

mayhem and violence, but Roberts didn't seem alarmed. He merely nodded. "Very well, milady. Any other instructions?"

"Just be sure to note anyone who shows especial interest in this lady and the earl, and find out where they are hiding themselves. Keep a particular eye out for this Murray."

"Right. Medium build, mousy-blond 'air."

"Exactly."

"And the woman, the one in scarlet?"

"Will be merely a decoy. As long as she's not in danger, you can ignore her further movements."

Roberts bowed and turned to the door. Elf remembered a detail.

"And, Roberts . . ."

"Yes, milady?"

"You can ignore that item in the locked room until tomorrow."

Did she imagine that he gave her an odd look? Nothing untoward showed in his voice as he said, "Very well, milady."

With that, he left and Elf puffed out a long, long breath. What on earth had she done?

On the surface it was a reasonable plan to draw the Scots out.

Murray and his men would surely be keeping an eye on Fort. They had to be. When Fort reappeared with a scarlet lady on his arm, they'd recognize the woman from Vauxhall. They'd see a chance to silence her and keep close watch.

She hoped they didn't stage an open attack, for that would ruin the other part of her plan—the one that would get her into Walgrave House, enabling her to steal the key and investigate the cellar.

The one that would make her Fort's lover.

Of course, she'd have to insist that he let her keep the mask on, but he'd been hot enough for her to accept any terms.

She hoped.

She remembered his kiss, his touch, his splendid body, then covered her mouth with her hand, appalled with herself. She couldn't suppress the excitement, though. Or the anticipation.

What a wicked woman she was, to be sure!

Composing her features, she walked briskly back to the drawing room, despite shivers of guilt. Surely the maid standing back to let her by, and the footman stationed in the hall must see how wanton she was. She felt as if her wicked plan was written on her back!

In the drawing room she picked up her embroidery, but immediately threw it down again to sit staring into space.

How could she? said her conventional part.

How could she not? asked the rebel who'd once been a hell-born twin.

Since the only man she wanted would never want her, she seemed likely to die a spinster. She'd be damned if she'd die a virgin. She couldn't imagine, however, joining her body with just any man merely for the experience. What other chance would she have to lose her virginity to a man so special to her and keep her identity secret as well?

And, she thought with a sigh, it was more than sex. She wanted so much to be with Fort again in his kinder form, the form he had shown to Lisette, the form she'd glimpsed at Sappho's. She wanted to see him in a state of joy.

Surely a man would have to be joyous in sex.

She wanted to see him naked again. She remembered him inviting her to do to his naked body all the wicked things she was imagining . . .

Elf waved her hand in front of her hot face.

Oh my. She now knew why people throughout history had made utter fools of themselves over members of the opposite sex.

Was she making a fool of herself?

Probably. And she didn't care a jot.

The only snarl in her lovely plan was her disguise. If

he recognized her, that would be the end of it. Would powdered hair and mask be enough at even the most intimate moments?

Hurrying up to her room, she found the loo mask and tied it on, studying her face. Yes, it really was enough. With only her mouth and chin uncovered, no one would recognize her. If she spoke French, he wouldn't know her voice.

It had worked before, and would again, particularly since he would be distracted by the throes of passion.

That reminded her that she had better make sure the strings were knotted very tight. It wouldn't do to have it come off when *she* was in the throes of passion.

Throes of passion. It was one of those phrases she didn't entirely know the meaning of.

But she would.

Tomorrow night.

The next night, Elf traveled to Lady Yardley's house in a stew of hot anticipation and chilly doubt. She was dressed as she had been at Vauxhall except for the domino. Tonight she wore a light, cream cloak. In fact, with her white hair and white half mask, she surely looked snowily demure.

What clear evidence that one should never judge by appearances! Virginal white merely disguised the "appalling" outfit Fort would surely recognize, and the wicked woman who hoped to be very unvirginal come morning.

"I'm surprised Chantal didn't leave your service," teased Amanda as the coach turned into Clarion Street. "She was almost in tears when you insisted on wearing that ensemble to a society affair. You do have dreadful taste, dear."

Elf pulled a face at her. "It's just that you all like to dress so dull. I weary of demure, pale shades."

"They suit you."

"I don't think so." As the coach drew to a halt, Elf flicked open the fan she'd had made especially for this evening. One side was mother-of-pearl, and matched her outer self. The other was red, black, and gold lacquer, the colors of her other persona. "Tonight I am again Lisette Belhardi, mysterious French enchantress, and I can dress as I please."

Amanda shook her head. "I still don't know what you think to achieve by this mischief."

Elf had come up with a story for Amanda, and now she repeated it. "I just want to meet Fort again on friendly terms."

"I think there's more to it than that."

"More than having fun flirting with my enemy?"

"Remember, love, I know you. You're up to something."

"Perhaps," Elf admitted as the coach came to a halt. She let the fan slither shut and descended, assisted by the waiting footman.

Mounting the steps to the brightly lit house, Elf chose the right moment to prepare Amanda. Once they were surrounded by other guests and attendant maids, she murmured to her friend, "Yes, I'm up to something, Amanda. If I slip away with Walgrave, don't try to stop me."

"Slip away!" Amanda exclaimed, then lowered her voice to a whisper. "Elf, do but think!"

Cloak gone, Elf flicked open her fan, colored side out. "Oh, I've thought. Believe me."

It hung in the balance, but then Amanda rolled her eyes. "Well, he's a completely eligible *parti*, my dear. If you want to conduct your wooing in this outlandish way, I daresay no great harm will come of it."

She sounded almost smug, which drove Elf to protest. "Amanda, I have absolutely no notion of *marrying* the man."

Her friend just shook her head with a maddening smile and led the way up to the ball.

Really, thought Elf, climbing the flower-decked stairs, it was infuriating. Amanda seemed to think she and Fort were *lovebirds*! Lovebirds did not peck at one another until the blood ran.

She'd be hard pressed, however, to say what they *were*.

Lady Yardley's ballroom was of moderate size, but well lit and heavily gilded. The glittering chamber swarmed with costumes and masks, both beautiful and macabre, and a wave of chatter and music hit Elf as she walked in.

Here, in a private home, more people had chosen costumes over dominoes or had merely added a loo mask to their regular evening wear. This should have made a black-clad Earl of Walgrave easier to spot, but Elf searched the room without success.

Stuff and bother. She'd hoped Fort would attend much as he had at Vauxhall, in ordinary clothes with just that narrow mask. If he were wearing a domino or one of the more cunning costumes, detecting him could be a challenge.

What if he wasn't here, and didn't come?

That possibility had plagued her ever since she'd hatched the plan. She'd even considered sending him a cryptic note from Lisette in order to draw him here. The risks to that were too great, however, and surely he must at least put in an appearance at his aunt's one grand entertainment of the year.

Still, she couldn't see him or anyone who might be him.

She shrugged and made herself calm. If he was here, he would surely spot her. He couldn't have forgotten this outfit.

Since everyone was supposed to be incognito, there was no question of greeting their hostess, so Elf and Amanda blended with the crowd to enjoy some anonymous fun. Immediately, a slender Tudor gentleman in tights and puff breeches bowed and begged Elf's hand for the dance. Though he certainly wasn't Fort, Elf happily complied. She spent the time plying him with questions to try to establish his identity, and he did the same with her.

Since it was the custom to act in part at these events, she spoke in French and he did too, though rather clumsily. They parted unenlightened, and Elf suspected he was a member of one of the embassies, probably from Spain.

Next, Elf accepted the company of a pirate of a century ago. She recognized Sir Cronan Darby, always a jolly fellow. His French was appalling, but his gaudy yellow shirt and lace-frilled breeches appealed to her, and when he teased her into a corner and stole a kiss, she didn't object.

Not as good a kiss as Fort's, she thought as he squeezed her close. Then she sighed over the fact that Fort had become her standard—her unreachable standard.

Sir Cronan invited her to find a more secluded corner. Elf playfully refused and returned to the ballroom so as to be visible. Though she hoped Fort would spot her, she didn't stop searching the crowd for tall men of the right build. As she danced with a domino'd gentleman too short to be her quarry, she continued to assess the men around. A number were the right type, but she felt strangely certain that none of them was Fort Ware.

When the set ended, she glanced at a clock, alarmed by how fast time was flying. It still lacked half an hour to eleven, but at midnight masks would come off as everyone went to enjoy supper. She had to identify Fort and leave with him before then.

Perhaps he hadn't come after all.

A sickening sense of disappointment settled into her stomach and it had nothing to do with rounding up the Scots.

Then she spotted a tall man in a brown domino. She supposed Fort might not wear black, particularly if he were trying to disguise himself. With a hasty excuse to her partner, she pursued the man into the small antechamber where drinks were set out.

As he accepted a glass of wine from a servant, Elf bumped him lightly so a few drops spilled.

"Oh, monsieur!" she exclaimed. *"Je vous demande pardon!"*

He wiped his hand with the cloth hastily presented by the footman and responded in excellent French. "No harm done, my dear. May I command you some wine of your own?"

It wasn't Fort. Elf made herself smile. "Oh yes, sir, if you please."

Now, she had to waste precious minutes talking to the man in brown. Reentering the ballroom, Elf encountered Lord Ferron in a toga and laurel wreath. He was one of her longtime suitors, but clearly didn't recognize her. Elf accepted his invitation to dance, thinking it would be a useful test of her disguise.

Dancing with him turned out to be a mistake, however. He didn't recognize her, but had great difficulty managing both toga and partner. At one point, the cloth slipped, baring his chest, and Elf noticed with surprise how narrow it was.

She'd always thought Ferron a well-set-up young man, but clearly he owed most of his charms to his tailor. His hair, she now noted, was thin and receding. No wonder he always wore a wig.

Really, she thought, as they danced down the line, it was completely unfair that men could keep themselves so modestly shrouded! A woman had to at least bare her chest and part of her arms, which inevitably told something of her form. A man, on the other hand, could hide everything but his face and hands.

He had to show his legs, she supposed.

She glanced sideways and saw, as she'd expected from his chest, that Ferron's naked calves were decidedly spindly and he must normally wear padded stockings. Of course, a spindleshanks with thinning hair could be a wonderful person, but a lady should know what hid beneath the covers.

Perhaps she would start a movement for greater exposure of the male form!

Executing a turn made awkward by the toga's drapery, a hooded monk caught her wandering eye. The long, black robe hid this man's form entirely, and yet something in the way he moved as he walked down the room suggested a naked body she remembered only too well.

If it was Fort, had he spotted her? Surely her flaming scarlet couldn't be missed.

If he had, he was not seeking her out. He was heading toward the door in the same autocratic manner as when he'd parted the crowds at Vauxhall.

He was leaving!

Elf excused herself to Ferron with a few mumbled words about a pinched toe, and dashed after the monk, silently cursing the chaos of the merry crowd. As she ran, gasping, onto the landing, she saw him already descending the stairs toward the hall and the door.

Running down and past him, she barred his way at the bottom of the sweeping curve of steps.

He stopped.

She looked up and saw her instincts had been right. The narrow black mask did not prevent her recognizing Fort.

"Madam?"

Standing two steps above her, he was painfully high. Elf moved up a step, even though it took her closer. *"Monsieur Le Comte."*

"You require something?" he asked in French, but as if speaking to a total stranger.

Well, he certainly hadn't spent sleepless nights longing for his lost Lisette!

Elf shook out her scarlet-striped skirts. "You promised me lessons in taste, my lord."

"I think you are mistaken." He stepped to the side to pass her.

Elf grabbed the rope around his waist. "I think not. A lady is allowed to change her mind."

He swung to face her, then gripped her arm and

hustled her into a small anteroom off the hall. "Are you completely mad?" he snapped as he shut the door.

Furious again. Just his ordinary, charming self. He released her arm, and Elf let go of his cord. "Why do you say that, my lord?"

He pushed his cowl back, revealing unpowdered hair curling loose on his shoulders. It made him look . . . untamed. It reminded her of him naked in a bedroom except that now he was angry.

A ripple of fear passed through her—an awareness that she might have stirred up more than she'd planned—but she placed an unsteady hand on his chest. "I'm truly sorry for running away like that the other night, my lord. But it was all such a shock. When I had time to think about it—"

He covered her hand. Captured it. "You realized the advantages?" He studied her so closely that she feared he would have to recognize Elf Malloren despite mask, powder, and foreign tongue. "I can't even be sure you are the same woman. You could be one of your relatives in the same outfit."

Elf was surprisingly upset that he held nothing in his memory of her except her dress. Which he thought appalling, the horrid man.

"Of course," he said, "I might recognize the taste of you."

Oh, the rogue! But Elf's feelings were soothed by this beginning of seduction. He was not indifferent after all.

She pretended to be coy. "I'm a little nervous at the thought of kissing a religious man, my lord."

He raised her chin. "I give you absolution before we sin."

His kiss was as thorough as last time, but in some subtle way mechanical. When he raised his head, she wanted to scrub at her lips. "That didn't feel very sinful, my lord."

"If you want to sin, Lisette, I'll show you the way to hell before the night is out." His voice contained no trace of seductive warmth. "Now, tell me the purpose for this."

So, even if he accepted her as Lisette, he was the man Elf knew too well—watchful, wary, and cynical. Perhaps the other night had been an aberration after all. What did this mean for her plans?

She had to at least accompany him out onto the street to draw out the Scots. But a night of seductive passion seemed unlikely.

She fought a betraying tremble in her lips, hiding them behind her fan. "I just wanted to see you again, my lord."

"Why? Having had the ingenuity to escape, I'd have thought you wiser than that."

She turned away coyly. "I'm sorry, my lord. I was just nervous. I thought, no matter what you said, you'd ravish me eventually."

"The chance of me ravishing you eventually is increasing by the moment. You're not making sense, Lisette. Who's behind this?"

"No one!"

Strongly tempted to hit him over the head with something, Elf turned to see that he'd moved to lean against the back of a sofa, arms folded. For some reason the pose sent shivers down her spine, and they weren't of fear.

"How did you get in?" he demanded. "I doubt Lady Yardley sent you an invitation."

"Well really! My cousin received one. She is titled."

"Is she?" He paused to consider it. "And your hostess is here?"

"Yes, my lord."

"Who is she?"

"Why should I tell you that?"

"Still trying to preserve your anonymity?" He smiled cynically. "So, the lady is as loose in her control of you as usual, and will not create a stir if I carry you off. We'll let that pass for the moment while you tell me just what you have planned. And be quick about it."

Elf took refuge in fanning herself. Why couldn't the wretch play his part and try to seduce her again, so she would merely have to put up weak resistance? Instead, it appeared *she* would have to seduce *him*.

"I . . . I just wanted to say that I was sorry, my lord. I was afraid I'd hurt your feelings."

He laughed. "Be at ease. I never gave it a thought other than to worry that you might have ended up in the gutter with your throat slit. I'd like my pistol back, though."

Elf realized she was glaring at the insensitive oaf and relaxed her features. "I will return it, my lord."

"You'd better, or I'll hunt you down and see you transported for theft."

He sounded as if he meant it!

He studied her for a moment, then shook his head. "I don't know what you thought to gain by taking it, anyway. Waving an empty pistol around is not much deterrent."

"I loaded it, of course.

"Did you, begad?" And now he looked at her with new alertness. Was that a flicker of recognition in his eyes?

She hastily lowered her chin and fluttered her fan. "My brother taught me, my lord. I didn't have to fire it, though, thank heavens. I'm not a good shot."

"Just as well." He moved so suddenly that he was on her, hand dangerously at her throat, before she had time to react. His thumb forced up her chin. "Just who are you, Lisette?"

Heart thundering, Elf stared up into his cool blue eyes wondering how he could not recognize her. But then, whyever would he imagine that Lady Elfled Malloren the Well Protected would be masquerading as Lisette Belhardi, a young lightskirt in search of a protector?

Half choked, she said, "I don't want to give you my full name, my lord."

He let her go but stayed close. "Very wise, though I'm no danger to you. Have you given thought to the man with the knife, though? He was not best pleased to find I'd let you slip."

Elf tried to assume profound ignorance. "But why would he care? What did he want with me?"

"He is afraid you overheard his private business. You didn't?"

"Business, my lord? I heard voices, but not the words, and my English is not very good. I was hiding from another gentleman. When I crept out onto the path, that man tried to seize me. When I ran, he chased. I was terribly scared."

"I suppose you were." His knuckles brushed distractingly along her jawline, then down her throat to the swell of her breasts. Before she could prevent it, he slid her bodice dagger out and tested the blade. "Not every lady wears one of these."

Elf decided it was wisest to remain silent.

"If you'd understood any of our business, I don't suppose you'd be here. Even you couldn't be so foolish. So," he added, sliding the small weapon neatly back into its sheath, "you came here for what? Did you truly rethink your decision about becoming my mistress?"

Even such impersonal contact near her breasts had set up a tingle there that summoned interesting memories. And now a faint warmth in his manner held promise that the night might, after all, end as she had dreamed.

It was only a distant promise, though. "Perhaps . . ." she murmured, praying that he'd begin a seduction.

"I need more certainty than that, Lisette. I've no mind to play the same scene over. Are you willing?"

Behind her fan, Elf gritted her teeth. Would it hurt the man to at least *pretend* a little loving softness? "Would you let me keep my mask on, my lord?"

His brows rose. "All the time? Your skin would rot."

"For the night," she whispered, trembling now that she had to put her fantasies into words. "For just one night, my lord."

His eyes became intent, intrigued. "Why?"

"Because I doubt the man I end up with will be as interesting as you."

He pushed the fan out of the way to study her. "You're interesting yourself, Lisette. Are you sure? Remember the terms. No marriage, even if there's a child. No false protestations of love."

"I remember, my lord, and I'm sure." She spoke the honest truth, but knew he mustn't guess the intensity of her certainty. "Will I still get the five hundred guineas, milord?"

As she'd planned, the mercenary question wiped away his lingering suspicions, and he laughed. "For one night? I'm afraid not, sweetheart. I have the feeling you should be paying me. But I'll give you a hundred, just to pacify your future husband."

Elf flicked open her fan and pouted, pretending to think about it. She still hoped he might try some ardent persuasions, but when he didn't she said, "Fair enough, my lord. Can we go now? The night's passing."

His brows rose. "Are you sure you're a virgin, Lisette? In some respects I'd rather you weren't, but I dislike being lied to."

"Yes, I am a virgin, my lord. I'm sorry if it displeases you."

He suddenly grinned. "You have claws, do you, though you've been trained to keep them sheathed. Perhaps tonight I'll let you use them."

She relished the prospect. She'd like to see some reaction from the man, even if just blood.

He raised her hand and kissed it, a trace of warmth softening his features. "Come along, then. This should be interesting, and I promise that at least it will be a night to remember."

Elf had no doubt at all that it would.

Discreetly expressionless, a maid brought Elf's white cloak and they exited into the soft summer darkness. Elf deliberately left the cloak hanging open so her people and the Scots could spot the scarlet lady.

She hadn't entirely forgotten her other purpose.

A quick glance around showed any number of loiterers, but no one she knew, Scots or English. It would be hard to tell here, however. Four houses besides that of Lady Yardley were brightly lit for entertainment. Latecomers were still arriving, and a few—like themselves—were leaving.

Coaches rolled up and down, and if the horses chanced to soil the street, urchins ran out to scoop up the valuable commodity. They'd sell it tomorrow to the market gardeners. Waiting servants leaned against railings chatting as they watched the lords and ladies come and go.

At the moment, most of them were watching the scarlet lady and the monk, knowing grins on their faces. Elf thanked heaven for her mask, for these servants surely made it their business to recognize the great and tally up their doings.

At the edge of the pavement, Fort paused. "My house is only on the next street, and I didn't bother with a coach. I wonder if it's safe for you, though."

"I'm not afraid, my lord, with your escort."

"You're better armed than I am, sweetheart. You have your dagger and I don't even have a sword. In fact," he added, drawing her against his side, "beneath this homespun robe, I am entirely naked. The notion amused me."

Elf became burningly aware of his torso separated from her hand by only a thin layer of cloth. Without intent, she moved her hand a little and he chuckled. "Interests you, does it?" He tilted her chin up. "I think you've chosen the right profession."

"I will doubtless marry, my lord."

"I wonder why." He touched his lips to hers in a velvet tease. "Perhaps I *will* offer you the position of mistress. Is that your plan?"

"No, my lord. In reality, I'm quite a conventional person." Elf enjoyed this opportunity to tell the truth.

"Really?" he said in obvious disbelief and began to guide her down the road. "Think, Lisette. You could be my mistress for a little while and then marry your conventional husband, handsomely endowed."

"I'm not a fool, my lord. A length of time with you would doubtless spoil me for other men. And I don't refer to my chastity."

"I do hope I can live up to your expectations, my sweet. But why marry at all, then, if it's not to your taste?"

"I told you, my lord. I'm conventional, and my family is even more so. Circumstances have arranged themselves so that tonight I have a chance to do just as I wish. It may be my only chance and I have chosen to spend it with you."

He paused to look at her, tracing her lips with his finger. "I think I understand you at last, Lisette. You are a most remarkable woman. Just one night, then. One night for ourselves alone. A night of freedom for both of us."

If Elf hadn't already been intent on wickedness, she would have surrendered to him then, conquered by his wistful need.

They continued down the street, arm in arm, walking a little faster now, both eager to reach their destination. Elf didn't forget other matters. She kept all senses keen, checking loiterers and passersby for lurking Scots or her own servants.

She saw neither.

What if the Scots didn't make an appearance? She couldn't imagine how else to draw them out, and the attack on the king could happen at any moment.

She remembered the item in Fort's cellars. Perhaps that would be a clue. Sometime in the night, once he was asleep, she would steal his key and investigate. That, after all, was the real reason behind this wicked plan.

That was *not* the reason behind this wicked plan.

She was hastening toward ravishment because of her restless needs, and because Fort's body next to hers, even here on the street, created the most delicious sensation she had ever experienced.

But she must try to remember to do her duty, too.

They turned the corner into Morpeth Street, and into sleepy quietness. No entertainments seemed to be taking place here tonight. A cart rolled slowly down the street, pulled by one tired horse, and in the distance two men walked briskly on their way. Otherwise, all was peaceful.

Elf looked around again, wondering if assassins lurked in the shadows, and whether her protectors were close enough.

Nothing happened.

Perhaps after all, the only danger she faced tonight was from her own tormenting desires.

She could marry Fort. Not could as in would be allowed to, but could as in him suiting her inclinations. He was not an easy man, no, but a strong one. And, at bottom, honorable.

If they came upon dragons, he had it in him to be a dragon slayer.

She wouldn't have thought that a few weeks ago, but now she knew Fort's sense of right and wrong was sound. He was unhappy, perhaps even tormented by something, and she didn't underestimate the power of that. It could even make him do things that went completely against his nature, but—

"Penny for them." His voice jerked her out of her thoughts, making her heart race with guilt as if he'd been able to read her mind.

"I was thinking about you," she said honestly.

"As I was thinking about you. You're an enigma, Lisette, and I still don't believe I have the truth of you. Perhaps I will by the end of the night."

I do hope not. "Why do you say that, my lord? You promised I could keep my mask."

"Sex is very revealing, my dear, and I don't mean of bodies. The mask won't hide anything that matters."

Pray God you're wrong! "Then will I find the truth of you, my lord?"

He smiled down at her. "Perhaps. But my experience gives me an edge. When my hand strokes your thighs open while my mouth pleasures your breasts, I doubt you'll be feeling observant."

Such casual words to make her turn hot all over, to make her ache in the places he spoke of. She made herself smile back at him. "Then perhaps I should stroke and pleasure you in turn."

His teeth flashed in a grin. "By all means, Lisette. The thought of your hand on my . . ." His grin turned very wicked. "What would you call it? My private parts?"

"Hardly entirely private tonight, my lord," Elf riposted, grateful for the mask hiding her red cheeks. She had never anticipated such a discussion. In fact, all her intimate imaginings had involved silence and darkness.

"Private enough, I assure you. Well, Lisette? Even an ingenue must have a phrase for the male anatomy."

Elf's French, though excellent, lacked such terms except for a baby name her French nurse had used for Cyn's little penis. She could only dredge up one literal French phrase. "Perhaps, your external organs, my lord?"

"Ah." He coughed slightly. "My *external organs* are certainly anticipating some stroking and pleasuring. I hope they are not alone. Contemplate, my sweet Lisette, those organs finding their home between your cream-silk and virginal thighs. Can you anticipate the introduction of my more outstanding external organ into your soft, moist, hot, and oh so empty internal space?"

Oh, she could. She could indeed! They were still arm-in-arm, still walking briskly down the street, and yet she felt as if he stroked her in impossible places. Elf's "internal space," feeling very hot and moist, became suddenly a second heartbeat. "You have a wicked tongue, my lord."

He laughed out loud. "You don't know how wicked, Lisette. But you will. Indeed you will. Having been chosen for your night of freedom, for your induction into the heavenly hell of lust, I intend to do my duty to the full. We're here."

Dazed, almost weak-kneed, Elf looked up the steps to

the door of Walgrave House, scene of her impending, and obviously thorough, debauch.

She shivered. Part of her was close to terrified. But nothing, not even threats to the king, could make her back away now.

"Last chance, Lisette." His crisp voice dragged her out of her daze. "If you come inside and get cold feet again, I will be very displeased."

He sounded as if her answer mattered as little as whether he had chicken or pork for his dinner. And yet something in his eyes, or perhaps in the way he shielded his eyes, made her think that wasn't true.

She didn't want it to be true.

It seemed, however, that she could walk away. She could put this wickedness behind her and return, still pure, to Lady Yardley's house.

She would never have to worry about her brothers finding out.

There'd be no danger of conceiving a child.

Amanda would be most relieved.

And yet . . .

She couldn't.

Deeper than the physical need that pounded between her legs, she wanted this night, perhaps the only possible night with Fort. She wanted the intimacy of sex which would reveal the truth of him.

But to have this night she had to be Lisette. Not Elf Malloren, who could perhaps love this man, and who wished to heal and comfort him. Tonight, she was Lisette Belhardi, a naughty creature who wanted only to exploit his body for her own sensual education.

So Elf cocked her head and smiled cheekily. "Cold feet, my lord? I'm the very opposite. I'm burning hot for you."

He laughed and ushered her into the house.

Chapter 9

From his seat on a shabby cart, Nat Roberts watched the scarlet lady and the earl stroll through the streets. He knew his people were at their posts nearby, but if any of them saw sight of Scots traitors it was more than he did. 'Course the streets were fair humming with people, but even so, if the Scots were around they were cunningly hidden.

He watched the couple go up the steps and enter the house. As the doors closed, he scratched beneath his tricorn with the handle of his whip.

Now what?

He'd figured right off that the lady in the red dress would be Lady Elfled. A quiet word with Mam'zelle Chantal had confirmed that milady had just such a gaudy outfit, and planned to wear it tonight to the masquerade. Gawd, but she was showing her old colors, for she'd been a rare handful as a child. He'd pondered telling that stiff-rumped Grainger his suspicions, but it went against the grain. And anyway, what could anyone do?

She was a member of the family. Were they supposed to lock her in her room like a naughty child?

Nat had brought in some extra people, though—this area was thick with them—ready to snatch her from the earl at any cost if she screamed. But she hadn't looked as if she wanted snatching. No. Not she. Judging from the way she'd been looking up at him, Milady wasn't no prisoner.

Scandalous, it was, the way the quality went on, but it wasn't his place to interfere.

Perhaps all that business of watching the earl had come out of female jealousy. Nat knew all about that, having a suspicious-minded wife.

But now what? None of his people had spotted anyone in particular watching Lady Yardley's, though he hadn't had a report since Lady Elf had come out with the earl.

He took a little sip from a rum bottle, contemplating the sticky situation.

He didn't think the marquess would be too happy at his sister spending the night—and a naughty night at that—in any man's house, never mind the Earl of Walgrave's. He doubted, however, that his employer would be any more pleased if Nat Roberts dragged Lady Elf out of there by the hair.

Even if he could.

"Women," he muttered, taking another swig. "Nothing but trouble."

Like those two there.

A couple of maidservants strolled down the street, arm in arm, singing a ditty, and winking at any man they saw.

They paused by the coach. "Hello 'andsome!" called out the blond one and moved right to the side of the coach. "Give us a sip at the bottle?"

Nat grunted something and passed it over, saying quietly, "What's up, Sally?"

Sally giggled as if he'd said something funny, then scrambled up beside him on the box. "Well, I don't reckon she was kidnapped, do you?" She winked as she took a real drink of his rum. A right handful was Sally Parsons, but a tempting armful, too, with her generous curves and merry eyes.

If he were that sort of man, of course.

She was also a chatterbox about some things, so he could only thank God she hadn't twigged to it being her ladyship.

"It was attack by the Scots we had to look out for, Sally."

"That didn't 'appen either. But—"

"But?" he asked, flashing her a quick glance.

She snuggled up against him. Gawd, there'd be hell to pay if his Hettie ever heard about this! "But, a group of street monkeys followed 'em."

Children! The streets were always full of ragged urchins, thieves most of them, and he'd not given them a thought. He looked around and saw two crouched in a gutter not far away playing some game. Dice probably.

"Them?"

"Could be part of 'em. Most of 'em ran off, though. Roger and Lon's following to see if they report to the Scots."

Nat muttered a few curses. "But still and all, they can't get at 'er in the 'ouse, can they?"

"Don't suppose so," Sally whispered into his ear, pretending to be enticing him. "But what's the problem? Roger and Lon'll follow the ratkins to the Scots. That's the point, i'nt it?"

"Aye, that's the point." But Nat was distinctly uneasy.

He remembered now that the scarlet lady was supposed to sneak a look at whatever the earl had in his cellars. Never mind her virtue, that could be bloody dangerous. "Look, Sal, I'll get this rig back to its owner. Can't keep the poor nag out 'ere all night. I'll be back as soon as I can, and we might 'ave to go in. You stay 'ere and keep your eyes open."

Sally fluttered her eyelashes at him. "Don't I always, 'andsome?" Then with a kiss on his cheek, she clambered down off the box, linked arms with Ella, and strolled off.

As he drove the coach back to the livery stables, Nat muttered to himself.

Women.

Nothing but trouble.

At the Peahen, Michael Murray, in his persona as the Reverend Campbell, listened to the leader of the pack of street monkeys. How wise he'd been to hire the urchins.

Besides being cheap, such ragamuffins went unnoticed by all, except that people held on to their purses and other valuables when they were about.

Yes, it had been wise to recruit the children, but he'd not expected such news as this. So, the scarlet doxy had turned up again, and at a society function. He knew that sometimes whores slipped into masquerades, or were sneaked in by their lovers, but everything about that creature unsettled him.

Pity the monkeys hadn't noticed her go into Lady Yardley's house. Murray would give a deal to know whom she'd arrived with.

Not Walgrave. He'd walked around alone in his monk's costume. Mack had been following him.

And now they'd gone back together to his house, happy as rats heading for their hole. Perhaps she was his mistress after all. Some silly young wife deceiving her husband when she got the chance.

But that didn't fit with those bloodstained garters.

Murray didn't understand it, and he didn't like that one bit.

He tossed the boy a sixpence to send him on his way, then sat there, chewing on his lip. No, he didn't like it.

His plan was ready. Even now, Jamie was putting the stone in a safe place. Soon he'd have the device. Tomorrow the Hanoverian Pretender would die. He couldn't abide uncertainties now.

He paid his shot and walked back to Lord Bute's house, fretting about the earl and his scarlet trollop. Walgrave had always been an uncertainty and Murray regretted ever making the connection.

Walgrave had been one of the names he'd been given, however, on a list of English people who had been secret supporters in the Forty-five. Most of them had never had to reveal their hesitant support of Bonnie Prince Charlie, and some of the younger ones were now in high places.

When Murray had realized that his relationship to Bute wouldn't get him close to the king, he'd started contacting people who had been particularly careless, ones who had left some evidence. In no case was it strong enough to force them into supporting him, but it was enough to make them very reluctant to expose him.

Murray sneered up at the fine houses as he passed. Half a dozen peers of the realm were on his list, and these days they sat in fine houses like these, worrying about Michael Murray and what he might tell.

But not worrying very much. No, they told themselves, patting their fat paunches and pouring another glass of brandy, the days of the Stuarts are over. That Murray is just a madman. Their youthful follies would not come back to haunt them.

Murray would prove he was not mad, and that those days were not over. Soon these haughty Hanoverians would be out in the gutter scraping for a living, just as honest followers of the Stuarts were today.

When he'd met with Walgrave, he'd found his tool. The incriminating evidence was strongest there—some firsthand accounts of a meeting with King James and Prince Charles. Of course, the evidence was against the present earl's father. That had been a shock to Murray, but the new earl had seemed much concerned about scandal, as well as being bitter about royal ingratitude. A wild young man, as well, much given to drinking and wenching.

A person easy to use, he'd thought.

He ducked into another house—a hovel really, cramped in an alley near grand houses—and quickly changed from his churchman's clothes into his normal wear. The old woman here gladly gave space and silence in exchange for a few pennies. Then, as Michael Murray, he left by another door and continued on his way to his rooms in the Earl of Bute's house in South Audley Street.

Yes, he reassured himself, Walgrave had been the right choice. Murray had only needed someone who knew the Court well enough to devise a way to get a lethal object close to George of Hanover. In that, the earl had done his part. Moreover, in the process he'd revealed his real driving impulse—a vindictive hatred against a certain marquess of Rothgar.

Murray had no interest in the marquess, but he'd been happy to know what rode the earl. He liked to understand people's weaknesses.

He'd been satisfied with the situation until he'd heard reports of too many casual meetings between Walgrave and the new Secretary of State, Grenville. That had led to the Vauxhall meeting, which in hindsight had probably been a mistake. But Murray still wished he knew what part that scarlet doxy had played. Had she been Walgrave's spy? And if so, what had been the point of it?

At Bute's house, he hurried to his small room before someone noticed the way his hands had begun to shake. He was so close. So close. Nothing could be allowed to upset his plans at this stage.

He pulled a miniature out of his pocket and opened it to look at the fine painting of a handsome young man with white powdered hair. Charles Edward Stuart. His friend.

Of course, Prince Charles was not so young anymore, and could not afford such a fine artist these days. That only made this miniature—a gift from the prince himself—a treasure. And a reminder of what should be. Murray's idol was reduced to wandering Europe, dependent on the charity of various monarchs.

That must change.

That would change.

The prince's father, James III, wasn't expected to live long. Then Charles would be rightful king.

King Charles III.

Murray intended to make him king, in fact, of Scotland if not of England. If only his careful plans had not been so dogged by mishap.

First the old king had died, appropriately suffering an apoplexy while trying to force his bowels. Murray rejoiced to see any of the Hanoverians dead, but it had not suited his plan. The old upstart had been a German autocrat in the true Hanoverian style. He hadn't been popular and his death would have been accepted with little upset, perhaps even with pleasure.

If George II's eldest son had lived to claim the crown, he would have sufficed. He'd have ascended the throne a dissipated middle-aged man.

The present usurper, however, George II's grandson, was a handsome young man, recently married to a dutiful wife expecting her first child. He had been born and raised in England, and didn't even have a German accent.

The English people would not like his death.

But in the end, it didn't matter whether they liked it or not. The king would die, and the stone would do the rest.

The Stone of Destiny. What the English—curse their thieving hearts—called the Stone of Scone.

Reputed by myth to be Jacob's pillow, it had been used as part of the coronation ceremonies of Scottish kings as long as memory could tell. In 1303 it had been wickedly stolen by Edward I, murderer of Wallace, as part of his attempt to seize Scotland as he had seized and subjugated Wales.

As further blasphemy, the stone had been incorporated into the coronation chair here in London, in Westminster Abbey. Every English monarch since then had been crowned while sitting on top of the sacred stone of Scotland.

It made no difference to Murray that these days the thrones of England and Scotland were joined. When James VI of Scotland had inherited the throne of England, he should have stayed in Edinburgh and governed his kingdoms from there! And he should have had the stone taken back to its rightful home.

If he'd done that, then surely the Stuart line would not have experienced such disasters.

But look what had happened. James's son, Charles, had been beheaded by those wicked Parliamentarians.

Charles's older grandson had eventually been restored as Charles II but, despite a virile sowing of wild oats, had failed to create a legitimate child to inherit the throne.

Then Charles I's other son, James, had shown signs of righteousness. He'd embraced the Catholic Church and even talked, so it was said, of restoring the monarchy and the stone to Scotland. Of course the English had turned on him and thrown him out, denying even that his son was his true child.

That son's son was Murray's beloved prince, who had led so valiant an invasion in 1745. It would have succeeded, Murray was sure, if only James III had sworn his coronation oath on the Stone of Destiny in Scone, in Scotland.

Charles III would do so, and so come in time into the right.

Murray chuckled. The English would grieve at their king's death, but they'd crown another one, never realizing the real disaster. They'd lost the stone. The new monarch would not be able to be crowned on the stone, which would be far away in France with the rightful king, awaiting its journey home.

They already had it in a safe place, just waiting for the box in which it would travel. In time, the Stone of Destiny would work its magic and the false line of Hanover would rot away without invasion or violence.

Which left just the last task, killing the king.

In the gloomy hall of Walgrave House, under the disapproving gaze of Roman senators and the blank one of a footman, Fort turned to Elf. "Do you require any refreshment, my dear?"

Strangely embarrassed by the impassive servant, Elf shook her head, reminding herself that she was masked and powdered beyond recognition.

"Come then." And he led her up the wide stairs she had crept down but a few nights since.

In moments she entered his bedchamber, and memories of her previous visit caused a frisson of fear.

Strangely, it merely seemed to add to the passionate excitement driving her.

Glancing at Fort, she saw the man who was going to guide her through the maze of carnal sensation. Because she'd demanded it. Perhaps, after all, she *was* Lisette the exploiter, not Elf, the nurturing savior.

She had no idea except that she wanted him, wanted all he had to offer. She wanted the fornication thundered against from the pulpit, and the guilty pleasures whispered about behind fans.

All thought shattered at the touch of his hands on her shoulders, thumbs brushing her collarbone. She looked up, helpless in the first winds of a growing storm.

"I would prefer that you take off the mask," he said softly. "I will keep your identity secret, my word on it. Carnal pleasure is best enjoyed with all barriers down."

For an idiotic moment, she was tempted, but she shook her head and he let the matter go. With a wry smile, he traced the edge of the soft leather, and the merest brush of his fingers sparkled on her skin. Then he cradled her head, teasing the edge of her jawbone with his thumbs.

"I do wonder who you are . . . But," he added, brushing his lips over hers, "it hardly matters now, and the element of mystery is intriguing."

He kissed her again, a dozen wayward, fleeting kisses, kisses so tantalizing that she stretched closer, seeking to trap and relish them. His smiling lips evaded hers, but his tongue touched. A flicker of hot moistness.

She laughed and did the same to him, dancing lips and tongue at play, until he snared her close. No mechanical, testing kiss this. It rendered her wax beneath his flame.

Warm, liquid, ready to be consumed.

At last he released her lips, and she turned her dizzy head against his chest, drifting under the touch of his hands. The wide sleeve of his dark monk's robe had fallen back to his elbow, revealing one strong forearm, sinuously decorated by raised veins.

She'd seen arms like that on the stable grooms. Were all gentlemen like that beneath the silk and lace?

Why had she never noticed before how beautiful a muscular arm could be? She curled up one hand to touch, to adore the entrancing masculinity.

A shift in position let her put lips to one line of vein and she traced it.

"What are you doing?" he asked, still for a moment.

"You have beautiful arms." She traced back up the vein with her tongue, then looked up at him, amused by the expression in his eyes. He almost looked embarrassed.

"I am pleased if I please you. You have beautiful arms, too." And he kissed from bare knuckle to naked elbow, then from bare shoulder—slowly—to the exposed swell of her breasts.

Letting the pleasure of his lips form the undertone, Elf continued her own exploration. She pushed up the loose sleeve to expose his upper arm, hard muscle beneath her hand.

Since leaving childhood, she'd never seen a gentleman's bare arms. Except Walgrave's a few nights before, she remembered. Then, however, she'd been distracted by the naked whole.

Oh, and Ferron's, revealed by his toga. No competition there.

Men's arms, she thought dazedly, pushing his sleeve all the way to his broad shoulder, deserved more attention. But it was perhaps as well they be kept veiled or women would be in constant danger of this madness of desire . . .

Her overdress fell open.

She looked down in surprise, then laughed. One-handed, he'd unhooked it. Now he escaped her explorations and slid it off her shoulders. Turning her, he began to loosen her laces.

For a moment, she felt deprived of touch and sight, but then the mere vibration of his touch, felt in her spine through layers of buckram and silk, wove its own special magic. Her eyes drifted closed . . .

"Look," he breathed, moving her slightly. "Look, Lisette."

Opening heavy lids, Elf saw a picture . . .

No.

She saw herself in a mirror. In a long cheval mirror she saw a white-haired, white-masked woman in a glittering stomacher and scarlet petticoat being undressed by a dark-robed, black-masked monk.

Lud. It was the stuff of wicked dreams!

Perhaps that was what made it so exciting.

For it was. Over and above any love, any lust, beat the wild drum of the forbidden. Of something wicked in the air.

Perhaps he heard it too. He looked up as he began to pull the laces loose, and smiled into her eyes in the mirror. "I think you're right, naughty Lisette, about the mask. Costumes do add a little something, don't they? But then, you're an innocent . . ."

That question again. How she must puzzle him. "I am a virgin," she said into the mirror. "But I don't feel innocent at the moment."

"You certainly won't feel innocent in the morning. That, I promise you." He had the laces loose enough, and now he slipped the shoulder straps over her shift, until it no longer compacted her breasts. In fact, he moved it just beneath them so they seemed to be bursting forth, nipples standing proud through the delicate silk.

Instinctively, she covered them.

He laughed and nipped at her neck. "Comfort them then, Lisette, while I make you pure white."

The bow of her petticoat lace surrendered to a tug, and it slithered into a scarlet pool at her feet. He pulled her hands from her breasts so the stomacher could follow it.

She was, as he had said, pure white now, from her

white-powdered hair, through her white leather mask, over white ladylike skin and filmy silk calf-length shift.

Even her stockings were white. White lace suitable, she had thought years ago when she bought them, for a bride. She'd felt defiant when she pulled them on tonight, but now it seemed so right.

Even her shoes were white, though gilded on the heels.

Only her lips and her veiled nipples gave color to the scene.

Unless black was a color. He stood, black-robed, behind her, like a shadow.

Or a devil.

Or a lover from her darkest dreams.

She shivered, but not with fear. She shivered from the look in his eyes. Surely every woman wished to be looked at in such a way by a lover.

He laid his hands on her sides—dusky against her pallor—and slid the silk against her flesh up and down her flanks. Elf watched in shocked fascination as the hem crept higher and higher, first showing her garters trimmed with white rosebuds, then exposing her pale thighs.

She'd expected to be naked, but not this. Not this slow, voluptuous exposure. She put her hands over his and challenged his eyes in the mirror. He just smiled and slipped his hands away. Her shift fell back to her calves and she idiotically straightened it. When she looked into the mirror again, he was naked and unmasked.

"Better?" he asked.

But he stood behind her. When she tried to turn, he stopped her, so she could only see his shoulders and his arms, which came around her. Brown muscular arms, paler toward the shoulders. He must spend time in the sun with his sleeves rolled up. Probably in the stables.

She wished she could see him like that in sunlight and simple activities.

He pulled her back against him, and hard heat seared

through the thin silk. Harder down low, where he clearly wanted her, wanted to burst in and invade her.

A tremor of fear shot through her, but it was easily swamped by the swimming pleasure of the moment.

Perhaps it added to the pleasure of the moment.

How strange to feel such pleasure from a casual embrace, for he merely rocked her in his arms, chin resting against her white-powdered hair, looking calm and in full control of himself. "Now, Lisette, tell me true. Just how wicked do you want to be?"

Faced with such an impossible question, the Malloren in Elf replied. "Very."

He raised his brows, perhaps disbelievingly. "Your wish is my command tonight. But my aim is philanthropic. I intend to give you pleasure, and nothing but pleasure. If it ceases to be pleasant, you must tell me."

"And you will stop?" She didn't believe it for a moment.

"And I will stop," he said, still swaying with her in a rhythm that sapped her sanity. "Stop whatever it is you do not like, that is. I'm sure I can find *something* you like, my bold adventuress."

Elf was sure he could, too. For example, she loved this embrace, this cradling. A week ago, she'd not have believed Fort could be such a subtle lover. What little she knew of these matters suggested most men took a more direct approach.

She'd expected him to be like most men.

Now, she didn't know what to expect, which both terrified and thrilled her. Indeed, she was at last having an adventure!

"Keep your eyes on the mirror," he said, and disappeared from view.

Though tempted to look, Elf obeyed until he reappeared in the mirror, placing an upholstered bench by her side. She did glance down, puzzled, but then his arms returned to cradle her.

He stroked her again, but softly and over silk, his right hand sliding down to her thigh. She glanced from hand to smiling, watchful eyes. Then he hooked his hand under her knee, raised her leg, and set her shoed foot on the bench. Elf gasped as her shift slithered all the way up to her groin, exposing her thigh entirely.

Instinct screamed, *cover yourself!* but she ignored it, relaxing back against him and waiting for the next move.

It came when he ran a finger around the flowery garter she wore beneath her knee, but he made no move to untie it. Instead he began to stroke up her thigh, brown hand against pale skin. "If you recall, I mentioned the delight of a woman's cream-silk thighs."

Elf watched his hand in fascination, entranced by sight and multiple sensations.

"Now that is a vision I find delightful," he murmured into her ear. "A woman relaxed in her senses. Add to it the feel of her beneath my fingers." Those long brown fingers danced high on her inner thigh. "Especially here."

Elf gasped and would have reached to stop him, but he snared her hands in one of his. "Don't. Don't fight unless you really want me to stop. Feel how it *feels,* Lisette."

A wicked dance on her most sensitive skin, that's what it felt like.

She could have broken free, but she relaxed in his hold, watching as his fingers gently played, feeling every touch a hundredfold because of the mirror.

"How does it feel?" he asked.

Elf wasn't sure there were words. Wonderful. Sinful. Dangerous. Promising.

"Wicked," she breathed.

"Precisely." He blew against her ear as he trailed his fingers across to her other thigh and back, watching her. "Do you feel it?"

"What?" He had just nipped her earlobe and she was drowning in sensation.

"The place where you *want* me to touch. Where already you want me inside you."

Immediately her mind isolated one place, and a growing need there. "Yes. But . . ."

His fingers continued that leisurely, tantalizing journey. "But?"

She moved her whole body against him restlessly. "But not yet. I don't know why . . ."

"Because then it would be over, clever one. You have an instinct for this game. It is urgent, demanding. Yet paradoxically, it is best enjoyed with torturing delay." He released her limp hands and touched her nipples, first one, then the other, watching her, watching her as she watched him.

Elf saw her own hands flutter up, flutter down, not seeking to restrain, but wanting something to hold on to.

"Reach back. Hold on to me."

Her hands found hot flesh. His thighs. The position made her breasts thrust. He untied the lace at the low neck of her shift and pulled the silk down to expose them, pink nipples bigger than she had ever seen them.

"My mouth wants your breasts, wants to taste them, I want to see and hear your pleasure when I suckle them. And they want me, don't they?"

A strangled sound escaped Elf as her body remembered, and wanted.

"But from here, I cannot tend to them that way. So, we delay. We have all night." Gently, he played with her nipples, stretching them. "I can wait."

"No. I want—"

"Patience, Lisette. We can sample every pleasure, every taste, every touch. Sometimes, waiting is the greatest aphrodisiac. Do you know what an aphrodisiac is?"

Scarce able to speak, she just shook her head.

"Something that stimulates or enhances physical desire."

His right hand settled between her spread thighs, pressing against the hungry place, moving slightly in a way that brought a whole new hum of excitement.

And need.

Could that woman in the mirror—gasping, moving,

stretching on tiptoe for some reason—really be Elf Malloren? "Then I don't think I need one . . . *Please!*"

Was that her gasping voice?

It was certainly her voice that protested when he took his hands away.

"Just a little adjustment," he soothed, moving in front of her to sit on the bench, so her raised leg arched over his like a bridge, anchored by his hand on her ankle.

"Put your hands on my shoulders."

She obeyed, glad of some support, loving the warm firmness of his flesh.

"Now, watch yourself be wicked, Lisette."

Elf only felt his touch between her thighs, for his back now blocked her view, but she could see his head at her breast, feel his tongue, his teeth, his lips tease and torment her until fevered sensations beat at her consciousness.

"Look!" He said it sharply to catch her fragmented senses.

Elf forced her eyes open. A wild creature gripped his shoulders, arms rigid, mouth loose with desire, breasts rosy from his loving. "Mercy on me," she whispered and let her eyes fall shut as she stretched like a bow, as if reaching, reaching for an impossible treasure.

Not impossible after all when he continued to circle his hand firmly between her legs and play with her nipples with his mouth. Reality disappeared, swamped by something she supposed could be called pleasure.

Shattering pleasure.

Though in fact, she thought as she realized he was holding her close, she needed a new vocabulary entirely to describe that experience. He moved her back a little to look at her, then slid her down so she straddled his hips, all the while soothing her with gentle touches.

But when she relaxed and smiled at him, about to thank him, he said, "More?"

In truth, a part of her wanted to say no, wanted to spend a day, a week, a month relishing that novel experience and recovering before sampling anything new.

But there would be no other time.

"Yes, more," said Lisette the brazen hussy and wriggled on his lap.

"What sweet words," he murmured, and moved her so that his erection pressed between her legs, pressed on spots still so sensitive that she flinched.

"Don't fight it." It wasn't the words that stopped her resistance, it was the hint of unsteadiness, of need. She recognized the need, tight-held, that drove him and it played on her senses as his hands had pleasured her skin.

"You want me, don't you?" he asked almost dreamily as she felt the push at the place that did indeed want. Despite the pleasure he'd given her, that place still wanted.

Then she realized that he needed her to say it. Perhaps he needed her to say more. Elf the chatterer had been almost silent throughout.

"Yes," she said huskily, as if her voice hadn't been used in a year. She cleared her throat. "Yes. I want you. What we did before . . . It was wonderful, but not—"

"Go on," he breathed, pushing just a little against her.

She licked her lips. She could still see herself in the mirror, disheveled and rosy, wanton in his lap. Could see his broad back. A very splendid back. She slid her pale hands down over it restlessly.

"It's like an ache," she whispered. "No, like an itch I cannot scratch. Inside me. Yes!"

She felt him inside her, just a little way.

She wished it went deeper, but it seemed churlish to complain.

"Keep talking," he said, "and I'll keep moving." When she looked down she saw a teasing challenge in his heavy-lidded eyes and laughed out loud.

"I could call your bluff."

Humor deepened. "One day you must tell me how an innocent comes to know so much. Yes, if you call my bluff, you'd win. But I'd like to hear you tell me how this feels. Let's pretend your words can drive my loving."

Abruptly, all words escaped her except a string of incoherent pleas she would not utter. "What you did before," she said desperately. "I liked it."

"You surprise me." It was a mere whisper against her breast, where his mouth played, but it carried laughter.

"I suppose that's why you watched. I always thought these things happened in the dark, you know, but seeing does seem to be quite exciting . . . *Oh!*" He had pushed forward a little more. "Yes! Er . . . that wasn't a cry of objection, my lord."

"I didn't think it was. Call me Fort."

"Fort."

Elf remembered imagining saying his name in the secret dark of a bed. They weren't in a bed or the dark, but the pleasure of speaking his name this way still entranced. She said it again, pulling his head up and kissing him, attacking him with the hard need still knotted within her, tormented by his nearness.

He returned the kiss, but when it finished they were little further forward.

"You're a wretch to tease a lady so!"

"You're a wretch to stop talking." A shudder rippled through him. "Have pity, Lisette, and tell me how you feel."

"As if I want to scratch you," she said, almost crossly. "Hot, sticky. Aching." Taking control, she wriggled forward. *"Ouch!"* She hastily squirmed back.

Hard hands seized her hips, pulling her back. Pain shot through her and she cried out again as he filled her completely.

Now she knew how deep it should go.

She sat rigid under astonishing sensations, some of them distinctly unpleasant. "I suppose I'm not a virgin anymore."

"If you start to complain at this point, I'll throttle you." A tension in him, almost a vibration, told her of his need. Did he feel as she had, hovering on the brink, aching for release?

She made herself relax. "No complaint except against nature who made women so." It felt a little better. The pain was subsiding and the feel of him, big and deep, was . . . was again beyond description.

His lips moved back to her breast, which helped, and she tangled her fingers in his hair. "I think I'm rather pleased actually, my lord. Fort. My lover . . . My first lover. Does it please *you,* I wonder, to know I'll never forget this?"

With a sighing shudder, he looked up at her. "You are a remarkable woman, Lisette. Despite your desire for the conventional, I might not let you go . . ." His hips flexed, and he moved within her so she shuddered too.

She kissed him, loose-lipped and hungry. "You cannot keep me."

"Perhaps you won't want to leave. Tell me how it feels."

"Tell me how you feel."

"As if I'm about to explode and fly into tiny pieces. But as if I'm going to be very happy, very soon. You're tight, and hot, just the right size and exquisitely responsive. I'm a lucky man. Or will be if you'll just talk to me."

"You're *impossible*! Just do what you have to do." But when he didn't, she added, "There's pain. But it's not too bad. More a fullness." She moved her hips, trying to adjust herself around him, then quivered as a new need stirred.

He groaned and she liked that. She wished she knew what to do to make him groan like that again.

"It's a strange sensation," she whispered, almost to herself. "But I think it's good . . ." He moved them both, and she gasped. "Goodness!"

"From good to goodness." But he stilled again except to suckle hard on her breasts, sending a new burst of power to explode along her oversensitized nerves.

"Mercy on me!" she gasped, thrusting her restless hips against his. He groaned again, so she did it again. Still he held himself rigidly still, jaw set.

"I want to stretch," she gabbled. "As if I could touch the edge of the world . . . It's like a hunger. A fierce hunger. As if I'm eating for the first time, but can't satisfy myself . . ." She seized his hair and turned his grimacing face to hers. "I could get quite cross about this, my lord."

"Fort. I insist that you call me Fort."

Elf looked into passion-dark, desperate eyes. "It would serve you right if . . . Fort, then. Fort. Fort. *Fort!*"

She chanted it as he rose, still inside her, to lower them both to the carpet. She chanted it in time to his thrusts, until breath and coherence escaped her. She chanted it in her mind when she could only grip him, tighter and tighter, for fear of extinction.

Then she sighed, "Fort," in dreamy surrender, remembering at last to say, "Thank you."

He laughed as if he scarce had breath to laugh with. "You can't imagine how delighted I am to have been of service, dear lady."

He had left her body, but sensations lingered everywhere to remind her. Flat on her back on the carpet, Elf stretched and smiled up at him. "You sadly underestimate my imagination, my lord. Fort."

Somewhat unsteadily, he pulled her to her feet, gathered her in his arms, and carried her to the undisturbed bed. He set her on her feet again in order to pull back the covers, but when he turned to her, he smiled and touched her lips with his finger. "I like that."

"What?"

"That smile. You look very pleased with yourself."

Her smile widened. "I am. And pleased with you, Fort." Cheekily, she added, "If you ever need one, I'll give you a reference!"

Laughing, he picked her up and tossed her onto the sheets. She realized then that she was still partially dressed, if a loose-topped shift, lace stockings, and one shoe could be in any sense called clothing. He plucked off the shoe and tossed it on the floor.

She moved to strip off her shift, but he said, "Don't."

She looked down at the stained and sweaty garment. "Why not?"

"A woman is most beautiful in sensuous disarray."

Elf didn't think she had ever felt more beautiful than at that moment in the mirror of his eyes. "What of you, then?"

"What do you want?"

She considered asking him to put on the black silk robe, but realized she liked the sight of his body too much to want it veiled. Strong body, tangled hair, and a face so relaxed she hardly knew him.

"What are you thinking?" he asked. "You can ask whatever you want."

"That a man is designed to pleasure the sight of a woman."

He grinned, and she thought perhaps he might even have blushed a little. "Men think it works the other way around."

"Which merely proves that God designed both sexes perfectly."

He leaned over to kiss her. "Don't bring God into this, sweetheart. Remember, I promised to show you the way to hell."

She discovered that his buttocks were available to her eager hands and explored their firm roundness. "I'll never think of hell in quite the same way . . ."

He pinned her to the bed with strong hands, but Elf relaxed in his grip. It wasn't a dangerous moment, just a lustful one. She would trust this man with her life.

That thought surprised her.

Naked trust.

Was that the truth he had spoken of? She did wish she could rip off the mask and be honest with him.

Deliberately, she moved matters back to the simply lustful. She licked her lips. "Do you have something else wicked in mind, Fort?"

He laughed out loud, and suddenly the universe shifted.

Just like that, thought Elf. Did a person fall in love just like that? Or was it realization that struck like Cupid's dart?

Her heart had started a new rhythm. A rhythm that had nothing to do with lust, only with love, with a fierce protectiveness and a need to be-with that pushed close to agony.

For she could not have him. If he knew who she was, he would not want her.

She would only ever have this one night.

But for this night, at least, she had her laughing lover.

As he relaxed down beside her, she snuggled against him, savoring perhaps the most precious moment of all—closeness, so relaxed, all barriers down.

This, she realized, was what she had really sought this night.

If only she could shed Elfled Malloren and all it entailed, and be Lisette. She'd do it in a moment to be so close to this man, to bring him laughter and pleasure every day and night, and be exquisitely pleasured in return. Just the thought of marriage, of this closeness through eternity, brought the agony of suppressed tears—because it could not be.

Or could it? She was a fighter, a Malloren. With a Malloren, all things are possible . . .

Fort pulled the covers over them and his arms came comfortably around her. "Sleep a little, Lisette. I promise I'll wake you later to continue your education in wickedness, but for the moment we both need a bit of rest."

She never could have imagined the beauty of sliding into sleep wrapped in his arms.

He kept his promise, waking her with kisses and nibbles and fiery touches. When she asked, he showed her how to touch him so he groaned and writhed. Though watching in the mirror had been exciting, this was perhaps even more delightful. The candles had guttered into darkness, and touch, taste, smell, and hearing were intensified beyond belief.

He did not enter her, but they shared pleasure anyway, inventively, wickedly, before tumbling back again into exhausted slumber.

When she woke to find herself smothered in dark cloth, encircled by strong arms, Elf thought he was up to yet more wickedness, but something she did not care for. She squirmed and tried to protest, but a hand clamped cloth down over her mouth, cutting off what little air she'd had.

Damn him, what did he think he was doing?

When the hand moved, she sucked in a breath through heavy, musty cloth and started to cough.

"Stifle it, or I'll throttle you," growled a voice. Definitely not Fort's.

A voice with a Scottish accent.

Chapter 10

Fear swamped panicked anger. Oh God, Elf thought, and it was a prayer.

How?

Why?

The world tipped and something punched her in the belly. No, she'd been tossed over a man's shoulder, head hanging down. Bile bit at the back of her throat, but she managed not to vomit, terrified that she'd choke to death.

Or that he'd carry out his threat and throttle her.

What was happening?

Where was he taking her?

Where was Fort?

Jerky movements told her the man was hurrying down the stairs. Swathed in the musty blanket, Elf could hardly breathe, never mind scream, and the thumping up and down once more threatened to make her vomit.

She prayed again, silent, incoherent pleas to any deity that might be listening.

Suddenly, she was swung around and dropped without care onto hard wood so she couldn't help but cry out. The blanket was pulled off her and she sucked in pure, fresh air. She was outdoors on a cloudy night in some kind of big box. Shadowy forms loomed over her . . .

A lantern opened by her face, so she flinched from the sudden light.

"She's a mask on. Let's see who she is."

With the snick of a knife, the mask was flipped back. "Nae one I ken."

The lantern was covered, creating dark again. Before Elf could try to move, something heavy tumbled on top of her. She squealed and a fist to the head knocked her dizzy. "I telt ye to be quiet!"

With a huge thump, the air changed. She was now in a closed box. A long narrow box.

A *coffin*?

Staggered by this thought, she heaved at the weight half over her. Cloth. Skin.

A *body*? A body in a *winding sheet*?

She was in a coffin with a body?

Oh God!

Fighting to escape the corpse, she couldn't stop whimpering. "No. Please. Help. Stop—"

No matter how she shifted, she couldn't find space. *Limp, cold arms and legs brushed against hers—*

Not cold.

She stilled. It was alive.

She ran her hands over face and hair.

"Fort?" In her panic she probably couldn't have made more sound than a whisper anyway. A moment later, she gave thanks for it.

He didn't so much as twitch. She shook him. "Fort!"

His slackness told her he was unconscious. Hastily she fumbled for his neck, for a pulse. She found it and sagged with relief.

She was stuck in a coffin in the hands of her enemies, but she was with Fort and he wasn't dead.

Elf took some deep breaths and tried to think.

They'd been taken prisoner by the Scots, but at least they hadn't been murdered.

That was good.

She hoped.

She could imagine some evil reasons they might want her alive, but surely they couldn't apply to Fort.

They were being taken somewhere. The box was moving. Or at least, she decided, the cart upon which the box rested was moving. She could hear the trundle of wheels and the clop of hooves.

She reached out to the rough wood and traced it around her. Shuddering, she realized it really *was* a coffin, with the traditional coffin shape.

A moan escaped, but she bit her lips to stop it and pushed up at the lid. She didn't have much hope, and as expected, the lid was fastened down.

Were they to be buried alive?

Her heart was already pounding, but now it began the mad race of panic. She wanted to beat on the box, to scream, but stopped herself—just—by biting on her knuckles. Screaming would do no good.

Surely their captors wouldn't just put them in a grave and throw on earth. Why would they do that?

It's an excellent way to dispose of inconvenient bodies, said a voice in her head. A murdered earl would be a national alarm. A disappearing one would just be a minor mystery.

How long, she wondered, before people realized that a marquess's sister had disappeared at the same time? The thought of the ensuing scandal appalled her, though she supposed she'd be past caring.

Her family wouldn't. How horrified and grief-stricken they would be at her disappearance.

Rothgar! He would be destroyed by her death. Again, pointlessly, she pushed at the coffin lid, weeping now with frustration. How could she have been so selfish as to put herself in danger, knowing how it would affect her brother?

Tears turned to rage.

Damn the Scots. She'd have their guts for garters for creating such a mess.

And damn Fort, for being embroiled in such madness. It was all his fault—

But abruptly, she couldn't feel that way. Though still muttering about his stupidity, she cuddled closer to him, checking again that his pulse beat steadily.

It was steadier than hers, for her heart still raced with panic. Or perhaps the air was beginning to fail. What did it feel like to suffocate?

She shook Fort, trying to wake him just to have someone conscious nearby. He moaned slightly, but no more than that.

Elf slumped against him, curling an arm around his torso, both protecting and seeking protection. After a moment, she snuggled closer and listened for his heart. Of course it had to be beating, but she needed to hear it.

She wiped away tears and kissed his chest.

Her lover. How strange to think of him that way, but he was.

Her beloved.

An even stranger thought, but he was that, too.

She recalled that moment of certainty, testing it. Yes, whatever love was, she felt it for this man. She cared for him more than for any other man, even her brothers. She needed his presence. Life without him would be arid. She longed for his body. Not particularly for the sexual games they had played, though they had been delightful, but just as contact, as presence, as if she was no longer whole when alone.

Nor was it a new thing. She'd been drawn to him from first meeting.

Such notions might terrify her at another time, but with death approaching, she could only be honest with herself.

She wondered if he felt anything similar. It seemed ridiculous that she feel so passionately and he be indifferent, but it could be so.

It could break her heart, that thought, but with death approaching such concerns were pointless.

With questing fingers, she found his features and traced them. She kissed his eyelids, his cheek, his lips.

"Mmmmm." Then the contented murmur cracked into a groan and he stiffened.

"Hush!" she whispered quickly. "Don't make a noise."

"What—"

Elf put a hand over his lips. His wits were disordered by that blow, but she didn't want him shouting out. If for some reason their captors opened the coffin to check on them, it would be useful if they thought him still unconscious.

He didn't relax, but something in his body suggested that he was aware of the situation. She gingerly moved her hand.

"What's happening?" he whispered, putting out a hand to explore. "Where the devil are we? Gads. My head . . ."

"It's a coffin," she whispered back. She couldn't put her fears into words, but an extra tension in his body suggested he shared them.

"Who?" he whispered. "Why?"

"The only voice I heard sounded Scots." She waited for his reaction.

He just became very still.

That answered any doubts she might have clung to about his involvement.

Where, Elf suddenly thought, were Roberts and her people? Then she realized that it was the middle of the night. They'd probably all gone home.

Elf began to suspect that she'd made a terrible mess of everything and could pay for it with her life. Clearly Fort deserved some of the blame, but she snuggled closer anyway.

That was when she realized he was naked, and she was as good as. They'd taken her in just her shift and stockings!

At the thought of that man carrying her like that, she wanted to cry. It was a stupid reaction, but she couldn't help it. For a moment, it seemed the most appalling aspect to the whole affair.

Then she became aware of her bare leg pressing against his. She could feel the rough, springy hair of his calf. Without any other place to put it, she still tried to ease away. It made no sense when they'd been so intimate, but for some reason their situation now seemed indecent.

Once or twice she'd dreamed of being naked in a public place. This felt horribly like one of those dreams. She should be worrying about death, but just now she fretted more about the lid opening to let in light and expose her state.

With a stifled groan, he shifted, gathering her thigh between his to make a little more room and wrapping his arm tighter around her.

Elf stiffened.

"What's the matter?"

"Nothing."

His hand wandered slightly. "Lightning blast 'em! Did they take you in just your shift?"

Suddenly tears threatened, but she swallowed them. "I still have my stockings."

He held her closer, muttering more curses, and now his touch didn't seem so wrong. "I think I'm wrapped in that damned monk's robe. As soon as we've room to move, you can have it. So, you think your Vauxhall pursuer is behind this?"

"Who else?"

"You might have vengeful relatives." He shifted again, easing her a little on top of him. "I sincerely hope this is not a case of Abélard and Héloïse."

"Who?" She eased her head into his shoulder, which seemed beautifully designed for the purpose.

"A pair of medieval lovers."

"A romantic tale?"

"Not really. Her relatives gelded him."

"Lud!"

"Indeed. And it's a true story."

"Well, I can assure you my relatives are not behind this." Though she had to wonder if they might be tempted to a similar vengeance when they found out. She'd intended to be back at Amanda's for breakfast. Now, even if she survived, the whole story could get out.

She thought of Chastity, who'd been caught with a man in her bed and ostracized. Lewd pictures of her had hung in every printshop window, and even after vindication, some people looked askance at the "notorious Chastity Ware."

And Chastity had been innocent!

The cart stopped.

Elf clutched Fort, scandal and modesty suddenly irrelevant. As they awaited their fate, Fort held her close in an illusion of protection that she needed anyway. With a jerk and an audible grunt or two, the box was lifted.

A moan escaped Elf. She couldn't help whispering, "A grave. I think they're going to bury us alive!"

" 'Struth."

They clung together as the box swayed and bumped. Then it landed with a thump.

But surely not in a deep hole.

Elf remembered to breathe.

A Scottish voice said, "Brace the rope, Mack."

They let coffins down into graves with ropes, didn't they?

"No!" Elf moaned into Fort's shoulder. He suddenly moved, thrusting up at the lid again and again.

"I think they're awake in there, Kenny."

"No matter. Get on with it."

With Fort still heaving at the lid, the box tilted and slid a noisy distance to land at an angle. The jolt clashed Elf's teeth together and made Fort grunt from the pain in his head.

They must be in the grave, though you'd think the coffin would go in straight.

Then the box shifted and went flat with another bump that made Fort curse and go still.

This was it, then. The end of the adventure.

A sudden calm settled on Elf. They were going to be buried alive. No one knew, so no one could help. Perhaps no one would ever know what had become of them. It seemed both silly and tragic, but beyond all help.

She began to pray that death come quickly, and that her brothers not suffer too much for her folly.

She heard a rattle and thump some way away, then

another rattle on the coffin. The first stones hitting the lid?

Metal against metal, but in the distance. Shovels? She tried to imagine the scene outside the stale darkness that had become her world, but then decided to concentrate on dying well.

"I'm sorry," she said to Fort, since she suspected this was all her fault.

"Why? I'm just sorry I don't seem to be able to break a way out of here."

Elf was wondering if she should tell him the truth when all sounds stopped. Only their own breathing, noisy in the cramped space, broke total silence.

After a moment, she asked, "What do you think?"

"Perhaps they had to leave to get tools . . ."

She waited, hearing each breath, feeling as if each breath found less air.

"They're going to wait for us to suffocate!" At that thought, she thrust her arms up at the lid.

It moved.

Hardly able to believe it, she sat up, pushing. The lid opened. She would have just shoved it out of her way, but Fort surged up and grabbed it, lowering it gently back. "I don't suppose it's an accident," he whispered. "But just in case, let's not tell the world we're free."

Free was a relative term. They had more space and fresher air, but absolutely no light, not even a cloudy sky overhead. Clearly, they were still inside something.

"Where are we?" she whispered.

"A crypt?"

She shivered at that thought, but then said, "Actually, I smell stale beer . . ."

"A cellar?"

They were both sitting up in the coffin now, and they arranged themselves facing each another, her legs over his as they assessed matters.

"I can't see *anything*," she said. "The walls could be close or far away. There could even be other people here, watching and listening."

"I think we'd know."

"At least there's air. And we're alive . . ."

Suddenly she threw herself on top of him, into his arms, and they were laughing and kissing in a mad ecstasy of survival.

"We're alive!" she gasped. "Alive! *Alive!*"

"Very much so." And he seized her hips and impaled her upon his rock-hard erection.

Elf gasped with shock and some pain, for she was still tender there, but he didn't seem to hear, and she didn't really care. She shared his instinct to celebrate life in this primal, savage way and met him thrust for thrust, finding her own explosive release even faster than he did.

They clung together afterward, quivering and sweating. "That," he said unsteadily, "wasn't part of the plan for the night."

"Are you sure?" she teased. "You promised me memorable."

"I promised you hell, too, but this wasn't quite what I had in mind." He held her closer and kissed her cheek. "Are you all right? You must still be sore."

"A little. I'm fine." That tender kiss almost broke her. She almost said, *I love you.*

"Not even slightly tempted to throw a fit of the vapors?"

"What good would it do?"

"You're a woman in a million, Lisette."

"Are you saying women are less able to bear shocks and hardship than men?" She was teasing, but was also serious.

"Don't tell me you're one of these women who think there's no differences between the sexes!"

"Oh, I acknowledge some differences." She felt bold enough to touch his now-soft genitals. "Just not all."

He seized her hand and pulled it up for a kiss. "Don't play with hellfire, sweetheart, or you won't be able to walk in the morning." He rubbed their joined hands against her cheek, then stilled. "What happened to your mask?"

Oh, dear heaven. "They cut it off."

"I'm glad." He traced her face as if he could see with his fingers. She did hope not. "We're both almost as naked as the day we were born. It's honest. I could become quite fond of this place."

Elf pushed away. "Don't be silly. We have to escape." That reminded her that she had to be home before morning to avoid complete disaster.

He helped her disentangle herself, and soon they stood in the coffin holding hands, each the other's only reality.

"You speak excellent English," he remarked.

Oh, Gemini!

Thinking back, Elf realized that from the moment of capture she had instinctively spoken in her native tongue. They'd been whispering most of the time and clearly he hadn't recognized her voice yet.

In such danger, it shouldn't matter, and yet they'd found something precious here, a fellowship brought on by shared peril. She couldn't bear to damage it with their family problems.

"Merci," she said, continuing in accented English. "I 'ave been well taught, I think."

"You've been well taught, yes, but which language, sweetheart? I suspect that *in extremis* people speak their native tongue." His fingers found her cheek, and then he kissed her lightly on the lips. "Keep your secrets for now, Lisette," he said in French. "The first thing is to get out of here."

Elf sent a prayer of thanks, though that "for now" held a warning.

Unfortunately, that meant that after tonight, Lisette would have to disappear. She'd only planned for this adventure to last one night, but now she could hardly bear for it to end.

What would happen if she confessed the truth? Could he understand? Could he put aside his malice and hate?

This man, the man she'd come to know tonight, had no connection with such evil emotions.

He released her hand and she heard him move. "The floor is flagstones."

Pushing aside wistful dreams, Elf scrambled out of her end of the coffin, extending every sense in a search for information. "I hate this darkness. Even a scrap of night sky through a window would be something."

"Or noise. If this is an inn, it's a strangely silent one."

"It is the middle of thc night."

"Even so."

Elf stood and one of her stockings fell down, reminding her that she was in a disgraceful state of undress. She groped in the box for the garter, and his body bumped into hers.

"Sorry."

She reached for balance and touched something soft.

Soft? Round?

She snatched her hand back. It was his intimate parts! For some reason, touching them accidentally seemed scandalous, when touching them deliberately had not.

He chuckled, and a moment later his groping hand found hers and guided it back toward him.

To cloth.

He put something into her arms and she recognized the monk's robe.

"Don't you need it? I have my shift."

"In the dark, I don't need a stitch. Put it on."

The thought of him wandering around stark naked did strange things to Elf's equilibrium. She fought it by pulling the habit over her head.

It settled around her, warm and concealing. She moved back to try to find her garter and promptly tripped over the hem.

"It's far too long."

He found her in the dark and fumbled for the hem. "Pox, so it is. And there's no knife here that I know of. If we had the cord we might be able to tie it up."

She slipped out of it and passed it back. "I'll make do."

He moved away but she heard no sounds of cloth against skin. "Are you not wearing it?"

"Why bother?" She could hear the laughter in his voice.

"So I don't contact your private parts again by accident?"

"I wouldn't mind."

"Well, I would!"

"My apologies, Miss Delicacy and Decorum." Now she heard sounds. "There. I'm decently covered."

"Thank you." Elf heard her ridiculously tight-lipped tone, but couldn't help it. She really couldn't cope with the image of him sauntering around naked.

"And you?" he asked.

"What?"

"Are you decently covered?"

Reminded, she hastily found the scrap of ribbon and lace and firmly rearranged her stocking. Then she tied the neck of her shift so it no longer sagged half down her chest. Again she winced at how she must have appeared to their captors.

"Insofar as possible," she mumbled.

If only she'd been less wicked and worn a cotton shift and stockings for this adventure. But no. She had to wear the finest silk and ridiculous lacy stockings. Exploring herself, she discovered the shift had been torn at some point in her capture, and a triangular flap now exposed part of her side.

Oh for a pin!

She put such concerns aside and set to work, exploring their pitch-dark prison inch by inch.

"I wonder why they bothered with this robe at all?" he said, clearly farther away in the room.

"Perhaps they needed it to carry you. Someone carried me over his shoulder, but you'd be too heavy."

"Probably. One puzzle solved. The rest, of course, is

still dense mystery. What do they want? Damme. I've no memory of the event. What happened?"

"I have no recollection, either. I woke up as they seized me. There were some noises. Perhaps a fight."

"I hope it was me." After a moment, he said, "I doubt it, though. Apart from my head, I've no bruises that I can tell, and my hands haven't hit anything recently."

He sounded aggrieved. Elf rolled her eyes at the way the male mind worked. "I hardly think that matters," she pointed out, "but I'm sorry about your head. Does it hurt a lot?"

"Yes." Was he terse because of pain or because he hadn't earned more honorable wounds?

She suppressed a sigh. "We need to escape before they do whatever they have planned for us," she reminded him. "Could you please apply your mind to that?"

"Lisette, you obviously have no idea how disconcerting it is for a man to go to sleep in his own bed and awake a prisoner with no blow struck!" When she said nothing, he added, "Oh, very well. Let's explore."

Elf continued to grope forward, having to suppress a giggle at his peevishness. "I suppose you wanted to be a knight in shining armor. Or perhaps a dragon slayer?"

"You're too fanciful. I just wish I'd broken some bones."

"Ugh. How horrid."

She heard a *clunk* as he moved something on the other side of the room.

"Ugh, how realistic. What do you think happens when that romantic knight in shining armor slams his lance into his opponent's body?"

Absorbed in this distracting conversation, Elf bumped into a barrier. Feeling side to side, she said, "There's a cask here. Big. From the size and smell, it's probably beer."

"And I've found some smaller ones. Probably wine but"—she heard tapping—"empty, I think. So, Lisette, if we win free and face our enemy, do you want me to be a gentle, perfect knight? Or do you want me to break some bones?"

"I'll doubtless join you in breaking bones." She tapped the cask in front of her. "This is empty, too. Staved in, in fact. Do you think—"

"Ah."

"What?" She turned toward his voice, though it served no purpose since she couldn't see.

"I've found the door. It is, of course, locked in some way." She heard some soft thumps. "Solid, plague take it. It's hard to imagine breaking it open with our bare hands."

Elf liked that "our." For this moment they were not Ware and Malloren, lord and lady. They were just two people with a common cause. Almost like Adam and Eve, she thought, naked in the Garden of Eden.

"Are you still wearing your robe?" she asked.

"Yes. I may not be concerned by modesty, but it's damned chilly. Are you sure you don't want it?"

He was right. Despite the season, the cellar was chill and dank. Her stockinged feet and bare arms already shivered with cold, and the rest of her was not far behind. "No, thank you," she said, absurdly touched by his gallantry.

And perhaps, she thought, leaning back against the barrel to rub her arms, she had things to smile about. They were alive when but a few minutes before, they'd expected death. For the moment, they had shed their pasts—their rank, their families, their feud—along with their normal clothes.

In a strange way, she felt closer to Fortitude Harleigh Ware here, prisoners in the dark, than even when making love.

"Anything else?" he asked, prompting her to continue her exploration.

Her foot touched a wooden bucket, empty. He reported some rags and rope. "Not enough to be of any use," he said, "even if I could think of a use for it. This is a damnably efficient prison."

Then Elf came to the ramp. "Of course," she said. "They always roll beer casks down a ramp. That's how they slid in our box."

He came to join her, reaching out so his hand brushed hers before taking it. She couldn't resist going into his arms.

He rubbed her shoulders. "You're cold."

"It can't be helped."

"It's another reason to get out of here. How long before your complaisant relative becomes alarmed?"

So he was thinking of scandal, too. "Morning, I suppose."

"And then what will happen?"

"I have no idea." Wanting to be as honest as she could, she added, "She might hesitate to complain to the authorities, but not for long."

He kissed her gently on her brow. "Then we'd best try to escape before morning. I'm going to climb the ramp."

She heard scrabbling sounds and then a rattle. "Fastened on the outside, of course, and almost as sturdy as the door. We could try to pry it open, but we'd still need a tool of some kind to have any chance."

He arrived back beside her, and they found one another again in the dark.

"Scared?" he asked.

Surprisingly, she had to think about it. "Yes, though not as much as I would be if I were alone. Are you? Scared."

"Yes." His hand rubbed comfortingly on her back, and she did the same to him. "Should I not admit it? Here in the dark, it seems ridiculous to posture. I don't want to die just yet, and certainly not with such lack of dignity at the hands of ruffians."

This approached interesting matters. "Do you think it's your Scottish friends who have captured us?"

His hand paused for a moment. "Perhaps."

"But why? And if they wanted to kill me, why sneak into an earl's house at night to steal us both away?" She prayed for an honest answer.

"I have no idea, which is worrying enough—"

"Especially since they are your colleagues," she snapped.

"Sheathe your claws, little cat. I honestly have no idea what is behind this. For the moment, we are on the same side, and our pressing need is to escape. I'm afraid that means crawling about the floor in search of some overlooked tool."

He would have moved away, but she held on to the rough wool of his habit. "I want to know everything that is going on."

"It wouldn't help."

"How can you know that?"

"You're just being curious, in typical female fashion."

"Curious! My life is in danger—"

"And you are delaying things by a pointless argument." He freed himself and moved away.

"Female fashion, indeed." Elf settled to her knees and started to work her way around the room. Her shift ripped further, so, muttering a curse, she knotted it near her waist. If a light appeared now and exposed her like this, she'd die of shame. "If you didn't know what was going on," she protested, "you'd be full of questions, too."

"I *don't* know what's going on. For example, I don't even know who you are, though there's something damnably familiar about your voice when you speak English. Why not start with your true name?"

Elf almost told him, longing to prick his bubble. She managed to resist.

"Who I am is not important." She reached tentatively beneath the huge cask—heaven only knows what might be there. As it turned out her fingers found only chips of broken flagstone.

"Then what's going on is equally unimportant," he said. "I've found a short stick—a broken broom handle, I think—but I can't see what good it will do us."

They took refuge in grumpy silence broken only by the scrabble of their search.

Chapter 11

Gradually Elf realized how absurd their behavior was and offered an olive branch. "It would be annoying," she said, having found nothing remotely like a tool, "to discover that axes and scythes are hanging from the ceiling."

She stood up, rearranged her shift, and headed back toward the box. And stubbed her toe against a rock, falling forward to bang her knees on it.

At her cry, he said, "What? What's the matter?"

"I just stubbed my toe." She sat to rub at various painful spots, then explored the obstacle. She'd thought it a raised flagstone, but it was many inches thick with metal handles attached. It was clearly no use to them, though.

"I hate this darkness," she said as she scrambled to her feet. "Do you keep rubbing your eyes, hoping to clear your vision?"

"Yes. Do you have moments of fear that you really are blind?"

"I would if I were alone. Have you found anything?"

"No. Come and sit on our coffin."

She felt her way forward carefully, already beginning to grow more skillful with her other senses. A dull thump told her he'd replaced the lid and when she got there and sat on it, his robe came around her shoulders.

Which meant that when he put his arm around her and pulled her close, she settled against his naked body. She didn't complain. The warm cloth was comforting, and he'd wrapped it lengthwise around both of them.

"What now?" she asked.

"We have to decide whether to attack that door at the top of the ramp. I think it opens outward and the lock might be weak. It's possible I can batter it down, though I'm not sure. I can't run at it. Since there's about three feet of headroom up there, I can hardly even swing at it."

"Anyway, you'd hurt yourself."

"For you, fair lady, anything."

She laughed, snuggling closer. "It really does offend you, doesn't it, not to be able to make a grand gesture?"

"Assuredly. It offends me even more, though, to just sit here waiting for something to happen."

During the search, Elf had been thinking about her people. Perhaps they were searching for her now. Perhaps they'd seen the capture but been unable to act immediately. But in that case, surely they would have planned a rescue.

Then she remembered that to them she was just some doxy hired by the Mallorens to seduce the earl.

"Do you think anyone is guarding that door?" she asked.

"It depends on so many factors. If it's important to hold us for a purpose, then yes, they'd post a guard and he'd already know we were up and active. If they just wanted to get rid of us for a while, then they might not. Clearly this place can hold us for many hours."

"Why would they want to do that?" Again she was begging him to be honest with her and tell her something of the plot.

"There could be reasons, but it wouldn't be safe for you to know."

At his tone, she remembered that Lisette had claimed not to have heard anything of importance at Vauxhall. The gallant man was trying to protect her. It made her smile in a way that would look very silly if anyone had been able to see.

"If there's no one guarding us," she suggested, "we could make a noise. Call for help."

"By my estimation, it's about three in the morning and this building, whatever it is, is deserted. Who'd hear?"

"Let's try anyway." Elf leaped down off the box. "I'll use the stick to bang on the door. You rattle the trapdoor."

"Impetuous Lisette." She heard him move. "Do you regret seducing me?"

"Seducing you?" Elf froze. "I most certainly did not!"

"Did you not? When a gentleman has no intention of dalliance, yet finds himself implored into pleasuring a lady, what else would you call it?"

Implored! "You seduced me on that boat, my lord." Elf groped to the door, found the stick, then banged out her anger on the oak.

"Alas. I'm 'my lord' again." He rattled the door at the top of the ramp. "*Help! Ho!* If I seduced you, Lisette, I was singularly inept."

"Were you?" She belabored the wood. "You caused me to rethink my decision."

"Ah. You restore my faith in myself. *Ho, there! Help! In the cellar! One hundred guineas reward to anyone who releases us!*"

"A hundred? How niggardly. *Help!*" Elf screamed. "*One thousand guineas to my rescuer! Help!*"

"Picayune. *Ten thousand guineas to free me from this rash, extravagant wench!*"

"I fear you are a man of limited resources. *Help! To me! A hundred thousand guineas to save me from this dastardly rapscallion!*"

"Why do I think you expect me to pay your debts? *A rescue! A rescue! My earldom for a rescue!*"

Silence fell, then Elf recalled the laughter in his last cries, and realized that the sounds of it continued. He was whooping. Oh, but she wished she could see him helpless with laughter.

It still shook his voice as he said, "A hundred thousand, indeed. You wicked, intemperate creature. Ah well, if no one's heard us by now, there is no one to hear."

Elf dropped the stick and leaned against the door. "But then . . . Will they just leave us here? Surely we can't starve to death within London."

"I'm sure it's possible, but I won't let it come to that."

"Will you not? You admit to being a poor sort of hero."

"And you are showing signs of being a sharp-tongued shrew! Desist. There are faint chinks in this door, and surely in daylight someone will have to be around. We'll think of something."

"I'm sorry." Elf fumbled back toward the box. "I'm not used to being so helpless."

"And you think I am? You clearly have no notion what it means to be an earl."

More than ever, Elf wanted to tell the truth, but the risk of weakening this camaraderie was just too great. "Daylight *will* be better, even if it's just the smallest chink. It's the dark that frets at me."

He sat beside her and gathered her into his arms, then pulled her down to lie half over him, on top of the box, the robe over them both. "Close your eyes and think of going to sleep."

"You think I can sleep here?"

"No. But with your eyes closed, the dark won't be so disturbing."

It *was* better, and she even felt warm and comfortable in his arms. She feared he couldn't be too comfortable on top of the rough wood, though.

"You're very kind, Fort."

"Am I? That would surprise many."

"Why do you say that?"

His hand soothed her back, but she thought he wouldn't reply. "I haven't been kind recently."

Cocooned together, they'd created a time for confidences. Elf wondered if she should permit it, for he would never talk this way to Elf Malloren. But she wanted to know him, to understand him, and she suspected that he needed to talk.

"Why haven't you been kind?" she asked. "It seems in your nature."

"Does it? I'm not sure I remember what my nature is. Yes, perhaps I used to be kind, if it didn't cause me too much trouble."

"I think you're too harsh on yourself. You've been good to me."

"Men are often good to women they want to have sex with."

"Aha!" Elf sat up straddling him, even though she couldn't see a thing. "You admit you wanted it!"

He chuckled."Yes. I wanted it. To be precise, I wanted *you.* God knows why."

"You can be very rude."

"I thought you said I was so good to you."

"You have the remarkable ability to be both good and rude at the same time."

"Are you talking about my nature or my sexual prowess?" But then he reached out, found her, and pulled her down on top of him, twitching the robe back over them. "I'm cold."

"You're . . . you're wanting again." She could hardly mistake the evidence.

"Rampant with lust would be a good term, yes. Don't worry, though, I'm not desperate."

Elf adjusted her position so as not to press on him. "Why do you want me, then?" she asked, letting her hand wander over his chest.

"Ah, the universal question. Perhaps, Lisette, I just hadn't had a woman in a while."

"Hadn't?" she teased. "That can't explain the last time."

He slapped her bottom. "Minx. That was a mad expression of relief at being alive."

"Very well. Why do you want me now?"

"Danger makes some men great."

"Great?" she said with a chuckle. "What interesting

words you use. Why hadn't you made love in a while? I'm sure you don't lack opportunity."

"Perhaps I grew tired of the incessant chatter of women."

He was doing his best to push her away with words, but Elf burned with the need to understand this man. "I'm sure you can pay a whore to be silent."

He pulled her close, hands hard on her buttocks. "I'm sure you're too clever for the silly innocent you play. And yet you were an innocent. Care to elucidate the conundrum, Lisette?"

Pressed tight to him, she could feel him growing bigger and harder between her thighs. He'd brought new weapons to bear in the attempt to shut her up.

A Malloren is not so easily silenced.

"My family is not mealymouthed," she said. "Why hadn't you had a woman?"

He shifted and pulled her head down for a silencing kiss. Elf kissed him back, turning it from weapon into pleasure until his hand gentled and she felt the tension drain out of him. When their lips parted, however, she whispered, "Why hadn't you had a woman?"

She had to choke back a scream at the way his hands tightened on her shoulders, but then they eased. "Because," he said softly, "I was hurting them."

"Hurting?" She wished she could see his expression.

"As I just hurt you." He rubbed at the places he'd bruised.

"You hadn't hurt me, until now."

"With you, it seems to be different. That's why. Why I agreed to make love to you."

Elf settled down, head snuggled between his neck and shoulder. "I'm glad."

"What?"

"That I'm different."

"At least you're not the type who likes bites and bruises."

"Do any women?"

"Ah! At last a touch of innocence. Yes, some women like pain with sex. Some men like it, too."

She shifted to kiss his jaw. "But not you."

He moved so he could kiss her lips. "No, not me. So if you have a taste for the rougher kinds of love, you'd better find another provider."

She turned her head away. "You may not like to bruise, but you don't hesitate to lash out with words!"

He lay still for a moment, then his hand touched her hair. "I'm sorry, but I told you I was not kind."

"I don't think it's your nature. Why are you so . . . so bitter?"

She'd asked the basic question, and as silence ran, she thought he wouldn't answer.

"I had a shock," he said at last. "It made me angry."

It told her little, but was a tremendous admission on his part. She caressed his chest. "I'm sorry for your pain."

"Pain? Yes, I suppose that describes it."

"A death?" she asked, risking a probing question.

She wanted him to tell her the root of his bitterness. Perhaps he had never spoken of it to anyone. She knew her brothers, particularly Bryght and Rothgar, found it hard to talk of their strongest emotions.

"Clever Lisette. Yes, a death."

He fell silent again and she waited, not sure how far she could push him.

"My father."

Elf tried not to react. It had taken so long for those two words to come out that she knew it had been hard for him.

"It can be very painful to lose a parent," she said. "My father died when I was young."

"How young?"

How much did he know of the Mallorens? Just in case, she added a couple of years. "I was nine."

"Almost too young to remember."

"Yes. I wish we had more of him. More pictures. More letters. He dictated letters to us all as he lay dying, but they're rather severe. Advice. Admonitions. I'm told he was a fun-loving man."

"I suppose death is a sobering experience. So, you have brothers and sisters?"

"Yes. And you, my lord?"

"You must call me Fort, you know, or I'll never tell you my secrets."

The teasing note made her smile. It also told her that she'd broken through, that he would talk to her. Her qualms returned, but she pushed them away. It would do him good to talk. "Fort, then."

"I have two sisters and one brother."

"And your mother? Is she still alive?"

"She died when I was quite young."

"But at least you have your brother and sisters."

"We are not very close."

Elf wanted to protest. Chastity loved Fort, as did the other sister, Verity. They would support him and assist him in anything, but he hardly seemed to realize it. Just because he thought he had failed them, he thought they could not love him.

"That's sad," she said.

"So, you are close to your family?"

"Yes, very close."

"You're fortunate."

"I think so, though it means they all feel entitled to interfere in my life."

"Really? I had the impression that you were inadequately supervised."

Elf knew she was drifting too close to the whirlpool of truth, but she couldn't resist being as honest as she could. "It's just that I am away from them at the moment."

"Ah, yes. And staying with your agreeable friend."

"You're not to sneer at her. She is not in favor of my actions."

"Then she should stop them."

"Perhaps I am unstoppable."

"Certainly I have found you so. To my delight." He

held her a little closer. "It would please me immensely, Lisette, if you would become my mistress. I like you, and I certainly seem to have no complications about my honest lust for your body."

"I wish I could," Elf said. "But once my family found out they would object."

"You misled me then." He sounded a little annoyed, as well he might. "Have you thought what they will do if you're with child? It's not inevitable, but it's possible."

Elf had thought. Indeed she had. "They would be upset, but they'd help me. I'd bear the child discreetly, and it would be raised by suitable foster parents. It is not an unusual situation."

"What a cool head you have. I hope your family is as understanding as you say."

So did Elf, and cool didn't exactly describe her feelings. The thought of being pregnant alarmed her. The notion of giving a baby, Fort's baby, up to strangers horrified her. Why hadn't she realized before how impossible that would be?

His voice distracted her. "Promise me something."

"What?"

"If you bear a child, let me know. I have two bastards that I know of, and I keep an eye on them. I don't think such children benefit from knowing too soon that they are born of a noble family, but I will make sure they have a good start in life."

She framed his face and found his lips with a kiss, able to feel in their relaxation his gentle mood, almost able to see his features softened by trust and good humor. "I told you you were a kind man."

"Is it kindness? They might be of use to me one day." But she felt his lips move in a smile.

"Why do you try so hard to appear heartless?"

"You are a romantic. I am merely trying to be honest."

"You have a false mirror. Tell me, then, how you see the Earl of Walgrave."

He shifted her suddenly, rubbing his erection along her cleft. "Rampant with lust."

Desire stirred in Elf, too, but she asked, "Why do you keep trying to distract me?"

"Because you keep probing at my wounds."

"What wounds?"

He groaned and silenced her with a kiss. She enjoyed it immensely, and never for a moment forgot the hot invader between her thighs, but when he stopped, she asked, "What wounds?"

"Shut up." He rolled her under him, spread her thighs, and thrust into her. She stiffened with shock and pain.

He froze, then pulled out of her, shuddering. "You see what I'm like. Even with you."

She gripped his hair before he could disappear into the dark. "You see what I'm like? Like a terrier, whether I'm after truth or a man."

Ruthlessly, she pulled him down and straddled him. "I want you." Fumbling in the dark, she found his erection, and despite a muttered protest that didn't sound sincere, eased herself carefully around him, loving taking the rigid fullness deep inside, even where she was so sensitive. "Am I doing this right?" she whispered.

A wild laugh ran through him like a wave. "Perfectly. Are you comfortable?"

Elf shifted a bit more, full of him, hips stretched wide over him. "What an extraordinary question. I'm not in pain."

She moved to try to improve her balance and felt the response in him, tense between her thighs. She remembered their lovemaking when he'd made her talk.

"What wounds?" she asked, gently rocking her hips.

"What?" She didn't need vision to tell his mind was not on practicalities at all.

She bit her lip on a giggle. "What wounds? Tell me some wounds and I'll move some more."

"That's whoring of the lowest kind."

"You won't deflect me that way. What wounds?"

"Don't. Don't . . ."

"Tell me. Wounds need to be opened to heal." In

time to her rocking motion, she chanted, "Tell me, tell me, tell me—"

He seized her, rolled her, pinned her brutally beneath him. "I killed my father," he said, before using her body for oblivion.

Shaken by his words, ravaged by his wild rhythm, Elf could only move with him helplessly until he collapsed over her, quivering still. She raised a trembling hand to stroke his back, which ran with chilling sweat.

What to say, what to say? He'd killed his father. *He,* not one of her brothers, had fired that shot.

Then she realized he was crying. Helplessly, wracked with it, he wept in her comforting arms, but all the while, she silently cried her own tears. *Oh, don't do this. How will you feel when you know who I am? How will you bear it? Don't do this . . .*

And yet she had caused it. She had broken down every barrier, never thinking how she would handle what lay caged within.

She thought back again to that terrible night at Rothgar Abbey. Her brothers had all been armed. She was sure one of them could have killed the old earl. Instead, they'd forced him—Rothgar had forced him—into that most heinous crime, patricide.

For the first time she was ashamed of something her family had done.

He lay silent now, surely at a loss. So was she. What could anyone say in this situation? What would Lisette say? Elf assumed a firm and saucy tone. "I'm sure your father deserved to die, then."

He laughed, very shakily. "Oh, indeed. But so do many. It is not condoned." He still sprawled between her thighs.

"Clearly no one knows of your crime or you would have been punished."

"Some know. It will not come out. You are not shocked?"

"No." She knew the dangers now, but she had to push

a little more to try to fix what she had broken. "Why does it pain you so much?"

"Why?" He seemed limp from sex and grief and was half-smothering her with his big body, but she could bear it. "God knows. Perhaps because he's the only man I've killed. That has to leave a mark."

She let the silence run, hoping for more.

"Probably because I hated him." He spoke so quietly she could hardly hear. "I hated, loathed, and feared him, and had all my life. I could tell myself I killed him because he was about to kill others. That's what my sisters said. But I killed him because I hated him, because I'd wanted to kill him since I was a young child, and I finally had the chance."

He raised up on his forearms and the words poured out of him. "As a child, I wanted to kill him out of powerless terror. It wasn't just the beatings, it was his impossible standards. Nothing I did was good enough. Every fault was picked out and waved in front of me, and in front of servants. When he whipped me, he would summon the servants to watch. He said it would break my pride. He, the proudest man in creation.

"But when I was a man, I was free of him. He didn't seek me out, and I avoided him as if he carried the plague. It was blatant cowardice. I did nothing to help my sisters. Nothing to stop his cruelty to servants and tenants. I was too terrified to interfere with him. And so, in the end, I killed him."

Shaken herself by these revelations, Elf stroked his damp arms. "He sounds like a monster."

"He was. But I should have killed him face to face."

"No, no. You could never do that. Yes, perhaps you should have tried to help those in his power. But perhaps you didn't know the depth of his cruelty."

"Because I chose not to know." His voice had settled to a more normal tone, and he shifted to slide his hand between her thighs.

She seized his wrist. "No."

"No? I don't think you found much pleasure in that recent bout."

"I think I've had my hundred guineas, worth."

"Don't forget. *I'm* paying *you*." When she continued to resist, he gave up and pushed into a sitting position. "Perhaps you intend to supplement it with blackmail now."

She moved to sit beside him. "Even if what you say is true, I have no proof."

"Thus I am saved from folly." Though physically they sat side by side, she felt as if he were moving away. "Are you proud of yourself, Lisette?"

Elf pulled the robe around her, shivering, and not entirely with cold. "No. After this, you'll never want to see me again, will you?"

"I never thought we were contemplating a durable relationship."

"You asked me to be your mistress."

"Ah. Yes, you're right. I regret that I must withdraw the offer."

She swallowed. "Don't hate me."

"I won't. I don't. I will just endeavor to forget you."

Elf pressed her lips together to stop tears. "What if we ever meet again?"

"Lisette," he said sharply, "you understand what has happened. Leave it be. This has been a strange night, and if we survive, doubtless neither of us will forget it entirely. But I'm sure we will both try."

She realized she had taken the robe, leaving him naked. She struggled out of it and held it out until it touched his body. "Take it. You must be cold."

Then he was gone, and his voice came from farther away. "Keep it. Try to get some sleep."

Swallowing tears he must not hear, Elf curled up in the robe, in the smell of him and sex, and tried to start forgetting.

It had been a long night with little sleep, and Elf must have dozed, for she awoke to loud noises. Struggling to untangle the robe enough to sit, she heard muttered voices along with bangs.

"Forced something in the keyhole, they have," someone grunted.

A touch made her start. Fort said, "Hush."

"Who is it?"

"I don't know. But not our captors. With luck, they're my people looking for me." He sounded relaxed and normal, but in an artificial way.

Or my people, looking for me, she thought. Then she remembered he was naked. She slid off the box and put the robe in his hands.

"I suppose I should wear something," he said, taking it. "I wish we had the means to share it, though. Your shift will be scanty covering."

Elf realized a trace of light gleamed around the trapdoor. It wasn't day yet, but must be past dawn. "Shouldn't we say something?" she suggested. "After all, if it's our captors, they know we're here. If it's not, they might give up."

"True. I'll go and communicate." She heard scrabbling noises, then his voice. "Hello out there."

The banging stopped. "Sir?"

Elf was easing up the coffin lid. They were about to be rescued and she *had* to try to keep her identity secret. Probably disaster was inevitable, but if she could put her mask on again, it was just possible that Fort need never know the true identity of his nighttime confidante.

That, at least, would spare him constant reminders of his confessions.

"This is the Earl of Walgrave. A handsome sum to the man who rescues me."

The lid was heavy, but she managed to support it one-handed as she groped around.

"Beggin' your pardon, my lord, but is there a lady there with you?"

She found the mask!

"Indeed there is. Are you in search of her?"

Elf eased the lid back down, absorbing the surprise in

Fort's voice. Oh, he was certainly in for some surprises. Especially as the mask strings had been cut. Damn and blast those Scots.

"Aye, well, in a manner of speaking." Elf recognized Roberts's voice. "Is she all right?"

"Yes!" Elf called. "For pity's sake, release us!"

Her main concern, however, was the mask. Plague on it. They'd cut the left string of the mask within an inch of the edge. With trembling hands, she tried to knot the broken string on to the fragment, but it was hopeless.

Hopeless.

Could she hold it against her face? No, that would look foolish indeed.

Bangs from the trapdoor threatened release at any moment, bringing light and terrible exposure!

Tossing the useless item aside, Elf tugged at her powdered curls, pulling them forward over her face.

"What's the problem out there?" Fort shouted.

"We've a man with us can pick locks, milord, but someone's jammed a lump of wood in the keyhole. And as the door opens out, it'll be a hard matter to bash it down."

"There's another door down inside. What sort of place is this?"

"It's a ruined tavern down near the docks, milord. There's been a fire not long ago, it seems. Took out the nearby buildings and charred this one enough to close it. We'll try to find the other door."

Elf heard Fort scrabbling back down the ramp.

"Where are you?" he asked.

"By the box."

In a moment she felt him at her side. He touched her gently on the hand. "I've been a wretch tonight, Lisette. Accept my apologies."

Elf took his hand, swallowing tears at the thought of what might have been—had they been other people or had she not broken down his walls. "I demanded answers to questions you didn't want asked."

He pulled her into an almost brotherly embrace. "Perhaps I was just ready to disgrace myself."

"I see no disgrace. And I just wanted to heal you. Forgive me."

"Of course I forgive you." He rocked her slightly, reminding her of their first embrace of the night, that delicious tender swaying in his arms which had led to other things that could never happen again.

No more, no more sounded like a dirge in her head.

"You're a kind woman, Lisette." Faint voices grew louder beyond the door. Any moment now and this would all be over. "Will you give me your real name?"

Elf wanted nothing more, but whispered, "I dare not." She clung to the remote chance of escaping unidentified. Perhaps then Elf Malloren might find a way to be with Fort Ware.

He cradled her head, tracing her features. "I wonder what it is you fear . . . ?"

But then, with a grating click, the door opened and torchlight flooded in.

When Elf hid her face against his chest, she simply wanted to spare her eyes. She realized immediately that she'd found an excellent position.

"The key was in the lock, my lord. My . . . my goodness."

Roberts had just managed not to say "my lady." How much did he know? And what on earth did she look like?

"Find something to cover the lady with," Fort said crisply. "Come along. One of your coats, and sharpish."

Elf found herself bundled in a frieze coat which was only slightly musty with sweat. Slipping her arms into the overlong sleeves she kept her head down and wished for a collar to pull up around her face. Then Fort lifted her into his arms and carried her through the door and she could again hide her face against his shoulder.

"I can walk," she said.

"The ground's rough here."

"You have bare feet, too."

"This seems to be my one chance to be the perfect, gentle knight. Don't snatch it away."

Reprieve.

Another few moments of untarnished closeness.

Elf relaxed against him as he climbed rickety stairs and threaded his way through the ruins of the old taproom. The place smelled of stale beer and charred wood, but then fresh air played on her stockinged legs, carrying a hint of the river. Turning her head cautiously, Elf saw gray dawn light through blackened, broken windows. How precious sight was after darkness.

Then he carried her through the doorway into a derelict wasteland edged by scorched buildings.

"Do you have a vehicle?" Fort asked.

"Aye, milord."

"Who the devil are you?"

At his tone, Elf sneaked a look and winced. They'd brought her own one-horse chair that she used to tool herself around town, generally with a footman up behind. A glossy blue with white-and-gold trim, it was no commonplace vehicle. Nor was Bianca, her white carriage pony, a commonplace horse.

She tensed, ready for the truth to come out.

"Name's Roberts, milord," said her servant phlegmatically. "Hired to find the lady."

Oh, bless you, bless you.

Fort didn't pursue his question, except to ask, "And how the devil *did* you find her?"

"Beggin' your pardon, milord, but can we chat somewhere else? If others were to return, we're not that many to oppose them."

Elf took time to count. Just Roberts and two other men, one holding the horse. She could understand why they'd not brought the two women, but there'd been two other men in her squad.

After a tense moment, Fort said, "Very well. But I will require a pair of shoes from one of you. The donor can hide around here until someone brings him a new pair. You, bring the chair here!"

The man led the open vehicle over and Fort lifted Elf into the seat. Then he turned to select from among the shoes being offered.

As she took the reins, Elf began to think she might get away with her deception after all. At the moment, the men stood between her and the only obvious road out of here, and she knew little of this part of London. But as soon as they entered a part of town she knew, she'd whip up Bianca and elude Fort once again.

Poor Lisette would have to disappear, but at least she might be able to continue to meet with him and tease him as Elf Malloren.

He chose the shoes of the man who'd been holding the horse and sent him to a nearby corner to make the exchange. He sent Roberts along to bring the shoes back.

And that was a kindness, she realized.

True, he had demanded the shoes as if by right, but he had not made the man limp into hiding barefoot over broken stone and glass.

Sighing, she admitted to herself that in her eyes Fort was close to perfect. Not that she *thought* him perfect, just that she had fallen under a spell that made him appear so.

A spell called love.

Hopeless love.

Amanda had been right. It was Romeo and Juliet, but it seemed they were at least going to escape with their lives.

Roberts came back with the shoes, and Fort put them on. "Now," he said, "by all means let us guide the lady home, wherever that might be. And while we go, you can tell me what happened, and how you found us."

He turned toward the chair as he spoke, and Roberts turned with the flaming torch. Before she could avoid it, Fort reached up to brush her tangled hair back off her face.

He was smiling quite tenderly.

She tried to turn, but he captured her chin, smile fading.

He blinked as if he couldn't believe his eyes, then turned her face full into the light. *"Elf Malloren?"*

Chapter 12

"I'm sorry." Elf made herself meet his shocked eyes, trying to send a message of love.

He let her go as if she burned him. "No wonder your voice seemed familiar! What a wonderful night you must have had, my lady. Not only do you get me to serve you as if I were a penny whore down on the docks, you have me blubbering my secrets like a maudlin boy!"

He lunged for her. Her two men fell on him, dragging him to the rough ground.

Legs and arms flailed in the flaring light of Roberts's fallen torch.

Curses and grunts flew out of the writhing mass.

Elf winced at the horrible sound of fists on flesh.

"Stop it!" she screamed at all of them, but they paid no heed.

She slashed at the raging heap with her whip but no one even seemed to notice. They were going to kill each other!

Then the barefoot man came running and in moments they had Fort overpowered, though still writhing like a madman. Singeing the air with curses, Roberts used belts and strips cut from the habit with his knife to truss Fort up.

He staggered to his feet, lip swollen and bleeding, and shirt town. "Now what, milady?" He sounded as if he'd like to throttle her himself.

Shaking, Elf sank her head in her hands. She had no idea.

She felt as exhausted and bruised as the men must be, and her mind floated, empty of all rational thought.

She could have him delivered to his house and leave

matters to fall as they would, but she remembered the look in his eyes. God knows what mischief he'd do.

Then there was the matter of treason. In all her probing, she'd forgotten to dig into that.

She took a deep breath and looked up. "What about the Scots?"

"It's a long story, milady, and we'd best not tarry here."

"True enough." Elf badly needed time to think. "Put him up here and guide me to Lady Lessington's."

Though silent, Fort resisted any attempt to put him in the seat, so in the end they laid him across beneath her feet. Elf even had to put her feet on him. "And it serves you right," she snapped, clicking Bianca into motion. "What a foolish demonstration."

He said not a thing.

They lurched out of the derelict area into a mean and narrow street, Roberts walking ahead with the torch, the other men behind, drawn pistols in hand. Since Fort didn't need the shoes anymore, they'd been reclaimed.

Doubtless woken by the fight, a few people peeped from behind tattered curtains or around slightly open doors, but no one interfered with them.

Elf looked down at the bundled body under her feet and fought tears. Yet again she'd created a problem, and must try to solve it.

"I never meant any harm," she said softly to her captive audience. "It was a complete accident, that meeting at Vauxhall. But I did overhear something about your plans. I couldn't let it go by."

He might have been a corpse for all the response she got. She persevered.

"I only played this masquerade tonight because I wanted to find out what you have hidden in your cellars. And I hoped to flush out Murray and his men. I thought they'd try to attack me if they saw me or at least follow me. Perhaps they did, and that's why they seized us. But I don't know why they didn't kill me . . ."

She was chattering again.

I love you, she could have said, but what point in that now?

What point in any words? He was doubtless too angry to listen.

Perhaps later.

If there was a later.

Lud, but she ached with tiredness. Her eyes itched with it, and exhausted chills shook her. She could hardly organize her mind for thought, but she must.

"Roberts," she said wearily. "Tell me what happened tonight."

As the horse clopped along the muddy lane, Roberts told his story.

"Well, milady, we kept close eye as you left the ball and walked to the earl's house. Nothing 'appened, though, and no one seemed to be much interested in you. Though Sally, God bless her, spotted some street urchins following close.

"So, we set about rounding some of 'em up. And it's like trying to catch eels, it is, with those little blighters. But in the end one of 'em told us as they'd been hired by a clergyman at the Peahen over near Cow Cross Street to watch Lord Walgrave. Since nothing else was 'appening, like, I went over there to see what I could find. Now I admit, milady, we didn't keep close watch on the earl's house, since we reckoned—"

He broke off there and gave her an embarrassed look. Elf could only pray the misty light hid her flaming cheeks.

"Well anyway," he continued, "we didn't expect anyone in or out for 'ours, you see. So when I got back, I was fair shocked to find such mayhem."

"Did you arrive as we were being taken away?"

"Oh no, milady. We'd surely 'ave stopped 'em! No, it was long over by the time I got back. You see, Sally and Ella 'ad 'overed near to the 'ouse. Woman's instinct, Ella said it was. When they saw some goings-on down the back of the 'ouse, they knew something were up. So Sally, she stayed to keep an eye on things, and Ella ran to get help. By the time Ella got back with Roger, the place was in uproar."

"Oh no." Perhaps matters were even worse. It was horrible that Fort knew her identity. It would be disaster if the whole world did.

"People thought it was just 'ousebreaking, milady. The earl's servants had woken to find rascals in the 'ouse, and fought with them. Mostly in the cellars."

He put no emphasis on the words, but Elf registered them. If the Scots had been in the cellars, it had been to steal whatever Fort had guarded there. She glanced down at him, seeing no sign of life, except perhaps an extra tension.

"Did they get it?" she asked.

"I reckon so, milady."

Fort twitched and Elf thought he might at last break his silence, but he didn't. What *was* this important item? And if the Scots had it, what were they doing with it?

"The man who'd been guarding it was bad 'urt," Roberts continued. " 'E'd put up a fight, though. There was a corpse, presumably of one of the villains. But in the end it seems they did make off with whatever was in those cellars, and you and the earl, too. The earl's servants were running around like panicked chickens with their 'eads chopped off!"

Elf was absorbed in trying to make sense of the story when Roberts spoke again.

"We found Sally in the garden, milady. Knifed."

Elf turned to him. "Dead?"

"Dead."

All other thoughts vanished. One of those women she'd spoken to in the office that day was dead.

Because of her.

This must be how it feels to be an officer, she thought, and to find that the soldiers you sent into battle are dead. She wished Cyn were here to tell her how to handle such a sickening responsibility.

"I'm sorry," she said, inadequately.

"We moved 'er," Roberts said gruffly. "Didn't seem wise to have 'er found there."

"I suppose not." Elf didn't think she could bear the pain of her suppressed tears. They tore at her chest, and stabbed pain all around her face, but she couldn't cry yet. If she started crying she'd fall apart, and there were things to do. Things to do if Sally's death wasn't to be in vain. "What happened next?"

Roberts cleared his throat. "Well, Roger and Lon ran to try to track the villains, leaving Ella behind to report to me. As soon as I 'eard her tale, I rousted out some more of our people and we spread out through the area looking for any 'int of you. I tell you true, milady, I were fair trembling at the thought of what might 'ave become of you."

And of what my brothers would have to say about it, Elf knew.

"I'm sure you did the right thing, Roberts," she said, because she had a commander's duty to encourage the troops.

They turned onto a wider street and she prayed they were close to Warwick Street. The sky was brightening, and already some people were about. Sooner or later, someone might notice a trussed-up monk hanging off either end of the floor of her carriage. Not to mention the fact that she was bare-legged, and dressed in little more than a man's coat.

"I tried, milady," said Roberts. "We didn't find anything particular, but then I thought of those urchins. I dug another one of 'em out of his 'ole, and a flash of gold shook lose some facts. They'd been curious, you see, about the clergyman who 'ired 'em. A Scots minister, a Reverend Archibald Campbell. Very prim and pious, but they 'ad their suspicions. So, when they didn't 'ave anything better to do, they followed 'im around. Went to Westminster Abbey a lot, 'e did, which perhaps was suitable. Also went to a crone's hovel, and she too old to be his woman. But 'e also went down to a burned-out area near the docks, and that struck 'em as fishy. So they kept an eye on 'im, 'oping to catch 'im whoring or something so they could demand more money to keep quiet about it. Anyway, that's 'ow we come to check the area out, you see."

"But what *is* Murray up to?" Elf asked, mostly to herself. "And who is this Scots minister? Westminster Abbey? Could they be planning to kill the king in the Abbey?"

Roberts swiveled his head, staring. "Kill the king?"

She couldn't bear to get into that now. "Oh, I don't know. Thank heavens. Here's Warwick Street! We must come in round the back."

Still shaking his head, Roberts guided the chair to the lane behind Amanda's house. All was quiet here, but as Elf drew up the rig in a quiet corner of the back lane, she saw the kitchen door open and a tousled, yawning scullion toss some slops outside.

She'd need Amanda's help to smuggle Fort in and stow him somewhere safe. Wishing desperately for a skirt, Elf climbed down. "Don't let him get away," she told Roberts and ran down the garden to the house.

The scullion—a lad of about ten—gawked at her.

Elf said, "I'm Lady Elfled Malloren. I am going to my room." The crisp words seemed to dumbfound him, for he made no move to stop her going through the kitchen and into the house.

She used the servants' stairs to reach the upper floor, then ran along the carpeted corridor to Amanda's room. She eased in, and arrived at the bedside before realizing there were two people there.

Amanda!

Then she realized that the man was Stephen, Amanda's husband, and they must have had a merry homecoming.

Elf backed away, but then stopped. She still needed Amanda's help, but if she woke Amanda looking in such disarray, she'd scream. And if Stephen saw her, there'd be hell to pay.

Silently bemoaning the passing time, she hurried to her own room and threw off her motley garments.

She wanted a wash. No. She wanted a long, hot bath.

She had time only to grab a new shift, a petticoat, and a plain gown. It didn't lie right without a corset, but the simple gown didn't need hoops.

Shoes! Where did Chantal keep her shoes?

She found them in a drawer, and started to put them on until she saw the rags that had once been her beautiful lace stockings.

Plague and damn and hell.

Angrily, she brushed away weak tears, tore off the dirty rags, and rummaged through more drawers until she found some plain cotton ones.

Hosed, shod, and dressed at last, she stuffed her ruined clothes in the bottom of a drawer, then spared a glance in the long mirror.

What a mistake. Her hair was a powdered rat's nest, her face and hands grubby, and she looked . . . She just looked different.

She was, of course, but she didn't want to look it.

Grimacing at yet more wasted time, she used the cold water on her washstand to clean her hands and face. Then she brushed her powdered hair into some sort of order and tied a frilly cap on top to hide it.

The mirror told her that the improvement was slight, but it would have to do. She hurried back to Amanda's room and gingerly opened the door.

They were still asleep.

Elf tiptoed over to Amanda's side of the bed and shook her. "Amanda," she said softly. "Wake up."

Amanda blinked, woke, then almost spoke. But Elf laid her fingers over Amanda's lips, and her friend managed to keep the words inside. She slid out of bed, pulling on a wrap, and hurried with Elf out into the corridor.

"What happened?" Amanda whispered. "You look terrible! I was so—"

"It's a long story," Elf interrupted. "Look, I have Fort—Walgrave—tied up outside and I need somewhere to put him."

"Tied up . . . ?" Amanda sagged back against the wall. "Elf, what have you done now?"

"Made a mess of things. You can scold me later. For now, you must have a cellar or attic—"

"Elf, this isn't a mansion like Malloren House. Every inch is crammed with servants' rooms! There's a spare bedroom, but how could we keep it from Stephen?"

Elf was trying to think of a way, when Amanda added, "And anyway, I told him you were at Sappho's."

"Sappho's?" Elf stared at her. "Why tell him that?"

Amanda grimaced and pulled Elf farther down the corridor. "Stephen turned up at Lady Yardley's looking for me! Of course, I was delighted to see him home so soon. It was only when he wanted to come home early"—she blushed—"that we realized you weren't there. He was going to make a fuss, so I said you'd left with a friend. When he asked who, the only person I could think of who was sure not to be at the masquerade was Sappho!"

It was Elf's turn to sag against the wall. "If I were to tear out my hair and giggle, do you think you could find me a cozy spot in Bedlam, please?"

"Well," said Amanda, "you have no cause to blame me! I did the best I could at the time. It was you who disappeared, presumably with Walgrave. I assumed you were enjoying yourself, and now I find you have him tied up! You're in the suds again, aren't you?"

"Deeper than you can imagine," said Elf with a sigh. She hugged her friend. "You're right. You've done everything possible. And perhaps Sappho is the answer. If not, I'll just take him to Malloren House and let the mess fall out as it will."

Amanda hugged her back. "You look exhausted, and not as if you've been having fun. Is there anything else I can do?"

"No, love. And," added Elf, turning toward the stairs, "some of it was fun. Lots of fun . . ."

Two more servants were up in the kitchen as Elf made her way back through, but Elf in reasonably normal clothing only warranted a sleepy glance and a "Good morning, ma'am."

At the end of the garden, she found Roberts with his pistol pressed to the back of Fort's knee. " 'E decided to be difficult, milady. I told 'im that even if 'e survived a shattered knee, 'e wouldn't like life like that."

Elf wanted to berate the servant, wanted to gather Fort into her arms and heal and soothe him. Being of a practical nature, she just passed Roberts his coat, climbed into the chair, and guided Bianca toward Sappho's house.

They hadn't far to go, and London was still quiet when she found the back lane. She jumped down and said to Fort, "Don't try anything stupid. It's not worth it. We can sort all this out when we have time."

Again, he lay as if deaf. Really, she wished she could sting him like the wasp he'd once called her. At least that would get some reaction!

She knocked at the kitchen door. To her surprise, the poet opened it herself, dressed in a plain gown, her hair tied in a loose knot at her neck.

"Lady Elfled?" Even a woman like Sappho showed astonishment.

"I need your help."

Sappho swung the door wide. "Of course."

The honest and complete response almost made Elf weep. "You don't understand. I have Fort—Lord Walgrave—outside tied up. I don't know what to do with him and Amanda said I was here. I've got to try to make him see sense. About the Scots. And the king. And us. The cellar. I didn't—"

She found herself in Sappho's arms. "Hush, child, hush . . . Cassie! Sweet tea. Put brandy in it." She guided Elf to a chair by the plain table. "Don't fret so. I'll have Walgrave brought in, and then we can sort this out."

"Don't let him loose!" Elf said, rising.

Sappho pushed her down. "Wild, is he? It doesn't surprise me, and it will doubtless do him good to be both wild and restrained for a while."

Suddenly strength drained from Elf's muscles and she sagged in the chair, watching numbly as a maid poured tea and added a large lump of sugar and a dash of brandy. When the cup was placed in her hand, the warmth of it felt good, and she cradled it.

"Drink up, ma'am," said the maid, guiding the cup to her lips. It was strong, hot, and sweet, and then the brandy kicked in, making her gasp. No longer needing help, Elf took another sip and another, feeling her brain clearing and her strength return. By the time Roberts and one of the other men staggered in with Fort, she felt ready to face her challenges once more.

Sappho had the men place Fort in an open part of the floor, then dismissed them. "Unless you need them, Lady Elf."

"No, I don't think so. Roberts, can we keep this quiet for a while?"

He rubbed the side of his nose. "Perhaps, milady. None of us'll talk. But with all the goings-on at the earl's 'ouse, dead bodies and all, London'll be in a uproar about it soon."

"I suppose so. Lud, but I wish my brothers were home! Do your best, Roberts." When the man had left, Elf turned to Sappho. "This must all seem bizarre."

Sappho sat opposite at the table and poured herself tea. "Let us say, intriguing. I can't wait to hear the story. I do hope," she said, "that the earl wasn't responsible for the bodies. 'Twould be a shame to see him dangle from a rope."

"They wouldn't hang an earl."

"They hanged Ferrers not long ago."

And that was true. Lord Ferrers had run mad and murdered his valet. Elf looked at Fort, who was not mad, but was quite capable of murder at this moment.

For a grubby man with bedraggled hair, in a torn monk's robe cut off at the knees, and trussed at elbows, wrists, and ankles, he looked astonishingly beautiful.

Even with the bruises and swollen lip.

She slipped from the chair to kneel beside him, touching the skinned and bloody knuckles.

"Oh, you . . . ! Well, you finally found a chance to hit someone, didn't you?"

"But not you, unfortunately." His eyes, hard and cold as stone, looked up at the ceiling.

Elf bit her lips, then addressed the maid. "Could I have some water, please. To clean his wounds."

"If I am given any say, I would rather you not touch me."

His chill hit Elf like a blow. She'd counted on anger burning out, but this cold hatred could last forever. Words hovered at her lips—explanations, protestations, apologies. They would fall limply off his hatred like flowers thrown against rock.

Sappho appeared on his other side, with a bowl of water and a cloth. "Then you will have to put up with me, my lord. I cannot let a guest remain in such poor condition." She turned his head toward her and gently cleaned away dirt, checking his eye. "No great damage done there." She washed his face and hands, then called for tweezers to remove some small stones from his knuckles.

Elf knelt there watching, wanting to take his other hand or stroke the hair off his brow. He had asked that she not touch him, but he lay limp and unresisting under Sappho's care.

Having cleaned both hands, Sappho moved and began to attend to his feet. Beautiful feet, Elf thought as the dirt was wiped away. Arms, feet. A man's body held unsuspected pleasures . . .

Suddenly, she hugged herself, remembering other pleasures she had shared with this man.

Who now didn't want to be touched by her.

She bit down on her knuckle, tempted again to rail, to plead, to beg. Later. He must be as exhausted as she, and he needed time to heal his spirit as well as his body.

"You have a cut here on your foot, my lord," said Sappho. "I've taken out the piece of a glass, but I'm going to apply brandy to clean it. It will hurt."

She pressed the pad of brandy to the cut, and Fort

hissed, clenching his fists. That was all, though. As Sappho bandaged the cut, he relaxed again into mute endurance, eyes closed.

Elf looked at her hostess, who met the glance and raised her brows. Her expression was enigmatic, but seemed calmly reassuring, as if she didn't see this as a great tragedy. Elf pushed wearily to her feet, hoping the poet was right.

Sappho rose, too, handing the bowl and cloth to the maid. "Now, my lord, we must do something with you. You are in the way where you are. Will you be reasonable and promise not to make trouble?"

He opened his eyes and smiled a little, though coldly. "On the contrary. I intend to make as much trouble as I can."

"Even to killing the king?" snapped Elf.

His eyes flicked to hers at last. "Hardly."

"Then tell me what's going on so I can put a stop to it!"

"But I don't want it stopped. Not anymore."

She was horribly tempted to kick him.

Before Elf could say anything else, Sappho laid a calming hand on her arm. "First we must find a slightly more dignified place for him. No man is going to be reasonable while prostrate at his captors' feet. And you, my lady, should eat something. Lord Walgrave may eat, too, if he wishes. He'd doubtless find it calming. Then we can discuss all these tangled matters further."

"I'm not sure we have time for niceties!" But Elf could see Sappho was right about his position. She grabbed a sturdy wooden chair and thumped it down near his head. "Let's put him up here."

Sappho shook her head. "Judging by the look in his eye, the first thing he would do would be to tip it over and knock himself out. That would hardly further communication. No, I think it should be the sofa. Cassie, get John and Margaret."

In moments, a sturdy older man and a wiry maid appeared. The three servants and Sappho picked up Fort and maneuvered him out of the kitchen, along a corridor, and up to the elegant drawing room in which Elf had encountered him over poetry.

Was it only four nights ago?

One of the sofas, she noticed now, had a back composed of elegant curlicued wood. The gasping porters dumped Fort on it, swung his legs to the front, then tied him firmly in place, passing belts and strips of cloth through gaps in the wood.

For a moment he clearly thought of resisting, but then he sagged back. It was hardly surprising. In addition to his scrapes and bruises, his head must still be throbbing from the blow that had knocked him out hours ago.

At Sappho's order, the servants undid most of his bonds so that only his arms were restrained by a belt just above the elbows. However, his torso was now firmly bound to the sofa back.

"There." Sappho settled into a chair opposite him as if it were a normal social occasion. "I think that's better for all of us. Cassie, we will take breakfast in here, please."

As the servants left, Elf sank into another chair. Her eyes ached, as did her stomach. As did a host of other places, some of which she'd scarcely been aware of before last night. She wanted a bath. She longed to just sink into sleep. Surely he must feel the same.

"Now," Sappho said, "what is this about killing the king? He seems an inoffensive young man."

Elf pulled her wits together. "Lord Walgrave has some connection to a bunch of Jacobite madmen who want to kill the king. Within the week, they said. A week that is nearly up."

Sappho turned to stare at Fort. "My lord! You astonish me."

"She's mad. We should dispatch her straight to Bedlam."

"If I'm mad," Elf demanded, "who stole us from your house, injuring one of your servants and killing one of mine?"

He met her eyes. "Jealous lovers?"

"Then they must have been yours, because before last night, I'd never had one."

He flinched, but kept up the sneer. "That, my dear, was not love. It was an entertainment as crude as bear-baiting."

The fight not to cry became harder by the moment.

"The king," Sappho calmly reminded them.

Yes, the king. The plot. Elf could deal with that and not feel torn into pieces. "You can't deny those Scots at Vauxhall. I saw you, heard you."

"You are delusional. Unless, of course, *you* are plotting treason and merely seek to put the blame on me. That would be a typical Malloren trick."

Before Elf could explode over this, Cassie came in with a large tray. Sappho helped her lay out brioches, butter, jam, coffee, and chocolate on a small table. When the maid had done, Sappho turned to Fort. "May I feed you something, my lord? It might sweeten your temper."

"I like my temper bitter."

"As you will." Sappho turned away. "Coffee or chocolate, Lady Elf?"

Hopelessly, Elf let Sappho provide her with chocolate and a brioche. Clearly Fort was in no mood to be rational, even about a threat to the king. Instead, he would pick fights and create as much damage as possible, even as the clock of disaster ticked the moments away.

It was all her fault, and she couldn't think how to put it right.

She nibbled on food which could as well have been sawdust, desperately seeking inspiration.

Joseph Grainger had not been in Malloren House for an hour yet, but problems and puzzles covered his desk. Then the door opened and another walked in.

Grainger shot to his feet. "My lord!"

The Marquess of Rothgar raised a brow. "I am aware that I am unexpected, Mr. Grainger. Is my appearance cause for alarm, however?" He looked down at his plain, dark riding clothes and boots as if seeking a peculiarity.

Heat flared in Grainger's cheeks. "No, my lord. I beg your pardon. It is just that there are so many things—"

"There always are." Rothgar settled elegantly into a plain chair and waved Grainger back into his seat. "Now, tell me what is amiss."

Grainger studied his unruffled employer, knowing his calm meant nothing and wondering what to tell him. It was dangerous indeed to try to keep things from Lord Rothgar, but why spill things that might never come to light?

He started with a minor matter. "I have just received word from Rothgar Abbey, my lord, that a mechanical device was taken from there nigh on a week ago. Launceston seems to think it was by your orders, and yet I do not recall any such matter being raised."

"Mechanical device?"

"The Chinese pagoda, my lord. The automaton."

Rothgar frowned slightly. "Taken? Stolen?"

"Not precisely, my lord. It was collected by some men claiming to be from Jonas Grimes, the clock maker. They carried a note from you explaining that the device was to be cleaned and checked before being given to His Majesty. I was about to send a message to Grimes inquiring about the matter, but I fear he knows nothing of it. I'm in a puzzle, however, as to why anyone would go to such trouble to acquire a toy."

"Puzzling indeed. And is that the only matter on your mind?"

Grainger cleared his throat. "No, my lord. This is even more peculiar. I have here a message from one of your private informants in government quarters. It seems that in some way the Stone of Scone has disappeared from Westminster Abbey."

"The Stone of Scone," Rothgar repeated. "If I remember correctly, it is a large and rather ugly hunk of sandstone. No wonder you seem distracted, Mr. Grainger. Perhaps it was a full moon last night."

"No, my lord. The moon is on the wane."

"Ah. Thank you. I can always depend on you for these details. So," he said, counting on his long, pale fingers. "we have a missing toy and a missing rock. Has any other strange item absented itself?"

Grainger shuffled his papers anxiously. "Not exactly an item, my lord. An earl."

Rothgar's brows rose. "An *earl*?

"Lord Walgrave. He has disappeared."

Now the marquess was attentive. "He has fled the country?"

"Not as far as anyone knows, my lord. He disappeared from his bed, taking not a stitch of clothing, and leaving a corpse and a badly injured servant behind."

Rothgar's dark eyes showed no particular alarm, but Grainger knew he was most dangerous when calm. "Do we know the identity of the corpse or the servant?"

Grainger swallowed. Here came the dangerous part, but he could see no way to conceal it. He thanked heaven that he had that note from Lady Elfled. "The corpse is unidentified, my lord, and the servant was not one of our people. However"—he cleared his throat—"there was another fatality. Sally Parsons, a maid in your employ."

Rothgar raised a long pale finger to his chin and as if by design, a shaft of morning sunlight caught his ruby signet ring, flashing red as blood. "She was, perhaps, enjoying the earl's favors?"

"Er, no, my lord. The earl had some other woman in his bed, and she's gone, too. Sally was there . . . She was thereabouts on the orders of Lady Elfled."

"I think you had better tell me all, Mr. Grainger, and rather speedily."

Thus prodded, Grainger raced through his story, which was brief enough. Into an ominous silence, he produced his saving note.

Rothgar held out a hand and Grainger hurried around the desk to give it to him, thanking heaven again that he'd had the foresight to demand it.

Rothgar read it, then looked up. "You requested this, Mr. Grainger?"

A new chill starting, Grainger cleared his throat. "I thought it wisest, my lord."

Rothgar rose. "Mr. Grainger, if you ever again question any order of any member of the family, you will be immediately dismissed. Continue with your duties."

Badly shaken, Grainger watched the marquess enter the inner room, wondering if he would ever understand the workings of his employer's mind.

In the private office, Rothgar slid Elf's note into a drawer, then stood for a moment in contemplation. He suspected that God had smiled on them when He had delayed Cyn and Chastity's departure. He rang the silver bell on the desk, causing the footman stationed in the hall to enter through that door.

"My lord?"

"Ask Lord and Lady Cynric to join me here at their earliest convenience, if you please."

Cyn and Chastity interpreted this correctly, and appeared within moments.

"Lud, Rothgar," Chastity said, gesturing at her traveling dress. "I haven't had time to change out of my dirt."

"My apologies." The marquess settled her in a comfortable chair. "Matters have arisen that might be urgent."

"Trouble?" asked Cyn, perching on the arm of his wife's chair.

"I fear so. And it seems Elf might be involved."

"Elf? She hasn't been in trouble since she put pepper in Great-uncle Faversham's snuff!"

"You forget Scottsdale."

Cyn rose, hand on sword. "Are you saying she's fallen into the hands of another adventurer?"

"I don't know what she's fallen into. I am about to visit Lady Lessington to find out. I thought you and Chastity might want to come."

"Of course. What reason do you have, though, for thinking anything is amiss?"

Rothgar strolled toward the door. "Merely the fact that one of our servants was killed last night at Walgrave House, and she was there on Elf's orders."

" 'Struth!"

"Oh. And did I neglect to mention that the earl is apparently missing this morning, along with an unidentified woman who was in his company?"

At the sudden silence, Chastity looked between the two brothers. "You don't think . . . But she doesn't like him at all!"

Cyn's grip on his scabbard tightened. "But he hates Mallorens enough to attack us through our women. I'll—"

"You'll come with me to Lady Lessington's," said Rothgar.

"Praying to God Elf's there," added Cyn grimly.

Amanda was trying to enjoy breakfast with her beloved husband, despite a sour worry about Elf. A message had come from Sappho's to say Elf was safe there, but it answered none of the questions seething in Amanda's mind.

Elf had Lord Walgrave tied up. What on earth did that imply?

And would her friend be able to escape scandal?

When the footman announced that the Marquess of Rothgar had arrived asking for his sister, Amanda nearly dropped her chocolate cup.

Stephen immediately rose to attend their callers, and Amanda hurried after. She thanked heaven that the formidable marquess was here to take charge of this tangle, but feared for poor Elf. What would Rothgar do to her when the truth came out?

As she entered the best reception room, she found that the marquess had not come alone. "Cyn? Good gracious, I thought you on the seas!"

Cyn shrugged. "Winds all awry, and then the ship

sprang some sort of problem. It was decided to put off sailing for a month and there seemed no point in kicking our heels in Portsmouth." Though he spoke pleasantly enough, Amanda couldn't help noticing that he was unusually somber. "We're here to speak to Elf."

Stephen turned to Rothgar. "I only arrived home last night, my lord, but I gather Lady Elfled decided to spend a few days visiting a poetess by the name of Sappho."

Amanda prayed that the story be accepted. Then she remembered that Elf thought Sappho was the marquess's mistress.

Oh heavens, what now?

The only sign that the information might be of significance was that Rothgar took time for a pinch of snuff. "Sappho," he repeated, dusting his fingers with a silk handkerchief. "Have you any idea, Lady Lessington, why she might have removed there?"

Fixed by those perceptive eyes, Amanda did her best. "Oh, she didn't *remove,* my lord! All her clothes are still here. I mean," she hastily amended, "*most* of her clothes, of course. We visited Sappho, you see. A few nights ago . . ." The more those dark eyes observed her, the more tangled her mind and tongue became. "Poetry reading. Quite unexceptionable! Elf must have taken a fondness for the lady—"

"So she left when?"

"Ah . . . Last night, actually."

Stephen turned to her. "Last night? I thought—"

Amanda forced a smile. "It was an impulse. You know Elf."

"I certainly thought I did," said Cyn. "What the devil's she up to?"

Stephen frowned at Amanda. "But you were at Lady Yardley's masquerade last night."

"Well of course we were, darling. That's where you found me!" Amanda scrambled for a coherent story. "Elf met Sappho there, you see, and—impulsively—took up her invitation to stay." She smiled fiercely at Rothgar. "You will find her there, my lord."

Rothgar smiled as if he believed every twittering word. And wasn't most of it true, after all? He kissed her hand. "Then we must proceed there, of course. My apologies for interrupting your breakfast, my lady. My lord."

Amanda watched the Mallorens leave, then turned to face her husband.

"Amanda, my love, I think you had better tell me what has been going on."

In the coach, the three Mallorens were silent, apart from Rothgar's command to the coachman that they be taken to Harlow Street. Then Cyn said, "Strange story."

"Extremely," remarked Rothgar. "Particularly as Sappho strongly dislikes masquerades and has never been known to attend one. And Lady Yardley, of course, is Walgrave's aunt."

At Sappho's Elf was feeling a little revived by food and coffee. Now she studied Fort, trying to detect any chink in his armor. Breakfast had passed without him showing the slightest interest in food. Surely he must at least be thirsty. Was the man human?

He must be sore and uncomfortable, but he sat perfectly still.

She knew her stare must be irritating, even though his gaze was fixed on the wall above her head. She hoped so. She wanted to irritate him. Any response would be better than none.

Sappho had left with the tray, so for a moment they were alone.

She rose to pace in front of him. "Did you mean to imply that the king is in no danger?"

When he didn't reply, she put her face in front of his. "Speak to me! This is more important than our petty differences."

He focused on her, and slowly, disdainfully, his brows rose. "Almost anything is. But yes. You can cease your fidgets. The king has been warned of the plot."

"Thank God!" she exclaimed, straightening. "So this means you weren't really involved in treason at all." She turned back to stare at him. "Murray was right. You were acting as an agent provocateur."

"Not at all. An agent provocateur seduces people into criminal activity and then turns them in to the authorities. I seduced no one. Unlike you."

Hot memories flooded her, not least of begging him for a night of pleasure, but she knew he wanted those memories, wanted her to feel uncomfortable. "Goodness," she said, hands on hips, "are you suggesting *I* acted as an agent provocateur, seducing you into fornication? But at least I have no intention of turning you in to the authorities."

"No? I rather thought you'd enjoy urging your brothers on to revenge."

"I don't deserve that."

"You deserve everything that's going to happen. If you don't intend to stir up trouble, be assured that I do."

She stared down at him. "What do you mean?"

He smiled, reminding her in a twisted way of his beauty. "I intend to tell the world about our adventures. In detail. Think of it. Items in the lower news sheets. Stories in the clubs. Cartoons in the print shops for the amusement of hoi polloi. It should all be vastly amusing."

"Until Rothgar kills you for it."

"I count on it, unless I am blessed by good fortune and manage to kill him."

Every scrap of good she'd done was undone, and she'd added a whole new set of wounds so that he was scarcely sane. "Oh, stop this," she begged. "Stop to think!"

At that moment, the door opened and she head Sappho say, "They are in here, my lord."

Elf turned, stomach churning, to see not only Rothgar, but Cyn and Chastity, enter the room.

Before she had a chance to say anything, Fort turned his head toward the door. "Ah, the family! Elf and I were just discussing how best to tell the world about our night of lascivious passion."

Chapter 13

Elf turned on him. "You *fool*!"

By then, Cyn's blade already pricked Fort's throat and Rothgar was firmly pushing it aside by the hilt. "He's bound, Cyn. Later, perhaps."

Chastity hurried over to Elf. "Is it true?"

Elf grimaced at her sister-in-law. "Unlike in your case, yes. Any suggestions?"

"Lud, no. I was a lamentable failure at handling scandal. I won't let them beat you, though. I promise."

Elf saw in Chastity's eyes that even months of freedom and marriage to Cyn hadn't wiped away all the fear.

"They wouldn't," she assured her gently. "They'll want to kill him, though."

Chastity went white, and Elf remembered that Fort was her brother. "I won't let them," she promised, taking Chastity's hands. She meant it, too, though she didn't underestimate the difficulties. She remembered the Scottsdale affair only too well.

"Nor will I," said Chastity, and went to stand behind her brother, facing her husband and Rothgar.

Elf thought of joining Chastity, but it would serve no purpose, and she wasn't sure where her ultimate allegiance lay. She remembered telling Sappho that in the end she would care for her brothers more than for Fort. Now she could only hope it wasn't put to the test.

"Bey," she said to Rothgar, "there are serious matters involved here."

He turned to her. "So I gather when corpses line the

path." He was not noticeably in a rage, but she knew him able to conceal the strongest emotions.

"It's a Jacobite plot to kill the king."

"In Walgrave's bed?" So, he was in more of a rage than he showed.

"No," she said crisply. "That is an incidental we can deal with later."

"An incidental," said Fort plaintively. "I'm sure you didn't think so when you howled for me."

Cyn stepped forward. Chastity grabbed his sleeve, but it was Rothgar's raised hand that stopped him. "Later," he said again.

Elf noted that this time he left off the "perhaps." She wished she'd had Fort gagged as well as bound.

Rothgar addressed Fort. "Since we apparently have matters of moment to talk about, Walgrave, please postpone your attempts at suicide. What of this plot?"

"Untie me."

"I think not. It is preserving your life. Tell me about this plot."

Fort's lips tightened, but then he said, "A man named Murray has an insane plan to kill the king and restore the Stuarts. He plans to stuff a gift with gunpowder and have it blow up in the king's presence. There's no real danger. Grenville knows of it, and the king's household has been warned."

"But the malefactors have been left at large?"

"Grenville wanted to catch them red-handed."

"Why?"

Fort resisted for a moment, then said, "Because Murray is a distant connection of Bute's, and presently living in his house."

"Ah. And a red-handed Murray would bring down Bute, leaving the way open for Grenville to become Prime Minister." He contemplated Fort. "I wasn't aware that you were of Grenville's party. How did you become involved?"

"That's none of your damned business."

"Your father's connections, no doubt. Are you aware that murder was committed at your house last night?"

"I understand that to be the case." Despite being bound and disheveled, Fort had relaxed into an excellent representation of a belted earl in boring company.

"One of the victims was a servant of mine."

"Doing a little pilfering?" Fort raised a brow. "On your behalf?"

"What could you have that I would want?" Rothgar queried, equally coolly. "Unless, of course, we are talking of a mechanical toy."

Toy? It sounded absurd to Elf, but a sudden tension showed otherwise.

Color touched Fort's cheeks, and he raised his chin. "Yes, I had it stolen from Rothgar Abbey for Murray to use in his plot. And yes, I hoped to cast some shadow over you."

"And the device does not concern you now?"

"Why the devil should it?"

"Because it disappeared last night."

Fort suddenly went pale. "God, I forgot . . . !" For a moment he looked at Elf, but flinched away as if he couldn't stand the sight. "But it still can't be the time. They had to get hold of some mystical stone."

"The Stone of Scone," said Rothgar, all illusion of laziness gone. "What, precisely, have the king's household been told?"

"The Stone of . . . The *Coronation* stone? It's *gone*?"

"What have the king's household been told?"

Flinching under that tone, Fort matched Rothgar's alertness. "To be careful of unexpected gifts." After a moment, perhaps in response to Rothgar's expression, he added, "Grenville didn't want to be specific, fearing the king would tell Bute, and Bute would chatter of it."

"And in your case hoping that some blame would attach to me. Which means, I suppose, that the toy will be sent from me and thus not be entirely unexpected." He turned to Cyn. "To Malloren House for our fastest horse, then all speed to Windsor to warn the king. Chastity, go with him and set Grainger to readying people to react on the instant. Send a message as well to Grenville."

As the couple ran out, Rothgar turned back to Fort, who was fighting his bonds. "The king, as you well know, was much taken with that toy. I had planned to give it to him on the birth of his child, and he knew it. Do you seriously think he will let his gentlemen prevent him from winding it up and seeing it work?"

"They have been warned. Damn it. Untie me!"

"There is nothing you can do that others cannot."

Elf interrupted the argument. "There was a large rock in the cellar where we were imprisoned."

Fort stared at her. "What? You never said anything."

"It was hardly of use in breaking out. It was about the size of a pillow." She turned to Rothgar. "The stone is that, isn't it? Just a flat boulder."

"Lightning blast you, let me free!"

Rothgar ignored him. "So, they stole the stone, then put Walgrave out of action. In this cellar, I assume? I wonder why they didn't kill you both."

"Because," said Fort, "a dead earl causes more questions than a missing one." He had ceased his struggles, and sagged wearily against the sofa back. "I'm sure they wanted as little mayhem as possible. The bloodshed is probably all your sister's fault."

"Really!" exclaimed Elf. "How can that possibly be?"

He turned to her. "Because in typical Malloren fashion, you meddled. Murray didn't know what to make of you, and it heightened his nervousness to panic. In addition, you brought your own people into it, and that's doubtless where the violence occurred."

"There may be some truth in that," said Rothgar calmly. "But since they half killed the guard you had set on the toy, you can't lay all the blood at our door. Do you know how long it would take to make the toy lethal?"

"I am not precisely in their confidence," Fort snapped. "They planned to pack the inner cavity with gunpowder and bits of metal so that when it was switched on, at a certain point it would explode, scattering shot all around."

"The chances being that if no hit was fatal, infection might carry the victim off."

Fort writhed once against his bonds, but then desisted, jaw tight. "I assume you intend to use this to destroy me."

"I? I am a singularly undestructive person. However, I do wish to have some words with you. Elf, leave us."

Elf looked between the two of them. "Not if you're going to hurt him."

Rothgar turned to her, brows raised. "He is bound. I wouldn't dream of it. But I could bear to know your feelings toward him."

She found it surprisingly difficult to give an honest response. "I . . . I do care for him. He didn't force me or seduce me—"

"Lisette!" exclaimed Fort maliciously. "Are you forgetting when I took you prisoner and tied you to my bed?"

"Oh, be quiet! I remember perfectly well that you didn't offend against me at all when you had me bound. And last night, I had the very deuce of a job to get you to agree to . . . to what we did."

"Sex on the floor," recalled Fort. "Sex in the bed. Sex on a coffin . . ."

Face flaming, Elf clenched her fists and let out a cry of pure exasperation.

". . . sex, now I recall it, *in* the coffin." He turned to her with a deceptively bland expression. "I'm quite surprised, actually, that you can walk."

Elf turned away. "I think perhaps I hate him."

"I think perhaps you don't," said Rothgar, gently touching her shoulder. "Unfortunately, I suspect he hates you or he would not try to shame you so."

She turned into his arms, and he held her close, telling her without words that, as always, all his strength and all his love was hers. She could have wept for shame at what she'd done.

"I am surprised," he said. "I would have thought you the last person in the world to inspire such bitterness."

"He has reasons, Bey. Not good ones, but reasons." She pulled out of her brother's arms and turned to meet Fort's cynical eyes. "I was disguised, you see, so he didn't know who I was. And when he was vulnerable, I pushed for answers to painful questions. I meant well, but he told me more than he'd ever want to tell a Malloren. I hope that one day he'll forgive me."

"My dear Elf," said Fort, "I think the excitement has turned your brain. There will be no 'one day.' Cyn is going to kill me. I must admit that I had not counted on him being around. As you remember, I fenced with him once before and though I've been working at it, he is surely still my master."

"None of my brothers will kill you unless I give them permission." She turned to Rothgar. "Will they?"

After a moment he said, "Not for this offense."

At that, Fort looked up at Rothgar. "I'm astonished at your inhuman calm. Can I at least look forward to the fact that you will beat her?"

"I doubt it. And you can take that in whatever way you want. Elf, go now."

Elf saw just how tight a rein her brother had on himself. Despairing of any words to make things better, she left the room.

Sappho waited in the hall, a pile of men's black clothing over her arm. "Is Walgrave likely to need these?" she asked. "I sent to his house for them, but a winding sheet might be more appropriate."

"I gather he's not going to die." Lips unsteady, Elf touched the coat, seeing buttons she remembered from Midsummer Night on his boat. "Oh, God. I've created a disaster!"

"Not at all." Sappho put an arm around her. "It is my philosophy to put all such disasters firmly to the credit of men, and to leave men to sort them out."

* * *

Rothgar watched his sister leave the room and studied the closed door for a moment before turning to look at Fort. "Don't brace yourself. I have no intention of touching you."

Fort rested his head back, eyes closed. "I gather I am just to be bludgeoned with words then. Don't you think, with a father such as mine, I have developed calluses against that?"

"I would be astonished to hear that he restricted himself to words. In fact, Walgrave, I need to offer you an apology."

Fort's eyes opened to rest on the older man. "Now you do surprise me."

"I thought I might. My feelings about my sister's involvement with you will depend largely on future events. That has little connection to my sin, which is that of misjudging you."

"I am bewildered but entranced. Go on."

Rothgar moved to sit in a chair a good ten feet from the sofa. "Before Cyn's involvement with Chastity, you were no more than a name to me, only of interest as the heir to a man who had become my enemy. I had assessed you to be the common sort of young buck, interested only in weapons, women, and wine."

"Ah, those were the days . . ."

Rothgar continued. "Having come into my inheritance too early, I lack experience of the tedium of living under the shadow of a father who will give his son no part to play. Our encounters over Chastity's affairs merely confirmed that you were uninteresting. Except, perhaps, after the fencing match."

"You were impressed because I didn't sulk when beaten?"

"Precisely."

Fort studied the marquess for a moment. "I don't recall a warming of your attitude."

"Few people ever do. Nor did I warm. I merely noted it, and subsequently forgot to take it into account. You are correct in thinking I did my best to make you the instrument of your father's death."

Fort sucked in a breath. "And now you think an apology will make all right?"

"Not at all. Apologies rarely change anything. I am apologizing to ease my own conscience, and in the faint hope that it might help you come to terms with your situation. And I am not apologizing for using you. It was a completely logical strategy."

"Oh, please. Tell me why."

"I intend to. I had no fixed plan that night other than to show your father the proof of his treason and thus compel him to agree to Chastity's marriage. Knowing your father's temperament, I did hope to drive him to kill himself, for he was a dangerous poison to leave loose. I did not expect, however, that he would try to kill someone else. I should have. Suicide is perhaps the greatest act of self-blame. Your father never blamed himself for anything."

"Another miscalculation. You must have been in an agony of self-blame. What a pity—"

"—I did not kill myself?" Rothgar smiled. "I have learned to handle guilt. I have, however, blamed myself for misjudging you. As your father raged in the hall, waving his pistol, you, Bryght, and myself were nearby with weapons of our own. I instantly decided that your father should die, but it really would have been inconvenient to have a Malloren do it. I and your father were known to be at odds, and in his ravings he was spewing lies about me and treason. I merely left it till the last moment, hoping you would prove to be the rather shallow man of action I thought you to be."

Fort shrugged slightly. "As I am. I killed him."

"You could have wounded him. You could probably have shot the pistol from his hand. You're a good shot and you were close."

Fort's jaw clenched. "I thought this was an apology, not an inquisition."

"Milles pardons." Rothgar inclined his head. "Of

course you had to kill him to save your family from ruin. The apology is because I misjudged you and gave no thought to you afterward. I assumed you to be the sort of clod who could kill a father—even a hated father—without a scar. I have come to see that is not so. As far as I can tell, your actions since becoming earl have been responsible and mature, except insofar as they concern my family. I have to suggest to you that as your father turned his own self-blame against me and Princess Augusta, so you are turning it against all Mallorens."

"So, you think I'm mad. Now that's a pot calling a kettle black."

"It really is quite pointless to jab at me, Walgrave. I am armored beyond any weapon you possess. Yes, the blood of a mad mother runs in my veins. Your father was not mad, except at the end. He was a man who loved power too much, and considered the effect of his actions too little. He was also handicapped by pride, an uncontrolled temper, and an inability to accept being crossed. I suggest you contemplate those flaws."

The marquess stood and straightened a snowy lace ruffle. "My apology is for misjudging you, and for putting you in a position that has caused you pain, then leaving you without aid."

"You think I would have accepted succor from you?"

Rothgar merely continued. "Your pain shows, however, that you have a soul. I would not reject you as a suitor for Elf's hand."

Fort laughed. "Are we, perhaps, finished? I'm damned uncomfortable."

"Yes. We are finished." Rothgar walked out of the room.

In a moment, Sappho came in and cut the ropes that bound Fort to the sofa. He moved his arms to the front, wincing, and stood with a groan.

"Would you like a hot bath before you dress, my lord?" she asked.

"Oh, call me Fort." He rubbed his battered hands over his face. "After tonight, any attempt to stand on dignity seems absurd, don't you think? But I must reject your kind offer. I have things I have to do."

Elf paced the hall, listening intently, but heard no shouting or sounds of mayhem. When Rothgar emerged, he looked unruffled. But then, he generally did.

Her mouth dried. She supposed now she would face the real consequences of her folly. He merely said, "I assume you wish to return home."

"Yes, please."

It had never occurred to her to question that she would return to Malloren House, but she realized many families would bar the door against a fallen woman. What *was* Rothgar going to do?

He merely took her hand to lead her out to the coach, which had returned for them. Once inside, however, he said, "I do have words for you."

"Yes?" Pain tightened within her and it was fear—not of punishment, but of his disappointment.

"I warned you once about Walgrave."

"I meant no harm," she said again.

"Those, my dear, are the most damning words in the language. You should have realized the rawness of his feelings and given him time to heal. Instead, you picked at him, demanding a response he was not capable of."

"Did I do that? He called me Vespa."

"At least he didn't call you Torquemada."

"Who?"

"An infamous torturer."

"I am beginning to feel very poorly educated!"

"You cannot blame me for that. You were educated with Cyn, but were always of a flighty disposition. I should have suspected the apparent change."

"Oh, Bey . . ." At the hint of humor in his voice, Elf brushed at tears in her eyes. She wasn't sure she deserved his understanding, and desperately wanted to soften his feelings toward Fort.

"He's a different person when not dealing with Mallorens, you know. That's what caused my ruin. Now, though, I'm not sure that person can ever exist for me."

"This time, you will have to give him a chance to heal."

"I've discovered that I am not of a patient disposition." Elf looked at the small scabs still remaining from the first step of this adventure. "I'm afraid of what he might do." She was equally afraid to tell her brother of Fort's threats to make the whole story public.

Rothgar took her hand and studied the marks, but he made no comment. "I don't say you must leave him be. I'm no oracle on these matters. Just be careful, and don't push for more than he is ready to give."

"Bey, what if I'm with child?"

"You must have thought of that."

"I did. I know these things happen. I can travel . . . But it will be his child, too."

"Then I think you must tell him. But I will not force a marriage. That would surely set the stage for tragedy."

"Would it? I think I was hoping that you would."

"Tush, tush. And you so independent. If you want him, my dear, you'll have to woo him for yourself. Just step carefully. Now, enough of that. We are home, and you must explain your part in this."

In an abrupt change of rhythm, he swept her into Malloren House in a whirlwind of questions and commands to hovering servants. Roberts, angrily grieving the slain Sally, was ordered to lead a party to the old tavern to see if the stone was still there and to scoop up any lingering Scots. A note to Grenville assured that a troop of soldiers would go there too, and that all ships sailing down the river would be stopped and searched.

In the middle of this, Bryght walked in. "I smell mayhem in the air. And since I received an urgent summons . . ."

He was tall, dark, and astonishingly handsome, and his eyes sparkled with interest.

"You're late for the action," said Rothgar, and gave

a brief account which made Bryght's eyes widen, especially when Rothgar made no secret of Elf's activities.

" 'Struth, Elf! And we're not supposed to kill the villain?"

"Not until she gives us permission. Which is unlikely to be provided, I fear."

"Pay attention, Bryght," said Elf, pausing in a restless pacing to face him. "*I* decided that I wanted Fort to make love to me. *I* chased him and insisted on it. He gave me a number of opportunities to change my mind. And when we did it"—she cursed the heat in her cheeks—"he made it very, very good for me. If I'd been able to be honest about who I was, I would have no regrets at all. I don't see why I should be denied all experience, all adventure, just because I'm a woman!"

"You should get your experience in marriage," Bryght pointed out.

"As you did, I suppose."

"It's not the same. You could be pregnant."

"And you could have caught the pox!"

"I was careful."

"Since there doesn't seem to be any way to be careful about pregnancy—"

"Actually, there are a few."

"What?" Elf stared between her brothers. "Do you mean to tell me there are things a woman can do so as not to conceive a child, and I don't know about them?"

"What use would they be?" Bryght demanded. "They're whores' tricks!"

Elf picked up a large, valuable Chinese vase and hurled it onto the floor. "The world needs changing."

"Probably," said Rothgar, amused. "At the moment, however, we need to make sure that some murderous traitors are dealt with without damage to our family's reputation. I don't entirely trust Grenville. I'm for Court. Bryght, you go with Roberts to see to the Stone of Scone and any malefactors who turn up there. I assume Portia is not with you?"

"No," said Bryght, still staring at Elf as if she'd grown

horns. "I left her at Candleford. Travel wearies her these days."

"Elf," said Rothgar, "you should rest."

"I'm going with Bryght."

"Why?"

"Because," said Elf, "this is my adventure, and I want to see it to the end. Have Tressia ready for me." She then swept up to her room calling for someone to clean up debris, and a maid, any maid, to help her into her habit.

Rage carried her up the stairs, but in her room, exhaustion and misery sank her limp into a chair. Oh God, oh God, it had all gone too fast for her to keep up.

And what of the future? It was one thing to face her brothers so boldly—even if she had been shaking inside. It was another to face the whole world. What if Fort carried out his threat to spread the story of their wickedness? She'd never be able to show her face in public, and even if her brothers didn't kill him, they'd want to. Every day.

Surely, on calm reflection, he wouldn't do it.

She just hoped he didn't spread the word before he had time for calm reflection!

She looked at her bed, so smooth and inviting, tempted to slip between the sheets and into sleep, to let others take care of everything. But that was the coward's way out. She intended to see this through to the end.

Even before the maid came, she had stripped to her shift, and stood ready to don corset, petticoat, and her finest gray riding habit with the silver-braided jacket.

Since nothing quick could be done with her powdered hair, she just crowned it with the habit's gray tricorne hat, jaunty plume flowing behind. In the mirror, with boots and whip, she looked the image of a proper lady. But pale. She hastily added some rouge to cheeks and lips.

Lud. Now she looked like a doxy.

Ah, plague take it. Telling herself she didn't care what anyone thought, she swept downstairs.

"The tides are right," said Bryght, still looking at her strangely. "We're taking the boat. Roberts says your prison was in Wapping, down in the port. He thinks Alderman Parson's Stairs should be close enough."

"Very well," said Elf. "Let's be off."

They rode down to the river, the servants jogging alongside, and found Rothgar's barge awaiting them, eight sturdy liveried boatmen already at their benches. Once everyone was settled in the covered portion, the boat shot off into the river traffic, speeding downriver on the tides toward the Port of London.

The curtains all around the covered area were rolled up, giving a view of the lively activity on the river. Commanded to make all speed, the boatmen rammed their vessel through narrow gaps, exchanging searing abuse with others of their sort.

Elf didn't know whether to giggle or swoon. This certainly wasn't the grand manner of travel the barge was accustomed to, but she suspected the boatmen were enjoying every moment.

Glancing at her brother, she saw his lips turn up in a smile of pure enjoyment. He caught her look and they shared a smile both of excitement and camaraderie. Suddenly, he held out his hand and she placed hers in it, tears threatening, especially when he gave her hand a friendly squeeze.

She really did have the best brothers in the world, though she suspected her twin was storing up a long and pointed lecture for her.

Then she looked ahead to see the almost solid barrier of London Bridge hurtling toward them. Most of the houses that had lined it since medieval times had recently been torn down, but the bridge itself was untouched. The nineteen broad stone arches were supported on wide rock starlings with only narrow passages beneath each.

"We aren't going to shoot the bridge, are we?"

"You wanted adventure," said Bryght. "Hold on!"

His eyes might be shining with anticipation, but Elf saw all the servants turn pale, and a few start to say their last prayers. People regularly drowned trying to shoot London Bridge, and the wise disembarked from their boats and crossed the barrier on foot, leaving their watermen to take their chances as professionals should.

Their speed seemed horrendous, and the gap they were aiming for impossibly narrow. With the oars, it was impossible. Surely they must crash into the stone starling—

She screamed and hunched down, even as oars fended them off and into the maelstrom. But by then the water's roar deafened her even to her own voice.

Into the dark roar.

Boat jars against stone.

Tossing wildly.

Bryght seizing her.

Clinging together as the boat spins . . .

Out into sunlight and wild water.

Boat tipping, twirling.

Oars digging.

Boatmen shouting.

Noise receding.

Water calming.

Laughter.

Everyone—boatmen, servants, and nobles—burst into wild laughter at the sheer joy of being alive.

Then the men settled to their oars, speeding them on down to Parson's Stairs.

Elf became aware that one side of her habit was drenched. "I have made one discovery," she said, pulling the clinging material away from her arm. "Adventure and vanity do not go hand in hand."

"Ah," said Bryght, removing his coat to wring out his sleeve, "but there is something so damnably attractive about a person living life to the full."

"Is there?"

He smiled at her. "For someone of the same inclination. I have this strange suspicion that you are not, after all, like our sister Hilda. She seems content with a dull husband and bucolic placidity."

"You've been buried in the country for months."

"With Portia. Who is never dull."

They were slowing, heading toward the busy wharves that lined the river here, the boatmen cleverly avoiding sand banks and shoals. The stairs ahead must be Parson's.

"One way or another," said Elf, "I doubt I'll end up with a dull, bucolic husband like Hilda's. Do you have your pistols with you?"

"Of course."

"Then I hope they didn't get wet. Give me one, please."

"Why?"

"I would just prefer to be armed."

With a sigh, he signed to a servant who clutched an oilcloth package. Unwrapped, it revealed a gleaming pistol case. Bryght opened it to take out two handsome guns.

"Oh, Gemini!" Elf exclaimed. "I never returned Fort's pistol. He doubtless *will* have me transported—"

"You can explain that later." Bryght handed her one gun. "It's loaded and primed, so be careful. And don't shoot anyone unnecessarily."

"I'm the gentle lady here, am I not?"

"I think the reason we don't give women guns is that they are dangerous enough without them."

"Ah, that reminds me of another complaint I have—"

"I quiver. For now, let's hope this Murray and the stone are here. If he's taking ship, they might be trying to catch the last of the tide."

The boat had to wait a moment for a wherry to discharge its passengers, but then it nudged up against the stairs, and Bryght handed Elf out. The scene appeared completely normal.

Not peaceful, no, in the middle of the bustling wharves, but with no sense of alarm.

Alderman Parson's Stairs were squeezed in between

wharves loaded down with goods coming and going to the great sailing vessels out in the river. Jostling watermen abused one another with cheerful insults interspersed with social comments such as "How's the missus?"

Watching a crane handle a huge cask, Elf could easily have been distracted, but Bryght said, "Roberts, where's this tavern?"

"This way, milord." Roberts led them away from the river and into a warren of streets that Elf thought familiar.

All such streets probably looked the same, however, lined with narrow houses, doors and windows open to let in fresh air. Grubby children stopped to stare at the strange party passing among them. Aproned women came to the doors, perhaps to protect their young, perhaps just out of curiosity.

Elf expected some begging, but then she realized this was no slum. These people were quite prosperous in their way, their menfolk all working down at the thriving port.

Then they turned a corner and found themselves in the small wasteland created by a fire. It was not deserted, for a few people rummaged through the already picked-over ruins. The ramshackle tavern stood to one side, walls still standing, and roof mostly intact, but windows completely gone. Clearly, even before disaster it had been a mean place.

Elf couldn't reconcile it with an interlude which had been, at times, positively romantic. Perhaps darkness was a blessing after all.

Bryght ordered his party to spread out and surround the building, adding a command to Elf to stay with him. Even as they approached the ruin, Elf noted curious children and even a few adults hovering nearby. She prayed no shots were fired, that no more innocents were injured in this affair.

Chapter 14

The Marquess of Rothgar made no attempt to ornament himself before setting off for Windsor in the carriage. This was not an occasion for glitter. With God's grace, Cyn would have alerted the king to danger. Now he must prevent damage to the family's reputation.

Even with six of his best horses in the shafts, it took more than an hour to arrive at the king's country palace, its ancient walls rising majestically over a mass of buildings added to and adapted by centuries of monarchs.

Almost anyone had to progress through a number of chambers to reach the king. Rothgar, however, progressed with remarkable speed. He was bowed through the paneled guard chamber, where the guards did not seem to be on special alert. Then a footman escorted him through the presence chamber and audience chamber, past a number of hopefuls lounging about admiring Verrio's magnificent ceiling, and the empty carved throne.

A couple of men tried to speak to him, but he indicated that his business could not wait. He recognized the envy in their eyes but had little sympathy for such petitioners. Most of them merely wanted a sinecure from the king to finance their expensive pleasures.

At the great gilded doors of the King's Drawing Room, the guards stood back to let him pass.

George, fresh-faced and bulbous-eyed, was pacing the room when Rothgar was announced. He turned to him fretfully. "Lord Rothgar!" he exclaimed. "Such goings-on!"

Rothgar, noting an absence of both mechanical device and brother, made a profound bow to the King and to the heavily pregnant queen who sat nearby, clutching a puppy. Then he bestowed lesser ones on Lord Bute and Charles Grenville, who were also present.

"You are well come indeed," said Grenville with assumed warmth. "We thought you out of the country, my lord, and feared for your reputation."

"God sent contrary winds, and thus I am here to set all right. The mechanical device?"

"Was delivered. But Lord Cynric arrived in time."

"He manhandled me!" George spluttered.

"I apologize on his behalf, Your Majesty, but I'm sure it was necessary."

"Well, I'm not! And if the device is so dangerous, how can that be when it is a gift from you, my lord? Eh? Can you make sense of this story, eh? Can you? Grenville says a relative of Lord Bute was involved, but Lord Bute denies any knowledge of it. The device came from your house, my lord, but you are ignorant of it. Lord Walgrave is involved, but acting on my First Secretary's orders, and innocent. And no one saw fit to tell me anything. I am displeased. Most displeased!"

The king dabbed at his sweaty forehead with a gilded, monogrammed silk handkerchief.

"Very understandable, Your Majesty," said Rothgar, forcefully projecting calm. "I assure you, had I known anything of this matter, I would have informed you in full immediately. Lord Walgrave, however, perhaps you can excuse. He is young and took the advice of older men."

"I am somewhat surprised to hear you defend him, Rothgar," said Grenville, no longer smiling. "You are no friend to that family."

"I try not to let my bias sway me, Grenville, and of course, our families are now joined. Walgrave's purpose, I am told, was merely to assist in rooting out the base of this plot to harm His Majesty."

"And as soon as we find Michael Murray," said Bute,

"we will have him! I am distressed, distressed beyond imagining, that I have harbored such a viper in my bosom."

"As close as that, were you?" queried Rothgar mildly.

The earl flushed. " 'Tis an expression, my lord."

"Ah, I see." Rothgar turned back to the king. "I have sent some men to a location where we might find Murray, Your Majesty. At the same time, I sent a message to Mr. Grenville's office suggesting that he dispatch soldiers there, and also search ships sailing down the Thames. I had no idea he thought it more important to be here."

Grenville flushed. "I left capable men in charge, Your Majesty. In fact, I left Lord Walgrave to assist them, since he was, most understandably, anxious to set all aright. I came here, feeling His Majesty had to be informed as soon as possible."

"Which it seems he is not." Rothgar turned to the king. "With your permission, Your Majesty, perhaps we may all sit and I will tell the tale as best I can. I'm sure Lord Bute and Mr. Grenville will add their mite."

"I know nothing," declared Bute fretfully. "Nothing." But when the king waved permission, he sat with the others, clearly trying to decide just where the threat to his position lay in all this.

The old tavern appeared deserted, but when Elf saw the trapdoor leading to the ramp, she knew someone had been there. It stood open, the lock forced in some way. Despite Bryght's cautioning hand on her arm, she leaned forward to peep in. Even in daylight, the windowless room was gloomy, but she could see well enough to know that it was now completely empty apart from the old casks.

The coffin had been removed.

No special stone sat on the uneven floor.

"It's gone," she whispered.

"Indeed it is," said a familiar voice, and Elf straightened to face Fort. He stood in the ruined doorway dressed in deepest black, and even with a battered face, he had regained all his aristocratic hauteur.

Suppressing a host of distracting emotions, she asked, "Where is it?"

Now she noticed the soldiers behind him, and altered by something in the atmosphere, she turned to see more appear from behind nearby objects, all eyeing the Malloren servants with suspicion.

Some of the hovering mothers grabbed their curious children.

"I have no idea," said Fort, "having only just arrived myself."

"Well, nor have we, since we have only just arrived, too."

Elf saw that Fort's attention was entirely on Bryght, and that if he'd been a dog, his hackles would be rising. She was sure her brother was reacting in exactly the same way. They were old enemies because of Portia. Goodness knows what folly they would get up to now if allowed.

Turning her back on them, she marched over to one of the nearby scavengers, a toothless crone, dressed in ragged clothes.

"If you please, ma'am, has anyone been here this morning to take anything out of that building?"

The woman's rheumy eyes shifted and she scuttled a few steps away, clutching her folded-up apron to her chest. "I ain't taken anything I shouldn't. 'Onest!"

"Of course not," said Elf with as reassuring a smile as she could manage. "No one wants to make trouble for you. It's just that we expected to find something in that cellar. Just a large stone, actually. And it's not there. Probably our friends were here ahead of us."

The woman's eyes turned sharp. "Friends, eh? And redcoats 'unting 'em? I don't want no trouble."

Elf heard footsteps behind her and knew they wouldn't be Fort's. "Bryght. Do you have a small coin?"

He put a sixpence in her hand and she held it out to the woman. "Here. Take it. You don't have to do anything for it. But if you do know anything, it would be a kindness to tell us."

The crone grabbed the coin, her eyes darting around. "Right, well, you seem an 'onest, sweet-natured lady, so I'll tell 'ee. Some men came by with a cart a while ago. Broke open that door, they did. Funny it was really, 'cos 'esterday the door wasn't locked at all, and the blinkin' cellar was empty of all but a few old casks. Then they 'auled out a bloody great boulder! I couldn't figure it at all," she said, getting into the spirit of her story. "Gawd knows there's enough rocks in the world if a body wants 'em. But this bob-wigged minister was leaping around, telling 'em not to scratch it. Never seen anything like it in all me born days."

Bob-wigged minister? But then Elf remembered Roberts saying the street monkeys had been hired by a Scots clergyman. Murray in disguise? "It does sound extraordinary," she said as if only mildly curious. "What did they do with this stone?"

"Put it in a box they brung up before." She cackled. "A coffin, it was, and a right funny scene. The clergyman was as fretful as if they was handling a corpse. Kept saying as they should 'ave put the stone in the box before bringing it up. Which was true enough if he didn't want it scratched. Stone, he kept calling it. Weren't no stone. Were a bloody great boulder."

"So, this clergyman. He wasn't here when the others started moving things?"

"Nah, he turned up later."

"And I suppose they put the box on a cart and drove it away."

"That's right!" said the woman, as if this were a work of deductive genius. "That's just what they did, mistress."

Elf looked in the direction of the river. "As you have guessed, ma'am, the poor clergyman is not quite sane. He thinks this boulder is of great value and intends to ship it to France as a gift to the king there . . ."

The woman cackled again. "Lord 'a mercy, I wish I could see that!"

"It would be less embarrassing if we could stop him before he sets sail. I wonder what wharf he would be most likely to use."

The eyes were sharp again. "Soldiers and all," muttered the old woman. "I doubt you're telling me the 'ole tale, mistress, but you look like a good 'un. I 'eard 'em say Harrison's Wharf. It's close by on the river."

"How long ago?"

"Not long. They won't have got orf yet, I don't think."

Elf took the woman's callused, dirty hand. "What's your name?"

The woman shied a bit, but then said, "Dibby Cutlow, mistress."

"Thank you for your help, Mrs. Cutlow. And if you are ever in need, come to Malloren House in Marlborough Square." Then she turned to Bryght. "The clergyman is probably Murray in disguise. *En avant!*"

She saw Fort, standing some way away but clearly able to hear, turn to his soldiers as if to give independent orders. She marched over to him. "This is a serious business with no place for rivalry. If we act in competition, we could well interfere with one another."

She really couldn't tell if his eyes were icy cold or flaming with anger. Perhaps it was icy rage. She only had a moment to study them, for he turned sharply toward Bryght. "What plan of action do you have?"

Elf could have hit him for so pointedly overlooking her, but this was no time for that either.

Later, she promised herself, remembering Rothgar saying that to Cyn. They, however, hadn't been talking about a chance to talk, to explain, to understand.

Oh, devil take all men and their codes of behavior.

"We should approach this wharf from both sides," said Bryght. "Three sides, in fact. Some of the soldiers can go on board our boat to stand out in the river in case they get the cargo out on the water."

"You came by boat?"

"It was fastest."

"You shot the bridge?" For a moment, Fort looked at Elf and she chose to believe that his flare of temper could come from concern for her. Immediately, however, he turned to his men. "Corporal, send four men with one of Lord Bryght's people to take position on the river."

"Aye-aye, my lord! What orders, my lord?"

"Stop any suspicious vessel. No, damn it. The river's too crowded—"

"I'll go on the boat," said Elf. "I can recognize Murray."

"It's too dangerous," Fort snapped.

"I agree," said Bryght.

"Such harmony of opinion!" She pulled out the pistol. "I'll shoot any man who tries to stop me."

Fort and Bryght gaped at her, then shared a look that came close to commiseration.

Without another word, Elf turned to the four chosen soldiers. "Follow me." As she led them toward the river, she heard Bryght say, "I knew it was dangerous to arm women."

She also heard Fort's response. "Of course, *ladies* are taught from birth to behave themselves."

She remembered a similar conversation at Bryght's betrothal ball, one that had almost come to blows. At the moment, she rather hoped they battered each another bloody over it.

The boat and the eight oarsmen stood a little way off the steps, but at her sign, it pulled in so they could embark. Elf gave Woodham, the leader of the crew, a brief explanation of the situation.

"So," she said at the end, "I need you to hold position on the river opposite Harrison's Wharf. Can you do that?"

The sturdy, middle-aged man scanned the busy waterway. "Aye, milady, though it won't be easy. Other boats won't want to go round us."

"Do the best you can."

* * *

As Woodham had said, getting out into the river under eight oars was easy enough, despite having to jostle for good water with the lighters and wherries ferrying goods to and from the ships. Holding place in the fast-flowing water without colliding with other boats was more difficult, but the oarsmen managed it.

Elf scanned the crowded river, looking for a boat carrying a coffin and a bob-wigged minister or Murray with his blond hair. She couldn't see any vessel that could fit the bill.

She turned to study the wharf.

She wished she had a spyglass, for the riverbank was a confusing jumble of jetties, warehouses, and cranes, all swarmed over by workers. Then she saw a flash of red that must be the soldiers. In moments she could make out Fort and Bryght coming from different directions, and could even mark their progress by the eddies in the human stream as men moved away from the military.

She studied the edge of the wharf where goods were being loaded into boats. It was hard to spot any one person, but then she saw a crane hoisting something off a cart.

A coffin?

"There!" she said to the soldiers. "See that box?"

It took a moment, but then they spotted it too. The crane was swinging the coffin over a lighter. Below on the wharf a white-wigged figure almost danced with agitation as he watched the operation.

"That's our target," she told the soldiers. "We must stop it being loaded on board a ship."

"Beggin' your pardon, milady," said one of the soldiers, "but on the river, that could be dangerous." She could see from the way he clutched onto the boat that he wasn't happy on the water. "If it gets onto a ship, it's no great problem. A vessel can be stopped and searched on its way down the river."

That was true. It could take days to sail down the Thames into the North Sea, and vessels were subject to various regulations all that time.

"Perhaps not, milady," said Woodham. "See that vessel there?" He pointed out into the confusing forest of masts. "The one flying the fleur-de-lis?"

Elf shaded her eyes and did see it. "What does that mean?"

"I reckon it's the ship taking the French ambassador back, and it's the only one that's yet to sail. Stopping vessels like that ain't usually done."

"Of course," murmured Elf. "That's why it all had to be last night. To travel on that ship. You say it's about to sail?"

He squinted at the great vessel. "Aye, milady. Anxious to be off on the tide, I'd say."

Excitement had fueled Elf, but at this crucial moment, it suddenly drained away, making it hard to formulate decisions. What-ifs and ifs only clamored in her weary head. She shook them away. "Block the way of that boat," she ordered.

"Aye-aye, milady," said Woodham, but he added, "That's a lighter they're putting that coffin on. A big boat, a lighter is. If it chooses to go through us, we'll be kindling."

Elf could see what he meant, but couldn't weaken. "Then we'll have to stop it before it goes through us, won't we?"

The coffin sat on the lighter now—a mere fraction of the cargo the huge barge could carry—and Fort and Bryght's parties had arrived nearby. From a sudden shift in the crowd—a surge away from the edge of the wharf—Elf knew something was happening. Like a line of toy soldiers, the redcoats aimed their muskets.

At whom?

At a man with a pistol.

Even as she saw that the man with the pistol wasn't Murray, fire spurted from the barrel as he fired, and the line of muskets belched flame and death.

The pistol-wielder tumbled backward into the river.

On the wharf another person fell.

Who? Dear God, who?

Elf stood clutching one of the stanchions, watching the lighter moving ponderously into the river, while on the wharf confusion seethed. But the barge was steering *away* from them, away from the French vessel!

"What's he doing?" Elf cried, trying not to even think of dead bodies. "Where's he going? Get closer to him!"

"Nay, milady," said Woodham phlegmatically. "He's heading for the French ship. Lighters are dumb-boats, see. With just one man and one oar they can't steer proper. They have to use the flow of the river. Lightermen know the ways of the river like you know your hand and he'll end up at the French ship in the end. Of course," he added, squinting at the crowded Thames, "that means that even if he don't *want* to crash right through us, there's not much he can do about it."

"Oh, God," Elf whispered.

She stole a glance back at the wharf, but saw only a milling crowd. The soldiers suddenly fell into line again and fired another round after the boat, but it missed. She prayed God their fire not injure an innocent person, and that Bryght or Fort stop them firing again.

If Bryght and Fort were both still able to give commands.

Who had fallen on the wharf?

Perhaps it wasn't either of them.

Why did she have this certainty that it was Fort?

She forced mind and eyes back to the lighter.

It was sidling and drifting its way over the river, and now it clearly headed toward the French ship. Which meant it headed toward them.

Then she spotted Murray.

He stood, one hand protectively on the coffin, gazing rapt at his destination. He wore clergyman garb, but Elf recognized him all the same. A pistol in his free hand pointed at the lighterman, so he couldn't be entirely caught up in the sight of the French ship. Clearly, the lighterman would not be allowed to turn back even if he tried.

There was only one thing to do.

Elf spoke to the soldiers. "Which of you is the best shot?"

One moved forward. "I am, milady. Pickett's the name."

"Well, Private Pickett, do you think you can kill the man standing in that vessel?"

He considered it, squinting. "If this boat don't move too much, it's an easy shot, milady."

"Woodham, keep the boat as steady as you can."

"Aye-aye, milady."

It shocked her to contemplate cold-blooded murder, but she had to stop the barge. Elf remembered Vauxhall, and the way Murray had pursued her, knife in hand. She knew he would shoot the innocent lighterman on the slightest pretext, and he was responsible for all the recent deaths, including Sally's.

Including Fort's?

She couldn't know that Fort had been the person who had fallen on the wharf, and yet she did, and chill sat heavy inside her because of it.

She cast one last harried glance at the distant riverbank, took a deep breath, and said, "Whenever the time seems right, Private Pickett."

The man knelt on one of the velvet-covered seats, using the back as extra support for his long musket, viewing down the barrel with great care. With a loud click, he pulled back the pin and removed the flint cap. Mouth dry, Elf saw his finger begin to tighten on the trigger.

Then another lighter passed between, blocking the shot, and creating a bobbing wave.

Pickett muttered something, then said, "Bob, keep an eye open for anything else like that, will you?"

"Right'o, Billy," said one of the other soldiers. "Looks clear for the next couple of minutes."

Pickett waited for the swell to die down, having to let the lighter get closer and closer. This would make the shot easier, but Murray had only to take his gaze off the lighterman and the French ship to spot the unlikely sight of the nobleman's barge among all these working ships. Then he would surely notice the red-coated soldiers on board, and the one aiming at him.

They were close enough now for Elf to make out the name on the lighter. The *Tilbury Troll*. It seemed suitable for such a cumbersome craft.

Hurry, hurry! Elf silently beseeched Pickett, even though she knew the soldier had to wait for the boat to steady.

Then Murray did move, shifting to look back at the wharf. As he turned back toward the lighterman and the French vessel, his gaze passed over Elf's boat. His mouth opened as if to shout something, but the thunder of Pickett's musket silenced everything. As the smoke cleared Elf saw the Scot sprawled back over the coffin containing his precious Stone of Scone.

The enormity of death froze her, but then she took in the *Tilbury Troll* gliding ever closer, the lighterman yelling, and Woodman asking—

"Yes!" she screamed. "Move! Move!"

Eight powerful oars thrust them out of the lighter's way, but only just, so the blood-soaked rag doll that had so recently been a man passed only feet away.

Everyone on the boat stared at the corpse, and Elf thought perhaps even the soldiers weren't hardened to such sights. Suddenly she realized she had the command here. She'd acted that way, giving orders, taking responsibility. But she knew there was more to command than that. She had to make this sit right for the men.

Wishing her hands would stop shaking, she said, "Well rowed, Woodham. Can you call to that lighterman to head back to Harrison's Wharf?"

"Right, milady. But it'll take him a while."

"No matter so long as his cargo doesn't end up on the French vessel."

As the shouted exchange began, accompanied by some lively language from the distressed lighterman, Elf turned to the soldiers. "Well done, Private Pickett. A clean shot. You doubtless saved that poor lighterman's life."

She looked closely at him for the first time, realizing he couldn't be more than twenty years old and was white with stress. At her words, however, he turned pink and bashful. " 'Tweren't nothing, milady."

"On the contrary. It was very important, and you played your part."

Woodham had finished conveying her instructions to the lighterman, so she turned back to him. "Take us back to the wharf, if you please."

And she finally felt able to slump down on a seat. Unfortunately, the release of urgency allowed fears for Fort to surge in like a river flood.

On the wharf, a coach had arrived. A doctor? Or a means of taking someone to a doctor? They wouldn't call a coach for a corpse, would they?

They probably would for the corpse of an earl.

Perhaps it hadn't been Fort who had fallen.

She was sure it was.

Perhaps he'd just tripped and fallen.

Perhaps . . .

Perhaps . . .

She knew, with an instinct beyond human comprehension, that he had fallen, had been shot, and was seriously injured.

Surely she would know equally clearly if he were dead.

She remembered at Sappho's house, with Fort bound and her brothers angry, she hadn't been sure where her deepest allegiance lay. Now she knew.

Hands clenched together before her mouth, she prayed as she'd never prayed before. Prayed for his life and another chance to bring joy into his life.

Then she saw the concerned attention of the soldiers and hastily lowered her hands, striving to appear normal. She had to play another part—that of a Malloren, cool commander of death and destruction.

Bryght waited at the stairs, alone.

He wasn't injured. She was relieved, of course, but not from her main concern.

She saw no sign of Fort or the soldiers who'd been with him. On the planks, red glinted in the sun.

Blood.

Heart racing, she leaped to her feet, desperate to be the first off the boat. As soon as the oarsmen had the vessel alongside she seized Bryght's hand and scrambled up onto the wooden jetty.

"Well done!" he said.

"Fort?" she demanded.

He sobered. "Took the ball in the leg. I don't think it's life-threatening."

All strength left Elf, and she collapsed into his arms, weeping for grief, for relief, and perhaps for sheer, bone-deep exhaustion.

She felt herself lifted and carried, but fell asleep before he found a means to take her home.

After two hours of explanation, questioning, and excuses, Rothgar emerged from the King's Drawing Room through a side entrance and asked a footman for his brother. He found Cyn under guard in a small room on a lower floor, but lounging around in reasonable comfort, drinking ale.

At Rothgar's entrance he raised his tankard. "How long do I keep my head?"

"Indefinitely, though His Majesty is still not entirely convinced. Congratulations on using your head to effect."

Cyn laughed, surging to his feet. "It was the most damnable thing, Bey! The blasted machine was sitting there, right on that big gilt table in the Drawing Room. It appears it had come with a cunning message from you, and the king had demanded it be sent straight up. His equerry tried to put him off, but wasn't about to forbid him to try the thing. The only reason the king hadn't already switched it on was that he'd sent for the queen to enjoy the treat! I got him out of there."

"Admirable military verve."

"Yes, well, with hindsight, I probably committed all kinds of lèse-majesté and, judging from his reaction, my chances of making major, never mind colonel, are decidedly dim."

"Perhaps we should convince him of your worth. Where is the diabolical device?"

"In the room next door. I insisted they put it where I could keep an eye on it."

Rothgar opened the door. The gaudy Chinese pagoda stood on a side table, its tiny figures frozen, waiting only the release of a catch to spring into lethal life.

"A pity, really," he said. "It is most cleverly made."

"Should we blow it up?"

"I gather it will blow itself up, given the opportunity. The trick will be to let it do so safely. Roll up your sleeves. We're going to carry it."

"*We* are?"

"Who else? It appears to have been carried up and down stairs without hazard. But in case, should we order others to take the risk?"

" 'Struth. If I didn't know better, I'd think you were feeling penitent."

"You think me beyond repentance?"

Cyn shook his head. "I think you're in a damned funny mood. Very well. Let's move the thing."

It was not heavy, but it was cumbersome, especially when they wished to move it with great care. Eventually, however, they could put it down outside the castle, on the grass near the river. Cyn pulled out a handkerchief to wipe sweat off his face.

Rothgar, unruffled, then summoned servants to bring old mattresses and a musket, and sent a message to the king to invite him to watch the spectacle from a distant balcony, if it so pleased him.

"Why?" Cyn asked.

"Your military advancement, of course."

As soon as the king and queen appeared and could see the pagoda, Rothgar supervised the servants as they piled the mattresses around the toy. Then, moving everyone to a distance, he handed the musket to Cyn. "I'm sure you're more of a hand with these things than I am. Try to get the ball through that gap we left."

Cyn carefully loaded the gun, then raised it, sighting down the barrel. With a click, he cocked it. His finger squeezed the trigger and with a boom and a burst of flame, the ball sped forward.

A moment later, a louder boom sent cloth and flock and pieces of gaudy metal flying in all directions.

"Damnation," said Cyn, lowering the butt to rest on the ground. "Imagine that uncovered and in closed quarters."

"Indeed," said Rothgar, and turned to the balcony. But the king and queen had already disappeared.

As servants hurried forward to take the musket and clear up the mess, he said, "The question is, would a replica of that toy be a treasured gift or send the king stark, staring mad?"

Cyn collapsed into laughter.

When they returned to the castle, they found not just their coach waiting, but a messenger from the king requesting Lord Cynric's immediate presence.

"Alas," said Rothgar. "He has remembered to have you beheaded for lèse-majesté. Do you wish to take the coach and flee the country?"

For once, Cyn did look alarmed. " 'Struth, Bey, what do you think he wants?"

"I suggest you go and find out. After all," he added benignly, "you have always claimed to want to deal with life on your own."

Chapter 15

When Elf awoke, she felt as if she'd been battered by the mighty Thames and thrown against the starlings at London Bridge. From dim memories of her dreams, she wasn't entirely sure she hadn't been.

Then she recalled tangled images of Fort sprawled bloodily over the box on which they had made love, dying because she had shot him . . .

No! She struggled for reality. That had been *Murray*, not Fort, and she hadn't fired the shot. But she'd ordered it, which came to the same thing.

Then her brain cleared completely and she remembered that Fort had, indeed, been injured. In the leg.

She forced open her gritty eyes and sat up.

A leg injury might mean anything from a little blood loss to amputation, but either way, infection and death hovered. Only last year, young Sir Francis Cornhallows had died of a trivial wound that turned septic because he would not let the surgeon clean out the bits of cloth forced into his flesh by the ball.

Her fumbling fingers found the bell rope and she tugged at it again and again, praying for Chantal to hurry.

She scrambled out of bed, easily able to imagine the arrogant Earl of Walgrave scaring away his doctors. And he had no one to gainsay him. Except her. A line of bright sunlight shot through the gap in her drawn curtains. It wasn't night yet. There might still be time to make him see reason.

Chantal burst into the room, with Chastity only a step behind.

"Milady! You are awake!"

"Elf, how do you feel?"

Elf clung to the bedpost, assailed by a fit of dizziness. "Dreadful." She could hardly speak for the dryness of her mouth. "Water. That would help."

"You need more, milady," said Chantal, and whipped away in a flash of dark skirts.

Chastity poured water from a carafe and brought it over. "I think I must echo your kind suggestion to me once. I suspect you would love a bath."

"Lud, yes." Elf drank the whole glass of water, then touched her hair. "Am I still powdered? I must look a veritable horror. But I have no time. I must go to Fort—"

Chastity pushed her gently to sit on the bed. "There is no need. He is in no danger."

Elf stared into her sister-in-law's eyes. "Has he been properly treated? Has the wound been cleaned?"

"Yes and yes. I assure you, I stood over him and bullied him just as much as you would want."

"He will recover?"

"As always, that is in God's hands. He's in pain. Fevered. But he seems to be healing."

The image of Fort in fevered pain had Elf off the bed again. "Surely it's too early to tell if he will heal. Why are you here and not there? You're his sister!"

Chastity eased her back down. "Elf, you have slept a day and a half. It's Sunday afternoon." She went to throw back the curtains, flooding the room with light, so Elf covered her aching eyes.

"A day and a half," she murmured, "and the world carried on without me. The king?"

"Is safe." Chastity refilled the glass and brought it over. "Cyn arrived in time."

"Thank God. And the stone?"

"Has been quietly returned to Westminster Abbey, with some story of it having been moved in order to repair the throne. I must confess, I wasn't aware of it being there at all. Do you believe in this idea of it conveying mystical kingship?"

Elf drank part of the water and stood again, more carefully this time. The dizziness seemed to have passed, so she moved about the room, feeling stiffness and aches in unlikely places.

That reminded her of a great many problems. She'd rather deal with the Stone of Scone. "I don't know. It didn't seem to do the Stuarts much good. They were crowned on it."

"True. Did you hear about Cyn?"

"What?" A score of horrible possibilities leaped into Elf's mind. "What happened?"

"Oh, nothing bad . . ."

But then Chantal hurried in with a coffeepot, along with a neatly peeled and divided orange and a selection of cakes. On command, she bustled off to see to the bath.

Elf eyed the elegant tray. "Ask for water, and I get a meal. Please, have some and tell me what Cyn's been up to."

Chastity picked up a piece of orange. "As for up to, he and Rothgar exploded that mechanical toy, safely outside Windsor Castle, of course. However, Cyn first had to ride hell-for-leather to warn the king. Would you believe he found him standing right by that thing, in a ferment to turn it on, and only waiting for the queen to arrive?"

"Saints save us!"

"In this case, Cyn saved us. He hustled the king out of danger with a fair degree of military brusqueness. At that point, His Majesty doubted Cyn's tale. But when he saw the thing explode into a thousand lethal bits, George summoned Cyn back, clasped him to the regal bosom, and declared him Lord Raymore!"

Elf stared at Chastity. "But why Raymore?"

Chastity was fighting to keep a straight face. "Apparently it's the name of . . . of His Majesty's favorite horse!"

They collapsed into giggles.

"And Rothgar," gasped Chastity, "would only say that Cyn shouldn't look a gift horse in the mouth! Particularly when the king accompanied the title by an estate to support the viscountcy."

"A viscountcy! That advances him over Bryght and Brand. What does Cyn think about this?"

Chastity grinned. "Of course, you know him so well. Mostly, he's embarrassed to be rewarded for merely doing his duty. He's also slightly suspicious that Rothgar somehow arranged it all. You know how he's always been about accepting support from the family."

"He carries it to extremes."

"I agree, but you know men."

Elf thought of Fort and Sappho. "I am beginning to." She turned to face her sister-in-law. "You know Fort and I were lovers."

Chastity's cheeks became a little pink. "Yes. I'm hardly one to throw stones."

"But you loved Cyn."

"True. Do you not love Fort?"

Elf turned away to look out of the window at the quiet of Marlborough Square. "Yes. It's so foolish, though, to give my heart to an impossible man."

"Perhaps all men are impossible. When I made love to Cyn, I believed marriage between us was impossible. I, too, wore disguise, though as it turned out he knew who I was. I gather Fort really didn't recognize you."

"Why would he even suspect anything so unlikely? And we spoke French nearly all the time." She turned back to Chastity. "I'm very afraid I'll be with child."

"You must have thought of it."

"After a fashion." A nervous laugh escaped, and she smothered it with her hands. "It seemed simple enough in theory. But now . . ."

Chastity became very serious. "Even if you are with child, Elf, I don't think he'll marry you."

That caused a pang, though she smothered it. "It would be unfair to expect him to. Our contract was clear."

"Contract?"

Elf waved the question away and moved restlessly around her room. "For a moment last night, I wanted Bey to force a marriage. 'Twas madness, and Fort would rather die. But surely we shouldn't just create a child and deny it its heritage . . . ?"

Chastity captured her and held her still. "Face battles when they come, not before. Advice from Cyn. Good advice."

Elf collapsed into her arms. "I suppose it is. It will be weeks before I'll know. Anything could happen by then." Including Fort's death from wound fever. Or—if he followed through on his threats and made a scandal—at the hands of one of her brothers. She wouldn't be able to stop them then.

" 'Tis a pity you didn't take some precautions," said Chastity, settling them both onto the sofa.

That reminded Elf of her last real conversation with her brothers. "Ah, yes. The whore's tricks! I assume you've been using them, since you've been married now over six months."

Chastity blushed. "Oh. Yes. Well, since we were expecting to travel to Nova Scotia, we didn't want me to give birth onboard ship, or even travel with the extra burden of a child within me."

"But how is it done?"

"A sponge soaked in vinegar is supposed to help prevent the seed taking root."

"A sponge soaked in vinegar," said Elf, puzzled. Then she added, "You mean, *inside*?"

Chastity nodded, quite red now.

"Goodness. But how does it . . . You put it there?"

"Or Cyn does." Chastity turned away to take a piece of bread from the tray. "I don't know quite what happened with you and Fort," she said, fiddling with it. "But it's not unusual for a man to touch a woman . . . there." She turned back sharply. "If they are lovers I mean!"

"Yes, I see. Goodness," said Elf again.

"It's not the word most would use. Many would call it wicked to try to avoid God's plan."

"I can't believe it would be God's plan to have a heavily pregnant woman on a naval ship crossing the ocean, never mind giving birth there. Thank you for telling me. I think we should spread this word to all women."

"Women and men do pass the word around. But it's not approved or foolproof. Nature's urge to conceive is not easily thwarted. In fact," she said ruefully, "I'm beginning to suspect that nature has overcome in my case. But don't tell Cyn. He might try to delay the journey, and I am as eager as he to see the New World."

Whether from loss again of her twin, or fear of conception, or longing for a child, tears ached around Elf's eyes. "Oh, I envy you!"

"The child or the New World?"

"The adventure of it all!"

Chastity hugged her. "If life here becomes too dull, just take sail and visit us among the forests and the Indians. We'll find you all the adventure you could want!"

"Ah, but will it be wicked enough for me?"

They shared teary smiles, both knowing that the only adventure Elf really wanted was Fort. But then Chantal came in from the adjoining dressing room.

Chastity rose. "Your bath is ready, dearest, so I'll leave you."

Elf went through to her dressing room and took a long, thoughtful bath. She counted her scrapes and bruises, but mostly fretted about the possibility of being with child. What would she do if she were?

It was all very well to think of bearing a bastard child abroad and giving it to foster parents to raise, but she would want to raise her child herself. She would want to feed it at her breast, rock it in the night, coax its first steps and words, and applaud its every little achievement.

She'd think a father would want that closeness, too. He had mentioned those two children he knew of, and that he had provided for them and kept an eye on their welfare.

Surely he'd want to do as much for a child of Elf's.

Elf knew she wanted more. She wanted them married and enjoying a child together.

What if she bore a son? He would be Fort's heir, but only if they married before the birth.

If she demanded it, her brothers would force Fort into marrying her, but she could imagine nothing worse than to tie a man for life against his will.

Oh, Lud, Chastity was right. Why fight a battle that might never arrive?

One matter could not be put aside, however. At the time, Fort's threat to make a public scandal had been serious. She'd put off telling her brothers for fear of what they would do, and now Fort was injured, perhaps he couldn't do anything. But it would be folly not to take steps to prevent disaster.

Elf rang for Chantal to wash her hair, then while it dried, she drank coffee and ate a slightly more substantial meal. Despite her long fast, however, her stomach felt too uneasy to accept much.

She hoped that wasn't an early sign of pregnancy. She thought it mainly came from anxiety about Fort. Despite Chastity's assurances, she desperately wanted to race over to see for herself that he wasn't at death's door. She wanted to wipe his brow and feed him nourishing broth.

He'd probably spit it right back in her face.

There had been that moment about shooting the bridge, though, when he might have been concerned for her.

She grimaced. It was so easy to delude oneself about such things. Now her hair was dry she must face more immediate problems.

She summoned Chantal to perform her usual magic, and soon Lady Elfled Malloren was ready to face the world, hair shining and neatly arranged under a lace cap, dressed in corset and hoops under cream lawn sprigged with forget-me-nots, and discreetly adorned with pearls. A glance in the mirror told her that no outward trace of wanton Lisette survived.

Then she realized she was dressed exactly as she had been when she'd waved good-bye to Cyn and the madness had all begun. Yet now, this suitable appearance felt like a costume, a costume even more absurd than Lisette's scarlet domino.

Who was Elf Malloren now? Perhaps she had better venture out and answer that question.

From a footman, she learned that Cyn and Chastity were in the garden while Bryght and Rothgar were in the office.

After a moment's thought, she headed for the latter, entering by the private side door that bypassed the busy clerks.

Rothgar and Bryght were working at the same desk, poring over papers that seemed unlikely to have anything to do with her adventures. So soon did the ripples of the explosion fade.

Both looked up and rose, showing no sign of anger or condemnation. She knew her cheeks were red, however, and just hoped they weren't flaming.

"I hope I'm not interrupting."

"Nothing important," said Rothgar, taking her hand and leading her to a chair. "You look much improved."

"Thank you. I gather I've slept the clock around."

"I think you needed it. Though we had to fight to stop Cyn sending for every doctor in town."

"Considering the worry I've felt over him for years, it's only fair that he fret over me at least once."

"My sentiment entirely. So, are you completely recovered?"

Elf knew she had turned a deeper red. A broken maidenhead did not mend. "I think so. Some bruises and scrapes, that's all. Chastity told me some of the events. Have the Scots all been rounded up?"

"As best we can tell." Rothgar resumed his seat behind the ornate desk. Bryght, more restlessly, perched on the edge.

"Murray died on the lighter," Rothgar continued. "You did well there, by the way. And one of his men was shot on the wharf. We think another was the dead man left at Walgrave's. A fourth corpse was found at the Peahen Inn clutching a declaration of loyalty to the Stuart cause. We assume he committed suicide when he realized the game was up. They seemed to be the only four deep in the plot, though they hired others as needed. The men who took the toy to Windsor, for example, were dupes. They believed they had truly been hired by me to deliver the gift. Since the king wants the whole affair kept quiet, they are not even aware of the true nature of their act."

"And Fort's part in it? Does the king understand that?"

Rothgar's eyes were all too understanding. "I think so. When I left, George was annoyed with Grenville for keeping him in the dark, and becoming a little suspicious of Bute. Not of his loyalty, but of his wisdom and judgment. That is as well."

Elf frowned at her brother. "You don't have political ambitions, do you?"

"Why the horror? Is it not the pathway paved with gold? But no," he said with a smile, "I have not. I have enough to do managing my tumultuous family. But I will not stand by and watch my country in the hands of fools. George is sound enough, but not under Bute's guidance. I suspect Grenville will take his place, and I reserve judgment. Of course, if Cyn had followed the path I laid down for him, he might one day have led the country."

"Heaven forbid!" declared Elf, knowing her brother was teasing, though that could well have been his plan once. She glanced at her other brother, the one chiefly responsible for the financial management of the family's affairs. "Now Bryght, perhaps. He might enjoy being First Lord of the Treasury."

"Oh no," Bryght said raising a hand. "Government

finances are far too chaotic for me. I'd be in Bedlam in a month. Speaking of which, we wondered if you'd care to take some of the burden off me—"

"Speaking of Bedlam or business?" Rothgar queried.

Bryght gave him a look. "Business." He turned back to Elf. "I admit to finding it hard to keep track of everything now that I want to spend more time down at Candleford. The silk trade, for example, could probably benefit from your expertise."

After a second, Elf's vision blurred, and a prickling ache all around her face warned of tears. Not only were her brothers not reproaching her for her wanton behavior, but they had detected part of the cause of her restlessness and were trying to help.

Bryght cleared his throat uneasily. "Of course, if it's too much for you . . ."

Rothgar just watched her.

"You are the best brothers in the world." She pulled a handkerchief out of her pocket and blew her nose. "I would love to try. But—"

"But?" asked Rothgar.

"What if I were to marry?"

The silence carried for a few heartbeats, but then he said, "Bryght has married. And though it has definitely affected the amount of time and attention he seems willing to apply to our aggrandizement, it has not proved ruinous yet."

Elf hesitantly asked, "What if I married Fort?"

"Whomever you marry, we would ensure that your marriage contract safeguarded your property and economic freedom."

Typically, her brother gave no indication of his true feelings on the matter. It was an unlikely prospect anyway, and a weakness in her to have mentioned it. It reminded her of other problems, however, ones that had made her seek this interview. "He threatened to make a scandal, Bey. To tell the world about us. He's capable of it. Articles in the news sheets. Pictures in the print shops . . ."

Rothgar did not seem alarmed. "Words spoken *in extremis,* I think, but we have people in his house who will alert us to any such actions."

"That doesn't seem right."

"But very practical. At the moment, of course, he is too ill to carry out any plan of revenge."

That swung Elf back to her major concern and brought her to her feet. "Oh dear. I wish—"

"No," said both brothers in unison.

"Elf," said Bryght, "it really would not help his recovery for you to try to nurse him. Trust us."

She glared at both of them. "Men are impossible!"

Rothgar said, "We are merely suggesting that you give him a few days to recover his strength before assaulting him again. It's only fair play, my dear."

"I have never *assaulted* him!" But there were mental as well as physical attacks, so perhaps her words weren't true.

She sat down, settling her pale, flowery skirts. "Very well, I will take your advice. But as soon as the battle will be fair, I intend to discuss this all with him. I will not let him be foolish."

Bryght looked skeptical, but just pushed a couple of ledgers over to the edge of the desk closest to her. "Let us distract you with silk. One of the main centers for silk weaving here is Spitalfields . . ."

Elf emerged from the office an hour later, head positively spinning with information and new ideas. From a life of fashion, and from experience running Rothgar's houses, she already knew about types of silk, the durability of different weaves, and possible trends in taste.

Now she had some idea of the state of change in the fabric industry and the money to be won or lost on decisions made about it.

After running through the family's existing involvement in the trade, she'd suggested that her role be expanded to include the management of other materials. Nowadays, there were so many cottons and cotton blends, so many new methods of printing and pattern weaving, that the whole industry could change.

She was particularly intrigued by improved weaving techniques, even though Bryght knew very little about them. She'd never given much thought to how patterns were made in woven cloth, but she could see the advantage in investing in improvements if they were practicable. It was surely worthwhile to find ways to make pretty, sturdy cloth cheaply enough for everyone to afford.

Though tempted to go to her room and read the two books Bryght had given her, she knew that would only put off an encounter with an anxious twin. The footman in the hall told her Cyn and Chastity were now in the morning room, so she gave him the books and headed there.

She found them playing cards, but Cyn leaped to his feet as soon as she entered. "I was looking for you!"

I'm sure you were, she thought, and tried to distract him. "I was with Rothgar and Bryght. They've given me a job."

"A job?"

"A part in the business."

His frown eased into a smile. "And you're glowing like a lamp. Poor Elf, has it been unbearably dull?"

Guilt. She could read it in his concerned eyes. "Not unbearable, no," she said gently. "I think it's just that a life of leisure palls eventually."

"And leads into disaster."

"I hope it won't come to that." Elf turned to Chastity. "Could I ask you, please, to visit Fort frequently and tell me how he goes on?"

Chastity rose, taking the hint. "Of course. In fact, I'll go round now and fluff his pillows." With a mischievous twinkle, she added, "I am so glad our sailing was delayed. I would have hated to have learned of all this months after it happened!"

She left, and Elf and Cyn looked at each other.

"I'm feeling guilty on a number of counts," he said.

"I know you are. Please don't."

"But if I'd not left to suit myself, I'd have been here with you."

"I doubt it. You'd have been tied to Bey's plan, studying law and entering politics."

"I'd have been close by," he said impatiently.

"And miserable."

"Instead, I left you miserable."

Elf dismissed his concerns with a wave of her hand. "Have I appeared cast down? It is only recently that I began to feel restless."

He wasn't convinced, and took a sharp-stepped walk around the room. "Very well, then, what about this? If I hadn't so absolutely rejected Bey's plans for me, he might have thought of giving you a role to play."

Refusing to fidget with him, Elf sat down on a sofa. "That's nonsense. I'm a woman, so he never thought of it. He thought I'd be like Hilda and settle early into marriage. I suspect it's still a bit of a struggle for him, but I would never accuse any of my brothers of inflexibility of mind."

Cyn came to a stop, facing her. "All right. What about Walgrave, then? His behavior to his sisters was *fueled* by inflexibility. Would you want to trust yourself to him?"

She gripped her hands together, knowing his feelings sprang more from Chastity's sufferings than from any cause of her own. "Don't hate him, Cyn. Please. And don't try to kill him. Our case is really no worse than yours."

"You forget. I saw the way he treated you at Sappho's."

"He was still shocked. And it all goes back to when he killed his father. That is not an easy thing to live with, especially when he wanted to do away with him. Cyn, his father was a monster. Far worse than we thought . . . That, of course, is just between us two."

"Of course." Cyn sat opposite her, somber now. "I do know something of the earl. Chastity's told me. It's hard to imagine what it must have been like to have such a father. He was a tyrant to his daughters. I suppose he was as bad to his sons."

"Worse. He used to whip him before the servants to break his pride . . ." She bit her lips to stop their quivering. "It must be hard to shake childhood terrors, even when grown."

"True. And none of us thought about how killing his own father had to affect him. Even Chastity didn't realize. Of course, she was distracted by the fact we were free to marry. We've been talking about it, this past day. There we were, practically dancing on the corpse and not giving a thought as to how Fort might feel. It was cruel, and damnably careless. But the damage is done. He hates all Mallorens, and always will."

She feared Cyn might be right, but said, "Time might heal. We'll never know if you kill him."

"I gather I still need your permission." He grimaced. "I do feel for the man but I couldn't stand by and see him try to hurt you."

"Then thank heavens you'll be on the seas before he's fit to fight. But I don't think he'll try to hit out at me once he cools down. I hurt him. He'd grown a shell to protect himself, and I chiseled at it until it cracked."

"And now he'll be growing it back, thicker than ever. People don't change that much, Elf. Why the devil did you have to choose *him* to lose all sense with?" He was back to pacing the room.

"Is it surprising our tastes are the same?"

He swung to face her. "There's no similarity between him and Chastity!"

"Come, come. There must be. Cyn, my body reacted to him before I found there was a man there I could like. Wasn't it the same with you?"

He tried to object, but then shrugged. "Perhaps. Chastity certainly presented a formidable appearance when I first met her, and yet she fascinated me. She even tied me to a bed, which I gather mirrors your adventure."

Elf didn't like the fact that her brothers had been piecing together her story, and yet she supposed it was natural. "There are many similarities. Chastity wore disguise, as I did. She didn't want you to know she was the notorious Chastity Ware, for fear you'd recoil in disgust. I didn't want Fort to know my identity for the same reason."

"The difference being that Chastity was pure and honorable and could be proved to be so. You are still a Malloren and always will be. No matter what happened between you, Elf, he will reject you for that reason."

"I suppose that's the male code!"

"No, it's the nature of the beast. In this case, the beast's nature is as inflexible as his damned father's."

"No! No, you're wrong about that. He's trying to fill his father's shoes, and he's built a shell around his feelings." She had to make him see, so she deliberately used an emotional weapon. "Beneath the shell is a person who can be kind, a person like Chastity who can laugh and give laughter if freed to do so."

It registered. When Cyn had first met his wife, she'd been hard and brittle because of her father's cruelty. "Perhaps you're right," he said gently, "but can he be that person with Elf Malloren?"

He meant to be kind, but it hurt like a blow. "I don't know."

"Will you promise me something?"

"If I can."

"If he can't find the whole person with you, if he can't be joyous in season with Elf Malloren, don't marry him out of pity."

She laughed bitterly. "He's not likely to ask me."

"He might come to his senses and beg on his knees."

The prospect both appealed and terrified. "Wouldn't that show—"

"No. It would only show that he knows he's wounded. Not that he's healed."

"Perhaps I could heal him . . ."

He shook his head. "Promise me, Elf. Promise or I'm not leaving these shores."

She didn't want to. She wanted to be free to marry

Fort on the most atrocious, demeaning terms if that was all she could have. But she steeled herself because she knew Cyn was right.

"I promise. It will hurt dreadfully, but I won't marry Fort unless it can be with true love and joy. It's mostly for his sake, though. He deserves to find someone with whom he can be joyous in season."

Chapter 16

Chastity entered Walgrave House with the usual shiver of distaste. It would always remind her of her hated father; of the scandal, the whippings, and the horrible feeling of having the hair shaved off her head. This time last year, it had reached halfway down her back in a thick mass of golden-brown curls. When she'd met Cyn, it had been little more than a stubble. Even now it only brushed her shoulders.

None of that disaster had really been Fort's fault, though. He'd been with the group who had caught her with Vernham in her bed. Why should he or anyone suspect it to be a contrivance to force her into an unwanted marriage, a contrivance abetted by her own father? During her suffering, when her father used his rights as an outraged parent to try to break her spirit, she had never imagined that Fort would ride to her rescue.

They had all learned in the nursery never to cross the will of the mighty Incorruptible.

Fort felt guilty about it, though, and she didn't know whether that was good or bad. It certainly complicated his attitude toward the Mallorens.

Mutual support lay at the root of the code that Rothgar had instilled into his half-siblings. Even Fort's brief stay at Rothgar Abbey must have shown him that, making stark the contrast with the Ware family life.

All this lay in the past, though, and brooding over it could do no good. If only she could convince her brother of that.

At Fort's bedroom door, she knocked and was admitted by his valet, the rather strange Dingwall. She had no idea why Fort kept him on. At least the man slithered away, leaving her alone with her bed-bound brother and another visitor.

"Jack Travers," Fort said, quite strongly, though he still looked feverish. "Jack, do you know my sister Chastity? Lady Cynric Malloren."

Chastity didn't miss the momentary startled pause before Travers kissed her outstretched hand. Though an explanation had been spread through society, and the queen and king had received her at St. James a number of times, there were still some who remembered Chastity Ware as the most flaming scandal of the decade.

"Lady Raymore, actually," she said with a grin. "The king gave Cyn a title for—" She bit her lip, remembering that the attempt on the king's life was to be kept as secret as possible.

"Oh, don't worry, chatterbox," said Fort. "Jack already has a good part of the story. It's whirling through town like wildfire. It won't appear in the news sheets, of course, and will grow stranger with every telling. So, what's this about a title?"

She ignored the bitter edge tingeing his voice, and leaned down to kiss his forehead. "The king gave Cyn a viscountcy for saving his life. I didn't tell you earlier for fear of sending you into a relapse."

He pulled a face at her words, but only said, "I might have known Rothgar would turn everything to his advantage."

"Then he should have gained himself a dukedom, don't you think? And he had nothing to do with it."

"Rothgar?" Fort laughed sharply. "He never does an unpremeditated act. He sent Cyn on that mission. He could have released me, and sent me."

"Heavens above! Never say you pine for a dukedom!"

He flushed. "Of course I don't. I'm merely pointing out that everyone knows what happens to people who bring the monarch good news."

"I would hardly call news that he was standing by a lethal object *good*. And isn't there also a saying about bearers of *bad* news?"

Fort leaned back into his pillows. "We're squabbling, sister dear. Very bad form before a guest."

Travers bowed. "In fact, I must leave, Fort, so you can squabble in peace. Know how it is. I have sisters, too. My lady."

With that, he left the room.

Chastity didn't mention Travers's obvious uneasiness in her presence, but Fort said, "I'm sorry."

"Oh, don't start that again," she said briskly, taking a chair by his bed. "None of what happened was your fault, and if you'd tried to interfere, Father would have destroyed you. After all, you weren't his only hope of dynastic succession. There's Victor."

"I should have done something."

"What? And looking back, I'm not sure I would want any of it changed. If Vernham hadn't slipped into my bed, I would never have met Cyn."

"The fount of all blessings."

Chastity stared at her tight-jawed brother. "You can't be jealous of Cyn!"

"Jealous? That would suggest tastes both illegal and immoral. But I wish *I* had rescued and supported you."

Chastity took his hand, wishing she knew a way to straighten all this out. In the end, it seemed, Fort was the only one left suffering. "Once you realized the truth, you did help me."

"As I remember, I tried to throttle you when I found you were Malloren's lover."

"An understandable reaction to shock. Now, how are you feeling?"

He accepted the change of subject. "Better than yesterday. Which isn't saying much. My leg feels twice its size, and under that damned cage, I can't see a thing." A huge wicker cage covered his lower body, keeping the bed covers off the wound.

"The doctor says it's healing properly."

"Damn sawbones." He looked up at her. "Chas, can I ask you to look at the wound? I know it's unpleasant . . ."

She could have cried with joy to be asked. They'd not been close before the scandal, and ever since, her place in the Malloren family had been a barrier.

"Don't be silly." She was already rising and stripping off her gloves. "Of course I will. Do you think it infected?"

"I don't know. I just don't trust them all. They never stop smiling. They say if I move too much I could start the bleeding again, but perhaps they just don't want me to know—"

She gripped his shoulder. "I'll look, and I'll tell you the truth."

She peeled the blankets off the cage, pushing him back down on his pillows when he tried to rise to see. "Trust me. I am your eyes." Then she lifted the wicker cage from his heavily bandaged leg. "I'm not sure if I should disturb all these dressings, though."

"Do it. We can always get someone back to dress it again."

"Are you sure? I can tell there's no sign of infection in the uncovered part of the leg."

"Don't bother then . . ."

But she could tell he was just trying to let her escape a task she didn't want. He must be fretting himself to death.

"It's no bother. I'll have to move your leg a bit to unbandage it, though."

"Just do it." He had flung an arm over his eyes.

Resolving to stop at any sign of bleeding, she gently raised his leg and began to unwind the bandages. "It might be stuck. I'm not going to rip it off. Am I hurting you?"

"No."

She suspected he was lying, but his need to know the truth seemed greater than any pain. She prayed silently that he was wrong, and that the wound was healing. What if he had to lose the leg?

The bandages were not stuck, and easily came off a final pad of cloth. "I don't suppose these are the original dressings anyway."

"Bryght Malloren bandaged me on the wharf. The doctors ripped those off."

"Ouch."

"Ouch, indeed. They were in a hurry to extract the ball. It was deep, they said, and came damned close to the bone. They've been under there twice since. So, how does it look?"

She carefully raised the pad to expose a jagged, stitched wound.

"You'll have an interesting scar," she said, but smiled at him. "Still red and puffy, but I see no sign of trouble."

He leaned up. "Get a mirror and show me."

Chastity straightened and looked at him. "Why do I feel you are not the ideal patient?" But she heaved an oval, gilt-edged mirror off the wall and held it so he could inspect his leg.

After a moment, his expression lightened. "It doesn't look too bad, does it? It feels worse. As if it's swollen to twice its size and oozing pus." He smiled for her, almost the lighthearted open smile she remembered from before disaster. "Thank you."

Chastity replaced the mirror, taking the chance to steady her lips. Fort deserved happiness, and she thought perhaps it lay within his grasp with Elf, and yet she knew the barriers between them might be too strong to be breached.

Steady smile in place, she returned to replace the bandages. "Do they think you will limp?"

"They say not, but I don't trust their unctuous reassurances. I'll be grateful, I suppose, to be alive and mobile. Perhaps I'll even be grateful not to be a suitable candidate for a duel."

Chastity was straightening the covers over the cage. "I would be very cross if you fought Cyn, you know."

"Have done. A sickbed gives plenty of time to think and I've been thinking. If the whole mess was anyone's fault, it was Father's, and he's beyond reach. I'm through with Mallorens. Instead, I'm going to use my energies and powers to put right what Father put wrong."

Chastity listened approvingly to plans to improve conditions on the earldom's land, and to support worthy causes in parliament. All the time, however, her heart ached for Elf, who was surely included in that wholesale rejection of Mallorens. It ached for Fort, too, who might never know the kind of love she had found.

If she could see any point, she might even try to delay their departure from England to help sort out the tangle, but she had little hope.

They moved on to chat of general subjects, but she noticed that he never mentioned Elf or showed any curiosity about her safety.

Perhaps he'd received a report.

Perhaps he really didn't care.

Dingwall returned, a doctor in tow. A smiling, bowing sawbones whom she would suspect if she were the patient. But Fort's treatment had clearly been effective, so she made no objection. She rose and took her brother's hand to say good-bye.

It wasn't until she opened the door that he broke.

"Lady Elfled," he said, "I assume she is well?"

"Oh, perfectly," said Chastity, and left with a grain of hope in her heart.

Elf welcomed the excellent report of Fort's progress, though she'd have preferred a message asking her to call. She knew just how likely *that* was. To preserve her sanity, she set about other business, the first being to call on Amanda and explain everything.

Her friend listened, mouth loose with shock. "Lud, Elf. Such things could only happen to you!"

"They happened to him, too," Elf pointed out, helping herself to more tea.

"You know what I mean. You are every bit as rash as you were as a child, and every bit as fortunate to escape with your life!"

Elf sighed. "I don't feel fortunate." She stirred a lump of sugar into her cup. "Except in my family, of course."

Amanda actually paled. "You mean they know? *All?"*

"Of course." Elf shrugged. "The foolish man insisted on making it clear to Cyn and Rothgar's face."

"Perish me! And . . . ?"

"And, what?" asked Elf in spurious innocence.

"And what happened?"

"They've given me a job."

"No! Don't tell me Rothgar's set you to scrubbing in the kitchen."

Elf burst out laughing. "Amanda! Of course not. I'm in charge of part of the family affairs. Would you care to come with me to inspect silk warehouses?"

"Silk. How delightful!" Amanda leaped to her feet but paused. "You mean that's all that happened? You plunge into mad adventure, end up in danger and scandal, and you're put in charge of buying the family's silk?"

"That's all." Elf didn't bother to try to explain the extent of the Malloren enterprises.

"Well, I think it abysmally unfair! I, quite the innocent party, received a stern lecture on folly."

"I'm sorry for embroiling you, then."

"Oh, don't be." Amanda broke into a smile. "Looked back on, we had quite a splendid adventure, didn't we?"

"Yes," said Elf with a sigh. "We most certainly did."

Some hours later, after a tour of London's principal silk warehouses, Elf returned Amanda to her house and ordered her carriage to continue to Sappho's house.

She made a more decorous entrance this time. Her footman knocked at the front door, and being informed that the mistress of the house would receive Lady Elfled, came back to hand her out.

A maid led her upstairs, but not to the drawing room. Elf was taken to a disorderly study strewn with books and papers and flooded with the light of three long windows.

Sappho, in a loose gown, her hair in a long braid,

came over to take Elf's hands. "My dear! You look much improved."

Elf smiled, surprised at the burst of affection she felt for this strange woman. "I doubt that was hard to achieve. I was a veritable wreck when I invaded here last."

Sappho drew her to a chaise, pushing off a drift of scribbled papers to make room. "I'm so pleased you felt able to come to me."

"I might not have even dreamed of it if Amanda hadn't said I was with you."

"But still, you felt able to come. And Lord Walgrave? How is he? I hear he was wounded."

Elf caught the question in the statement. "Lud, *I* didn't shoot him!" She gave a simple version of the Scots plot and its ending.

"Well," said Sappho, leaning back in the chaise, "I think I am quite cross with you both. No one thought to invite me on this adventure. I'd have liked to have been on that barge in the river."

Elf chuckled. "It never occurred to me that you would wish it. I apologize."

Sappho waved an elegant hand, heavy with unusual rings. Elf wondered for a moment whether she could take to wearing loose clothes in rich oriental fabrics and heavy rings in fantastic shapes.

"I don't think so," said Sappho gently, as if she could read her mind.

Elf knew she was blushing. "I suppose not. I have neither the height nor the looks for it. I do wish, though, that I had a style of my own." She spread her pale green skirts with dissatisfied fingers. "Whenever I choose clothes to suit my own taste everyone swoons with horror, so I end up wearing things like this."

Sappho tilted her head, studying her. "Very often, you know, we think an outward change will bring about an inner change that we desire."

"You mean—?" Elf stared at her. "Are you suggesting that my taste for bright materials is because I want my life to be brighter? That seems . . ."

"Strange? Indeed it does, but there is truth in it. And there is truth in the deed, as well. I suspect that your adventures were not carried out in cream and pale green."

Elf shifted uneasily, thinking about her scarlet outfit and her lacy stockings, and the moods she'd been in when she'd bought them. "But what does that mean? It would mortify my friends and family if I were to go about in gaudy clothes."

"Yes, we have to balance our needs with those of the people we love. What outfit would you want now, today?"

Elf pondered it, then laughed. "I don't seem to care. I've just gone through four silk warehouses with Amanda. She wanted to buy up the entire stock and I hardly felt any interest at all. Certainly none in the purples and scarlets."

"Perhaps you are different inside, then?"

Elf tested it. "Perhaps I am." She was not content, for Fort was a nugget of frustration deep within, but she recognized a new steadiness in herself, a degree of calm.

"But still," said Sappho, "what outfit would you choose today?"

Elf raised her skirt to study it. It was a corded green poplin with a gray stripe so narrow as to be hardly visible and tiny leaves worked between. "I'm tired of these little motifs," she said. "They're . . . timid. They're also girlish, and I'm no longer a girl."

Sappho just nodded, encouraging her to continue.

Elf leaned back and closed her eyes. "I suppose I've become afraid to choose boldly, and my maid feels it safest to be—well—safe." She tried to let her mind summon a gown that would please her but after a while she opened her eyes and shrugged. "Perhaps I just don't have the talent for it."

"And yet your brother says you choose materials for the houses with great skill and judgment."

She must mean Rothgar. Elf felt a strong temptation to ask Sappho about Rothgar and his place in her life, but she managed to restrain herself. "That doesn't seem so set with pitfalls."

"It proves, however, that you can choose wisely in the right circumstances."

"I suppose it does. I shall just have to think of myself as a tester bed and decide what hanging will do best!"

Laughing, both women rose, and Elf turned to Sappho. "I do thank you, for everything."

"I help women," the poet said simply. "But you are more like a sister to me."

Now Elf felt compelled to ask. "Because of Rothgar?"

"Of course."

It seemed as if Sappho was inviting the question, so she asked it. "What is he to you?"

"Certainly not my protector," said Sappho with a smile. "What we have is not easily named, but very precious. We are close friends. Sometimes we are lovers, but it is an extension of friendship, not the force that ties you and Walgrave together."

"Ties us together!" Elf exclaimed with a bitter laugh. "Pushes us apart, more likely."

"No, that is another force. But this is beginning to sound like a lecture at the Royal Society."

Elf chuckled and pulled on her gloves, a final question niggling at her. In the end, she asked it. "You will not marry him?"

"It bothers you?"

"No," said Elf, though it wasn't entirely true.

"We will not marry," said Sappho, leading her downstairs. "Our bond is strong, but not the bond that would make a good marriage."

Elf paused at the door, for the question of good marriages interested her greatly. "Why not?"

"Think, Elf." Sappho gestured around her home with one of those strangely beringed hands. "I am content in my place, as he is in his. Neither of us would be happy in the other's. What we have, we can have without marriage and without loss."

"Does marriage involve loss, then?"

"Oh yes, and should only be undertaken if the gain is equal to or exceeds the loss." Then she laughed. "I am sounding scientific again, and love does not blend with science. Please call again, Elf, whenever you wish."

"I will. Thank you."

Elf returned to her carriage, head full of yet more new and challenging thoughts. Perhaps she'd be put out of her misery by her head simply exploding.

As soon as she arrived home, she summoned Chantal and conducted a thorough review of her wardrobe. Yes, definitely. The garments were pretty, but dull and safe except for the few odd outfits purchased in one of her fits of rebellion.

And "odd" certainly described them.

She fingered a gown in a vivid print of tigers. As a fabric it was rather splendid, but both the mantua maker and Chantal had been right to protest that it wouldn't make a good gown. Perhaps, she thought, she'd just been in a mood to snarl at the world.

She came across a gown of sulfur yellow and winced. Heaven knows what inner turmoil had prompted that. She'd certainly never worn it.

There weren't actually many disasters left, because last year when Chastity had turned up in rags, Chantal had taken the opportunity to get rid of most of Elf's nightmares. Elf still pined a little for the raspberry silk, but Chastity looked magnificent in it and it didn't suit her own coloring at all.

She gave Chantal permission to dispose of anything she wished and the maid almost wept with joy. Perhaps soon she would find the courage to order new gowns entirely to her taste and see just what resulted.

It would be something else to distract her mind and pass the days until Fort was well enough for her to assault him yet again.

Chapter 17

Patience was definitely not one of Elf's virtues, and despite regular reports from Chastity, she had to fight every day not to invade Fort's house and force herself into his presence. Even if he cursed and threw things or glared at her with icy disdain, she still would see him. She would be able to reassure herself about his health with her own eyes.

And they had been able to talk once, when she was just Lisette. Why could they not talk now and find a way out of their situation?

Sometimes she felt it would be easy if they were only face-to-face, but then she would note that Chastity did not encourage her. That gave her strength to stay away. If their next meeting would be conducted with the noise and smoke of open warfare, she must surely wait until he could face her on his feet.

Some days she weakened and wrote letters to him. Thus far, she had found the resolution to destroy them unsent.

Every night, however, lonely in her bed, she was tormented by a thought. Could she have found the one man she would love intensely and forever, only to be barred from him by family history?

Romeo and Juliet seemed truly to be the story, and it was depressingly likely that the end be sad.

She'd fight, though. She'd fight for happiness. But not, unfortunately, until he was on his feet.

To keep her sanity, she flung herself into work, new

and old. Running Rothgar's various households took some of the day, as did her work for the business.

In addition, she pursued her idea about self-defense. Soon she and Chastity were quite skilled with a pistol. Rothgar had made no objection, and had even commissioned a gunsmith to design weapons suited to their smaller hands, including tiny ones able to be safely carried in a pocket.

He'd dissuaded them from learning swordplay, however.

"It's a dying art, Elf, only of use in duello. You are unlikely to be challenged to a duel."

"Perhaps I'd like to challenge someone."

The look in his eye told her that he knew whom she had in mind. "In that case, choose pistols. It evens out strength and reach. For general use, however, you may want to consider a knife, since you seem to favor them as evening ornament."

So another adviser appeared, this time Hunot, a taciturn black man who taught interesting ways to kill and maim with a short blade. Cyn took an interest in these lessons, and soon they were all developing a good eye for a throwing knife.

One day, having sent her knife quivering into the heart of the man-sized target set up in a spare bedroom, Elf heard applause and turned to see Rothgar clapping, smiling slightly.

"Do you want to try?" she asked.

He held out a hand, and she placed a knife in it. In moments, it *thunked* beside hers. "How do you think I knew about Hunot, my dear? I like to be as well-armed as possible without unsightly bulges. Cyn has only missed these skills by taking himself off into the crude military world."

Cyn laughed. "I'll take you on. Cannons at twenty paces."

Rothgar bowed slightly. "I regret that I must decline. Elf, papers have arrived from Lyons."

So Elf hurried off to the other matter that kept her days crowded—her part in the Malloren affairs.

She was beginning to understand the excitement Bryght found in business affairs. Cyn considered it dull stuff. He needed open air and physical activity. Rothgar, she thought, saw trade and finance as a means to an end—power and security for his family. But Bryght, and now she, saw it as a challenge, as a great game.

Bryght had been a gamester in his day, and found the same thrill in business. Elf had never been much enthralled by the roll of a die or the turn of a card, but placing money on a likely invention or sending out ships in search of profit—that could excite her.

And knowledge.

Knowledge in itself was a delight.

Now she knew the way silk varied according to country of origin and the way it was processed. She knew about throwing and doubling, and the full meaning of denier. She had visited the silk weavers in Spitalfields and watched and listened, learning about different qualities and finishes.

In one of these discussions, she had picked up the name of a certain Jacques de Vaucanson in France. He, apparently, had already developed the improved method of weaving used in Spitalfields. He was said to be working on other projects.

A servant of the Mallorens was already in France investigating Monsieur Vaucanson and the potential for investment.

She listened, too, as Rothgar talked about legal and Parliamentary situations. Plans were afoot for Britain to ban the import of finished silk. If that came to pass, silk weaving would boom. If it didn't, expanded production facilities could lie idle.

After fretful consideration, she made her first significant decision, and recommended that money be spent to set up a small workshop in Norwich for some of the Spitalfields silk weavers who wished to leave London.

She found it rather alarming when Rothgar didn't hesitate to authorize the funds, and wished Bryght were still in town to give a second opinion.

"Don't furrow your brow," said Rothgar. "I think you've neglected one lesson. In this game, no one expects to win every time. Some of your decisions will be disastrous. You must take the long view."

"I find that hard. It's my nature to tread cautiously."

They were in the office, though he was dressed in courtly magnificence, ready to attend a royal levee. "I don't think so, my dear. You have learned to be careful so as not to endanger others. Shall I admit that perhaps I overreacted to young Scottsdale?"

He must have spent time going over the past, seeking flaws in his management of the family. She took his beringed hand. "Bey, you are not responsible for everything that happens to us. Some of our problems we create for ourselves."

A smile twitched his lips. "And some of my decisions will be disastrous. I should take my own advice, yes?"

"Yes," she said, returning the smile. Then she released his hand and sobered. "Speaking of disasters, Chastity says Fort will soon be out of his bed."

"A disaster, is it?"

"You know what I mean." She turned to pick up the papers relating to Norwich, nervously tidying them into a pile. "I am not going to let him slip away without effort."

"I would be disappointed if you did."

She turned to look at him. "You won't mind?"

"You dragging him into the family by the hair? I will survive. Now, I must off to St. James or George will grow anxious. Really, nurturing kingship is far more exhausting than dealing with troublesome twins."

The door closed gently behind him, and Elf smiled, counting her blessings, as she did every day.

Thought of blessings suddenly reminded her of the old woman down near the docks. She'd never come for help, but now it occurred to Elf that perhaps she was afraid to. Or it could be a daunting journey to cross London without chair or carriage.

Elf went to give the documents to Grainger, who was

still rather distant with her, then ordered her coach. When she encountered Chastity, she invited her along on the trip down to Wapping. Soon they were on their way, escorted by two armed footmen in addition to the coachman. Elf was past being foolish about these things.

The area had not changed, and the grand coach brought out a small army of gawkers, but again no one begged, and the people looked reasonably fed and clothed. Elf, however, was in search of the less fortunate.

She halted the carriage on the edge of the charred wasteland. Scavengers still picked over it, but today they seemed to be children searching more in play than desperation. Elf called for the door to be opened and descended, skirts raised clear of the rubble. She made her way toward one of the children, who looked up, startled and wary.

"Don't be afraid," Elf said. "I'm just looking for an old woman I met here. Dibby Cutlow, she said her name was. Do you know her?"

The girl, who must have been about eight, nodded.

"Do you know where she lives?"

Again, the girl nodded.

"If you bring her here, I'll give you a penny."

Eyes suddenly narrowed in suspicion. "Show me."

Elf dug through the slit in her outer skirt to find a penny in her pocket, then showed it to the child.

"Right then." The girl flew off over the uneven ground like a nimble sheep.

Elf watched her go—young, strong, and healthy—and wondered just who had decided that females were frail. As children, boys and girls were as active and strong as they were allowed to be. Women surely could be trained for many more jobs than were currently thought suitable, and thus be less likely to fall into poverty or prostitution.

She must add that to her inquiries and revolutions.

To think that a few weeks ago she had been restless and bored. Now there weren't enough hours in the day for all she wanted to accomplish. She threaded her way back to the coach and ordered it moved in the direction the child had taken, hoping to shorten the old woman's walk.

Chastity was studying the broken-down tavern. "Is that where you were held?"

"Yes. In the cellar. Isn't it strange how one can think fondly of such a decrepit location."

"I have fond memories of a dusty attic, myself."

They shared a smile, and Elf said, "Does the feeling dull with time?"

"Which feeling are you referring to?"

"The need to be-with, I suppose."

"I think it must, or we'd all live as if shackled together. But I think part of the easing comes from security. If I wasn't sure Cyn would be there for me, I would be more inclined to cling."

"Oh, for the chance to cling!" Elf smiled at her desperate state. "I spend time, you know, wondering if I could have done anything differently. Better. I was wild and foolish to create Lisette Belhardi. But without her, I would never have met the real Fort."

"Are you sure you know the real Fort?" Chastity turned to study her.

"Are you, too, going to try to warn me off?"

"No, not that. But it's easy to see our beloved through a veil of illusion. I remember you laughing when I described Cyn as sensitive."

"It was a startling concept. But I suppose he is, for a man."

"Indeed. But he is also ruthlessly practical, and tough as boiled leather, which I should have known a soldier has to be."

"Does it bother you?"

"Not now, but it takes time to learn all dimensions of a person. Fort is his father's son."

"Fort is not at all like the old earl!"

"Yes, he is. And he knows it, which is one of the things that galls him. He's proud to a fault, hates to admit to any error, and believes in his divine right to do as he pleases."

"You can't expect a Malloren to quibble at the latter."

Chastity shrugged. "I'm just warning you to plan your assault on the real man, not on a memory that lingers from here. Is that your old woman?"

Elf turned to see Dibby Cutlow hobbling down a rutted lane.

She seemed in slightly better form, and Elf realized she wore new boots and a fresh, untorn apron. Could sixpence buy all that?

Elf went to meet her. "Mrs. Cutlow. I wanted to be sure you were all right."

The old woman's eyes shifted around, still anxious and wary. "Doing fairish, ma'am."

"I thought perhaps it might be a bit far for you to visit me in Marlborough Square if you were in need."

" 'Twould be a fair way, ma'am, yes. But I'm fair set. 'Is lordship saw to that."

"His lordship?" Had Rothgar had taken over this matter for her?

"Lord Woolgive, or somin'," said Dibby. "Seems 'e was with you that day, and 'e sent a crown. Said as there'd be another every week, and there has been, Gawd bless 'im."

Fort! Well really, what business did he have stealing her charity case? Just because she'd let the matter slip from her mind for a week or two . . .

Elf determined to take her cause back.

"And do you have a good place to live, Mrs. Cutlow?"

"I 'as a room."

"Would you like a place in the country? Far away from here."

The old woman stepped back. "Don't take me away, ma'am. I don't want to leave 'ere!" Her gnarled fingers clutched her apron and it looked terribly as if she were going to cry.

"No, no. Of course not! No one will do anything you don't want . . ." Elf felt like crying herself. She just wanted to help this poor woman, and yet everything was going wrong.

As it had with Fort.

Was she really just a clumsy meddler?

She looked around, and the germ of an idea came to her. She touched one of Dibby's clenched hands. "I'm pleased Lord Walgrave is seeing to your welfare. Don't worry about anything else. But my offer remains. If you have a problem or are in need, just send someone with a message to Malloren House in Marlborough Square, and I will do what I can."

With that, she gave the impatient girl her penny, and returned to the coach.

As the coach lurched its way back to the road, Chastity asked, "She is not in need, then?"

"She doesn't seem to think so. Probably because your brother has made her his pensioner at a crown a week."

"You sound rather aggrieved."

"I think he did it just to contest me!"

"Perhaps a little. But he is genuinely kind, you know. He's made many improvements since becoming earl. The servants are better treated and paid. I gather he's visited all the estates, and dealt with long-standing grievances of the tenants. Our father was *not* kind, and from being blackmailed, he'd become a veritable clutch-fist."

"I'm pleased he's being responsible." Elf meant it. She loved to hear of Fort's virtues. She was still aggrieved, however, by his interference in her business. "I have a plan . . ."

Chastity pulled a face at her. "What now?"

Elf chuckled. "Oh, nothing wicked, I assure you."

"Are you sure?"

Alerted by something in Chastity's voice, Elf asked, "Yes. Why?"

"Because I visited Fort this morning and found him finally out of his bed and on a chaise. He'd been refusing to make the change of scene if it involved being carried, but apparently he managed to hobble across the room with the aid of a crutch. You did say that when he was vertical, you would feel free to assault him."

"He's not vertical on a chaise!"

"I'm sure he'd struggle to his feet if you entered the room."

"And doubtless injure himself."

"Elf, are you scared?"

Elf looked at Chastity. "Well, of course I am."

"He won't hurt you, I'm sure. He's developed a certain balance in his feelings."

"I might upset his balance, mentally and physically. What if I push him into bitterness again, and he tries to make it all public? Now he's up and about—"

"He wouldn't be such a fool."

"Are you sure?"

"No," Chastity admitted. "But truly, he seems to have put it all behind him. He's much like the brother I knew before Father's death, but better. More mature."

"And where does that leave me?"

Chastity sighed. "I'm not sure there's any hope. He appears to have put you behind him, too."

"Out of sight, out of mind?" Elf tried not to let her pain show. "Perhaps in sight, in mind . . . But that's why I'm frightened. Now, I can hope. I can dream of it all coming right. Once I put it to the test, I might find that you're right . . . Anyway, it isn't fair to sting him when he can't run away."

"He could have you thrown out," Chastity pointed out. "I think you should put it to the test. He's talking of removing to Walgrave Towers as soon as he's stronger."

That hit Elf with panic. She'd gained some comfort from the knowledge that Fort was only streets away. "And we'll soon be at the Abbey. No one stays in London in the summer. Lud, anything could happen if I let months go by. Oh, this is worse than a visit to the tooth-puller!"

Chastity laughed. "Now, there's a fine romantic sentiment. Shall we go visit him, then?"

"Now? Oh, I don't think so . . ."

Elf's hand went to her hair to check if it were tidy, and she assessed her outfit. She was wearing the dull forget-me-not dress again and a plain cap, and a flat, flower-trimmed hat made little improvement.

Dull, dull, dull. Spinsterish dull. Why hadn't she pursued the matter of bolder clothes? In a few days, she could have something better.

"He wouldn't admit me . . ."

"I hope he wouldn't be so impolite, but we'll never know unless we try."

"Lud!" Elf's heart raced with panic and longing, and her hands were probably soaking her cotton gloves with sweat.

"Courage," said Chastity. "Where's that Malloren spirit?"

Elf rolled her eyes, but the prospect of seeing Fort after more than two weeks was too tempting to refuse, even if all she saw was the cold, unforgiving earl.

As they headed toward the better part of town, she spotted a flower-seller. Stopping the coach, she called the woman over. Soon she possessed a pretty nosegay of sweet-smelling roses.

"What's that for?" Chastity asked. "I assure you, his sickroom is not noxious."

"When a person goes a-wooing, aren't they supposed to take flowers?"

Fort was pleased enough to hear that his sister had arrived, for convalescence was a damnably boring business. Various friends visited to play cards and gossip, but they couldn't fill all the hours of the day. He had books he should read, and his secretary, Jellicoe, kept bringing papers to do with the affairs of the earldom or matters arising in the House. For some reason, he found it hard to keep his mind on such stuff.

And his idle mind had a wretched way of wandering to Elf Malloren. Or rather, to Lisette in this room, masked, disheveled, melting under his touch, driving him to ecstasy with hers.

He found it damnably hard to blend that delightful creature with Milady Elf of the sharp wit and even sharper tongue. And yet for some reason the notion of having Elf here, sandy-haired and maskless, of doing with her the things he'd done with Lisette . . .

Plague take it!

If he could think of a reason to give, he'd move to some other room. Any other room. He looked around with distaste at heavy furniture and somber hangings. He could claim the room was haunted. It wouldn't be far from the truth. The ghosts of his father and Lisette made very strange bedfellows, though.

He was smiling at that thought as Chastity came in, carrying a nosegay. "Roses? Charming, but an unusual gift for a gentleman."

She leaned down to kiss his cheek. "I don't see why ladies should be the only ones to be given flowers. Anyway, they're from Elf." A still watchfulness belied the casual way she tried to say the words.

Having no idea how to react, he looked away. "How . . . quaint."

The roses were tossed into his lap, their perfume suddenly assaulting him.

"Gentlemen are usually polite about gifts."

He gazed at the simple country bouquet of assorted roses, pink, cream, and yellow. "Only to the giver," he pointed out.

"She's below stairs. Shall I call her up?"

"God no." His heart started a sudden staccato of panic.

"Afraid to see her?" Chastity was as tight-lipped and angry as she had been in their worst times, and he could put that to Elf Malloren's account.

"Perhaps I prefer not to hang for murder."

He knew the accompanying gesture in this melodrama was to toss the roses to the floor. Instead, of their own will, his fingers touched one cool, soft petal.

Soft as Lisette's skin.

As Elf's skin.

'Struth, most women had soft skin. One wench or another, what did it matter?

"You'll hurt her feelings."

His sister sounded a little less irate so he looked up, and he made himself speak calmly and logically. "Chastity, it would not be wise. If Lady Elfled is capable of rational thought, she too will realize it's for the best."

She rolled her eyes. "Lud, but you sound just like Father. Bone-headed and insufferable!"

"That at least reflects well on the honor of our late lamented mother." Then he realized he had raised the flowers and was inhaling their musky perfume. Giving up pretense, he met his sister's eyes.

"Why are you fighting this, Fort?" she asked softly.

"Perhaps I've decided against self-destruction as well as murder."

"And turned instead to melodrama and insanity!" Then she bit her lip.

"Don't let the idea torment you, my dear. I no longer fear inherited insanity. As I was told, Father was not mad except insofar as he was mad for power, an affliction none of us seem to have caught from him. Pushed far enough, I suppose any of us could be driven into a form of madness, but that is not the same as having it in the blood." Deliberately, he added, "As the Mallorens do."

Chastity sat with a flounce in the chair by his chaise. "The Mallorens do *not*, as well you know. Only Rothgar bears that concern. The others have a different and sane mother."

He inhaled the perfume of the roses again, thinking that perhaps such smells were healing. What a heartless world it was that lavished them on women and denied them to men.

His sister's voice broke into his whimsical thoughts. "So, what is your attitude to Rothgar these days?"

He lowered the roses and met her eyes. "I promised Elf to put aside the feud. I told you the same thing. As long as he doesn't interfere with me, he can go to hell in peace as far as I'm concerned."

"What if he pushes for you to marry his sister?"

"I would consider that interference of the most malignant kind."

"Fort, what if she's with child?"

That possibility tormented him, but he would not let it show. "We discussed it before our charming jousting session. I agreed to provide financial support if needed, but made it clear I would not marry her."

"Then you had best be careful not to spread the story, hadn't you? Or you will force Rothgar to act."

It took a moment for her words to make sense, so far from his mind were they. Then he laughed. "Devil take it, is she still concerned about that? Tell her I've come to my senses. She need not fear that Mr. Hogarth will turn his cruel pen to her adventures. I told you, I no longer desire death, and I certainly don't desire marriage to a Malloren."

His sister frowned at him with something close to pity. "You're making a terrible mistake, Fort."

He pulled out a rose, one as creamy as her lovely skin, and offered it to her. "I do thank you for caring, Chas. But I know my own path best. My apologies to Lady Elf, but I am not up to a visit from her today."

She took the rose. "Just don't do anything foolish."

"What on earth do you mean?"

"I don't know. But I fear it's a family trait."

"Malloren or Ware?"

"Both."

Elf had made herself sit quietly in the reception room, even when enough time had passed to tell her Fort would not see her. She was tempted to go up and force herself upon him—she knew the way, after all—but force was unlikely to work any miracles.

And anyway, it had belatedly occurred to her that meeting him in that room with that bed, that bench, that mirror might prove to be too much for her nerves.

So she was not entirely devastated when Chastity returned with one rose in her fingers.

"So he didn't throw them out the window?"

"He's pretty well confined to his chaise still." Chastity shrugged and passed the rose over. "It wasn't clear, but I suspect he wanted you to have it. He won't see you, though. He seems firm about it."

Elf rose and took the flower to inhale the sweet perfume. "Did he say why?"

"Not too coherently, but he mentioned not wanting to commit murder or suicide. Perhaps time . . ."

"No, not time," said Elf, leading the way out of the house. "Time just lets some things set harder."

They had sent the coach home, so set to walking the few streets between Abingdon Street and Marlborough Square.

"But what can you do?" Chastity asked. "I don't think it would help to force yourself on him."

"Sting him," said Elf.

And when they passed a toy shop, she went in and bought a ball and cup, the ball attached by a long string. She ordered it sent to Walgrave House with the compliments of Mademoiselle Lisette.

Fort was dismissing Dingwall.

"Have I failed to give satisfaction, my lord?" asked the man. For once he was showing a reaction, and it seemed to be hurt.

"I'm sure you satisfied your employer, Dingwall. But he is dead. I have decided it is time to bury him."

"Bury him? My lord, are you suffering some minor instability of the mind—"

"Running mad? Like my father? You would love to have charge of me in chains, wouldn't you? On the contrary, I am coming to my senses, and I realize I don't need a resident penance anymore. I will instruct Mr. Jellicoe to pay you your wages and a handsome gift for your long service. I am trying to correct my father's errors and omissions."

Dingwall was probably in a rage, but it merely showed by a quivering about his mouth. "It is my job to watch over you! I must—"

"You must take your dismissal."

"You are not worthy to take your father's place."

"Then I am sure you will be happier serving a better master." Fort picked up the toy, let the ball fall out to the length of the string, then flicked it. The ball missed the cup.

He smiled up at Dingwall.

"You are right, my lord." The expression in the man's eyes might even be compassion. "I have tried, but there is nothing I can do."

He bowed and left.

Fort flipped the ball again and it settled neatly into the cup. "One ghost dealt with," he said.

Chapter 18

Jack Travers arrived at his friend's room to find him idly flipping a wooden ball into a wooden cup.

"What the devil's that?"

"A toy."

"Yes, but why?"

Fort looked up at his friend. "Perhaps it's a message. Does the ball seek the cup, or seek to escape? Is the string a fetter or a guide?"

Jack looked around, concerned. "Has that damned sawbones been giving you new medicine?"

"Not at all." Fort put down the toy, but picked up a bouquet of roses. "I am forcibly made aware of the fact that no one thought to sweeten my prison with flowers."

"Flowers?" Jack was ruining his neat hairstyle. "Look, my dear fellow, perhaps we had better have the doctor back . . . Where's Dingwall?"

"I dismissed him."

"Well, then." Jack smiled. "Perhaps you *are* in your right mind. At last."

"Quite. I am merely in a strange mood from being damnably bored. Play hazard with me."

"Of course," said Jack, relaxing. "I know it must be tedious having to just lie about." He pulled over a chair and a small table, adding, "In fact, a group of us thought we could have a party up here if you're willing. Wine, wenches, and high play."

"A delightful prospect, but leave out the women. I'm not up to it, and have no desire to watch you all making fools of yourself."

"Oh, of course." Jack flushed slightly, and Fort realized that as far as his friend was concerned he was still sunk in his strange apathy toward women.

That needed to be corrected, too.

Fort picked up the dice and rolled them. "When I am fully recovered, let's stage a magnificent orgy in honor of the occasion."

Jack grinned in relief. "That's the spirit! The best damn orgy since Heatherington's do at Rood House."

The next day, Tuesday, not long after breakfast, a scroll arrived, a pretty item on pink paper tied with silver ribbon and decorated with a spray of tiny silk roses. Unrolled, it proved to be poetry, presumably written out in her own hand and cleverly decorated with blossoms and flying birds.

To a Nosegay on Lord Walgrave's Breast.

"Must you alone then, happy flowers,
Ye short-lived daughters of vernal showers,
Must you alone be still thus blessed,
And dwell so well on Walgrave's chest?
Oh, would the gods but hear my prayer,
To change my form and place me there!
I should not sure so quickly die.
I should not so inactive lie;
But ever wandering up and down,
From swelling shaft to fading frown,
Enjoy ten thousand thousand blisses,
And print on each ten thousand kisses."

With a laugh, Fort recognized a play on a poem by Jenyns, but that one had been written to a lady addressed as Pancharilla. In the original, the fanciful wandering had been restricted to her breasts!

He read it again, his "shaft" indeed swelling at the words. If he were weak enough, with just a few words he could make fancy fact. He could have Lisette/Elf on his breast, showering various appreciative parts with ten thousand kisses—

He crumpled the paper into a ball and hurled it across the room.

Vespa indeed.

The damned woman was impossible! Just like all the Mallorens, she thought her will was law.

When Wednesday passed without another intrusive gift, he thought he was safe. He knew himself to be oddly disappointed, but that was doubtless just because of boredom.

He'd settled in bed for the night when the singing started.

Cursing, he seized his crutch and hobbled over to the window to peep around the curtains at the torch-lit group. Venetian-style, the musicians beneath his window were cloaked and masked in a way designed, surely, to remind him of Vauxhall and Lisette.

He rather thought the singer, whose voice was truly exquisite, was the castrato Gioletto, currently the adored star at the Opera House. Two guitar players and a flute accompanied him. No figure looked like Elf.

Damn, but the music touched his soul, even if the song was some silliness about a rejected lover languishing in misery, fading away for lack of sight of the beloved . . .

He came to his senses and staggered back to the bed to ring his bell and command that the caterwaulers be driven away.

On Thursday a small box arrived containing a fine topaz ring with a wasp engraved so as to appear to be trapped within the jewel. It fit his ring finger exactly.

He had kept the crumpled poem and the roses, though the latter were now beginning to droop. He was loath to part with this offering, but in the spirit of the game, he replaced the jewel in its box and called for paper and pen.

His note was brief.

Lord Walgrave regrets that it would not be proper for him to accept such a valuable gift.

He sealed it and sent box and note to Lady Elfled Malloren at Malloren House.

Moments after his footman had left, he knew he'd made a tactical error. He had acknowledged her existence. Her plan was working, too, in that he was now obsessed by her gifts, heightening his obsession with her.

It was lying about in this room that had trapped his mind in nonsense. So, gritting his teeth, he grasped his stick, pushed himself off the damned chaise, and began to move around the room.

Recently his doctor had urged exercise, though he had instructed that a footman be on hand in case the leg gave way. Be damned to that. Fort defied pain and worked his way out into the corridor, heading toward the stairs that would lead to the outside world.

To freedom.

He reached the top and halted, clutching the carved knob on the newel post, already running with sweat. That's all he needed, though. The outside world.

He'd order his chair and be carried to one of his clubs. Perhaps he'd even be carried to the House. A boring, long-winded debate about the slave trade would at least stop him thinking about Elf, wondering what the next gift would be . . .

How was he going to get down the stairs, though?

Should he put his injured leg down first so it had to bear his weight, or the good leg first so the injured one had to bear his weight? There should be rules for this.

He shifted his weight to the wounded leg and immediately desisted with a hiss of pain.

Someone knocked at the door, giving him an excellent excuse to put off the trial until tomorrow. I would definitely be beneath his dignity to be caught trying to hobble crab-wise down the stairs.

He turned back toward his room, then paused. Perhaps the knock heralded the ring flying back to him. However, it was merely a liveried messenger with some papers to do with business of Parliament. Fort scuttled hastily back to his room, his overexerted leg already hurting like blazes. He didn't want the footman to find him like this.

He staggered back into his room and collapsed on the chaise. He'd study the papers seriously, though. It would be a distraction. Moreover, he was determined to rebuild the honor of his family, even if few people knew just how badly his father had tarnished it.

It was a lonely task. Chastity had her own life, and would soon be gone. Verity was already abroad with her military husband. Victor was in Italy.

He had friends, but he couldn't involve friends in family or political affairs. His friends were the friends of his carefree youth.

Strangely, the closest he'd come to a new friend, a friend of his new self, was a certain scarlet lady. If only she truly had been a doxy called Lisette, looking for a rich protector. He'd pay her handsomely to be his mistress, and treat her as well as a wife . . .

Marry Elf Malloren, said a tempting voice. *Then you can have it all.*

"Never," he said out loud. "Never."

On Friday the package came in the regular postbag. He opened it to find a narrow box and a neat little note.

Vespa regrets overstepping the bounds of propriety, and can only offer as excuse the power of her feelings. She prays that Lord Walgrave will accept this trifle in place of the ring.

The long narrow box proved to contain a silver-and-black fan. He took it out, shaking his head. Some fops had taken to using fans, but he wasn't one of them. It would be an unexceptionable gift, however, from a suitor to a lady, and she'd borne in mind his habit of wearing mourning.

She couldn't know that he'd given it up and was wearing colors again.

He idly flicked open the fan, then laughed out loud.

It was decorated with a series of pictures of a lady in scarlet stripes slowly raising her skirt to tie her garter, all the time smiling at the observer in a most inviting manner.

He turned to look at the other side and found it to be an unexceptionable picture of Vauxhall Gardens. Unexceptionable, that is, if Vauxhall did not hold memories.

Damnation, but he was hard again, swamped with memories of Lisette and the loving they'd done in this room. Some of the best sex he'd ever enjoyed . . .

Then he saw a paper in the box and unfolded it to find another poem. This time he did not recognize the derivation.

When I remember where our paths have led,
From park to prison, to voluptuous bed,
I am unable to arrest my mind
From appetites of the most scandalous kind.
Dark monk assaulting gently my most delicate skin
As he entranced me down the road of sin.
I pray, my lord, that when you are restored,
You'll summon once again your scarlet bawd.

'Struth, but there was nothing coy about Elf Malloren! Was she seriously offering to return as his plaything?

But then, who had been playing with whom?

He couldn't decide whether he felt delighted or disgusted by this bold behavior, but it certainly made him nervous. What would she do next? The woman was clearly capable of anything!

He was contemplating the scarlet lady on the fan when Jack appeared.

"We're all set for tonight, Fort! Of course, we're happy enough to hold our revels up here, but wouldn't you be more comfortable on the ground floor now you're a bit mobile?"

Fort riffled the fan closed. "An excellent idea. In fact,

I'll have a bed put down in the study for a while. What point in being up here at all?"

"That's the spirit!"

"And this room has very disturbing memories."

"Your father, eh?" Jack looked around. "Why not have it refurnished? Brought up to date. This heavy oak and velvet ain't really the thing. Is that a fan?"

By way of answer, Fort spread it, Vauxhall side out.

"Oh-ho! Buying gifts for the ladies, eh? There's life in the old dog yet." He went over to the side table that held glasses and decanters. "Sure you don't want us to bring along some pretty wantons for your pleasure?"

"Completely." Fort made an abrupt decision. "In fact, I suspect I might soon be married."

Jack turned, a half-filled glass in hand. "*Married?* You gave no hint—"

"I've had time to think on it. Lady Lydia North should do admirably."

Jack stared at him. "Lady Lydia? Ain't she that simpering chit with the big eyes? Never knew you were interested."

"Her father has been wooing me assiduously. Though without particular imagination, I must confess . . ."

"What?"

"Ignore my whimsy. Let us just say that I have suddenly developed an interest in Lady Lydia."

Jack turned back to fill his glass, but after a moment he said, "To be honest, Fort, I think she'll bore you to tears in a week."

"One never knows what lurks beneath an image of maidenly modesty. But at least she'll be a shield against other ladies."

Jack came over to press a glass of wine into Fort's hand. "Don't do anything rash, old boy. Trust me. Wait till you're up and about. This room is turning your wits."

"Surely Lady Lydia is exactly the kind of bride I am expected to choose."

"Aye well, why start doing the expected now?" Jack

sat and shook his head. "Ever hear the story about the man who shot himself for fear of catching the plague?"

Fort savored the wine. "Ah, but can't you see the appeal of choosing your own form of demise?"

Cyn wandered into the drawing room in Malloren House, a piece of paper in his hand. "I've a strange invitation here."

Elf and Chastity looked up from their stitchery and chat. "Why strange?"

"It's to Walgrave's for an evening of cards."

"He's better, then," said Elf, bright-eyed.

"Must be improved at least. But why invite me?"

"Will you go?" Chastity asked.

"Of course not. I'd likely throttle him."

Elf paused in her needlework. "If only we were identical twins . . ."

He caught her meaning immediately. "Don't be foolish. And a man and a woman can hardly be identical, can they?"

She pulled a face at him. "Very close in looks, then."

"Well, you are," said Chastity. "But not close enough for anyone to mistake one for the other, no matter how dressed."

"And women can't dress as men. It's never convincing."

"Well . . ." said Chastity, with a mischievous twinkle at her husband.

"I spotted you within moments, love."

"That was before you advised me to stuff some padding down my breeches. That fooled those ruffians in Maidenhead."

He pulled a face at her. "Need I point out that you're putting ideas into my hen-witted sister's head?"

Chastity stared at Elf. "You *wouldn't*!"

"I don't *think* I would . . ." Elf made them both wait a moment, then laughed. "But only because I'd be caught." She looked between the two of them, sobering.

"It is very . . . bothersome not to have seen him for so long."

Chastity leaned over to squeeze her hand. "I understand. But if he's holding entertainments he must be finding it easier to move. We'll soon have him out among society again."

"And then he'll remove to the Towers."

"If he does, you'll just have to practice patience. Even if you have to wait months to encounter him, nothing important is going to happen."

"I have discovered that I am not of a patient disposition!"

Elf would have invaded Fort's entertainment if she'd believed for a moment that she could get away with it, but she had no intention of making a fool of herself.

Again.

Instead, she dispatched to his house a gaudy handkerchief of red silk trimmed with gold-and-black lace.

Lord Coalport was clearly delighted to be asked to Walgrave House, and to hear Lord Walgrave ask for his daughter's hand. To Fort's irritation, he did not immediately grant it.

He received Coalport in the library on the ground floor, where a narrow bed sat behind a screen. Fort was settled comfortably in a chair, his leg supported on a cushioned bench. It was a significant improvement, but he felt for all the world like a victim of the gout.

Coalport was not a likely candidate for gout. His build was trim and healthy, his actions brisk, and Fort doubted that he ever overindulged in anything. Not a bad stable for a wife.

"You see, my lord," said Coalport, crossing one leg over the other, "I've promised my wife that our little Lydia will have her say on the matter. Now, I'm sure it's just a matter of you courting her a little, for you're a fine, handsome man, particularly now you've put off your blacks. But I can't settle the details before you have her interest."

"But I am tied to a chair most of the time, Coalport."

"Aye well, there's no hurry." Coalport leaned forward and patted Fort's hand. "I assure you, Walgrave, she'll not go to another before you have your chance. There are others interested, I'll not deny it. Doubtless you'd not believe it if I were to try, for she's quite the prettiest lady on the town this decade. But you have my favor, and will have your chance."

Fort felt like cursing the doting father for he was now in a fix. He could hardly go after another woman who would agree more speedily, and yet he was in no shape to court anyone.

"I confess to some urgency," he said, hoping he looked like a love-struck fool. "Soon all the world will be leaving London, and your estates are far removed from mine."

Coalport nodded, much struck by that. "True enough, my lord. True enough. My wife does talk of leaving within the fortnight." He scratched beneath his neat gray wig. "I could have you over to the house, for you could sit there as well as here, but I tell you, Walgrave, it would look a little too particular if your first venture out were to call upon Lydia. I'll not have her pressured."

"Then perhaps I had better take up some general social moves," said Fort, forcing a smile. "I am much improved. Not up to dancing, of course, but as you say, I can sit as well in company as alone."

"That's it, my lord! And if you tell me where you plan to be, I'll see that Lydia attends if it be suitable."

"Thank you, my lord. I think we will soon find everything just as we would wish."

Coalport grasped his hand and shook it. "I believe it will be so, Walgrave. Indeed I do. And there isn't a girl in the world to match my Lydia."

And so that night, despite hating to appear such a figure, Fort ordered his sedan chair, and had himself carried into the gaming room at White's, where he hobbled to a chair.

He was immediately surrounded by friends and the

merely curious, telling the approved tale of a madman down at the wharf who had fired into a crowd and unfortunately hit him. In fact, soon he was having a grand time and silently blaming Elf Malloren for keeping him trapped in his house for a fortnight.

Until Rothgar turned up.

Fort eyed him, both wary and cool. It was, after all, the first time they had met since that encounter at Sappho's.

The marquess's brows rose slightly, then he strolled over to Fort. "I am delighted to see you about again, Walgrave."

"It is a relief to me, too," Fort said. "I feel more in control of my life."

"I rejoice."

"In fact," said Fort, suddenly determined to seal the matter, "I'm thinking of marriage."

"Indeed." Rothgar flicked open a gold snuffbox one-handed and presented it.

Fort took a small pinch. "Nothing is settled of course," he said and inhaled, letting the powder create its own moment of well-being. "But the young lady's *father* gives me reason to hope."

Rothgar did not so much as pause in his own use of the snuff, and took the time to wipe his fingers on his silk handkerchief. Then he smiled approvingly. "Accept my felicitations in advance of the happy event."

With that he bowed and moved away leaving Fort prey to sudden doubts. He should have realized that Rothgar wouldn't want another alliance between their families, even when Fort and Elf had enjoyed the privileges of the wedded state.

By escaping Elf, Fort could be doing just as Rothgar wished.

For a moment, the old urge returned, the urge to do anything that would make life difficult for Rothgar. He pushed it aside and concentrated on cards. He'd given up judging his every act by its effect on the Mallorens.

* * *

The next morning, Elf was poring over financial statements when Rothgar strolled into her study. Rather than change her boudoir into a place of business she had taken over a spare room for an office and it had now become one of her favorite places.

" 'All work and no play . . . ,' " her brother remarked. "The same applies to Jill as Jack, I think."

Elf smiled up at him. "Perhaps this is play."

"You are distressingly like Bryght, aren't you?"

"I suppose we are all a mix of the same ingredients. Did you know that if we were to buy—"

"No," he said, raising his hand. "I have no interest in it. Explain it to Bryght. I think you should be out in society."

"It's so dull. People never talk of interesting things."

"Like trade and profit," he said dryly. "Walgrave is breathing fresh air again."

Elf put down her pen and paid attention.

"I encountered him at White's last night."

"I'd hardly describe that as fresh air."

"I assume he passed through the streets to get there."

"Was he walking?"

"With a cane, and with some difficulty. He let his chairmen carry him almost up to the table."

Butterflies had suddenly taken up residence in Elf's stomach. No, not butterflies—wasps. Buzzing there, and likely to sting her. The time had come to act.

But she might see him.

At last, she might see him.

"How did he look?" she asked.

"Well, all in all. Rather less under a cloud."

"That's good. I wonder . . ." She wondered where else he might turn up, but didn't want to say it. Heaven knows but she had no pride left over this with her family. They all knew her desperate need. Still, she didn't want to say it.

"I believe he might be attending Lord Coalport's picnic at his Chelsea villa."

"A *picnic*? White's I can believe, but an alfresco meal

probably largely attended by ladies? Can a pistol ball in the leg change a man that much?"

"Perhaps he is just craving fresh air." With that, Rothgar left, and Elf sat chewing her lower lip.

Since her brother had come specifically to tell her about the picnic, he doubtless had made inquiries and thought Fort would be there. That didn't necessarily mean that Rothgar thought she should attend.

So should she?

She looked down at the neat columns of figures that told the story of income and expense in a certain warehouse for upholstery fabrics. Life could be seen as neat columns, too. If she didn't attempt to see Fort, she might as well just admit that she lacked the courage to pursue her aim.

She'd have to leave him be.

It was tempting, for that's what a lady was supposed to do, what she had been trained to do. She should sit at home demurely and make him woo her. A lady's rights lay solely in the acceptance or rejection of an offer.

She didn't think Fort would woo her, though. Even if he wanted her.

He *must* want her. Surely he must be drawn to her as she was to him. And the problems were her fault for so mishandling that intimacy. So she must put it right.

Immediately she knew she'd reached the correct, the only decision. As they were all discovering, she was a complete Malloren. She could not help but try to steer the ship of fate.

She pushed back from the desk and stood, then frowned at an inkstain on her finger. Lud. Perhaps lemon juice would help.

As it turned out, Chastity knew of her brother's intention to attend the picnic.

"It's not so strange," Chastity said. "He attended such affairs at home before—"

"Before he killed his father."

Elf had been astonished to find that the whole family knew Fort had shot his father, and everyone had assumed that she knew, too. She had been involved with Princess Augusta, however, and had missed some important meetings.

After the death, Chastity and her sister, Verity, had spent a great deal of time with Fort. They had done everything they could to persuade him that it had been a necessary act to protect the innocent, not a heinous sin.

They hadn't succeeded, but Chastity had always believed he'd see it that way in time.

Elf knew—or hoped at least—that their disastrous talk in the dark cellar had helped to crack the shell of guilt and anger around him, and started the healing. If so, it had been worth it, even if it had cost her any chance of love.

More than possession, she wanted him free to be himself.

"So?" prompted Chastity, pulling Elf out of her thoughts. "You want to attend this picnic?"

"Quite desperately. But is it wise?"

"I honestly don't know. He doesn't speak of you. But he still has some poems, a fan, a toy, and a horribly gaudy handkerchief. And it was only a few days ago that he let a maid throw out the remains of some roses."

Elf couldn't suppress a smile. That did sound hopeful. "Then by all means, let us go. At the very least, I will see him."

She hurried to her room, glad she'd taken the trouble to order some gowns to her new taste. She was still rather unsure of herself in this regard, but at least neither the mantua maker nor Chantal had blanched at her ideas.

Two gowns had arrived so far, and the amber one might be ideal. The striped taffeta had caught her eye and she had felt sure it would harmonize with her difficult hair rather than fighting it. With rust-brown trimming and rich cream lace, she thought the effect strong but pleasing.

And Chantal did not protest when ordered to produce it.

However, remembering the way Fort had looked at her scarlet and gold and called it "appalling," Elf could easily have been persuaded back into the safety of paler shades.

Waiting for Chantal to bring the gown, she paced the room restlessly. Half of her wanted to cancel her plans, to put off this meeting till another day. But her need to be with him again, even among a crowd, overwhelmed even her terror of having him look coldly at her or even turn his back.

He had kept her gifts.

She hugged that thought to her as Chantal returned with the outfit and began to help Elf into it.

She remembered, so long ago, telling Chastity that men often needed a bridge to cross the gulfs they themselves created. She'd been talking then of Cyn and Rothgar, who had created a chasm over the issue of whether Cyn should be allowed to join the army. It might apply to Fort too, though, mightn't it?

Elf didn't look in the mirror until the gown was fastened, then she turned to the glass. She released her held breath and smiled. "It does look well, Chantal, doesn't it?"

The amber-and-brown silk created a rich effect that might have been a little strong for her pale skin except for the cream lace at neck and sleeves. "In fact," said Elf, turning this way and that to check the line of the gown over her wide hoops, "my hair *is* pale amber! That sounds so much better than sandy."

"Yes, milady. The whole is good. It is . . . interesting."

"Interesting?" Elf echoed with a wry smile. "Is not that what they say of ladies of a certain age?" But with sudden confidence, she knew she looked well.

Looking back at the mirror she could see that the gown did as she'd intended. It expressed Elf Malloren. It reflected the way she felt about herself these days—a woman, confident and moving beyond the tighter expectations of society. A person excited by the prospect of interesting things to do with her life.

"What hat do you wish to wear, milady?"

"Oh, the large leghorn to shade my face, I think."

As Elf waited for Chantal to find the straw hat, she continued to look at herself in the mirror. It was not vanity, just a satisfaction with a job well done.

One among many.

The burned-out piece of land down near the port had been purchased by the family and she had already met with the architect who was to build almshouses there. Dibby Cutlow and others like her would have a good place to live out their lives, but would not have to leave the area in which they felt comfortable.

In the future, other similar places would be constructed around London. Too often, the old were forgotten.

She was still considering ways to spread information about means to delay childbearing until the right time.

She placed her hands on her flat abdomen. At least the prospect of inconvenient motherhood no longer troubled her. She'd had her courses. She didn't carry a child. Her sensible part had rejoiced, but a tiny rebellious corner of her mind had wept. She could not be sure of winning Fort, and a child of his would have been something of him to cherish.

It would have tied him to you, said stern honesty.

"Yes, that too," Elf whispered to the woman in the mirror.

Then Chantal returned with the straw hat, deftly tying amber grosgrain ribbon around the crown. She brushed Elf's curls, added a delicious lacy cap, then set the hat on top, tying a big bow beneath the chin.

"Charming, milady!" declared Chantal in what seemed to be honest approval.

Elf left the room hoping the maid was right.

Chapter 19

Elf and Chastity took the boat upriver to Chelsea. Elf soon realized that this wasn't wise, for the boat held far too many memories for such a day.

Fort *had* been upset to hear Bryght had shot the bridge and put her in danger.

It was from this boat she'd watched him fall, and known he was wounded.

It was from here that she'd ordered the execution of a man.

Despite these thoughts, she managed a flow of light chatter throughout the journey.

The boat conveyed them to Lord Coalport's boathouse—a miniature cottage, complete with deep thatched roof. From there they climbed the steps to his pretty garden, which was in full summer bloom. Elf told herself that it was nothing like arriving at Vauxhall for a midsummer masquerade.

It was daytime, for a start, and an ideal one for a picnic. They were blessed by a cloudless sky, but also by a light breeze to cut the heat. Tables of food and drink sat beneath shady trees, and ladies and gentlemen strolled paths and lawns, chatting. To one side, a small orchestra played peaceful, soothing music.

A perfect English summer day.

As they went in search of their host and hostess, however, Chastity swatted with one hand. "Wasps. That's always a problem with picnics."

Elf sighed, seeing it as an unfortunate omen.

She wore amber jewelry with her outfit, and the large

pendant around her neck contained a winged insect trapped there through the ages. It was similar to the effect created by the wasp engraved in the topaz.

Were she and Fort both trapped in a situation they could neither enjoy nor fully escape?

Her Malloren soul said there was always an escape for the brave. But did courage always bring victory?

They headed toward the house, where Elf saw Lord Coalport standing by his wife's chair near the terrace steps.

She suddenly stopped dead.

Chastity turned back. "What's wrong?" She followed Elf's eyes. "Oh, there's Fort. What has you so shocked? You expected to encounter him here. Is it that he's in colors again? I must have forgotten to mention it."

Certainly it was a small surprise to see Fort in blue silk, but that wasn't what had frozen Elf to the spot. Couldn't Chastity see? Sitting beside him was London's latest darling—Lord Coalport's daughter, Lydia.

The girl had arrived in town in the spring and created a sensation. Pictures of her had appeared in the print shops—not scandalous pictures, but idealized ones of angelic beauty. Soon her every appearance and the details of every gown were in the newspapers. At one point the Horse Guards in the Mall had been called out to intervene to control the crowds of people wanting to catch a glimpse of her.

Elf had not paid the girl much attention, for she'd seen such beauties come and go. But that did not deny the fact that Lady Lydia possessed extraordinary beauty. Glossy dark curls, a perfect heart-shaped face, huge eyes of an almost violet color . . .

Even this catalog of perfections did not do her justice, for it was all put together perfectly and accompanied by grace and a charming youthful modesty.

Lady Lydia, in an exquisite blue-and-lilac dress and a hat that appeared to be composed entirely of lace and flowers, sat beside Fort smiling up at him as if he were a god come to life. He was smiling back at her as if she were the most fascinating person he had ever met.

Charming though she was, the girl could hardly put together two coherent sentences, so what had him so absorbed?

As if that wasn't obvious. Elf wanted nothing so much as to flee back to the boat and go home.

Such a retreat was unthinkable, however, so Elf drew upon years of social training and smiled and chattered as she continued toward her host. Lord Coalport greeted them affably, so Elf supposed she was saying and doing all the right things.

She could hardly tell when she was so rattled by fear and anger.

She would have to go over and talk to Fort. What had possessed her to come here with his sister? Otherwise she could have ignored his existence.

Of course, she'd never intended to ignore his existence. She'd come here to woo him, damn his black heart.

Unless the girl moved—a likely event, to be sure!—she would have to talk to Lady Lydia. It would be a remarkably one-sided conversation, she thought with appropriate waspishness.

She saw no point in putting it off. As soon as they could move on from the Coalports, Elf summoned every scrap of Malloren spirit, and went over to smile and chatter at Fort and his lovely companion.

"I'm pleased to see you recovering, Walgrave."

Perhaps, just perhaps, he had a little trouble meeting her eyes. "Thank you, Lady Elf. Are you acquainted with Lady Lydia?"

Elf smiled at the girl. "A little. What a lovely property your family has here."

The girl blushed as if she'd been paid an outrageous compliment. "Yes, it is, isn't it?"

"Especially now the city grows so hot and dusty."

"Oh yes, it is, isn't it?"

Elf couldn't help herself. She flashed Fort a look of disbelief.

He met it with a look of his own, a challenging one.

Then she understood.

This was a direct move to counter her persistent stinging of him. Dear God, had she pushed him into peril again?

With a resolute breath, she sat on the bench beside Lydia, leaving Chastity to talk to Fort. He gave her a thoughtful look, as if wondering about her intentions, but then turned to talk to his sister.

Elf smiled at her rival. "This has been your first visit to London, hasn't it, Lady Lydia?"

"Yes, my lady."

"And have you enjoyed it?"

The girl looked around. "Everyone has been most kind."

Elf's competitive instincts abruptly became protective. Gemini, but the child should still be in the schoolroom! "Perhaps a little overwhelming?" she suggested gently.

Lydia turned back, a spark of relief in her huge eyes making her even more breathtaking. "Oh, yes! Overwhelming expresses it perfectly. Everyone *has* been most kind, such flattering attention, but"—color rushed into her cheeks—"I will be glad to be home again."

Elf reached over and squeezed Lydia's hand. She couldn't imagine what it must be like to be just seventeen and cause a crowd to gather even when walking down the street. "Next time you come to town, you will be more at ease, I promise."

"I suppose so." But Lydia looked down and fiddled with the trimming of her lovely dress.

"You do not want to return?"

The girl glanced up as if considering the wisdom of a frank answer. She was not at all stupid, Elf realized, just very young and appropriately shy. "I suppose it will be different if I return to London as a married lady."

Elf's mouth dried. "Is that likely?"

Lydia blushed. "A number of gentlemen have expressed their admiration." But her glance slid betrayingly to Fort.

Pain around Elf's heart made it hard to breathe. She'd expected to find Lydia a pretty bird-wit quite unworthy of Fort, but she was charming, innocent, and honest. Too young, though. Surely too young. What were her parents thinking of?

When she spoke, she felt only an honest desire to help.

"There can be no hurry, surely. If I were you, I would enjoy the single state a little longer. I assure you, you will not lack for offers in a year or two."

And Lydia laughed, doing so as charmingly as she did everything else. "That's what my mother says. But having begged to be brought to London . . . And . . ." Lydia glanced again at Fort, who appeared to have all his attention on Chastity and a gentleman who had joined them.

Clearly it had to be spoken of openly. "Lord Walgrave is a handsome man," Elf said.

"Yes, he is." But Lydia did not speak like an infatuated girl. It was a simple statement of fact.

"And one of the most eligible men around."

"Indeed."

"He can be a pleasant companion."

"Oh yes. He teases me and makes me laugh."

Elf wanted to burst into tears. Just briefly in the cellar he'd teased her, and when they'd been shouting for help it had come to laughter, but teasing was a side of Fort she'd never really known.

Yet it seemed it came naturally to him with Lydia.

She knew she should wave the white flag, should surrender the field of battle. This was what she wanted for him, wasn't it, someone who could make him joyous in season? But in her opinion, Lydia was still too young for marriage, too young to know her mind.

She smiled at the girl who might steal the man she loved, and spoke as honestly as she could. "Let me give you some advice, my dear, unasked for as it is. You are very young. Do not rush into marriage for any reason other than the deepest devotion. But if you feel that devotion for Lord Walgrave, accept him now. I doubt he will still be available next year."

Lydia considered her, then said, "Thank you, Lady Elf. I think that is sound advice."

Elf had the horrible feeling that the girl could read the situation too well by far. No, not stupid. A treasure in fact, and if Fort could win her, she should wish him all success.

She had done what she could and with the best of intentions, and so she excused herself and rose to mingle with the other guests, chatting to this group and that. They were all old friends and acquaintances and put no strain on her.

The strain came entirely from the man sitting in the shady spot with a treasure by his hand, ready to be claimed. But really, she thought—despite her charitable intentions—could he seriously want to share the marriage bed with a delightful infant?

Why, thought Fort, had he believed he could marry a mere child?

Oh, she was beautiful almost beyond belief, and charming with it. But if he did marry her, he didn't think he'd be able to touch her for years. And even having let years go by, he couldn't imagine ever enjoying with Lydia the sort of wild loving he'd explored with Elf Malloren.

Elf looked well. Perhaps a little less animated than usual, but it seemed more a matter of calm than subdued spirits. He tried to resist, but couldn't help stealing glances at her as she walked around chatting to this person and that.

She was wearing a different style of gown, he realized. No, not the style, the color. A stronger color, but one that suited her.

Then he had to suppress a laugh.

Waspish colors.

Gads, but she'd be the death of him if he wasn't careful.

He'd seen her as soon as she entered the garden, as if drawn by a sixth sense. He'd promptly turned to Lydia and concentrated on her as if she were his sole hope of salvation.

Which perhaps she was.

What ease she had in this world . . . Dammit, he was looking at Elf again.

Unlike Lydia, who seemed scared to leave his side.

But that was unfair. Lydia was being kind to an invalid. Elf was eight years older, and had been raised by Rothgar to fill the position of hostess to him. She was up to anything. Lydia could be the same in time.

Or could she? He dragged his attention back to the girl, who was talking to a young friend. Suddenly they giggled over something, hands over pretty mouths.

A child.

But children grow.

Elf had been a child once. A hellion, he'd heard. She had a twin brother, after all, and from things Chastity had said it appeared that the two of them had shared adventures from birth.

At age eight, Cyn and Elf had climbed down the ivy on the north wall of Rothgar Abbey and been whipped by Rothgar for the crime. He was sure Lydia had never contemplated such a rash act, and equally sure that her doting parents had never needed strict discipline.

This should be to her credit.

He remembered "Lisette" talking about using his pistols. Yes, he believed Elf Malloren could load and fire a pistol. He was equally sure Lydia would be horrified at the mere idea. It shouldn't matter. His wife would never need to protect herself.

Yet the contrasts between the two women troubled him. Elf seemed like a fine sword—flexible steel, ready for action, and potentially lethal.

Lydia made him think of a silk cushion—pretty, comfortable, and ready to conform to his every need.

Any man of sense would prefer the cushion to the sword.

"Do you not like Lady Elfled, my lord?" Lydia's voice demanded his attention.

He looked back at her. "Like? Why do you ask?"

"You were frowning at her."

He made himself smile. "Perhaps the sun was in my eyes. Lady Elf is sister to my sister's husband. We are family in a way."

It was clear Lydia saw the evasion in this—he'd been pleased to discover that she wasn't dim-witted—but she did not pursue it. "We had a charming conversation."

"Conversation is one of Lady Elf's chief skills."

"I wish it were one of mine," said Lydia with a rueful smile that could take any man's breath away.

Gads, but she was astonishingly beautiful. There wouldn't be her like in a decade. Why did he have any doubts? She would mature, and she could be taught to be stronger, taught to be sharper-tongued, taught to enjoy lovemaking in all its forms . . .

"You are a delightful companion," he assured her and raised her hand for a flirtatious kiss. "A chattering woman soon drives a man to drink."

He thought about kissing her lips. Lydia's pretty, full, soft mouth should be tempting him. Instead, however, he could only think that she'd be shocked, hesitant, and quivering, and that it would be a devil of a bore to have to coax her into relaxing. He wished he were mobile enough to draw the girl into a secluded spot and test the theory.

What if she turned out to be the sort who wanted the lights out, who was repulsed by intimate experiments?

He'd set up a mistress. It was the accepted solution.

He was looking at Elf again, remembering Lisette. Damn, but he wished Lisette had been real. He could even forgive her for wearing him down to tears if he could have her as his mistress. Trouble was, he'd not want to drag himself away to spend duty time with his lovely, quivering wife . . .

"I think I bore you."

He snapped his attention back to Lydia, fearing he was actually flushing with guilt. "Not at all."

She didn't look hurt, merely honest. "It's not surprising. I am very young still, and what interests me does not interest you."

She suddenly seemed a great deal more appealing. "What interests you, then? Tell me."

"Such a charming couple."

Elf smiled at Mrs. Dettingford, thinking that the movement of her lips must surely look more like a rictus. "Lord Walgrave and Lady Lydia?" she asked, having long since given up trying to say, "Who?"

"After his tragedy," said the plump young woman, "it would be so fitting to see him capture the prize of the year!"

"You refer to his father's death?"

"Of course. So sudden. Such a loss to the nation."

"It was certainly sudden."

"And so touching the way his son wore deep mourning for so long. But now he is emerging from the shadow of grief to claim his prize!"

Elf contemplated the satisfaction of throwing a fit and upending a large bowl of pureed fruit over Mrs. Dettingford's head, but the silly woman was merely the most effusive of the company. Everyone was delighting at the romance in their midst—London's premier beauty, won by its most eligible young man. One who, moreover, had been obligingly injured in some mysterious but doubtless heroic way.

Did none of them see that Lydia was unready for marriage? Did none of them wonder about a "romance" between two people who had never been observed to even speak to each other?

Elf knew she was being unfair, however. *She* knew Fort had not been in the habit of attending the sort of events where he would meet such a tender young miss. It doubtless wasn't obvious to others. Others hadn't been obsessed with the man for months.

She escaped Mrs. Dettingford and moved on to another group, but found that they too were gossiping about the likely match.

Eventually she decided she had been at the picnic long enough and could leave without causing comment. She collected Chastity from an animated conversation with friends, friends who did not seem to harbor doubts about Chastity's old scandal, thank heavens.

"Oh, I'm completely restored now by Cyn's noble act," said Chastity as they made their way over to their hosts to say farewell.

"But no one knows of it."

"Elf, it's not like you to be naive. Cyn has a title impetuously bestowed upon him by the monarch. Fort is wounded. A hundred stories are being invented to explain it, each more glorious than the next. They are both heroes, and Cyn just wants to set sail and escape!"

Elf chuckled. "Oh dear. I've been so absorbed in other matters, I'm out of touch. Of course, everyone wanted to talk about the heroic tryst under the beech tree."

Chastity pulled a face. "For what it's worth, I told him he was being a damned fool." Then she straightened her face into a smile and thanked Lord Coalport for his kind hospitality.

"Aye, well, it's turned out very well, Lady Raymore, I won't deny." He beamed at Fort and Lydia. "Everything as it should be."

Elf was speaking to Lady Coalport, who rolled her eyes slightly. "Dear Lydia is the apple of her father's eye. Our only daughter, you know."

"She is very beautiful, and charming besides."

"Yes, the poor child has every gift of the gods."

Elf couldn't help but chuckle at the wry tone. Now she knew the source of Lydia's wit and wisdom. With such a mother, she surely wouldn't be allowed to do anything rash.

That didn't mean, however, that an engagement to marry might not be drawn up, with the betrothal to last a year or two.

So be it.

But she had one last thing she had to do.

Tonight.

Fort enjoyed Lydia's chatter once she ceased being tongue-tied, but he felt less and less inclined to marry her. Oh perhaps in a year or two, but if he had to languish unspoken-for for years, he'd doubtless do something foolish.

If he wasn't doing something foolish now.

Out of the corner of his eye, he saw Elf laugh at something Lady Coalport said. When had she ever laughed for him? Abruptly, he had an image of her in bed, laughing with him over some fanciful game.

He went so hard, he had to glance down to be sure his long waistcoat covered him decently.

He watched as Elf and Chastity strolled down to the boat. Once they had gone, the afternoon suddenly seemed a great deal less interesting.

Nonsense. He concentrated on Lydia again, wondering why he couldn't feel any passion toward such a beautiful creature.

"Is something the matter, my lord?"

He feigned a wince. "My leg begins to pain me a little. I think I should summon my carriage and make my slow way home."

She leaped to her feet. "Oh, of course! I will send a servant."

In moments she returned accompanied by her parents and a footman. He said his farewells, then set about making a figure of himself by hobbling across the gardens to the road. The footman accompanied him, but so did Lydia.

That would cause talk. Were they trying to force his hand?

By the time he made it to the carriage drive, his leg was truly hurting and he wished he was home in his bed. What mad impulse had driven him out too soon?

Then he remembered his purpose, and looked at Lydia North.

She was eying him with genuine concern. "Your coach is still not here, my lord, and I'm sure you shouldn't be standing. Thomas, go and fetch Lord Walgrave a chair."

The footman hurried off, and for a brief moment they were alone.

Had she deliberately arranged this moment, hoping for a declaration? He'd as good as arranged all the details with her father.

What did he want?

What should he want?

Their talk, and the sense of intelligence and kindness he'd found in her, let him ask the question.

That evening, Elf went to the opera, then on to a supper given by the Duchess of Derby.

She returned home after midnight, which was why she had arranged for Hunot to be in the mews of Malloren House at one o'clock. She met him in some clothes she'd sneaked from Cyn's room. The breeches were rather tight in the hips and loose in the waist, but otherwise fit quite well. She was a few inches shorter than her twin, but that merely meant the sleeves of the coat hung down a bit over her hands.

Dark-skinned Hunot was almost invisible in the shadows of the mews, but she could see him shake his head. "You'll not fool no one in a good light, milady."

"I'm not planning to. I just thought I'd be safer if I dressed as a man."

"With me, you could walk the streets in your shift and no one would touch you. You just like to play games, you Mallorens."

Elf flashed him a grin. "And there, you might be right." She led the way down to the nearby street. "It's not far. I just thought I'd be prudent and take a bodyguard."

"Prudent," he said. "Uh-uh."

Elf chuckled, enjoying strolling through the dark streets safe from the bosky gentlemen and the hovering cutpurses.

She was completely safe, for she had Fort's pistol in her pocket. A sheathed knife snuggled alongside the pistol, and another nestled in her right boot. And she had Hunot, who could handle a small army with his knives and his lethal hands.

She wasn't really happy, though, for she dreaded what she was about to do.

She was going to set Fort free.

Perhaps she didn't have him trapped, but just in case, she was going to give him his liberty.

She could have visited him during the day with Chastity as chaperone, but he was quite capable of again refusing to see her. And anyway, she couldn't imagine having an honest talk with him during the day. No, night was their time and she had his pistol, an excuse of sorts for a clandestine visit.

In Abingdon Street, they avoided the front of Walgrave House, and headed for the back, looking for the gate Elf remembered. It still wasn't locked and so they slipped through and down the garden.

As she'd expected, the house was quiet. Fort, still an invalid, would go to bed early, and the servants would take the chance to get a good sleep. She couldn't be sure they'd all be in their beds, though, which added a little spice to the moment.

Elf paused to inhale the sweet smells of the dark garden, and to admit that she was enjoying this last adventure. In fact, she enjoyed adventure. The excitement was like wine—sweet and liberating.

Yes, she was very like Cyn.

Hunot was watching her, and she could see well enough to know he was smiling. "God help the man who marries you."

"Perhaps I'll just save any man the trouble. You stay here. Don't worry, the worst that can happen now is that I'll get thrown out on my ear. Prepare to catch a flying Malloren!"

He laughed as she slipped toward the house.

It was a hot night, and she was relying on there being some windows open. She'd expected to have to climb the scullery roof to get at a higher floor, but she spotted a small window there left ajar.

His servants need a firmer hand, she thought, then grimaced at the direction of her mind.

The window opened farther without squeaking, and she eased through onto the stone sink. Soon she was in the familiar kitchen.

The big room was quiet, though again a few figures slept rolled in blankets on the floor. Surely all the other servants would be in their beds. A faint meow made her look down, where she saw a familiar dark cat. She crouched to stroke behind its ears.

She daren't speak, but she hoped it understood her apology for using it to escape, and her thanks.

At least when she rose to make her way across the kitchen, it didn't follow. Nor did anything else happen to prevent her making her way through the servants' quarters and up the stairs to the first floor.

It was easy from there. She knew the way to Fort's bedroom.

Gingerly, heart beginning to race, she eased open the door to a pitch-dark room. He must be asleep. Carefully, she worked her way to the bed and touched the surface. Her wandering fingers found only a smooth surface. He wasn't there!

Irritated, she pushed back the heavy window curtains to let in a glimmer of moonlight. Not only wasn't Fort here, this room was unused. No water stood ready on the washstand. No towels hung on the rail.

For a horrified moment she thought he might be dead, but then sanity returned. This was not a house of recent death.

So where on earth was he?

With a woman?

Jealousy threw up that suggestion, but reason immediately quashed it. He surely was in no state to enjoy a woman, or to be traveling over town in search of one.

So, he had moved to another room.

Elf caught sight of herself in a mirror, surprised at how much like her brother she looked in his clothes. Then she remembered other images in that mirror and wondered if Fort had simply fled the memories this room held.

Fled to where? If she'd expected this problem, she would have asked Chastity.

She eased into the adjoining room, but it too was unused.

The ground floor.

She shook her head and laughed at herself. Of course, a man with a wounded leg would not use stairs if he didn't have to.

In moments she was downstairs trying to remember her earlier explorations, and choose a likely room. She made her decision and walked boldly into his study.

Fort lay in bed, reading by candlelight.

He started and half-rose, but then relaxed back on his pillows. "Trying to terrify me to death? I thought you were Cyn."

Elf's heart beat so fast she feared she'd turn dizzy. "You don't seem surprised to see me."

He closed his book and put it aside. "I'm surprised. But with you I've come to expect the unexpected. To what do I owe the honor of this visit?"

He was decorously clothed in a white nightshirt, and neatly tucked into the narrow bed. But his brown hair hung loose, and the reflective candleholder close to his head gave it a golden aura. A wave of love and lust engulfed Elf, threatening her mission.

Then she noticed the frame holding the bedclothes off

his leg and she just wanted to take care of him. "Does your leg still pain you?"

"Frequently. I thought Chastity took back regular reports."

"Regular, but not detailed. I'm sorry you were shot."

"I don't think you were responsible. Were you?"

"Of course not!"

"With a Malloren, all things are possible." He threw the family saying at her like a knife. Just like old times. Squabbling again.

Elf carefully extracted the pistol and put it on the desk. "I wanted to return this."

"Thank you. You could have sent it as you sent other items, however."

"I wanted to speak to you."

"We spoke today."

"In private."

With a sigh, he spread his hands. "I am here, and you would have to sting me viciously to persuade me to move. By all means, say your piece."

Elf sat in a chair, forcing herself not to show how much his words hurt. She'd expected this, hadn't she? Clearly he didn't feel the same powerful attraction that she did. To him, she was merely importunate. Doubtless he planned to marry Lady Lydia, and thought the fact that she was a sweet innocent a bonus rather than a handicap.

So be it.

"First," she said, "I want to apologize for anything I might have done to hurt you."

"Accepted."

"Second"—and she looked at the scrolls, the fan, and the toy on a table by the bed—"I will bother you with no more gifts."

He too glanced at her offerings. "Ah. They have enlivened the tedium of convalescence. Why stop now?"

"So you won't offer for Lydia North in retaliation."

He looked back at her then. "You do think me a shallow fellow, don't you?"

"No!"

"No? You think I would spoil the life of a charming girl merely to hit back at you?"

Elf shook her head, trying desperately to understand. "You wouldn't spoil her life. You'd make her a wonderful husband."

"Are you carrying my child?"

The question caught her unawares, though she'd planned to tell him. She knew she was flushing as she said, "No."

He leaned back, watching her from beneath lids so low they effectively blocked interpretation. "We were lucky, then."

"Yes, very."

If he wanted it this way, she could play the game. She crossed her legs as her bother would do. "So, you have no intention of marrying Lady Lydia?"

"Not in the near future." He shrugged. "Next year, or the year after, who knows? She is a delightful young lady."

"But young."

"Desist!" In a completely different tone, he added, "I kissed her today."

Elf caught a breath. "And escaped uncommitted? A miracle!"

"I'm sure you have been kissed many times and yet escaped bondage."

"But then, despite the clothes, I'm not a man."

"And such matters are much more hazardous for us. Unfair, really, wouldn't you say?"

They shared a smile that Elf couldn't interpret, yet treasured. They had slid into talking as friends, or even as she might talk with Cyn—something she had never experienced with Fort before.

"We were left alone for a few moments, and I wanted to kiss her. I had already discovered that very proper ladies can be a surprise in these matters."

Elf swallowed, knowing she was blushing.

"She, it turned out, was just as eager to experiment.

I started very gently, of course, but at her insistence became a little bolder. She made no objection, but soon pulled back."

"She didn't like it?"

"Your astonishment is flattering. It wasn't clear, but she did say that she thought she'd wait before permitting other men such liberties."

"One day, she will make some man a truly remarkable wife." Elf had not intended the question in that "one day," but it rang out.

He looked at her without any obvious artifice. "Elf, I don't know. I don't know anything. I feel as unformed as a babe."

It was horribly unsatisfying, but it was honest, so she rose, smoothing down her man's coat. "And I'm stinging you when you can't retaliate." She'd come to set him free, and now she must do it. "Did Chastity tell you I've taken over part of the family business?"

"An estate?" His brows rose with surprise.

"No, part of our industrial concerns."

"I didn't know the Mallorens had concerns other than making my life a misery."

Elf stared at him. "How strange. But we don't spread the word, I suppose. Yes, we are busily engaged in many matters to do with industry and trade. I have charge of fabrics of all kinds. It started with silk . . ."

A little while later, she stopped. "Oh, Lud. I'm chattering like a ninny!"

His lips twitched into a smile. "Just like an Elf. I'm glad you're enjoying all this hard labor."

"Well, I am." Something in his manner had her blushing and fiddling with the cuff of her coat. She made herself relax and tell him the whole of it. "I quite see that my interest in trade makes me even less of a perfect lady. As does my ability with a throwing knife." She pulled the one out of her boot. "Hold one of my poems up against the wall."

After the briefest hesitation, he picked up the pink

scroll and held it out at the full extension of his arm. "Bear in mind that I already have one wounded limb."

"At least you're not suggesting I could kill you by mistake at this distance." She was surely mad, Elf thought, but she couldn't back down now. It would just be like throwing at a target. Praying for a steady hand, she flicked the knife, and it thudded into the wall through the paper.

"Thank heavens!" she exclaimed.

He released the paper. "If I'd known you were so uncertain of your skills . . ."

And they shared a smile. Not a lovers' smile—something more.

"Friends?" he said.

She nodded, fighting tears. She relished the precious moment, but knew it might be the end of other things. She almost asked whether friends could ever enjoy a physical relationship, perhaps just in fun, but she stopped herself. It could never be just in fun for her, and so it would tear her part.

And probably in a year or two he would marry Lady Lydia.

She walked over and pulled her knife out of the wall, sliding it back down into her boot.

"We do seem to have come full circle," he said.

"Except that I'm in the breeches, and you're in the robe."

"A half circle with more to go?"

She looked down at him. "I don't know, either."

And that was a strange admission. She'd felt so sure that she wanted him, that they belonged together.

Then she'd felt so sure that she could let him go.

Now she wasn't sure of anything.

He held out a hand. "Kiss me, Elf. The Earl of Walgrave has never been kissed by Lady Elfled Malloren."

She sat on the edge of his narrow bed. "He won't be now. I'm still in disguise of sorts."

"What is real, what is disguise?"

Elf looked at him, lying back on his snowy pillows

in a pristine white night gown, his wavy hair loose on his shoulders.

She chuckled.

"What now?" he asked resignedly, but with humor in his eyes.

"It's just that with me here in men's clothing, I'm sure this looks like one of those scandalous pictures of the amorous suitor about to ravish the trembling maiden."

He fluttered his lashes. "I'm prepared to scream, sir. But I might permit a kiss."

"If you scream, they'll probably make me marry you." She leaned forward slowly to put her lips to his.

It was true. They had never kissed like this before, in honesty and without urgency. Bracing herself on one arm, she threaded the other hand through his hair, exploring the silky, springy texture of it as she enjoyed the soft firmness of his lips and the familiar taste of his mouth.

His hand touched her neck, drawing her gently closer as he deepened it, as his tongue greeted hers in play.

Almost, she collapsed down on top of him, but she made herself stop. Even if he wanted it, even if he were capable of it, now was not the time. She pulled back, straightened, and stood to give him a formal court bow. *"Au revoir, Monsieur Le Comte."*

With that, Elf turned and left before weakness could make her stay.

Chapter 20

The box arrived just before Christmas.

Elf was in the middle of last-minute preparations for the grand Christmas masquerade they always held at Rothgar Abbey in mid-December. Servants and family had spent the day outside gathering traditional greenery. Now they were transforming the great house with it all, creating an indoor forest—a forest twined with scarlet-and-gold ribbons, and hung with mistletoe kissing boughs.

Spontaneously, the servants were singing traditional Christmas songs and she saw some of the younger ones sneaking nuts and oranges. That was allowed on a day like today.

Elf put the box aside for a moment to give instructions to the maids hanging the gilded nuts among the boughs on the staircase.

A squawk alerted her, and she turned to see Portia, her five-month-old son on her hip. Red-haired Portia was slim and petite, and her son was growing so healthily he seemed almost too much for her to carry. Despite the fact that Elf knew Portia was much stronger than she looked, she reached to take the child. She received a bright smile from both mother and little Francis. She carried the wide-eyed child around the hall, showing him the gilded ornaments and the scarlet ribbons.

"Elf," said Portia, "this package is from Fort."

Elf turned back slowly. She'd learned to put him out of her mind, she'd thought.

Now, immediately, her heart raced.

Not long after their last meeting, he'd removed to Walgrave Towers in Dorset. At the same time, Cyn and Chastity had finally left for Portsmouth and shortly thereafter, sailed. They'd been in Nova Scotia now for months. Their first letter had been enthusiastic, even if Cyn had been annoyed to find out halfway through the voyage that his wife was with child and had concealed it from him.

Elf's revived pain at saying farewell to Cyn had been soothed by time spent at Candleford and the birth of Portia and Bryght's son.

At some point, however, it had dawned on her that she missed Fort more than she missed Cyn.

That was an ominous sign when Fort had made no attempt to contact her.

With Chastity gone, Elf heard little about the Earl of Walgrave. He'd already left the country for Italy when she learned about it.

It shouldn't have mattered whether he were one hundred miles away or five, but it did. Elf had been hard-pressed to keep up her cheerful manner, but since she wanted to assure her family that she was completely happy, she did.

And she *was* happy, more or less.

Her days were filled with business she enjoyed, including a certain amount of mingling with friends and relatives. She was a wondering and devoted aunt. The first of the Spitalfields silk weavers had settled in Norwich, and the business there was prospering.

Just last week she had journeyed to London to celebrate an early Christmas in Prince George's Almshouse, down near Harrison's Wharf. Dibby Cutlow ruled the seven other elderly inhabitants, considering the place virtually her own establishment.

The king had graciously permitted them to name the charity after his newborn son. These days, he beamed on all things Malloren. He had been delighted when informed that Portia and Bryght's son had been born on the same day as his own. He was already talking of the two being companions in a few years—a suggestion that did not appeal to Portia and Bryght at all.

Bryght had even been heard to mutter that Rothgar must have had a hand in it.

Rothgar had merely remarked that if they didn't like the situation, they should have planned with greater foresight.

Whether by accident or foresight, Bute and Grenville were openly contesting for power and the king's favor. This had made George even more devoted to the undemanding Marquess of Rothgar. In fact, the king was here at Rothgar Abbey, complete with wife, child, and entourage, looking forward to the masquerade.

There was still much to be done, but Elf walked over to return Francis to his mother and look at the box.

She felt a strange reluctance to open it. She'd found a kind of equilibrium, and wasn't sure if she could handle any disturbance to it. But she commanded a pair of scissors from a maid and snipped the string. Pulling off the lid, she revealed scarlet and gold.

"Oh, it's a costume," Portia said. "Gaudy, to say the least."

"And inappropriate. You know that tonight we have to be in character."

"You could go as a Covent Garden whore."

Elf flushed, and covered the thing, wondering how she could have ever thought it appealing. More important, why had he sent it? She'd assumed it had been thrown out.

"I suppose this must mean Fort's back," Portia said, setting Elf's heart racing once again. She hadn't thought of that. "Did you send him an invitation?"

"I'm sure we must have, as a matter of form . . ." Now Elf's heart rate teetered on the edge of panic. Surely he wouldn't come.

Why not?

He might *want* to come.

Oh no. She pushed that aside. Foolish hopes and dreams were just too painful.

"If he comes, he comes," she said briskly, knowing that if a dark-clad monk appeared tonight, she'd quite likely faint.

Elf carried the box up to her rooms and summoned Chantal. When the maid came, Elf gave her the package and rather enjoyed the shriek of horror when it was opened. "Milady . . . no. Please!"

"Definitely not. But don't throw it away, Chantal. It holds memories."

Then Elf turned to look at her costume for the night. Layers of filmy silk swirled in brown and yellow, making up a loose gown to be daringly worn without hoops or corset. A kind of harness over her shoulders was included, however, to support the diaphanous wings.

Her mask was also yellow and brown, and included delicate gold antennae.

She was going to the masquerade as a wasp.

They held no formal dinner on the night of the masquerade, but Elf and the other Mallorens in residence—Portia, Bryght, Brand, and Rothgar—were invited to dine with the king and queen and their senior attendants. This inconvenient honor necessitated a *grande toilette* of its own. Elf attended in massive hoops that supported deep blue silk and a lot of silver embroidery and lace.

It was as well that tonight she didn't need to chatter over awkward moments, for her mind was almost numb with panic. The king and queen, however, neither of them normally garrulous, wanted to talk about babies. Portia and Bryght were happy to support that conversation. They even managed to do so without implying that their child was even prettier and cleverer than Prince George.

Elf, seated between Lord Hardwicke and Lady Charlotte Finch, was relatively comfortable, though she could hardly stomach a mouthful of food.

Would he come?

What would he wear?

Had that costume been a message? Should she wear it?

No. No matter what his intent, she would not wear it. That belonged in another life.

But was Lisette the only aspect of Elf Malloren that really interested him?

As soon as the event finished, she hurried to put on her wasp costume. Part of her urgency was practical, for she should be available to deal with any last-minute problems. Mostly, however, she felt that the sooner she was dressed, the sooner it would begin, and the sooner she would learn her fate.

Gown, corset, hoops, and headdress were quickly disposed of. Elf looked in the mirror at her undisguised shape covered only by her white silk shift and experienced a sudden blinding vision of another mirror.

When Chantal, in a dark gown, appeared behind her, she almost shrieked with shock.

"Milady! What is it?"

Elf put a hand to her unsteady chest. "Just nerves, Chantal. Don't ask why, but I am all on edge. Come, let's make me ready to sting."

She discarded her white shift and put on one of flesh-colored silk. The wing harness went on next, fixed securely around her shoulders. Then the fine silk slipped on top. It had been dyed to her order, not precisely in rings of yellow and brown, but in a swirling pattern. The skirt floated in a ragged end around her bare calves, and for shoes, she wore simple sandals of a Grecian design.

She'd tried on the gown before without any unease but now, Fort in mind, she felt overbold. No lady exposed her figure in public so close to its natural state. Even the most brazen whore wore corset and hoops.

She ran her hands dubiously past waist and over hips. Her breasts were so shamelessly *round*. The shape of the nipples could be seen. "What do you think, Chantal?"

The maid's eyes opened in surprise. "But, milady, it is magical! Everyone will be entranced."

"You don't think it . . . bold?"

The maid firmly turned her from the mirror. "Not at all. There will be others there in classical style or dressed as fairies. Come sit, and I will put on the wings and headdress."

Remembering the lady at Vauxhall—the one who'd dressed as Titania and had trouble with her wings—Elf had consulted people at the Drury Lane theater about the design of hers. She wished to be comfortable. Chantal carefully attached the sparkling shapes of wired gossamer to the harness. Elf felt no additional weight and when she stood, she was hardly aware of them. Even some dancing steps did not make them wobble or come loose.

"Excellent!" she declared, and risked another look in the mirror. They really were delightful wings—noticeable, pretty, but not so large as to be inconvenient. She refused to study other things again.

"Sit, milady!" commanded Chantal. "We must do the head."

Again the mask covered half Elf's face, but this time secured by a gold filigree cap which included the antennae. When she looked in the mirror again, she smiled. It really was a wonderful costume. The mask, again made in the theater, had large black eyes, just like an insect's. With the antennae and wings the whole effect—though wildly fanciful—was indubitably wasplike.

And, suddenly, it was right. This, including the body revealed, was an important part of Elfled Malloren, a part she did not want to deny.

"C'est bien," she said softly.

"Bien sûr, milady," said Chantal.

Of course, everything was in perfect readiness.

Elf wandered restlessly through the chain of deserted reception and anterooms and into the grand ballroom hung with ribbons and greenery. The number of candles in the chandeliers had been reduced in order to give a kind of mystery to the place, but bright lights surrounded one corner. The corner containing the new automaton.

Very different from the disastrous one, this was a silver tree with bright enameled leaves. On every branch sat tiny feathered birds, some in nests, some poised as if ready to fly. At the base, leaning against the trunk, a shepherd and shepherdess sat cheek to cheek.

Elf found the switch and it sprang into life, filling the air with birdsong. The birds all moved, some just to turn a head or open a beak, but a few to stretch and flap their wings. Then the shepherd and shepherdess sprang to life. His hand rose to rest on her shoulder, and both heads turned so that lips gently touched lips.

Then they slowly moved back to their original positions and the whole thing settled back into silence.

"Do you think they ever curse the clock maker who gave them so short a spring?"

Elf swung around to find Fort behind her. For a moment he looked almost distant, but then a smile began, and grew, until it was controlled. His lids lowered secretively.

Elf studied him hungrily, heart pounding. No monk tonight. Was that significant? He still wore black, however, the rich sleek black of a Renaissance gentleman, puffed in satin, hung with jet.

What should she read into that? "An assassin" she guessed, wanting to say so much more, but not sure where to start.

"Not at all." He dug in his short puffy breeches and produced a small skull. "The gloomy Dane." Pure, wonderful mischief twinkled in his eyes, and she bit her lip on a laugh, on joy she could not trust as yet.

"I do hope you don't see Rothgar as your wicked uncle."

"Rather that than peevish Laertes, or sententious Polonius." His eyes passed briefly, appreciatively, over her. "I'm delighted to see you haven't taken yourself to a nunnery, Vespa."

"Just to good works." Needing to move, Elf walked

away from the automaton and caught a glimpse of Portia—dressed as Good Queen Bess—anxiously peeping around the door. Portia hastily disappeared, and Elf heard a masculine laugh. Doubtless Bryght teasing his wife for being a worrier.

Were they all out there, all her protectors, making sure Fort didn't murder her?

She took his hand and with a conspiratorial look, drew him behind a screen of pine boughs. It concealed a side door. She tugged him through it and along a corridor.

As busy servants pressed aside to let them pass, he said, "Do I get to ask questions?"

"Just one."

They'd paused at the bottom of some narrow servants' stairs. "Are you happy?"

Elf turned. What answer should she give? If she said yes, he might assume that she didn't want to change her situation, didn't want him. But at this point, she could only be honest. "Yes. All in all, I am."

Then she pulled him on up the stairs.

At the top, she opened the door into the corridor that led to her rooms.

"Where are we going?"

"One question, remember?"

"It's just that I left my rapier at home, and I am in the den of the Mallorens."

"At least Cyn is an ocean away." She opened the door to her bedroom.

"For which I give sincere thanks." He closed the door, but stayed there, against it. "I didn't come here to seduce you, Elf."

It hurt, so she hit back. "I don't expect you to. We've done the penny whore down at the docks, haven't we?"

He closed his eyes. "I see I have much to make up for."

Oh God, her unruly tongue! She took his hand. "No! I'm just in a state of nervous insanity. Don't pay any attention to me."

He smiled. "Impossible. That's an unignorable costume. I've never before thought insects quite so erotic."

Glad for a mask to hide her burning cheeks, Elf looked him over in turn. "Yours does show your legs to advantage . . . Lud!"

She'd finally noticed his codpiece. Discreetly embroidered in black, it had not stood out from his velvet puff-breeches in the dim light of the ballroom. Now, the long horn-shaped bulge snared her attention.

"Our forefathers were a boastful lot, weren't they?" he commented, and his narrow mask did reveal a flush on his cheeks. "Actually, it's rather useful. For example, it disguises the fact that I'm big and hard just looking at you. Satin breeches can be damned embarrassing at times."

"But informative." She looked at him intently. "I've missed you. It's just that . . . that I'm not sure who's come back."

He took her hand to kiss it. "A better man, I think. But yes, you must find out for yourself. Does that preclude a kiss or two?"

She shook her head. "Any gentleman may be allowed that."

"Really? Methinks you are too free with your favors, my lady." But he was teasing, and his lips silenced her retort.

Elf relaxed into his embrace, relishing a kiss so like their last one—gentle and friendly—but experiencing again the rapid surge of desire that plagued her with this man.

His hands played restlessly over the silk gown. "This is a damnable thing to sting a man with, Vespa. Especially one who's been celibate for far too long . . ." His hands slid up her ribs and both thumbs flicked over her nipples, only covered by two thin layers of fine fabric.

Elf stiffened under a sharp jolt of desire, and reached for him. But he stopped and drew her into his arms. "No. We know we can drive each other mad with our bodies. We need to talk about other things."

That sounded ominous. Had he come just to tidy up loose ends before pursuing Lydia?

Before she could speak, he added, "Honestly. As ourselves. Whoever those selves may be."

Then she understood him. "You want us to meet without disguises?"

"Yes. Beautiful as you are as Vespa, exciting as you are as Lisette, and charming as you are as a man, when we talk about serious matters, I want it to be us."

"Naked in the cellars?" She'd do it too if he wanted it, and surely his words were grounds for hope.

He laughed, shaking his head. "I never have decided if that was the ultimate truth or just another illusion. No, we presumably are going to live our lives as lord and lady, as Elf and Fort."

"We've never met like that, have we? We were Malloren and Ware."

She pushed aside delirium to consider it all. He was right. There was more to a life than games and lust. They needed to talk. "When?"

"When else but at dawn?"

"At twenty paces?"

Humor creased his eyes. "We'd have to shout. You can choose weapons, though, as long as it isn't knives."

"Truth."

He nodded. "And the location?"

"Here, of course."

"Formidable, indeed. I depend on you to defend me from rampaging Mallorens. And to come without seconds."

He slipped out of the room and Elf sat with a thump. He was back and, she thought, healed. He was capable of laughter and joy in season.

But would it be with her?

The masquerade was a huge success. The king and queen, presumably by design, were dressed as the shepherd and shepherdess beneath the mechanical tree. When it was formally presented to George as a Christmas gift, he applauded with delight, then kept the lads designated to wind it busy all night.

Fort appeared to have left, for which Elf gave thanks. She'd love to dance with him, but she was having trouble enough keeping her mind on practicalities. She just wanted the event over and the arrival of dawn. If she could have wound the spinning earth and sun like a mechanical toy and made it go faster, she would have done.

She was pleased Amanda was here with Stephen, for Amanda and Portia were the only two people she felt could begin to understand her feelings. Even Amanda and Portia, however, could not guess what Fort had in mind.

At midnight, the masks came off, and disguises were admired over a series of suppers. Elf's wings were much commented upon. She wished she could use them to fly through time.

At two in the morning, as people began to leave or seek their beds, Lord Ferron proposed. At least he'd not worn a toga this time, but a more concealing Harlequin costume. Elf turned him down gently, wondering if she'd regret it.

If Fort intended to put an end to her hopes, she might in time want a poor substitute. She'd discovered that she very much wanted a husband and children . . .

But no. It wouldn't be fair to marry when her heart was set on another. Perhaps in time she'd forget and be able to go to another man heart-whole.

Elf immersed herself in the business of tidying up the event.

She made sure coaches were coming around for neighboring guests, and that all were supplied with hot bricks for warmth. She found mislaid cloaks, coats, and canes, and one broken pearl necklace. She came across a few gentlemen in corners, rather the worse for drink, and arranged for their comfort. She detected some spills and other damage requiring quick care, and set servants to deal with them.

She should be growing tired, but she didn't think she'd sleep this night.

Occasionally she encountered Rothgar in similar activities, making sure the event ended as harmoniously as it had begun. Eventually, weary peace settling, he drew her into his study—one of the few rooms kept locked during the masquerade—and poured them both wine.

He raised his glass. "Magnificent as always, Elf."

She mirrored the toast. "A true Malloren effort. And the king seems pleased with his gift."

"Since he's ordered it carried up to his room, it would seem so. Will the poor queen have any sleep tonight?"

"Probably not," she said with a grin. "I heard him tell her that he intended to go farther than the shepherd beneath the tree."

"An education for the winding boys, to be sure."

"Bey! They wouldn't!"

"Monarchs are strange creatures." But he smiled. "Don't worry. I sent the lads to bed hours ago and put a couple of middle-aged stable boys in their place. Even if George wants to claim his marital rights to the sound of singing birds, he'll not shock those two."

He wasn't going to mention it, so she did. "Fort's around somewhere."

"So I understand."

"He seems much improved."

"I am delighted."

"I'm meeting him at dawn."

He paused in the act of sipping. "I really would rather not have another Earl of Walgrave die here during a masquerade."

"We're not dueling!" Elf said with a laugh. "Or at least, not with weapons."

"Almost anything can be a weapon, my dear. Do try not to reopen his wounds."

She turned away and put down her half-empty glass. "Bey, I don't know what he wants. He was maddeningly ambiguous."

"Do you know what you want?"

She turned back. "Oh, yes. I want him, quite desperately. In all meanings of the word. But only if I can make him happy." She rubbed her hands nervously over waspish silk. "I suppose I should get out of this costume so Chantal can go to bed. He wants us to meet in normal clothes."

"Surprisingly wise. *Bon chance,* my dear."

Elf paused at the door and looked back at him. "Bey, just for once will you be frank about something? What do you think about this?"

"I? I am recognizing that the one area I cannot control is affairs of the heart. But if Walgrave wants to marry you, and you can both be happy in that state, I will be pleased. We did him harm, and it would be right to do him good."

"I think he'll fit into the Mallorens remarkably well."

"Oh yes. That is what made him so dangerous."

As she opened the door, he added, "If he is to be part of the family, see if he'll take over the wine and spirit division."

Elf was still laughing as she ran upstairs to her room.

Chapter 21

Elf drove a weary Chantal to distraction trying to choose exactly the right outfit for her crucial meeting. What represented the real Lady Elfled Malloren?

She was tempted by her remaining safe gowns, the pales and pastels with pretty little prints. At least they *were* safe, and perhaps that's how Fort thought of her. After all, apart from that one encounter at Lord Coalport's villa, he'd never seen her in her new wardrobe.

Her new clothes, however, were more true to her now. But not a grand gown. That would be inappropriate, besides being unnecessarily uncomfortable during hours of waiting.

"Milady! Why don't you want to dress for your bed?"

"Don't question me, Chantal. I have my reasons."

Not the amber again. She didn't want waspish.

The cream with black-and-gold design?

The dusky red print?

The clear blue just edged with embroidered flowers?

In the end she settled on the green-and-cream stripe. It was cut in a rather plain form with closed bodice but skirt open over a leaf-green quilted petticoat that took the place of hoops. It was the sort of thing she'd wear for an ordinary day, and green, they said, was the color of hope.

Once into it, she sent Chantal off to bed and sat on a chaise in front of the window, praying for an early dawn.

But the earth and sun cannot be hurried, and in late December, the sun will not rise before eight, not even at the command of a Malloren.

In the end, she slept until the glow of sun on her eyes awoke her.

She blinked gritty lids, then saw Fort lounging on the padded window seat in front of her. He was dressed casually in buff breeches, long fawn waistcoat, and dark brown coat—what he'd wear for a casual day on one of his estates.

"It's a long time since I've watched morning," he said, turning his head to look at the golden sky. "A humbling experience."

She sat up, rubbing her eyes. "I thought you were just the sort to seek your bed with the dawn."

"Only in my wild younger days." He looked back, unreadable. "Do you want to put this off?"

Again, that sounded ominous. "No. But I'm going to have a drink of water. Do you want some?"

"No, thank you." As she walked over to the carafe and glass, he added, "I've cheated, in fact, and had breakfast."

As she returned to the chaise, he added, "With Rothgar."

Elf sat. "I thought he wasn't going to interfere."

"Perhaps he can't resist. Perhaps he didn't interfere."

Elf didn't believe it for a moment. "What did you talk about?"

He thought. "About the situation in Portugal and in the West Indies. About the king's art purchases from Italy, and some of my own. Oh, and we discussed suitable disposition of the worthy Roman senators who stand in the hall of Walgrave House. Unless, of course, you have an attachment to them."

Elf was startled by the switch in direction, then cautiously hopeful. "No. No attachment." She studied him as if he were a conundrum. "Did he ask about wine and spirits?"

Now he was puzzled. "No. Though I gather you have interests in a vineyard in Portugal."

"Probably. I wouldn't know. I have enough to do with silk."

"He did explain more about your family's business concerns. It's an intriguing notion. I have Victor to think of."

Elf couldn't stand this inconsequential talk any longer. "What of Lady Lydia?"

"I don't think she'd care for trade."

"You know what I mean!"

He looked at her for a moment, and she held her breath. "She's too young," he said, "and I'm not inclined to wait."

She needed more than that. "Surely you would wait if you thought her the woman for you."

"I suppose I would. Tell me, what is most important to you these days?"

"What?"

You, she thought.

"Elf, we hardly know each other." That devastating teasing humor shaped his eyes. "What if you love glee singers and braised heart?"

"You don't like glee singers and braised heart?"

"Can't abide them."

"I'll give them up for you."

"Ah," he said, mock-melancholy. "But then I'd have to bear the burden of having deprived you of things you hold so dear."

"I don't hold them dear."

"Then tell me what you do."

You, she thought again, but she saw she'd have to answer the overt question.

"My family, of course. My work." She knew this might be a problem. He had used to be a conventional man. "My involvement in the family business is very important to me. It's challenging and exciting."

He didn't faint with horror, so she kept going. "I'm still training with pistols and knives, and generally go about armed. I like the feeling of not being entirely dependent on others for my safety."

Still no obvious dismay.

"I'm funding a pamphlet about ways of avoiding unwanted pregnancy. It will be passed around discreetly. The problem is that so many women can't read, so we've done it with illustrations, but—"

"Schools next, I assume," he said. "Does all this have Rothgar's approval?"

"Do you care?"

"Not particularly. I'm just curious."

"Yes, it does. Though if it didn't, I'd still be doing it. In fact, Sappho's handling the pamphlet."

"Then Rothgar must approve, I suppose."

"You can't really think they are like that."

"No." His smile was rueful. "I started going there just to annoy my father. I did so many things simply to annoy my father. Then, after, I went seeking a means to injure Rothgar. I think she knew. She never tried to stop my visits, but I never encountered him there. In time, almost accidentally, I learned to enjoy good music and poetry, and to appreciate clever women. I have a lowering feeling that I was deliberately educated."

Elf didn't know what to say, for he was almost certainly correct.

"Almshouses," he said. "I visited Mistress Cutlow."

"Oh, yes. If we're to dig over all the old coals . . ." She drained her forgotten glass of water. "When you arranged to pay her a crown a week, was it simple kindness or a move against me?"

He thought about it, looking out at the brightening garden. "It's hard for me to understand my mental processes back then. Probably a bit of both." He looked back. "You *had* forgotten her."

"I admit it. And so," she said, tossing the challenge back at him, "what is important to you these days?"

He moved to face her directly, the sun gilding the rim of his tied-back hair. "My family. Chastity and Verity seem to be well settled, so there's only Victor of my siblings. He seems to be less marked by our childhood than the rest of us and should do well. There are any number of family dependents, though."

"Everyone has those."

"True, but to look after them requires money, as does catching up on all the work on the estates that Father neglected. The amounts he spent on royal gifts alone are enough to turn my hair gray." He looked at her. "A frugal wife with mercantile interests would not come amiss."

Her heart fluttered up to panic speed. "Frugal? I'm a Malloren." Then she bit her lip, wondering if she'd leaped too far ahead.

He didn't pounce on it. "I assume that your portion is grand enough to support your extravagances. Are you saying you won't make me rich?"

She couldn't stand it. "Are you saying you want me to marry you?"

Silence. Was he going to say no?

Then he smiled, but wryly. "No man likes to set himself up for disaster, least of all me. I confess, I'm still afraid . . ." But he slipped off the window seat onto one knee. "My dearest Elf, after long and careful consideration I have come to see that you are the only woman who can make my life complete. Will you accept my hand in marriage?"

She placed her hand in his, steadier now they had come to the point. But she frowned. "You almost sound reluctant."

"Do I? I'm sorry." He kissed her hand, but lightly, and looked into her eyes. "I'm nervous. Frightened, even. You are, after all, a Malloren, and I've learned to expect stings. But you *are* everything I want in a wife. I knew that when I found myself thinking of ways to turn Lydia into you. But I knew I had to untangle myself before I could make a clear-headed decision. If you don't marry me, I doubt I'll marry elsewhere."

"That's hardly a fair weapon!"

"I hoped we were beyond weapons."

Flushing with shame, Elf slid down to the floor and into his arms. "You're right. I think I'm nervous, too. We've been squabbling far longer than we've been talking rationally. I keep waiting for the answering sting. When did you first think . . ."

And sitting there in the brightening day they relived their encounters, the bitter and the sweet.

"You know," he said at last, arm comfortably around her, their backs settled against the chaise, "you still haven't answered my proposal."

Elf dug in her pocket. "Give me your left hand."

He did so, brows raised, and she slid the wasp ring onto his third finger. "Now you are mine, *Monsieur Le Comte.*"

With a laugh, he captured her left hand, pulled a ring out of his pocket, and slid it onto her finger. "Will you make everything into a contest?"

"Oh, probably." Elf gazed through tears at a beautiful emerald. "I knew I was right to wear green. For hope." She looked up at him. "I love you quite desperately, Fort, but this frightens me. I am a Malloren and I've come to like being in control of my life."

"The warning is duly noted. I won't beat you for insubordination."

"No, you won't."

He laughed and kissed her lips. "Elf, the war is over. I love you, and I love you strong, bold, active, and even chattering. We can find a way."

Then they were kissing as they had never kissed before, with wondering hesitancy and knowing familiarity. And, like the glow of the sun, with the added savor of leisure, of lifetimes, of security.

Eventually, the sun full up, they drew apart. Elf wanted more and she was sure he did, too. She was equally sure they would wait.

"Can it be soon?" she asked.

"Today would be nice."

She leaned laughing on his chest. "We'd need a Special License."

"I have one."

She looked up at him. "Overconfident, perhaps?"

"Just prepared. And I told myself that I couldn't feel this intensely about anyone and it not be reciprocated."

"I've felt that way for over six months."

There was a complaint in it, and he responded. "If I hadn't been abroad, I'd have come to you sooner. Much sooner. You have been a void in my heart."

Irresistibly, they sank back into kisses. "Today *would* be nice," she murmured, half over him, his cravat loose in her fingers because she wanted to be skin to skin.

He moved her and stood, raising her with him. "Then why not? With Mallorens and Wares, surely it is possible. There are still guests. Even royalty. We can be as grand as we please or we can slip down to the village church and be very private. What is your desire, my lady?"

Warm, blue, laughing eyes. Smiling lips.

You.

"Private is tempting," she said. "Especially as it could be now. But I'm a Malloren. By all means, let us be grand."

And grand they were.

The king and queen, who had witnessed Cyn's wedding the year before, and actually hosted Bryght's wedding not long after, were amused to be again involved in a hasty Malloren march. The guests who had stayed were happy to delay a few hours to witness the vows and partake of a grand breakfast made up of rather unusual dishes. It was mostly made up of the leavings of the previous night's supper.

Rothgar, appearing benign, murmured something about funeral baked meats furnishing the wedding feast.

Fort and Elf were standing hand in hand, trying to pretend they weren't burning with lust. Did all married couples feel this impatience? she wondered.

"You see," Fort said, "I knew it was Hamlet."

"Amanda thought it was Romeo and Juliet." Elf thanked a plump dowager for her warm and slightly risqué wishes.

"A foolish story."

They were married. The event was almost over. The guests had been fed and were finally leaving. What else was there to do but chatter? "Then she said it was Benedick and Beatrice."

"Closer, but a scrambling plot in that one." They both spoke briefly to a departing couple.

"Which play do you choose, then?"

"Why not make up one of our own? And a merry Christmas to you, Sir Charles. Yes, an impulsive wedding does save a great deal of fuss. *Bon voyage.*" Fort turned back to Elf. "A lighthearted comedy, I think, with somber moments at appropriate times, and even elements of farce. But always, always, with a happy ending."

"In iambic pentameters?" Elf thought for a moment. *"Behold brave Fort, and lively chattering Elf / Waving off guests, but wishing only to be by them self."*

"Not well scanned or even very grammatical."

"Then you do better!" Elf had to turn away to kiss good-bye to Aunt Kate.

"Those evenings at Sappho's must have taught me something," he murmured. *"Her vows all said, the baked meats all consumed, / The bride and groom wish only to be roomed."*

Elf fought laughter. "It might scan better, but it lacks something of elegance. Thank you, Lady Garstang. And a happy Christmas to you, too. *The vows all said, the bride and groom thus wedded, / They chatter nonsense, impatient to be bedded.*"

"You may not have noticed, but it is only just past noon."

"I noticed. *For I have known you in the dark of night, / And would now know you in the sunlight bright.*"

"And I have stripped you by the candle light, / And"— he screwed up his face and laughed— *"And can't now think of how to make this right."*

"Isn't that what marriage is for, to make this right? I do believe that everyone of importance has left."

They looked at one another, suddenly somber, but

somber in the happiest possible way. "Then let's escape," he said, "before anyone thinks we want to engage in polite chatter or a game of cards."

Feeling like guilty children, they slipped away and ran upstairs hand-in-hand to her room. By her orders it was well-heated by a leaping fire, and even this early, her bed was turned down invitingly.

"I never asked if you wanted a wedding journey." He leaned back against the door as he had the evening before. "I must warn you, my lady fair, I have come here to seduce you."

"I know. You're wearing satin breeches."

He laughed, glowing and flushing with it. Or perhaps with embarrassed lust.

Despite their impatience, it took time to extract her from the layers of formal clothing. It took less time to strip him of his. They stood naked in winter sunlight and she reached up to tug off his ribbon and set his hair free.

"There. That is how I like to see you. Though black silk is appealing, too."

"If I please you, I am delighted." He took her hand and twirled her, as if in a dance. "Do you realize that I've never seen your naked body before? It is perfect."

"You're blinded by love, sir."

"Indeed I am. But it is perfect. Golden hair in interesting places. It flatters the sun. Will you dance in the summer sun for me, out in the woods where elves belong?"

Now she was blushing at the thought. "Perhaps, if you dance naked with me."

" 'I know a bank whereon the wild thyme blows . . .' " Perhaps it was *A Midsummer Night's Dream* all along."

Elf tugged him over and down onto the waiting bed. "No, it was always something wicked. Show me. Show me something else. Something wonderfully, deliciously wicked . . ."

Author's Note

It's scary, really, how these things work out.

I can't remember quite why I decided to weave the Stone of Scone into this story, but probably the only reason I was particularly aware of it was a dim memory of its theft by Scottish Nationalists back in the 1950s. (I was a small child at the time. Honestly!)

As I wrote the book, it did seem interesting to me that there was a link with *Braveheart*, which was proving so popular. I was surprised and excited, however, when not long after sending the finished novel to my publisher, I opened the paper to see the headline STONE OF SCONE HEADING HOME.

My rather whimsical plot line had suddenly become one of relevant current interest!

The Stone of Scone, as you will have gathered, has been of almost mystical significance to the Scottish people for over a millennium, but especially since it was stolen from them by Edward I of England in 1296—yes, the wicked old king in *Braveheart*. (In fact, you could say that the theft incited Sir William Wallace to lead the revolt against English control of his homeland.)

The stone had been used in the coronation of Scottish kings since at least the ninth century, and it was said that the stone groaned if a true king sat upon it, but stayed silent otherwise. The injury to Scottish pride was made worse, therefore, when Edward had the stone put into a chair used in the English coronations.

Wallace was defeated at the Battle of Falkirk, and executed in 1305, but his struggles were continued by

Robert the Bruce, then King of Scotland. When Edward I died in 1307, his son succeeded him (only then marrying Isabelle of France, by the way), and began to lose England's hold on Scotland. The English army was resoundingly defeated by the Scots under Bruce at the Battle of Bannockburn in 1314. In 1328, at the Treaty of Northhampton, the English recognized Bruce as King of Scotland, gave up their claim to feudal supremacy, and promised to return the stone.

The promise, however, was never kept.

In fact, this Scottish success proved transitory, and civil war in Scotland between Bruce and Balliol almost let England win. However, in 1342, Robert the Bruce's son took hold of his country and established Scottish independence. It would only be the linked bloodlines in the sixteenth century that would lead to the joining of Scotland and England under one monarch.

However, the Stone of Scone, or the Stone of Destiny as many Scots prefer to call it, would only return to Scotland once. This was in the 1950s when some Scottish students managed to steal it from Westminster Abbey one Christmas morning and get it back across the border.

It was soon found and returned, but in the meantime, it had been broken. The students asked a Glasgow builder to mend it. Shortly before his death, this man claimed that the stone returned was not the real one but an imitation. The students denied that. There is always the possibility, however, that the real Stone of Destiny is still hidden somewhere in Scotland, its location known only to a few honored Scottish nationalists.

Whatever the truth of that, British Prime Minister John Major has promised that the slab of sandstone currently sitting beneath the throne in Westminster Abbey will be sent back to Scotland.

True to form, however, the Scots are feuding about it. Some of them want it returned to Scone Palace, which is near the ruined abbey that once housed it. Others want it to be placed in Edinburgh Castle, Scotland's premier tourist attraction.

Wherever it ends up, it will be returned to London for coronations. I wonder if it groans?

Sounds a little like a medieval whoopee cushion, really, doesn't it?

I love to hear from my readers. Please write c/o The Alice Orr Agency, 305 Madison Ave #1166, New York, NY 10165. An SASE is appreciated.

Or e-mail me at wp823@freenet.victoria.bc.ca.

Or visit my web page at http://www.writepage.com.

Read on for an excerpt from
Jo Beverley's brand-new historical romance
about the Malloren family

A Most Unsuitable Man

Coming from Signet in February 2005

December 27th, 1763, Rothgar Abbey, England

Almost away.

Damaris Myddleton sat in the speeding coach, hands clenched, wishing she could see behind, see if anyone raced after her to drag her back. The crunch of her coach wheels and the pounding of the horses' hooves blocked any sound of pursuit—or perhaps she was deafened by the pounding of her own frantic heart.

"It'll come to disaster. I know it will," her maid prophesied, for perhaps the twentieth time. Maisie was plump, plain, and generally merry, but today every line of her round face curved downward. "How're we going to get all the way to Worksop without being caught, miss?"

Damaris would scream at her except that Maisie could be the only friend she had left in the world. Oh, why had she behaved so atrociously?

"I told you. We only need to reach the London road and take a public coach. I'm of age. I can go where I want. The Mallorens can't drag me off a public stage."

Maisie's grim silence said *I wish I were sure of that.*

Damaris felt the same way. She wished she'd never fallen into the clutches of the Mallorens at all.

She'd grown up in genteel poverty, believing that her absent father was a failed adventurer. Last year, upon her mother's death, she'd discovered that he'd made a fortune in the Orient and left it to her. He'd also left her in the guardianship of Lord Henry Malloren, part of the rich and powerful Malloren family.

Once she'd recovered from the shock, Damaris had

ventured into her new world with growing optimism and hope, even looking forward to a future as wife of an aristocrat purchased with her fortune. Her trustees had drawn up a list of the grandest and neediest, and she'd picked the handsome Marquess of Ashart. She'd believed the matter settled except for the proposal, but yesterday, however, everything had crashed around her.

Ashart had announced his betrothal to Genova Smith, a penniless beauty. Instead of maintaining her dignity, Damaris had screeched her objections, and then—oh, God—she'd tried to claw Genova Smith out of Ashart's arms.

Or would have done if his blasted hanger-on, Fitzroger, hadn't overpowered her and carried her away. She was sure that had been a pretty sight for the observers—an audience of most of the guests at Rothgar Abbey.

The coach swayed as it turned out of the park of the Abbey. She'd escaped! She'd never have to face any of those people again.

Then movement in the corner of her eye whirled her to her right.

A rider thundered by her window. Fine horse. Fine rider. Wild blond hair flying in the wind.

Fitzroger?

No, it couldn't be!

The wretched man cut off her coach. It shuddered to a halt and the coachman said, "Trouble, sir?"

The reply came in that crisp, cool voice that had dogged her for days. "I need a word with Miss Myddleton."

Maisie moaned. Damaris wanted to. Instead of a means of escape, the coach now felt like a trap.

Fitzroger rode to the window and looked in, presenting the very picture of a vagabond. His blond hair curled loose about his shoulders, his shirt lay open at the neck, and he wore no waistcoat beneath his plain blue jacket. He was as good as undressed!

His ice blue eyes seemed . . . what? Exasperated? What right did Ashart's penniless friend have to be exasperated with her?

Damaris let down the window, but only to lean out and call, "Drive on, Briggs!" Cold air cut at her. Briggs, plague take him, didn't obey.

Fitzroger grasped the edge of the window frame with his bare hand. He couldn't hold back the coach by brute force, but that commanding hand unnerved her, preventing her from raising the glass between them.

Bare hand. Bare neck. Bare head.

Grimly, she hoped he froze to death. "What do you want, sir?"

"But a moment of your time, Miss Myddleton."

He released the coach and swung off the horse. He called for the groom to come down and take the horse, which snapped Damaris back to action. She leaned out farther and yelled at Briggs, "Drive on, you spineless varlet!"

She could have saved her frozen breath. Despite the extortionate bribe she'd paid him, her guardian's coachman was abandoning her at the first challenge. If she knew how to drive, she'd climb up on the box and take the reins herself.

The wide-eyed young groom, in his frieze coat, gloves, and hat, appeared outside the window and took the horse's reins. Fitzroger opened the door smiling—but at Maisie, not Damaris. "Return to the house behind the groom. I'll bring your mistress back shortly."

"No, he won't. Maisie, do not dare to obey him!"

Maisie, the traitor, scrambled toward the door. Damaris grabbed her skirt to stop her. Fitzroger chopped sharply at her hand, shocking it open, and pulled Maisie free.

Damaris gaped at him, her hand still tingling. "How *dare* you!"

Pure fury blazed and she reached for the holstered pistol by her seat. She knew nothing of guns, but surely one had only to point them and pull the trigger. A strong hand closed over hers. He said nothing, but she was suddenly unable to move, frozen by his bare hand controlling hers and his cool, steady eyes.

She pulled free and sat back, folding her arms and directing her eyes to a spot behind his head. "Whatever you have to say, Mr. Fitzroger, say it and be gone."

He leaned out of the window. "Walk the horses, coachman, and you might as well turn them."

Back toward the house. She wouldn't return. She wouldn't. But right now she didn't see how to prevent it. Tears choked her but she swallowed them. It would be the final straw to cry.

He raised the window, cutting off the bitter winter air, but trapping her in this enclosed space with him. Their legs could hardly avoid contact and she could almost feel his heat.

"You don't really want to run away, you know."

She responded to that with silence.

"I'm impressed that you persuaded Lord Henry's servants to carry you away," he continued. "How did you manage that?"

"Guineas," she said flatly, "which I have in abundance, and you, sir, significantly lack."

"Whereas I have understanding of this world in abundance, which you, Miss Myddleton, significantly lack."

She fired a look at him. "Then you understand that I am ruined."

"No, but this mad flight might do it."

"I won't be here to find out."

But her hands had clenched with desperation. How could she escape? Fitzroger looked impervious to reason, bribes, or tears and over the past days she'd found him to be a formidable opponent.

"You have a fighting spirit," he said, "but a fighter needs to understand the terrain. Running away won't help because you'll have to meet all those people again one day. Unless you intend to live like a hermit."

She slid away from that. "It's Ashart who should be ashamed. He was supposed to marry me. You know he was."

"He was supposed to marry your money."

It stung like a whip, but she raised her chin. "A fair

bargain. My wealth for his title." Was that the reason for this interference? "I'll not trade my fortune for less, sir, if that is your plan."

If it stung him back, he hid it well. "I wouldn't aspire so far above my station. Think of me as Sir Galahad, Miss Myddleton, riding to the maiden's rescue with pure and noble motives."

"I don't *need* rescue, only to be allowed to go on my way."

"Run away and society will laugh about it for years. Return and play your cards right and you'll have sympathy on your side." He took her hands. She tried to tug free but strength seemed to have deserted her, and her vision was blurred by tears. "Flee, and your bad behavior will be fixed in people's minds for eternity. Return, seem in good spirits, and everyone will doubt their own memory of events."

She blinked, trying to read truth or error in his face. "Every detail must be etched in their minds."

"Every detail is etched in yours. In the minds of others, it's part of a tumult of fascinating drama, and for the most part you were the injured party. We can return you to that, to the point where people sympathized."

She snatched her hands free. "With a pitiable creature, jilted because all her jewels and riches couldn't compensate for a plain face, awkward manners, and inferior birth!"

She froze, unable to believe that she'd just exposed those thoughts to this man, then covered her face with a hand.

He swung over to sit beside her and gently tugged her hand down. "Begging for compliments, Miss Myddleton?"

Damaris had to look at him, but she could hardly think for his body suddenly so close in the confinement of a coach seat. She'd lived most of her life in a world without men, without their effect at close quarters. Now this man pressed against her at leg and arm, and his strong, warm hand enfolded hers.

"You can't compete with Genova Smith in beauty," he said. "Few can. But plain, no. And I've seen nothing amiss with your manners except when strain over Ashart rode you. Come back with me. I promise to stand by you, to make sure everything turns out as you would wish."

Tone as much as words shivered along her nerves, weakening her will.

"How can I? What am I supposed to do?"

"Face them and smile."

Damaris's mouth dried, but she was being offered a second chance. She realized she had to take it, to prove something to herself if nothing else. She would not be a coward.

Logic didn't defeat fear, however, and she had to fight a tight throat to speak. "Very well, I'll return and put on a glad face. But I hold you to your promise. You will stand by me?"

His smile was remarkably sweet. "I will."

He had to have an eye on her fortune—no other reason explained his apparent kindness. "Before you go any further, Mr. Fitzroger, please understand that while I appreciate your help, I will never, ever offer you my hand and fortune."

"Not every man who does you a service will be after your money."

She wished he'd be honest. "Are you claiming to have no desire to marry riches? I cannot believe that."

He shrugged. "I'd take yours if you offered it, but you won't do anything so foolish, will you?"

"No."

"Then we know where we stand."

How could he agree with everything she said and still tangle her in knots?

"Lord Henry is taking you to London for the winter season, isn't he?" he said. "You'll have your pick of the titled blooms there. A duke, even. Think of it. As a duchess, you'll outrank Genova, Marchioness of Ashart."

He seemed to see right into her petty soul, but she couldn't deny the appeal of that. That list of the needy, titled gentlemen had included a duke—the Duke of Bridgewater.

"What are you plotting now?" he asked in lazy amusement. "You make me nervous."

"I wish that were true."

"Any sensible man gets nervous when confronted with an inexperienced lady weaving plots."

"Inexperienced?" she objected, but in truth she could hardly claim otherwise.

"Very. Are you experienced enough, for example, to choose your husband wisely?"

"Are you offering to guide me?" she asked with a disbelieving smile.

At that moment, perhaps from some reaction of his, she recognized that she'd spoken flirtatiously. She would have said that she didn't know how to flirt, but she was doing so and it shook her.

If she was going to flirt, it should never be with this man. If she'd asked her trustees to draw up a list of the *least* suitable men she might meet in polite society, Octavius Fitzroger would have been near the top of it. He was penniless, and without employment, and she'd heard rumors at Rothgar Abbey about some dark scandal in his past. She'd been too intent on pursuing Ashart to pay attention, but some of the guests were surprised, even shocked, that he was allowed in the house at all.

All the same, when he took her hand and raised it to his lips, when he murmured, "I could be your guide in many things . . ." Damaris's grasp on common sense faltered.

He's kissing your hand, nothing more, she told her misty mind, but it didn't help. Her heart pounded and moisture gathered in her mouth, forcing her to swallow or drool. When he leaned closer she recovered enough to put a hand on his chest. "No, sir!"

"Are you sure?"

No. His body felt like fire beneath her palm, for only

his shirt covered his hard chest. If she slid her hand higher, her fingers would touch naked skin at the base of his throat. . . .

"Practice," he murmured, "leads to perfection."

"Practice?" she squeaked. "At what?"

"Flirtation." He raised a hand and brushed his knuckles down her slack jaw. "If you're happily flirting with me, no one will be able to believe that you're still pining for Ashart."

"Why would I ever choose you over him?" The question was rude, but the desperate truth.

His eyes danced with wickedness. "For Christmastide amusement. You're a rich heiress who is soon going to London to marry well, but for the moment, you amuse yourself with me."

They were fixed in place, he stroking her jaw, she holding him off. It created a strange illusion of being within a magical circle, one she didn't want to break.

"Very well," she said, but clung to reason. She pushed at his chest and said, "There's no need to embrace here."

Her push achieved nothing but to press her hand harder against his heat and make breathing more difficult.

"No kiss as a reward, fair lady?" His fingers brushed between the fur lining of her hood and the skin of her neck. "Chinchilla," he murmured, making the word sound like a whisper of sin.

Oh, he was wicked, and she should push harder, even scream for help, but she wanted his kiss. Her mouth tingled for it.

"Just a kiss," he said softly. "Nothing more, I promise."

He dislodged her hand that was still feebly trying to hold him off and took her into his arms. She couldn't remember ever being touched like this before, with such tender power.

Resist, resist!

He caught any protest in a kiss.

She was powerless, but his embrace felt not at all forceful, except as a force of nature. Thought evaporated, and Damaris let him tilt her head so he could deepen the kiss, then let him crush her to his strong, hard body, enfold her, protect her.

His lips freed hers. Damaris opened stunned eyes to look into his. Silver blue around dark, endless empires. But he looked insufferably pleased with himself.

She gripped his hair. His eyes widened—good. Before he could resist, she pushed him back against the side of the coach and kissed him as thoroughly as he'd kissed her. She'd never done such a thing before, but let instinct rule as she whirled with him back into the storm.

When she broke the kiss to pant for breath, she realized she was straddling him. Her breasts ached and she pressed them against him, returning stinging lips to his again and again and again—

He twisted away. "Damaris, we have to stop!"

"No."

"Yes."

Then she heard what he'd heard.

Gravel. They were nearing the stables!

What had she been thinking?